Fire
in
Beulah

Also by Rilla Askew

Strange Business
The Mercy Seat

Fire
in
Beulah

RILLA ASKEW

VIKING

VIKING
Published by the Penguin Group
Penguin Putnam Inc., 375 Hudson Street, New York, New York,
10014, USA
Penguin Books Ltd., 27 Wrights Lane, London W8 5TZ, England
Penguin Books Australia Ltd, Ringwood, Victoria, Australia
Penguin Books Canada Ltd., 10 Alcorn Avenue, Toronto, Ontario,
Canada M4V 3B2
Penguin Books (N.Z.) Ltd, 182–190 Wairau Road, Auckland 10,
New Zealand

Penguin Books Ltd, Registered Offices:
Harmondsworth, Middlesex, England

First published in 2001 by Viking Penguin,
a member of Penguin Putnam Inc.
1   3   5   7   9   10   8   6   4   2

Library of Congress Cataloging-in-Publication Data

Askew, Rilla.
Fire in Beulah/Rilla Askew.
p. cm.
ISBN 0-670-88843-5
I. Title.

PS3551.S545 F57 2001
813'.54—dc21   00-043366

This book is printed on acid-free paper. ∞

Printed in the United States of America
Set in Bulmer MT
Designed by Nancy Resnick

For Travis
and Marlene
and Ebony Rose

Acknowledgments

My gratitude, always, to my husband, Paul Austin, first reader, final critic; and to my sister Ruth, who receives all. Friends and family members have sent articles and clippings about the Tulsa Race Riot through the years, and I appreciate all of them. Warm thanks to my agent, Jane Gelfman, who asks the right questions, and to my editor, Paul Slovak, for all their good work. A special word of gratitude for my friend and teacher, the late Dr. Nancy Vunovich, who in the months of her final illness read these pages with enthusiasm, interest, miraculous patience. For the facts of the riot I've used a number of sources, and have drawn particularly from Scott Ellsworth's seminal work, *Death in a Promised Land: The Tulsa Race Riot of 1921*; Eddie Faye Gates' gathering of oral histories, *They Came Searching: How Blacks Sought the Promised Land in Tulsa*; Hannibal B. Johnson's study of the Greenwood district, *Black Wall Street*; and the contemporary eyewitness account of the riot by Mary E. Jones Parrish, *Race Riot 1921: Events of the Tulsa Disaster*. Finally, a note of sorrowful indebtedness: although the characters here are entirely fictional or, in the case of historical persons, fictionally portrayed, the incidents of racial violence are all real; they took place almost exactly as described, perpetrated by Americans, on Americans, in this promised land.

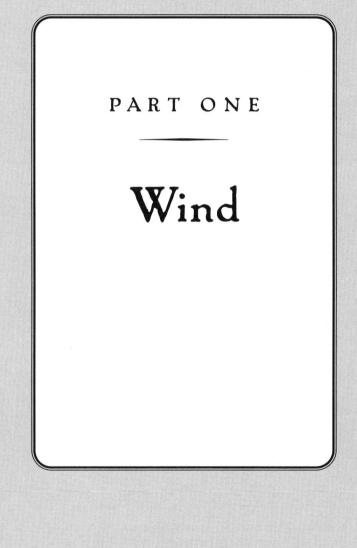

PART ONE

———

Wind

Near the Deep Fork River
south of Bristow, I.T.
September
1900

A high, hot wind had been blowing from the south for seven days. It
blew morning and evening and did not lay at night as it should but
cried and fingered at the windows till the sun rose, and then it went on
blowing. A constant wind, an unremitting wind, it did not gust or fall but
blew one monotonous gritty speed. Water could not be kept in the
troughs for the animals but evaporated almost as quickly as it was
pumped and had to be pumped anew each time the cattle started bawling.
Washing on the line did not flap and dance but held a steady northward
angle and dried bone-dry in less than twenty minutes. The older Whiteside girls complained their lips and cheeks were cracking. Their mother
stayed indoors, though it was more miserably hot inside than out, because
she feared the wind would suck the life from her unborn child.

She prowled from windowsill to windowsill in her tiny room, touched
the rolled rags laid end to end across the cracks to hold back the dust, and
pressed them against the openings, tighter. She paused, her hands entwined beneath her belly, stared out the glass at the bluestem grasses
bowed and bending toward her, the stunted blackjacks (those ugly trees)
hunched close to earth like dwarves or gnomes, their gnarled fingers
reaching earthward: dear God, how she despised them! Beyond the jacks
the brooding Deep Fork River crawled west to east, its meandering path
made plain by the paler bark of river trees, the cottonwoods and syca-

mores, within the arc of hickories. Rachel raised her eyes and searched the sky for the moon's pocked face. For a week she'd watched it growing full, swelling as her belly swelled, rising a little later each day to hang above the trees, the blanched sky bleeding through its very features. The daymoon frightened her. For all its grinning, it seemed a malevolent thing: a ragged oval, frayed a little on one side, but soft and permeable, and growing in its porous membrane, like a great ruptured reptile egg, giving forth that cursed wind. Her eyes turned left, and right, straight up above, but the empty sky showed only windspun dust in ruddy light. On the north side of the house the motherless calf was bawling. Lord, couldn't one of the girls go feed that thing, or knock it in the head and leave it for the crows to eat, or something, anything, just shut up, shut up that useless bawling. Rachel eased over to the door and yanked the knotted pull-rag. The door slapped back against the wall. She called down the stairs, "Estaleen! Go feed that thing!" The woman turned, treaded heavily across the roseprint rug toward the southern window.

In the crowded downstairs parlor room, her eldest daughter Estaleen gazed round the room at the frowning faces of her sisters. Each kept a downcast eye upon her embroidery hoop or darning needle or crochet hook, but for the baby Kay playing by herself on the rag-rug floor, and the very middle of the seven girls, Aletha Jean, who stood gazing out the window.

"Lethajean!" the eldest called, though the girl was but five feet away. "Go feed Pet." She turned her face down to the sampler in her lap, but her eyes cut slantwise at her sister's back. Aletha Jean ignored her. Estaleen called again, "Lethajean! Go feed that thing!" Still the girl stood motionless at the window.

"I will!" piped up Winema, the next-to-youngest, a sweet-faced, wiry, amber child of eight, but Estaleen, who was mother to them all, said, "You will not. Letha, go do like Mother said."

Without turning her eyes from the dust-smoked prairie, Aletha said, "Told *you*, not *me*."

"*I'm* telling you," the eldest said, and swept her mothering gaze around the room to see if this rebellion might be joined from another corner. But blond Prudence met her gaze in timid complicity, and pale Dorcas kept her eyes on the embroidery hoop upon her knee, and redheaded Jody, who, at twelve, was hardly a year younger than Aletha Jean and therefore especially resentful of her dreamy, high-and-mighty sister, glared at the dark-haired middle daughter's back with a vehemence outshining Estaleen's own, so that the eldest's pique was in fact enhanced, and she snapped in exact imitation of their mother's former power, "Aletha Jean Whiteside, don't make me have to get up off this chair. Go right this minute and give that calf its ninny."

Aletha continued staring out the window. The calf's bawls came from the corral in a piteous honking wail, the sound so loud it rose above the wind and circled the clapboard house, came in through the shut-tight windows. It had been a fortnight since the old brindle cow tore her bag on a barbed-wire fence, ripped one tit from end to end, and the infection had set in, clabbering her milk right in the bag, the tit so sore, oozing yellow, that she'd kicked the calf away and wouldn't let it suck. The girls' father had tried to turn the calf to another cow, but none would take it, so he'd penned it up and fashioned a teatbag from an old cleaned-out cow stomach and fed the calf one morning before he left the house on his sorrel mare, riding north and east to Bristow. When their father didn't come home the first night and the calf stood in the pen bawling long and weak and pitiful, it had been Estaleen who'd announced that she would save the red calf on her own. She'd gone to the barn at dawn, at noon, and dusk, and nursed the calf for almost a week, and the calf had fallen in love with her and followed her around the pen like a starving pup.

But then the hot southwind had come (though not yet their father), and the days blew dry and full of dust, the burning coin of sun cracked Estaleen's lips, made the buttermilk washes she used on her face to fade the freckles entirely useless, and for the past few days she'd parceled out every one of her outside chores among her younger sisters. In all fairness, if fairness could be had in that household of female wants and needs, it was Aletha's turn to feed the calf, but Aletha was the orneriest of the girls and could be made to do very little on the best of days, and this day was a bad one. She traced the distant trees with her eyes, saying to herself, *Y'all can go to aitch-ee-double-ell.* She had no intention of doing what her sister said. She hated everything there was to hate about that sucking calf. Oh, she'd watched it many times, had stood outside the gate and watched the creature's thick-tongued slobber, the frothing milk trickling out both sides of its mouth while it sucked and pulled at the bag in her sister's arms, its long red tail a-twitching. She hated the way it followed Estaleen from one end of the corral to the other, nudging, bawling, long after the milk was gone, and she cringed to think of its nuzzling snout prying at her private self. The calf bawled and bawled but Aletha's eyes never left the line of river trees; she stood with her jaw clenched and her spine as straight as a hoe handle. *No way on earth,* she thought, *in hell, or under God's blue heaven. I ain't going out there.*

Winema, her heart breaking with the poor calf's distress, begged to be allowed to go feed it, but the older girls told her to hush, and shot their daggered stares at Aletha's back, until she turned at last and faced her sisters. Six pairs of lightbrown eyes, even the baby Kay's by this time, were focused plain upon her. Aletha's thoughts fell self-consciously to her bony arms and washboard chest, but the sisters did not see. She felt it then, as she felt it always: her own worthless invisibility, and with that useless sense came a rush of sorrow for herself. *Ain't one of them can see me,* she thought. *That damn slobbery calf out back gets more attention.* And then, wordless in her mind, she saw her mother prowling the narrow room upstairs, absorbed within her swollen self, and Aletha's self-pity was overswept by anger. Immediately she pushed away from the windowsill and flounced across the room without a glance at her sisters; she stomped through the kitchen to the porch, swiped up the full milk bucket and the disgusting teatbag, and stormed out the back door.

She paused, stricken, on the wooden steps. In the west the sun floated above the lip of earth in a fiery ball; in the east, the moon was rising. Its forehead lifted swollen, full, above the horizon, reflecting the crimson of the setting sun. The sky north and east and west and straight up above was clear of clouds, depthless, wrong in color—saffron, olive, berylline—and exquisite beyond all telling. For an instant she took within herself the strange sky, the reddened synchronous moon and sun, stood trembling on the brink of change: almost, the girl was transformed by the prairie's turning beauty. But Aletha was, in more ways than either understood, her mother's daughter, and in the next instant she frowned against the spitting dust, drew her eyes away from the skies, marched down the steps and out across the pasture.

The barn sat on a northwest rise behind the house, so that Aletha had to angle through the gale to reach it. Flax-colored homespun billowing, brown braids snapping, lifted to her very toes sometimes, Aletha fought and floated through the wind to the small corral beside the barn. She reached between the slats to pull the latch, and then had to fight to keep the gate from being torn from her hands by the wind; in the struggle the bucket tipped and sloshed milk on her skirt, darkened the swirling, manure-spat ground.

She said aloud, "Damn it. See?" as if there were a witness who might, now convinced, agree with her how wronged she'd been. Looking down at the greasy milk streaks on the homespun, thinking she'd have to scrub till her hands were raw with lye to get them out, she squeezed past the gate, shoved it shut with all her strength; she squinted toward the far side of the pen, where the calf stood with its back to the wind. The first trembling hint of fear nudged up within her. The calf's head was lifted and cocked, nostrils flared; it had heard the clang of bucket and creak of gate, and now waited in the wind like a blind thing, all senses homed on one awareness only. Without signal or warning, the red calf turned and, leaning sideways, began to trot toward her.

The little thing was stark-ribbed, knob-kneed, solid red (the ferocious color of the setting sun), and as poor as any calf might be and breathe, but in Aletha's eyes it could as well have been a rutting bull. The urgency of its coming scared her. Pushed northward by the wind, yet hungering east toward its dinner, the calf came loping, dancing, bawling, prancing, sometimes purely cockawhoop sideways, rapidly toward her. The milk pail fell from Aletha's hand, she whirled around to the gate, and couldn't get the gate to open. Nor could she feel the slosh of milk on her skirt and shoes, the sting of windflung dirt upon her face, the lashing whips of her own two braids—but only the rising burn and dark of fear inside her body. The gate's latch was jammed, and though the girl clawed at it and was truly terrified, there was at work a far more compelling force than rusted iron and wind, or the beauty of the prairie sunset sky: in those frantic seconds the girl's soul thrilled to the dark sweet rush of danger.

The calf shoved its snout against her skirt. He smelled the milk; he knew the scent and shape of the teatbag beneath her arm; he knew the smell of young human female and claimed the smell as owed him. He pressed against her with the full weight of his bony flanks, demanding, seeking, pushing, and Aletha, thinking herself in actual danger, thinking her terror a terrible thing and not the delicious, alive sensation that, in truth, it was to her, began to scream.

Inside the house, her sisters' working hands fell still; twelve pale brown eyes stared wide across the parlor. The baby Kay, holding to the hassock, her bouncing stopped by the curdling scream, collapsed her face and began to cry. It was this, not Aletha's screams, that finally roused the mother.

Rachel lay on the bed upstairs in a stuporous, halfwaking dream, numbed by the ceaseless groan of wind, pressed into the muslin sheet by the moist weight of her own body. She heard the bawls of her youngest child and tried to ignore it, as one tries to dismiss a mosquito's whine when it hums into the depths of sleep, but at last she rolled sideways, lifted her terrible weight, and placed her swollen feet upon the floor. She made her way to the door and pulled the knotted rag, started down the steep pine stairs. It wasn't until she came into the parlor, where the toddler girl had fallen to the rug, wailing, and the other five were staring wide-eyed and silent at one another, that she recognized the distant terrified shrieks as something real and not the residue of her own unhappy dreams. The others looked up in fear, for Aletha's screams were horrible to hear, and the older girls, at least, believed she was being murdered. The mother lifted Kay and made a move to put her on her hip, but with her belly so far advanced and wide, there was no hip for the toddler's thighs to clutch, and so she dropped her, still sobbing, into Estaleen's lap and turned, as in a dream, and went rolling side to side through the open doorway, the kitchen, the cooling porch, and didn't pause when she stepped outside and lost her breath for an instant to the sucking wind, never looked right or left to see the full moon rising as the red sun set, but headed straight up across the pasture.

She made a broad target for the wind, but her very bigness anchored her to the earth so that the wind became, in fact, more aid than hindrance, buoying her gently north. The rise, however, held her back. Its slope would have seemed slight enough to a woman who did not bear such weight, whose lungs were not pushed up and crowded against her heart, but to Rachel Whiteside the slant was steep as the pine steps to her upstairs room, and a thousand times as far. She climbed, one loglike leg before the other, her labored breathing drowning, almost, her daughter's screams.

The girl's mind had raced past the first rush of fear, past panic, to pure, unbridled hysteria. She screamed, feeling for the first time the rough post oak beneath her palms, the calf's warm breath through the cotton skirt, the warm, sticky milk upon her legs. She screamed, seeing with quickened eyes the serpentine color of the sky. She saw the moon swimming, pure yolk yellow now, above the dark horizon; and nearer, in a closing circle on the rim of earth, blackjack limbs like gnarled screams against the brightened sky. She smelled manure and dust, the calf's sweet hide, a thousand autumn pollens released like sperm, the pecan trees in the distant grove. She smelled her mother, heard her mother's breath and groans. Aletha began then to scream in earnest. She screamed for all her imagined loss and grief, for having wanted, wanted all her life, and never got; for being her own private self within the world. And then she felt her mother's hands. For a fleeting moment the girl knew gladness; she surrendered to the rough skin of her mother's palms, felt their warmth encase her own, and though the calf still pushed against her hips and bawled, Aletha ceased her struggle.

She sagged, deflated against the gate, felt herself shoved back, her wrists clamped within the cuffs of her mother's hands. The big belly pushed through the opening, and then her mother was inside the pen and the teatbag was on the ground beneath her mother's skirt and the calf was struggling to get at it. Her mother slapped her across the mouth, let go her hands, and Aletha had only the space of a heartbeat to feel the bafflement and pain and, quickly, a righteous flare of rage against this clear injustice, because the red calf then, consumed with its own frustration, turned fully away from mouthing at the mother's hem and whipped its head around, up once, and down, and kicked Rachel with all its hungry might right in her swollen belly.

There came a little sound, like *hoomph,* like sudden air expelled. The mother did not cry out but released that unwilled sound and stood perfectly still on her leaden legs. The calf came at her hem again, grabbed the teatbag in his mouth and tossed it up into the wind, and trotted over to where it landed. The mother stared down at her body. Her whole belly was shoved to the side. Unbelieving, she reached to stroke her stomach where it ought to be, high and huge before her. Her hands fell, lost. The wind pressed her skirt against her so that there appeared, clearly visible though in all ways unreal, the outline of the unborn babe like an overstuffed saddlebag slung at her side, riding low, halfway round toward her kidneys. Beneath her feet a wet spot spread, darkening the red dust.

Late in the night, as the mother lay groaning her terrible labor, the wind changed. Near midnight it fell still, and for some several hours the prairie around the Whiteside homestead waited, stunned with sudden silence. The snarled clutch of blackjacks on the rise, the eerie Deep Fork bottoms, too, were suspended in stillness, and the moon, high and small and very white, cast perfect shadows. The shadows were still. But at three o'clock—the human hour of guilt and the mind's repetition, the hour of human fear—the wind returned. It had shifted shape and become a new entity. It swept down from the north, and in its scent was no salt sea breath but the smell of deep blue, of ice and indigo: the roiling breath of the great northern plain. Not steady now but a spitting, cold, fretful thing, it rose and fell, gusted and died, and gusted again, and pushed before it high, tarry clouds that tumbled between earth and the face of the moon. On the prairie, the moon's shadows chased one another.

Inside the lone clapboard house there were only two whose senses were quick to this change. Aletha Jean knew the moment the wind ceased, and in the hours between the wind's death and resurrection, she suffered. For her, there was a kinship between the dying wind and her mother's travail in the small bedroom at the top of the stairs. She thought this strange, noisome labor had somehow sucked away the wind's life as it tried to suck the life from her mother—and both, she believed, were caused by her own selfish terror.

The other in the Whiteside home whose senses grew alert when the wind stopped, who listened and knew it would come again moments before it roared down from the north, was the Creek woman who'd been fetched from Iron Post to help with the twisted birth.

Wind come like this, come down like something blue and fierce—

Tell me which is it you want then, the wind or the little whitegirl. You the one talking about the wind, *I* don't concern myself with none of it. All right. Here then.

The little redheaded whitechild come, face pinched up like a fox face and white as that moon yonder, she's so scared. She say, My mama got kicked by a calf and she's dying. It was near on to first dark. I went and told Bluford I was going and he just nod his head, even though I hadn't seen him for two weeks because he'd just got back. He was the best thing. I believe he was the best of the three of them, though they each was good men, but Bluford was the gentlest. Oh, he had a touch. I thought I'd die when he died, but I didn't, I just went on and lived and come down to Boley finally and married Tim—

Well, what do you want me in here for? Ain't that like whitefolks, think I got time to drop by and tidy up their story. Think I don't have my own life to tell. You never seen my daddy black as pitch and smarter than any of them allowed, a horse trader deluxe, and they whipped him for that, I know it was mainly on account of that, and that's how come him to carry my mama to this Boley town and quit that Deep Fork country. You never seen my mama no taller than a fencepost and poor as sin and better in her heart than your idea of God, and I don't guess you'd know them if you did see them, much less care. All right, all right, I'm here now, let's go on.

That woman lied. She called me Creek, and I am part Creek, but you look how this colored blood dominate. My daddy was a black man, and my mama was part colored, part Creek, part French, and she was born on the Trail to a slave mother. I'm a Creek freedwoman is what I am. You hear that word? Freed. From slavery. It wasn't my Creek blood got that name. Make up your own mind why that woman lie. But, yes, my husband Bluford Tiger was a Creek-and-Seminole man, and we lived on his allotment up toward Iron Post. I loved them people. It's been many a year since I lived around Indians—and I don't go around whitefolks at all, I stay right here in this good colored town, try to, anyhow, till some ghost woman come around and drag me out to try and make me talk—but I always did claim Indian, married me two of them and loved their families like my own, and not just because of my own mama, not because it come down in me so I got good hair and this pretty mahogany-color skin, but because I known them in my heart and eat with them and went to stomps and danced, and my mother had it in her from her mixed-blood dad. So I was, what? Thirty then. I never had no children, that was the main cross the Lord give me through my life to bear, so in their place, in them unborn children's place, He give me three good husbands and a gift to heal, and that's what I was doing then.

So. The little foxface whitegirl come, and I wrapped my head and went, and yes, we walked through that wind and I don't know what you got on your mind about that. A seven-day wind ain't nothing new in this country, and that quick change ain't nothing new. But I heard when it died along about the middle of the night, and I raised up my head, say to myself, Bluford's ax finally done its work. Quick as he got back from Okmulgee that morning Bluford set that ax in a tree stump with the cutting edge facing south, and I ask him what he do that for and he say it's to cut the wind. So that's what I was thinking in that whitelady's bedroom, I's thinking Bluford's ax finally done its work. But we jumping way ahead. You better let me back up.

I followed the little girl up the stairs and see that mama crouched naked on the floor, holding to the bedspread like she get down and can't get up and got no ambition to try. Bloody water leaking all over that nice roseprint rug. First thing, I got to get on my knees and pray. I never see such a twisted-around kind of mess. Ain't no human help for *that,* I tell myself, and I pray, Lord God have mercy Thy will be done. The whole bunch of whitegirls done trooped up the stairs behind me, I gets up off my knees, turn to shoo them back down. Give my scissor to the little foxface girl, tell her to boil it up good, though I didn't have a hope in the world that baby's going to get down that way. Whitewoman's insides must've looked like stopped-up plumbing, though I guess I hadn't seen plumbing pipes up till then, but in my memory that's how it look. Tell that little fox-face girl, say, 'Fore you bring that scissor back up, y'all send to Bristow for the doctor. Tell him to come quick. I figured we going to have to cut that woman sure. I didn't believe she's going to last till somebody get to Bristow and back, but I sent anyhow, and proceed on with getting that woman up on the bed. She weighed a ton, but I was a big woman myself then, and I just about hoisted her up, say, You git on up here now and lay like this. Propped her sideways on the pillows, that baby raised up like a boil out her side. She one of these women never let scared come on her face. Her belly twisted plumb around to her backside nearly, and her face just look like she's mad. All that come out of her mouth be this low grunting moan.

Lord, that room stink. Any birthroom do, but this one was different and worse, and I lay that onto that stopped-up plumbing and so much blood. There's been just a few times when I seen so much blood. All births is bloody, make no mistake, they completely violent events, and I done see and smelt plenty, cut more than a few babies out their mamas' bellies, and that sure do make some blood, but this one was different, I believe because that woman bleeding way up high somewhere. Time it get down through them twisted pipes, the blood done start to clot and stink. Well, I expect for sure she's going to die and that baby going to die, but there's nothing for it but just work on her and pray that doctor get down from Bristow before she give up the ghost. She don't want to let me touch her. She flat snarl at me any time I get close. I know I got to rub the baby around and down where it belong. Looks to me like she been carrying high anyhow, but you couldn't say a thing for sure, time that calf got done. I spend maybe the first hour moving slow, talking smooth and soft, sneaking in close, same as with a injured animal if you don't want to get bit.

Birth's a slow, tedious thing sometime, unless you talking about an old-timer going lickety split, which she ain't generally going to send for the birthwoman anyhow—but most times you just got to get into that rhythm. You can't be expecting to rush it along, even when you think they going to die. So I was used to moving slow and waiting on God and the baby's time. I was breathing with the woman, I's trying to love her, because you do best to love them, I already known that then, know it better now. But it's hard to love somebody you never laid eyes on till you see her crouched down naked on her roseprint rug, plus which, she's white—though I did not yet have so much bitterness in my heart as come later, because I had not yet seen out of whitefolks what I seen before it was all done, but I finally coax that woman to let me rub her belly. You got to do like this, see: you got to breathe with her while her pains coming, you got to talk to her while you breathing, say like this: Here it come, mama, ride the top of it, ride with it, yes, mama, easy, mama, eeeeasy, eeeeasy, and so. That's the same for any. At midnight the southwind die, and I remembers Bluford's ax, say, Un-huh, ax done its work, and me and the woman just keep on in that time outside of time. I'm praying for the Lord to deliver her safe, plus that doctor to hurry up and get down from Bristow.

Windchange come along way up in the night. Afterwhile I adds another prayer, say please God for Bluford to go out and turn his ax around, because this new wind bringing in something fierce feel like it want to freeze the blood in my bones. That whole house is shaking. Windows rattling, upstairs shuddering, floor just shivering underneath my feet. I look up and see her then, not the little foxface but a darkhaired middling girl, two long brown braids, she's standing on one foot beside the door, got her other foot wrapped behind at the ankle, her hand crammed in her mouth, and that girl is shaking the same way as the house. She's bleeding. I mean, she bleeding just like her mama, out herself all over the rug. Look like she got her monthly but she don't know it. Long bloody streaks down her skirt, little red plops on that roseprint rug. I say, Sister, there's enough blood in this room already take Moses to part it. You best go clean yourself up. Girl look down at herself then, and she do what I certainly do not expect. She pull her fist out her mouth and start to laugh. Laughing like a crazy child. I walk over and tug on the pull-rag, that little door slap back against the wall, and, Lord, the northwind do in that moment rise up and wail. I nudge that girl out the door, but not before I hear the whole rest of them girls downstairs wailing, like to sound near as loud and boiling as the wind, and I thinks to myself, I have never seen such a pitiful house. I turn back to the whitewoman, but she don't know anything about it. She all turned in on herself, like any laboring woman got to do. Everything settle down nice and quiet then, the woman moaning regular, and that is all, because, for her, time and everything stop. The same so for me.

You don't know how it go. Time don't run in a line forward but spiral around and dark and up, till change come, and you don't know because you in it to breathe it and live it, and only outside of birth and dying do you think it's some other way. Woman let me in close now, she in no condition to stop me, and I touch hold of her belly but I can't tell if the baby's living or dead or where its head is, because that belly twisted around so, and I know I got to put my hand inside to feel it, but she ain't about to let me, she still sensible down there, and I think then it's going to be a long time longer, because her pains stay the same, not closer, not spiraling for the change coming, and I just hold on and touch her on the outside when she let me, rub her lightly, rub her and chant real soft and pray that doctor come up the stairs.

Keep on, keep on, and afterwhile I see it's getting close to daylight and that woman's pains don't get no closer together. Then, seem like they getting farther apart. Then for true and certain they coming farther apart, you could piece a quilt-top nearly in between how far they come. And that doctor ain't arrived yet. Window curtains get light. The woman begin to wake out herself, and she look up at me and see me, which scare me plenty, because I don't think she ever before that moment known I was there. That's when I finally see it on her face. She's scared. She and me both scared. I pray to Jesus it don't show on my face like it do on hers.

That woman ain't got pain one. You can see it. She's not laboring, she just sweating. She put her lips together, quit groaning, quit with any kind of sound. She way past mad, her eyes just nothing but fear. Well, you know labor don't up and quit like that, not for a loosed-up practiced woman like this one, got children strung like seedcorn all over the house. Labor pains don't quit unless something is mighty bad wrong, guaranteed. I thinks to myself, That child sure enough dead now, and I guess she know it. Maybe it's been dead a long time, maybe that's what stink so.

But I watch the woman's face awhile, and I see stopped pains ain't what put the terror in it. Might be the signal but it ain't the cause. The cause is inside that woman's belly, and that's what make it so bad. You think I don't know? Listen. Me, here, Iola Bloodgood Bullet Tiger Long, I have seen every type of human fear. I seen Laura Nelson and her two children dragged out the Okemah jail in 1911. Yes, ma'am, I will tell it. Again and again I'll tell it. Them whitefolks hanged Laura Nelson and her little boy off a bridge west of town, left that baby crying by the side of the road. I was witness to that, I don't care if folks do lie and say it ain't happened. Stood right there in the alley, me and six other womens from the church, watched them carry her up Main Street, she's screaming—Lord, them screams be in my dreams for eternity—trying to get loose, get hold of her children. She know what's going to happen, we all know, and her fear different from the little boy's fear, different from us churchwomen's, and I seen all three kinds. I seen the kind when you afraid to lift your head, not because somebody's going to do you body-harm but because they going to do you soul-harm, because they going to shame you, make you feel like a worm, and you more scared of that than a licking, so you can't find strength to move. I'm not talking about I felt it, though the Lord do know I have, I'm talking about *seeing* it, how you look at it and see it and know what kind of fear. I have seen children terrified of their fathers, grown men terrified of witches, people terrified of each other in all kind of ways. And I tell you this: that whitewoman's fear been different from any other, and I'll tell you how. She ain't afraid of something coming at her from the out-side. Even them that's dying and know they dying without Jesus, they're afraid of something outside theirself, which is Satan or Hell or God's Judg-ment or pure blank empty nothing. But this woman scared of something inside her own skin. My whole life there's been just one other time I see the kind of fear like I seen on that whitewoman, and that was in Wetumka in 1907, time I see Curtis Monday on Main Street, drunk as seven lords, screaming about he got tarantulas crawling out his knees.

The woman is hunched up on her nether side sort of, her right side—she can't lay on her back nor any other way on account of how that baby's slung around so—and she's peeking over her great big titty, down around and back, like she's looking for some mess somebody told her been smeared on her. Face so white it's gone to clear nearly, you can see every blue vein in her neck, see little red threads popping underneath the skin. Right then it look like she's fixing to go mad—I don't mean mad an-gry, I mean mad loco insane. She take in to moaning, but not about pain, them moans ain't about body-hurt, they about the lowest sorry you ever believe. Reach back with both hands, touch that swelling like it's not a baby but a blob of something too terrible to talk about that somebody take and smear upon her. Whispering to herself. I can't hear what she say. But something happen to her face, it go from fear to something entirely dif-ferent, run through madness and sorry right quick, like she got no time to pause with them, they not important enough to tarry, and she lean over with some kind of terrible grunt and spit out the side of her mouth, spit blood and some pieces of teeth off the side of the bed, down on that ru-ined rug. When she come up, her face covered with the purest—I don't know what you call it—*aim-to-do-it* I ever see. She saying the Lord's name over and over, in all its magnifications.

Well, lady, I taken to praying to Jesus outloud, say, Sweet Jesus, have mercy on this your poor servant and her poor friend a sinner. I was scared,

I don't know what's going to happen, the way that whitewoman blas-pheming the Lord. Wind howling around the house, girls wailing down-stairs, two of us womens saying the Lord's name outloud. You have to see what happen to know what that whitewoman doing, because she just say like this, like you cuss a dog in the biscuits, she say, *Christ Almighty, you so and so*—she don't say *so and so,* but I don't talk such a way, even in telling—she say, *You so and so, GET on out of there, Jesus Lord God, take it, take it, take me.* She say, *Dear God Holy Christ Almighty God Son of God Son of Man Heavenly Host Lord God Holy Ghost Almighty Father Lord Jesus Christ Almighty Holy Christ Father,* and on and on. Oh, she's sweating, she got her mouth clamped, spitting out Christ' holy name. She touch that swelling with the tips of her fingers, touch it like ten spiderlegs tapping. I look there, I see it: her twisted-around belly start to ripple. Oh, it's huge, you know, big white mound of flesh, purple popped veins run-ning through it, been this huge pale naked mountain in them soaked sheets all this time. But now it look delicate as glass. More so than glass, like a soap bubble, like you could touch it and pop it, like a floatable, frangible, airy thing. And that belly rippling, moving like waves of pond-water pushed by the wind, and I swear to you right now standing before the face of the Lord, you could see inside that pregnant womb. Her skin gone to clear, right there while she praying.

Don't believe me. I don't care. You ask me to tell it, I tell it.

Look now. See that baby's head, huge as a mushmelon. See them big veins. Looky. Looky. It's pressing down. See the butt there, belly stretched so clear you can see the crack between them two little round mounds. Look there, that's a elbow poking out. Baby is living, and, Lord, I don't see how. Baby is swimming. Look at it. Swimming around the side of its mama, wriggling like a great white fat tadpole coming, swimming side-ways, wiggling down. Only time in my life I ever see such a thing. That mama don't even appear like she's pushing. You expect a woman going to start to want to push soon as she come up on peaking. Peaking! Shoot. That woman slide right past any notion of peaking, she's going for the whole shooting match right now. And she don't push like a normal woman, like she's fixing to pop a vein out her behind. Best I can tell, this woman is pushing out of her head. I don't mean she gone out her mind, though she been teetering on that for a long time, I mean she's not push-ing with her teeth and jaw and bowels and belly and inside muscles so strong they ought to be laid on a workmule and still yet hid so deep no human eyes ever going to see 'em. Oh, womens will push with they eyeballs, I'm telling you, every particle inch honed to the one purpose of pushing that child out into the world, but this woman do not have her whole entire body set on pushing, but only her mind. I'm telling the truth now. She's laboring with her thoughts, her body don't have nothing to do with it, I don't know how to describe it any better than that. Look like she's praying to God and cussing that child at the same time, like she depending on that child to get its ownself out and God to help if He care to.

I's standing on that bloody rug thinking, Lord, this whitelady's body done gone to pieces, her interior muscles is wore out. Say to myself, This child know its mama ain't helping, this child know it's going to have to get out on its own. I look yonder and see that woman haunched up on her frontside. She done roll over. I don't know how she turned that big old white mountain around on that soft bed and I didn't see, I's looking right at it but never mindfully seen it, but next thing I know, she's crouched up on her knees. Rocking. Got her face in the pillow. Weeping. Weeping like Jesus in the Garden. She's not weeping with pain—this is the kind of woman, you could slice her ear off, she'll turn and spit at you. She's weeping with sorrow. I don't know what kind of sorrow, it's no kin of any sorrow I been familiar with. Now I look back I can get mad if I let myself—that poor whitewoman and her poor pitiful sorrow—but I trust all that to Jesus and the Hereafter, let others do what they will.

Sure enough, this is how she going to give birth, up like that, rocking on her knees on that old soft featherbed, big belly hanging to the red sheet, blood just a-pouring. What am I going to do but get myself up behind that woman? Oh, everything, everything all twisted around, it don't pleasure me to be at the hind end in that smell and blood and excrement, but it's how God seen fit to put it, and the baby's head swelling toward me. Ordinarily, baby's crown is going to show and slip back, show and slip back, maybe just twice or three times for a practiced woman—sometime it'll slide back more times than you or the mama either one care to speculate—but this baby ain't going to do nothing like most. That head swell toward me blueblack as my daddy's bald pate, whole mess of hair matted down purple, and Lord God, it is huge, and it never stop, pause for nothing, I think the child's fixing to land on its neck and break it, that big old purple head coming so fast. Jesus Lord have mercy, it tear that woman plumb asunder, you can hear it, hear the flesh rip same as you'd tear a old sheet for wrappings. She never let out one scream. Just keep on with *Lord God Almighty Christ Jesus Lord.* You know once any child's head get through, the whole rest going to slip out quick, I got to catch it, so, slippery bigheaded thing, got to try and keep it from dropping, can't get a grip anywhere without I'm afraid I'm going to mark it. I opens my two big palms, slide 'em under. I can't get hold of the child's shoulders, child *got* no shoulders to speak of, skinny, skinny butt, don't amount to nothing, but I catches him, palm the child up toward its mama's belly.

Ease my hands down to the blood sheet. Look here, see what you got. Boychild. No different to what I fully known and expected. Frequently I known the child's sex before I seen its peter if it's a boychild, I don't know why. Girl babies, I'd be guessing right up to the last minute, and I don't really mean guessing, because when you trying to help a child into the world you don't be thinking about boy or girl, you thinking *baby,* that's all. Most boy babies, same way, the majority of them, but when I did know beyond doubting, it's invariably been a male child.

This male child laying faceup beneath his mama's belly. Don't make a sound. But he's wide awake, breathing. Now's when I get me a good look at the child's face, and this here is what it look like: a rutabaga turnip turned blueblack from frostbite. The same. Its neck swoll up the same size as the head, that broad across, plumb even with them skinny shoulders. Eyes like two dried plums set in pudding. Got no nose, can't make out the lips hardly but for where they open and you can see that black tongue. Look like two completely different children joined against each other, top part the color of a overripe mulberry, bottom part white as heavy cream, all except for its little purple privacies swelled up so fat. This is the extent of the damage that calf done.

But I ain't got time to study that neither, because here come the after-birth slithering out, long skinny red thing, look like a slaughtered hog's entrails more than what it supposed to be, laying there midst the blood and all nature of bodily fluids—we all three smeared red, look like that featherbed and rug and my own dress all going to be ruint, because you know blood is one element in nature don't want to come out. Woman give a little grunt—she quit saying the Lord's name, I don't know when she quit it, just notice upon that grunt that she have quit—and she pro-ceed to start 'flating down like she's fixing to let all her air out and col-lapse. I think she's going to lay down upon that baby and smother it like I seen a mare do once when she gived birth to a little mule. I guess a sound must've come out my mouth, because, just in time to keep from killing it, she groan and roll off to the side and lay flat, like a man do when he fin-ish the marriage relations.

Now here come the pause. Here finally come the pause when me and her, and—believe it or don't believe, I don't care—that infant, too, all taken stock. We all three blinking at ourselves. Gray light come in at the curtains, that coal-oil lamp on the table look weak, pee-yellow, how it do in daylight, and I's thinking then it was just past dawn and this all happen in a minute, but later I find out it was almost straight-up noon. We all three blinking, that baby alert as anything, still tied to the mama by the birthcord. The woman look at the child. Look at him. Look at him.

I done back off the bed now, standing, my knees feels like water. Woman look up at me, her face blank like somebody sandpaper every feature off it. Look back at that child. She just taken and roll over, turn her back to it. She don't care about that cord going to jerk its belly or nothing, just roll over and put her face to the wall. She say, Take it. Take it out to the ravine and smash its head in. Her voice completely even. She say, I never in my life wanted to give birth to a monster such as that. Lay still then, big naked whitewoman red from the waist down. Baby lay there breathing, that's all, never cry when that birthcord tug its belly. Never let forth a sound.

But I did hear something then, and at first I put it off to the wind, because that northwind is still picking and prying at every window around that little shakeshingle house. But what I heard wasn't no wind. I don't know how it's possible I never felt her. Never sensed her one iota, I don't have any idea how long she been standing there in the doorway. Don't know when she creeped back up the stairs and come watching. Might've been a long time, because, from the look of the bloody streaks all up and down the front of it, she never even yet changed her dress.

PART TWO

Kin

Tulsa, Oklahoma
Wednesday
September 1, 1920

It began in such a small way.

The girl had been with them three months then. From the beginning there'd been something about her that bothered Althea. On the first day, when the girl had stood quiet in the dining room, tall, big-boned, her high slanted face gazing impassively as Althea gave instructions for polishing the sideboard—even in those first moments she'd felt troubled by the girl. It wasn't just her slow pace, though that was part of it. Althea sometimes watched from the parlor doorway, following the girl's languid movements invisibly, inside her own body, aching to prod her along like a dawdling milk cow. But the girl did her work well, deliberately and thoroughly, and her slowness was really only a vexation. It was something more.

Once, early on, the girl had turned when Althea stood watching behind her. She'd neither smiled nor looked shamed, as so many of them did when they felt themselves watched by a white person, nor changed the indifferent pace of her movement. Her face was serene, and completely unreadable. Althea had smiled quickly, startled at the warm blossom of shame opening inside her, and asked the girl to touch up the flatware when she'd finished. The girl's head tipped forward in a barely perceptible nod, and she'd turned back to the silver coffee urn she was polishing.

After that, Althea hid herself more perfectly when she kept an eye on the girl. Or she would walk abruptly into the room where the girl was cleaning, half hoping, she knew, to catch her at something, though she could never quite lay her mind on what.

The girl's given name was Graceful. That, too, irritated Althea. The aptness of it. The slow elegance of the girl's movements grated on her, and she would find herself gritting her teeth as she watched the girl move placidly from mantel to highboy with her duster, her arm reaching in a slow arc, her hips rolling luxuriously beneath the cotton skirt. Yet, when Franklin began to call the girl Grace or Gracie when he spoke to her, Althea corrected him.

"Her name is Graceful," she would say, outside the girl's hearing. "The least you can do is call the girl by her rightful given name."

Certainly she'd never thought to ask Graceful's surname. Like so much that had never occurred to her, the idea that the girl even had a last name never crossed Althea's mind. If anyone had asked—a neighbor, say, or someone from the Auxiliary, which of course never happened—Althea would have dismissed the question with a shrug of her shoulders. Graceful's family name would be some dead president's, more than likely, Washington or Jackson or Lincoln or Johnson. She'd never thought about the girl's life, or her family, where she'd come from. Never dreamed there was anything more to the girl's existence than her slow, placid movements and the vague stirrings of unease she produced in Althea.

And so when the letter came, delivered by a grinning roundfaced colored boy of about ten, who ducked his head and grinned wider when Althea told him to wipe his feet before stepping onto the porch floor, there was more than a small stab of surprise in Althea's heart.

Graceful had gone to do the shopping, had left an hour before, bareheaded, though a light rain was falling (another source of irritation—other women's housemaids went about with their heads wrapped properly in white cotton rags), the produce basket on her arm. Althea, passing near the pantry, heard the light rapping on the back door.

The boy stood on the steps, reaching up with one hand to swipe at the droplets beading the tight nap of his hair. His other hand was tucked in the fold of his shirt. Behind him, in the side yard, her rose garden was obscured in the grayness. Althea could just make out the spreading boughs of the elm tree in her backyard.

"Yes?" she said, and the boy grinned, hunched his shoulders. A chill passed through Althea, brought on, she thought, by the dampness seeping through the screen, and she turned, crossed the screened-in porch, stepped into the kitchen.

"Well," she said when she turned to close the inner door and saw that the boy still stood outside the screen, "Come in, boy." And then quickly: "Wipe your feet first!"

The boy dug his feet into the soaked doormat, vigorously, over and over, grinning, until Althea said, "That's fine, that will do," and he pulled the screen open, stepped onto the smooth gray-painted planks of the porch floor. He kept one leg behind him, close to the door, as if to make sure he could dart back through it should the situation turn dangerous.

"Yes, what is it?" Althea assumed him to be a neighbor's yardboy sent with a request or an invitation, and she was annoyed at having to answer the door herself—and then was doubly irritated at her own quick irritability. It was with her so often now, she didn't know why.

A flicker of uncertainty passed over the boy's face, and he looked past Althea's shoulders into the kitchen. "Graceful?" he said. His eyes turned to Althea again. "This here where Graceful Whiteside work?"

"What?" Althea said, startled, hearing it and dismissing it within the same heartbeat. "Who?"

"Do a woman name Graceful work here, ma'am? Is what I mean to say." He shifted his weight to his back leg.

"Yes," Althea answered, less sharply. "A girl named Graceful works for me."

"She here, ma'am?"

"She ought to be back in a little while. She's gone for the shopping. I'll give her a message, or—" Althea glanced at the boy's muddy shoes; she went on in a tight voice. "If you want, I guess you can wait."

"I got a letter here I'm suppose to deliver."

The boy removed his hand from the front of his shirt, and as the brown hand pulled free from the threadbare white cotton, a foreboding passed though Althea, a feeling of dread, of something irrevocable begun. The boy held a wrinkled, pale blue envelope toward her. Althea took it from him. The envelope was damp, the inked letters blurred at the edges. But there it was, clearly written in a delicate backhand scrawl:

Miss Graceful Whiteside
Care of Mr. Franklin H. Dedmeyer, Esq.
1600 Block So. Carson
City

"Ma'am?" the boy said. "Ma'am? You could give that letter to Graceful?" He cleared his throat lightly behind his hand. "Ma'am? You could give it to her for me?"

"Yes," Althea said finally. "I'll see that she gets it."

"Thank you much, ma'am." The boy backed through the screen door, turned and jumped down the four steps to the wet ground. He landed on his feet and took off running.

"Boy!" Althea rushed across the porch, and the coiled spring twanged loudly as she shoved open the door. "Boy!" she called.

He stopped halfway across the yard, his shoulders hunched against the mist, or against the sound in Althea's voice then. After a long moment he turned around.

"This name here," Althea called. She held the envelope toward him, though she knew he could scarcely see it for the rain and the distance. "Is this name right? This name Whiteside?"

"Yes'm," the boy called back.

"Whiteside is Graceful's last name? You're sure of that?"

"I guess so, ma'am." The boy grinned, a white flash in the grayness. "That's alla us last name."

Graceful did not seem surprised to find her mistress standing in the middle of the kitchen with an envelope in her hand and the back door open, allowing into the house the sweltering dampness from the screened-in porch. She nodded in the slight, irritating way she had, crossed in front of Althea, and opened her arms to allow the soggy bundles she carried to fall onto the counter next to the sink. Althea watched the long square of the girl's back as she lifted the full produce basket and thunked it onto the counter. She watched the girl's fingers moving among the packages, untying strings and rolling them into small, tight balls, pulling moist tan paper from red slabs of meat.

"A letter came for you," she said finally, and lifted the envelope, creased now in the center from where she'd held it so tightly. Graceful stepped from the counter and took it from her hand. Without a word of thanks or a glance at the inscription she slipped the envelope into a loose pocket of her apron, turned back to the counter.

"You're wet." Althea was beginning to come to herself now. "You'd better get out of those wet things, and then. . . ." Her eyes swept the kitchen, the pantry, the open doorway, landed finally on the brown smears of mud on the gray porch planks by the door. "And then see about cleaning up that mess out there before you start dinner."

Graceful nodded again, the barest gesture of acknowledgment. She walked across the kitchen and disappeared into the back hall, toward the maid's room. Althea stood awhile longer, alone in the kitchen, seeing in her mind's eye—as she'd seen it for the past hour, appearing and disappearing, swimming in some invisible place before her—the image of a flax-colored dress she'd owned once as a girl.

In the evening Althea tried to speak of it to her husband. She sat propped against the feather pillows in the four-poster bed, her dark hair loose upon her shoulders, a new novel loose in her long hands, lying open on the coverlet. Franklin stood before the mirror, his great blond head lifted toward the ceiling as he worked to unclasp the button tight at his collar.

"A boy came today," she began. She fell silent, and the sound of the hard rain in the yard filled the space of the silence.

Franklin glanced over his shoulder, his fingers tugging at the collar. "Well?" he said. "Damn this thing." He turned back to the glass.

"Yes. To bring a letter to Graceful."

"Well," Franklin said. He pulled the button free finally, and his fingers flicked down the shirt front, freeing the others. He went on, seeming to have hardly heard her. "Ran into L.O. Murphy this afternoon. I don't know. He acts like he knows a little too much about that unfortunate business Saturday night." Franklin frowned, shaking his head. "You'd think he'd keep a little tighter lip, the way the papers are talking."

Althea stirred beneath the sheet, irritated; she didn't want to hear any more about that awful lynching. Tulsa had talked of little else for days. It was boring, stupid, ugly. She ran her fingers along an unread page of the novel.

"They tell me the governor's trying to get the names of the ringleaders, though I don't believe it, but they're liable to call in anybody can't keep his mouth shut. That'd be L.O." Franklin glanced at his wife. "He bragged for an hour on that new pool at Bigheart, says they're pumping thirty thousand a day."

His brows came together, frowning, but his eyes were lit bright from the inside. Althea knew this look in her husband, this blend of jealousy and hope warring always in his face at news of the success of another. Delo Petroleum had made creditable strikes, had secured leases for several minor pools, but none of his little company's discovery wells had touched anything like the wealth foretold by the Nellie Johnstone or the Ida Glenn. Still, Franklin never doubted that the next well was going to be the bonanza gusher, that he and his partner were just days or inches, moments or miles away from the big strike, and so news of another's success both confirmed and threatened his faith, for it declared that there was still plenty of the earth's black blood flowing in the hidden sands of Oklahoma, and it whispered secretly, urgently, Hurry, hurry, it will all be gone soon, you'll miss it, fool, hurry, you're going to miss out. "L.O. swears Bigheart's going to be as big as Cushing, bigger than Glenn Pool, but you know what a braggart L.O. Murphy is." The abiding hope and envy did battle in Franklin's face as he shrugged himself out of his linen shirt.

Althea turned her eyes to the window, where water streamed down the glass in dark, trembling sheets. She thought again of the boy and the letter, and Graceful, asleep now, she supposed, in the tiny maid's room downstairs. She tried to think how to bring it up. She told herself it was nothing, there was no reason to tell Franklin. And what would he care? Very little sank into his awareness that did not have to do with oil. She had no reason to tell him. Well, she would mention the thing casually, like a shard of gossip from a neighbor. She thought of several ways to put it and opened her mouth several times to speak it, but in the end Althea could find no casual words for this information that had so stilled her she'd stood for an hour after the boy had disappeared in the grayness. Stood alone in the center of the kitchen, staring at her own family name on an envelope addressed to a colored girl.

It's stupid, she thought, her eyes tracing the rain's trembling. *There's absolutely no reason to mention it.* Anyway, she knew where darkies got white names; it hardly mattered (and deep in her mind a thought jerked: *What matters anymore? What matters?*), and she shut that away and said nothing. Franklin's trousers fell to the floor, the suspenders clunking softly on the carpet. He reached for his nightshirt.

"Jim's wanting me to come to Bristow tomorrow, says he wants to show me a spot down on the Deep Fork."

A sudden tightening clamped Althea's chest, and her mind closed down as sudden. She sat very still, her face composed, her mind empty.

"Gypsy's got most of the lease land sewed up down there, but . . ." He turned toward her, his blue eyes bright, lit with hunger. "Jim's really hot for me to come down."

Althea stirred almost imperceptibly, thinking perhaps she would get up and go wash her face again; it felt sticky, covered with a light film from the

oppressive humidity. Thinking she would go downstairs and make sure
the girl had closed all the windows. But she made no move to rise; rather,
she lifted her knees beneath the white eyelet coverlet and settled the book
upon them. Her eyes glided left to right, following the letters on the page.

"Nobody's 'catting down in that direction lately, but maybe that's a
good sign. Might be a good sign. Or not." Franklin's voice was studiedly
casual, tight with deception, even against his wife, who paid him no attention. He turned back to the mirror, ran both hands though his thick hair,
smoothing it, his fingers sweeping along either side of this head. "I don't
put too much credence in it, really," he said. "Those old Deep Fork bottoms don't seem likely, if you ask me, but I'll have a look-see."

A terrible restlessness pushed through Althea, though it showed only
in the way her fingers picked at the corners of the book's pages. She sat
quite still against the pillows, her eyes steady now, her face a white mask,
her fingers stroking the slightly nicked edges of the thin paper. Her husband's gaze was on his own face in the mirror, and he didn't see—nor
would he have thought anything of it if he had seen, for in their many
years together he'd never come to understand the meaning of his wife's
habits. Althea grew outwardly rigid when her heart was in turmoil, her agitation revealed always through small, pettish tics. But Franklin thought of
his wife as a serene woman, a transformation of the bold girl he'd married:
she'd grown tranquil from grief, he believed, and his eyes never saw anything in her to conflict with this idea.

He went on talking, his voice pitched with excitement, his words
guarded, but Althea didn't listen. She turned inward toward the roaring
inside her, the rush of blood in her ears. The mention of her husband's
partner could sometimes set the outward stillness upon her, but it was not
the speaking of Jim Dee Logan's name now that held her. Althea's mind
slid over it as over a small stone in silt, and crashed instead against the
words *Deep Fork* like a boulder. The name of the brooding river she'd
grown up beside caught hold of her and kept her, forcing memories upon
her she was unwilling to yield to. Her mind flailed, reaching for something to think of that would push away the images rising, but she could
find nothing to seize upon, and she could not will her mind blank. She
looked at her husband's slight paunch pressing the inside of his under-
shirt, his thick neck and golden head turned toward the mirror, and she
hated him then, as if he were conspiring with the letter and the flax-colored
dress and all that she'd sheltered so long from her memory: as if he knew
and were adding with intent to this chasm opening inside her.

She slapped the book shut and placed it on the nightstand, sank down beneath the covers. But she couldn't keep the stillness on her surface now, and she rose up again and threw the coverlet to the side, saying, "Lord, it's hot in here. Don't tell me that idiot boy's lit the furnace already."

Her husband paused, one arm half thrust in the sleeve of his nightshirt. His reflection stared at her from the mirror. "What's the matter with you?"

"Nothing. It's hot. It's suffocating in here. I can't breathe, can't you open a window?"

"That's a blowing rain, Thea. And it's not hot in here—matter of fact, it's damned chilly." He turned fully around and looked at her, hard at first, and then his face softened, his forehead tilted slightly. Althea hated that tilt of forehead that indicated Franklin was concerned and, to her mind, disgustingly sincere. He came toward her, pulling the nightshirt around him. "What's the matter? Are you sick?" He reached to feel her brow for fever, but she shrank back, shaking her head.

"No. No, it's nothing. I'm hot, that's all. Just crack the window a little at the bottom."

He stood over her a moment, and then turned and crossed the rug and pushed the glass up an inch. The sound of pounding rain washed into the room. He finished buttoning his nightshirt as he moved toward the doorway, paused with his hand on the lightswitch, frowning at her. Althea gazed back at him. Her heart was stiller now.

Franklin turned out the light, and she heard the soft shuffle of his feet on the carpet. She felt the mattress sink as he crawled beneath the sheet, and then, soon—too soon, long before she was ready—the tips of his fingers brushing along the silken edge of her gown. She lay rigid on her back, staring up into the black space over her head. Her husband's fingers came at her like some snuffling night-thing, prying, poking, trying to get in. "Franklin," she said aloud in the darkness. His hand stopped, expectant, very still and waiting. Then the weight of the bed shifted as he soundlessly rolled onto his side away from her.

Althea held her eyes open, waiting for the streetlamp in front of the house to balance the sudden extinguishing of the light. Franklin's breathing slowed and grew regular. She was glad. Maybe he would sleep soon and there would not be the silent stiffness between them. She listened to the drumming on the roof, the splashing in the yard below. The day's spitting mist had given way at evening to a rolling thunderstorm driven east by fierce winds across the prairies, and now the great crashes and low rumbles had moved on, leaving behind this gorged, steady drumming.

She waited, waited, she knew not for what. *For the streetlight,* she told herself, though she understood this was not it. Still, she was glad when the thin bluish glow began to give form to the objects in the room, and she looked with relief at the familiar shapes dissolving from the dimness into the lives of themselves: the scrolled wardrobe along the west wall, the mahogany vanity near the window, with the low stool crouched before it and the high oval mirror glinting silverish in the poor light.

Althea had dismissed memory with the sudden closing of the novel, the gesture of placing it on the nightstand; she'd succeeded, with long-practiced skill, in forcing the past into a walled-off place far from her consciousness. And yet the restlessness was here. The monotonous thrumming of the rain drove at her and into her, and she gritted her teeth against it; she tried to force a softening into her limbs, but the easing would not come. She wanted to rise and close the window, wanted to stand at the glass and raise her fists and shout at the glutted heavens, Shut up, shut up, shut up! Convulsively she reached out and touched her husband's back. Immediately he rolled toward her. Immediately his snuffling fingers crept up beneath her gown.

Afterwards, she listened to him sink toward sleep: the ragged intake of breath, the long wait, the plosive exhale. His weight was dense beside her. She moved only slightly, and Franklin roused, grumbled, "For God's sake, Thea." He reached for her and wrapped his arms tightly around her, as if he would muffle her tension, bury it with himself. She held still, and Franklin settled again, his snores at last covering the rain's rhythms. Quietly, hardly breathing, she slipped from his grasp, from beneath the sheets, stood and walked in the blue light's trembling.

The house was silent but for the steady drumming on the rooftop. There was no ticking, no settling of this new house in the coolness of night. In her thin silken gown, her feet bare, she groped toward the bathroom at the end of the hall. She felt the sudden release, the warm clot rolling down, followed by the slow trickle, like blood. Like relief. Like the loss of all possibility. The warmth cooled on the inside of her thigh as she edged forward in the darkness.

Her feet left the smooth surface of wood, touched the tiles of the bathroom. In the darkness she found her facecloth, still damp from the evening's washing, draped on the side of the tub. She wet it with cool water from the lavatory and wiped her face, lifted her heavy hair and washed the back of her neck. Then she raised the front of her gown and washed herself roughly, scrubbing the cloth hard back and forth. Though she almost believed now it would not happen, could not happen, she knew from long experience that sleep wouldn't come until she'd washed away the smell. She rinsed the cloth again, shook it, and folded it neatly over the tub's porcelain lip, and then she turned in the small, dark room, went out into the darker hallway.

Down the stairs, her right hand touching lightly the cherry banister, a moment's pause in the foyer, and then she turned left into the parlor. Laced light crosshatched the carpet through the sheer window curtains. She looked at the pieces she'd placed just so in the room when they'd moved into the house: her small tables and treasures, the silk brocade fainting couch, the high-backed wing chair, the velvet divan. Only a year ago, and the pleasure in it, the newness and luxury that had delighted her for a short time, seemed old now, dried up and sullen. What had she come in here for? She couldn't remember. She turned and went back into the foyer, where colored light streamed from the oval stained-glass window next to the door. *Not here,* she thought. *Nothing here.* In rising agitation she crossed the hallway, stumbled through the dark library into the dining room.

The heavy damask drapes at the French doors smothered the room in darkness. Althea felt her way to the dining table, and began to move slowly in a great circle around it. She paused a moment with her back to the oak breakfront, pressed her palms to the front of her chest; she circled the table again, touching the smooth lip of polished wood with her fingertips, her pelvis bumping the backs of the chairs. Abruptly, she stopped. What did she want here? For an instant she couldn't remember where she was. She stood in swimming black space, with no sense of right or left, up or down. Untethered and terrified in the darkness. Then a pale rectangle of light calmed her from the far side of the room, and she moved toward it. She stepped through the narrow passageway into the kitchen.

There was light here; the white floor grasped the faint glow falling through the uncurtained window and enlarged it, and Althea was relieved a moment, standing in the center, in the same place she'd stood staring at the crumpled envelope for an hour in the afternoon. Such a long time ago. She could hardly remember. It seemed like a dream now. But the sense of that standing—not the mind's memory but the body's recollection— pushed the restlessness on her again. What did she want here? What had she come for? She searched her body with an inward turning of her senses. Was she hungry? No, not hungry. Not hungry on any level.

She stood in the pale box of the kitchen, disoriented, empty. Her mind traced and retraced itself, seeking old comforts: the slow smile and rising gaze of a stranger on the street; a certain woman's arched eyebrow at Althea's entrance into a chandeliered hall, and the immediate stir in that goldenlit room, the turning of a hundred faces toward her. She tried to call up the deep sensuous pleasure, as she'd first known it, at the touch of fox fur, delicate porcelain, sculpted wood, but these failed her, and so she turned to the fail-proof pleasure: the secret dream she'd cherished for years. Jim Dee Logan's name, the thought of his face, a word of him—that, at least, had always been able to raise the small rush of pulse and pleasure. She waited for the sly, familiar warmth at the recollection of his image—but the image itself would not even come. *What now?* the words said. *What shall I want now?*

Quickly she turned and left the kitchen, back through the dark dining room, the library, into the foyer once more. She reached for the polished wood of the banister, but even as her hand lifted, she turned her eyes, unintended, toward the south wall, and at once she stopped.

Street light tumbling through the stained-glass window lit the gilt mirror over the hall table in a trembling chiaroscuro of reds and blues and yellows. Althea's hand fell to her side, and she moved as if bidden to the mirror, stood before it. Reflected in the colored light she saw her own image: the pale oval haloed in darkness, the two elegant curves of her brows, her ivory neck, the angular line of her shoulders beneath the silk gown. But in the trick of light and shadow, the smooth bodice began to coarsen, turn to muslin, darken with glistening streaks; she watched the curve of her face narrow and sharpen, the bone of jaw jutting, teeth gritted, against the sickness inside her mouth. Panicked, she willed herself to escape, but the sense of being ungrounded, without source or direction, trapped her, and she couldn't tell where to run.

She felt the girl's presence first as a square of warmth against her back in the cool hall, and then, in incremental degrees, the dark face took form beside her own in the glass: the luminous eyes first, reflecting light, and soon the planed cheeks, the broad nose and backtilted forehead. The girl's brushed-out hair radiated wildly, without definition against the cavernous foyer, and for a moment longer Althea still could not be sure she wasn't dreaming, for the features were completely immobile, but then the mouth opened, the soft voice said, "Ma'am? You all right?"

Violently, as if jerked awake, Althea whirled around, and from her own mouth there spat forth a sound, profane in its essence, though it had no English meaning. As quickly as the curse erupted, Althea clamped her mouth closed. Graceful stood a few feet from her in a white cotton gown. The expression on the girl's face was as placid, unsurprised, unmoved as ever.

"What the devil's the matter with you?" Althea hissed. "Sneaking around out here in the dark!" Instantly she drew back her shoulders, raised her chin, composed the mask on her face. "Did you close the windows in the library? I'd better not find rain on my carpet in the morning, hear me?"

Graceful's head tilted up only the slightest fraction, but Althea saw it: the soft sheen of light on forehead and cheekbones, the little lift of defiance. It was enough.

"Don't you dare sull up at me! Don't you dare! If you're not the laziest, sneakingest, slowest damn excuse for a housemaid—Shut that sulky mouth! I'll pinch a plug out of it. Get back in the bed this minute. You'd better not ever let me catch you creeping around my house in the dark. Never! Do you hear?"

But the girl had already turned away.

As she watched the ghostly gown disappear down the dark hall, Althea received a new sensation, burning her dulled senses, past the emptiness and the familiar prickling irritation: she hated the girl with a dead white heat.

By morning Althea had managed to do with the previous night's encounter what she did with all uncomfortable recollections: pushed it quite comfortably to a confined corner of her mind, and dismissed it. This was an old trick of memory in her, one she'd developed in the beginning by force and now continued by habit, but on this occasion she'd achieved the separation entirely in her sleep, so that by the time she awakened to the earthy after-rain smell and the sunlight streaming through lace curtains, she had no more sense of her fears of the night before than the vague stirrings of a half-remembered bad dream. This, too, she struggled away from, scrambling from the bedclothes as a cat claws free from water, and she crossed the carpet quickly and reached inside the oak wardrobe for her wrapper.

Franklin, of course, was already up, either downstairs at breakfast or gone now to the office at the Hotel Tulsa or to the Robinson, wherever his leasehound instincts told him to hurry off to downtown. Althea glanced at the window to discover the time, and seeing the full morning light, she moved rapidly, though in a smooth, controlled manner, to the vanity and picked up her hairbrush. Seated sideways, so that she faced not the tall mirror but the nearby window, she brushed her hair with long, brusque strokes and twisted it up and pinned it. She glanced to see that no stray hairs had slipped from her fingers, that the thick brown knot was straight, and then she stood up quickly to dress.

Downstairs she found that Franklin had indeed left. Her place was set at one end of the table. The house was quiet. The clock on the breakfront as she swept past it told her it was already nearly eight-thirty. Relieved at her husband's absence, yet annoyed with him somehow, as if it were his fault she'd slept late, she sat at the table and poured coffee from the steaming china pot. The damask drapes were drawn open, and even with the overhang of the porch roof dulling the panes in shadow, she could see the sun's strength in the side yard. The sudden heat after so much rainfall had coaxed the pink buds to life on her wild-rose bushes near the street. She could see hundreds of small red clusters bursting on her climbers.

A sense of urgency came on her then, a pressing at the day's escape, and Althea's thoughts moved rapidly. She would have the girl do the wash while the sun lasted. Thunderclouds might roll in from the west again, spill a torrent before the washing could be brought in from the line. The season's turning toward September could mean more thunderstorms, the drop of forty degrees in an hour, an unforetold deluge of wind and hail. Althea had grown up with the vagaries of the Territory's weather, and she lived always in expectation of sudden violent change. Of course, this steamy September warmth could stretch well into October; there might be sultry weather for many weeks yet, without a sign of rain. One could count on nothing about the weather in Oklahoma except unpredictability and change—so, yes, the wash this morning, and the girl could do the mending while the wash dried, and then, of course, the ironing. Maybe there would be time before Graceful started dinner to wax the staircase banister and the foyer floor. Althea had observed the dulling of the old wax as she'd come down the stairs and noted it to herself, a task to give the girl. But, no, it wasn't likely Graceful would get to the waxing, the poor creature was so wondrously, exasperatingly slow. It was a good thing she'd insisted on the shopping being finished yesterday, Althea thought then. Otherwise there'd be no telling when the wash would get done.

A small disturbance fluttered in Althea's mind, as if a hand had for a brief moment flicked aside a curtain. She sat very still, staring out at the side yard. Delicately she ran her fingers up the back of her upswept hair, feeling for stray strands, pushing the hairpins in tighter. The curtain swung back in place. She drank her coffee and busied her thoughts with the small details of the day: she would tend to her garden before the heat fell too heavily, and then there was the sorting of clothes to be mended and those to be discarded, and she really must settle the question of whether to give the faded green sateen to Graceful or donate it to the Ladies Auxiliary League.

She heard a faint clink of silver and the rustle of the girl's starched apron coming through the passageway from the kitchen. At once the dread of the afternoon before, the night before, rushed fully formed on Althea. She pushed herself back from the table, touched her fingers to her hair, reached again for the thin china cup, and sipped from it. She calmed her outward face, sat motionless while the girl unburdened the silver tray of covered dishes. Graceful clamped the tray beneath her arm while she poured more coffee, snapped loose the folded napkin and held it out, swung the tray horizontal again to receive the silver tops from the chafing dishes. Her movements were smooth and rhythmic. *Slow as sorghum in winter,* Althea thought. She waited with gritted teeth for the girl to have done with her business.

"You be wanting bacon, ma'am, this morning?" the girl said in her soft, rising inflection.

"Bacon?" Althea was startled at this breach of habit. She always had bacon with her eggs in the morning. But it was a distraction from the dread swimming inside her, and she seized on it. "You mean you haven't cooked the bacon?"

"I didn't yet, ma'am."

"Well," Althea said after a moment, her voice cool and distant, "pray tell, why not?"

"Mr. Dedmeyer say he don't know if you want much breakfast this morning."

"Did Mr. Dedmeyer say why he thought I might not want bacon since I always have bacon?"

"Just that you wasn't feeling good last night."

Althea slowly raised her eyes to the girl's face. Graceful revealed nothing. There was that infuriating, placid stillness, of course, but it was no different from normal. The girl showed no hint of recollection concerning Althea's tirade the night before—except possibly in a certain narrowness in her eyes as she gazed calmly back at her.

"Yes," Althea murmured. "Yes, I . . ." A profound confusion blurred her thoughts. What was it they were trying to settle? And then she remembered. "Oh. Well. Yes. I mean, no. No. Eggs and biscuits are fine this morning." A dull tingling pricked at her face muscles, urging her to motion, and she longed for the girl to leave so she might ease it in some manner. At last Graceful swung the tray under her arm and disappeared through the passageway, her back a high, hard square, like a working-man's, her hips rolling beneath the maid's-uniform skirt.

Althea forced herself to remain at the table. She reached for the serving spoon and scooped scrambled eggs onto her plate. She broke open a biscuit and dabbed it with butter. She closed the biscuit and placed it carefully beside but not touching the soft yellow mass of eggs. Then she wiped her fingers on the linen napkin and folded her hands in her lap. She sat so for a long time, listening to the small thunks and clatters in the kitchen, the sound of the faucet turning, the cold water groan, and then gurgle, and then gush. A muscle trembled along her jawline. Her mind was entirely empty. Abruptly she stood and moved to the French doors, looked past the porch swing, past the shadows, to her rose garden in the side yard. She would work. Yes. That was it. She had much to do to prepare her garden for winter. There was the pruning, the mulching, the cloths to be wrapped at the base of her prize Cimarron Tea Rose—though winter was months away. The first hard freeze might not come before December. But one never knew. It might come sudden. Might come in the night without warning, before she was ready. Althea went back to the table, stirred the eggs around on the plate, smushed them up and scattered them over the delicate blue print in the china. Standing, her pelvis pressed hard into the walnut edge of the table, she took a bite out of the biscuit and laid it back on the plate. The bread was dry, it nearly choked her, and she took a swallow of coffee to force it down her throat.

Steam rose from the soaked ground and drifted in knee-high wisps as Althea walked the footpaths, her pruning shears tight in her fingers. She passed from rosebush to rosebush, from bloom-covered trellis to scraggly low scrambler, from the tall free-standing Cimarron Tea Rose to the new hybrid Pink Ophelia to the climbers sprawling along the white fence in the back. Occasionally she snapped her shears in the open air, or she'd kneel and lift a freshly opened rosebud and cup it in her fingers. The front of her dress was filthy from where she'd knelt in the wet black loam, but she didn't pause to swipe at it. She moved almost as a sleepwalker, as if she hunted in her dreams, unconscious, not knowing what she looked for, and it was only in the occasional pause and kneeling, the sudden snapping of shears from time to time in the muggy sunlight, that she showed any sign of presence in her body.

An automobile passed on the street, sputtering, trailing gasoline fumes, and Althea stopped to watch it disappear north toward downtown. The auto backfired somewhere up around Fifteenth Street, a loud bang like a gunshot, and Althea jumped at the sound of it. She reached a gloved hand to her brow to wipe away the perspiration. The sun beat down, a merciless hellfire. Althea felt it through the wickered straw of her sunhat as if it had just begun its burning: a small, round scalded place on the top of her skull. She turned from the street at once, as though she'd at last found her purpose, and bent to the nearest rosebush and began to snip savagely at the blossoms.

"Althea Dedmeyer, what in the sweet name of Pete do you think you're doing?"

The voice jerked Althea to awareness, a sudden plucking of her nerves like fingers yanking open purse strings. She held still for a long time, her gloves among the thorny branches of a climber, and then she stood up, very calm upon her surface, and slowly turned around.

The woman posed on the stones of the footpath as if the sea surrounded her. A magenta cloche hat hugged her auburn hair; a filmy pink scarf swirled at her throat and drifted to the hem of the pale sheath she wore. The crepe-de-chine skirt was almost vulgarly short, hardly covering the midpoint of her calves. In one hand she held a pair of lace gloves, and she fanned her face with them as if the flimsy material could really move the sodden air. A sly, expectant look touched her features. She smiled at Althea. "Hot, isn't it?" she said.

"Hello, Nona."

"Is this a new idea, to scalp a rose garden like a red war party?"

Nona Murphy laughed, a tripping sound like water. Her small head dipped and turned prettily as she surveyed the rose garden. Althea followed Nona's eyes, her own eyes taking in the destruction. In a ravaged half-moon around her, the remains of a dozen rosebushes clawed the steaming air, scraggly, raw, bleeding sap. Green leaves, twisted green stems, wilted petals, dying rosebuds lay in scattered circles at the bases of the bushes. The prongs of the living branches were cut close to the mother stumps; the stumps were hewed close to the ground.

Lord God have mercy, what on earth have I done?

"Yes," she said aloud. "I . . . I've been pruning my garden." She bent and gathered an armload of wilting green, unheedful of the thorns, and carried the branches to the fence and dropped them. "The blooms are supposed to come back stronger if you prune them back hard in early fall."

"Well, I hope you haven't killed the poor things," Nona said, and her laugh trickled through the air again. "It's not *fall* anyhow, child, on the second day of September." She stood fanning herself with her ridiculous lace gloves as she glanced toward the house. "Might's well be the Fourth of July from the feel of this heat." Now her eyes swept Althea from sunhat to gardening gloves, and the sly smile tipped her features. "Honey, I hate to say it, you look like a fieldhand."

Althea felt on her face the sun's ruthless light, which the straw hat's speckled shade could not soften; she felt the sweat beading her upper lip, sliding down her temples. She saw the ragged hem on her gardening skirt; her muddied shoes, the heels run down to nothing; her gloves blackened with earth, and wet and heavy. She forced a laugh. "Well," she said, "gardening does that." She smiled at Nona with the surface of her skin. "I guess I'll give that murky muck that passes for Tulsa tapwater a chance to show something for itself afterwhile." She bent, gathered another armload of branches, dropped them over the fence.

"You don't look a bit worse than L.O. did when he got home Saturday night. That road was pure mud. Or that's what L.O. *said* anyhow." Nona's voice was buttery with innuendo, slick with implied meaning. "*Some* of us know how to stay out of the mud, though."

Althea ignored her. She had no desire to hear Nona Murphy go on about that lynching. Would people never find something else to talk about? In any case, it had nothing to do with her. Franklin had been home Saturday night, as he was every night when he was in town. They hadn't known a thing about it till the *World* came Sunday morning, and didn't care about it then, Althea didn't, and she didn't want to hear about it now.

"Law, it's muggy, isn't it?" Nona flipped her gloves all around her face as she peered around the garden, scanned the side porch, seemingly looking for something. "I thought the rain'd cool things off some, but I declare it's just made me more miserable."

Althea moved swiftly through the humid air, gathering the cut stems, and Nona followed after her along the stone path, stepping primly in her high patent shoes, prattling on about the weather, the lynching, the Auxiliary League benefit a week from next Friday. Althea would not ask her what she wanted, though she knew she wanted something. Nona Murphy never came without secret purpose hidden in her trickling laughter.

"I said to him, Honey, you're going to spoil me silly, and he said—oh, you know L.O.—he said, What else is it good for? If I can't throw you a little party now and then I might's well pump that oil right back down in the ground. And I said . . ."

Althea closed her mind to Nona's simpering chatter. For a moment she stood looking at the pruned branches, the crushed and fragrant petals gathered on the pile. A grief like the grief of death began to rise in her. She turned and picked up her pruning shears from where she'd dropped them by a fencepost, moved across the garden toward her wild roses near the street.

Nona followed, though more slowly, as she picked her way along the meandering footpath. "Well, I said, October is the absolute soonest if you aim it to be *that* big a shindig, and he said, Sweetheart, I aim it to be the biggest whingding this town's ever seen, and if it takes you a year to get ready, why, you take a year. No, honey, I said, this is a celebration. We've got to celebrate while the news is new, don't we? He just laughed." Nona came up directly behind Althea, where she stood before the ragged hedge of pale pink wild roses. "Two months, going on three, it'll be old news practically as it is."

The new Winton parked at the curb caught Althea's attention, and she lifted her eyes and looked past the roses to the dark leather seats, the brilliant trim reflecting sunlight. Nona Murphy *would* drive over here for whatever sly purpose she held in that mind of hers, would drive though she lived no more than two blocks away. Would drive because her Winton was brand-new and lovely, because she must show off that she *could* drive, that she knew herself to be a scandal in Tulsa because her husband had taught her how to operate an automobile. Althea made up her mind suddenly that, whatever it was Nona wanted, she would not let her have it. Her eyes returned to the rosebush.

"He took me up there last Sunday, my stars, Thea, it looks like a *city*. I mean those derricks march off across those hills like an army or something. You can't even *see* the horizon. You can't see the end of them. It's the most thrilling thing. I said, Honey, it looks like *Glenn* Pool, for heaven's sake, and he said, Sugar, the Ida Glenn was a little duster compared to what's under this spot. Believe it, woman, he said, that's our million-dollar future out there."

Was this what Nona had come for, to brag of L.O.'s strike? Althea glanced up; her fingers paused on a faded bloom before she snipped it. No. She dismissed the notion. Nona never approached a subject directly but always sidled up sideways, tiptoeing around by way of Robin's barn to sneak up on it. And she never came simply to relay information but always—somewhere in her monologues that ran on without pause for answer, some way in a sentence that carried no question mark—always, somehow, finally, to ask. Althea pinched the head off the rose with her fingers. The faded pink petals fluttered to the muddy ground as she reached for another.

"He held me right there by the waist, swept his big old hand across like he was drawing me a picture, and he says, We're going to inaugurate that little ballroom, sugar, quick as you can get ready, and I said, What are you talking about, L.O. Murphy? and he says, I'm talking about a masquerade ball big as this whole country, that's what. I want you to plan us a party the likes of which this little town's never yet seen, and I said, *Bigheart?,* and he got so tickled, I thought he'd never quit laughing. No, now, you know I mean Tulsa, he said. We're going to throw us a party fit to make that town's head swim, and I said, Lord, L.O., that'll have to be going some, and he says, You can believe that, sugar."

Nona prattled on, her voice high and excited, her green eyes darting around Althea's property, looking for something; she turned again toward the house. Her lips never ceased for a moment to talk, but her gaze returned and settled finally on Althea's swiftly moving fingers. Althea felt her. She deadheaded the roses quickly, waiting for Nona's manipulation to complete itself.

"I've been nearly beside myself trying to figure how in heaven's name I'm going to get everything done. That girl of mine's slow as blackstrap. I swear she moves like that three-toed sloth we saw at the Saint Louis Zoo last summer. You could just stand for an hour and watch her lift a duster."

Althea nearly laughed. She'd thought the same thing of Graceful, Lord, how many times.

"Well, of course, we'll bring in a whole crew of niggers for the party and to decorate, whatever, but I'm talking about I don't know how I'm going to get out the invitations and do all the planning and keep up with all my engagements and run a household in the meantime." She sighed with the burdens her sudden wealth had laid upon her, and bent to sniff languidly at a crimson rose near her waist.

God, she's coarse as a stick. Cold contempt rose in Althea, increasing her irritation. She'd long held the secret fantasy that L.O. had found Nona in one of the brothels on First Street and fixed her up like a mended china doll before he paraded her around. Or that he'd come across her in some little hick Southern town and bought her off her parents as quick as she reached puberty. Wherever he'd found her, there wasn't an ounce of breeding in her— The distant flutter sifted in Althea's mind, and she held herself still. She bent to her work again. One thing was certain, poorbred or not, Nona's silly exterior covered a feral mind: slow, sure, full of grace, endlessly stalking its prey with perfect stealth. Althea moved fast along the walk, but Nona followed.

"They're every one slow as sand anyhow, I don't know what I can do about that. L.O. says that whole bunch in Little Africa's just worthless, he says if this state'd ever taught niggers their place in the first place we wouldn't have to have these lynchings, keep people and the papers all stirred up." Althea glanced back, the irritation so prickly and strong she felt that she'd love to just slap her. "Of course," Nona went on airily, flipping her little gloves, casting her eyes about the garden, "that wasn't a nigger the other night, he was white as my foot, but he was sure defiant as a bad nigger, you should have seen him, he lit a cigarette and stared us right in the— Oh!" She opened her eyes wide, touched her fingers to her lips as if she'd let a secret slip out. Then she tipped her vulpine features sideways and tucked her chin, smiling. "Oh my," she said, "guess I let that little kitty out of the bag."

The urge to slap her was so profound Althea feared she might give in to it. She turned away, snapped her shears brutally at the untamed hedge along the fencetop. This, surely, was part of Nona's sly purpose: for Althea to see her as she saw herself, a brave and slightly reckless female, defiantly childless, flaunting her wild acts at the limits of feminine respectability. She wanted Althea to quiz her for details, to be shocked or envious, to react. It was not all Nona wanted from her, but it was part, and Althea would not rise to it. She would not. Her clippers flew at the rambling hedge.

"You should have seen him, Thea. I hate to say it but you practically had to admire the man. He acted like it didn't matter to him one way or the other." She laughed. "But he was guilty as sin, you could see that. I told L.O. on the way home, I said, if ever a man was a coldblooded killer he was. You could see it right in those brazen eyes."

It's no different from her driving over in that Winton, Althea thought. *From how she brags shamelessly about L.O.'s strike.* But it was different. It was odious, vile, monstrous . . . it was . . . what? What was she thinking of? A bitterness crimped at her, an ugly pinched smallness, and she turned despite herself, said, "That's no cat out of the bag, Nona." Her voice was withering with contempt. "Half of Tulsa was out there, from what I hear."

"Oh, well, it was quite a turnout." Nona lowered her voice to a near whisper. "But you won't catch anybody admitting it this week!" Her smile was outright flirtatious. "The police were directing traffic, of all things! Folks were selling pop and little cut-up pieces of rope for keepsakes. Now, of course, butter won't melt in nobody's mouth. I guess it wasn't a soul from *this* town hung that scamp!"

Althea turned away, nearly faint with loathing, and began hacking at the wild roses again. The silence was broken only by the quick snips of the steel shears as she honed the rambling hedge to a tight, domestic neatness. At last the irritation grew so savage within her that she stopped, turned and glared directly in the wide, calculatingly innocent green eyes. "What is it, Nona?"

"What?" The bright eyes opened impossibly wider.

"What do you want? Why'd you drive over here in that ridiculous contraption—" She jerked her head at the Winton, which was not ridiculous at all but beautiful, stunning, and Althea did not even want to see it from the corner of her eyes. She tilted her head so that the sunhat shielded her sight, and she glared a moment longer at Nona. But Nona's soft pink beauty, her of-the-mode dress and stylish cap, her slim ankles and narrow waist and darting, hungry eyes were unbearable to look at, and Althea turned to stare across the garden, but there before her were the mauled and razed rosebushes, and so her gaze fell at last to her own filthy hands, the dark smears on her gardening dress. She saw not black loam but streaked bloody smears down the front of herself. Her vision began to go dark, as if she would faint or fall into a fit in the next instant, and she steadied herself with a hand on the fence beneath the thorny hedge.

"Thea? Are you all right?"

"No, it's nothing. Never mind. I just don't feel . . . The heat. Come back another time," she said. "Tomorrow . . ." Her voice trailed off, and she looked at the shade on the side porch, the swing motionless, the potted begonias and the impatiens brilliant in the shadows. She walked away from Nona without a word of explanation or apology. Without having learned her sly little purpose, without caring. She could hear the light heels tapping along the walk behind her. Althea stopped, said in a low voice, without turning, "Go away, Nona." She could feel the green eyes staring at her back, but that, too, did not matter. She walked on.

"Well. I never. You're going to give yourself a sunstroke, honey!" Nona called after her. "Why'n't you have Frank get you a gardener? Thea?"

Althea stepped up into the porch shade. She sat in the swing and began to rock. She didn't look at Nona again. The Winton's motor started up finally, but she didn't turn to watch Nona drive off. She rocked herself in the porch swing, rocked a long time, and her trembling pulse began to slow. Her clammy palms cooled. Her mind settled, grew calm, grew entirely blank.

Later—Althea couldn't have said how much later: perhaps half an hour, perhaps longer—she stood up and went to the French doors. She didn't wipe the mud from her gardening shoes but entered the house with driven urgency and hurried through the dining room, leaving a trail of ugly smears on the hardwood floor that faded to dull blotches by the time she stepped onto the kitchen's gleaming tiles.

Graceful was not in the kitchen. Althea looked in the pantry, which was likewise empty; she'd started toward the entrance into the back hall when she heard the slow, metallic grinding coming though the open back door. Without breaking stride she shifted course toward the screened-in porch, but stopped short in the doorway, took a stealthy step back.

The girl stood at the wringer washer, running a bedsheet through the rollers into the galvanized tub. The washer was angled so she could look out the screen as she worked, and only half her face was visible. A veiled expression touched her features, so that her almond-shaped eyes slanted more deeply, the lids partly closed. As always, she held her head high, tilted backwards nearly. She wore not her regular maid's uniform but a sleeveless cotton shift, and her clavicle bones showed above the scoop of neckline. The sinews in her arm lengthened, drew taut with each turn of the crank. Her hair had been brushed straight and pomaded, pressed tight to her skull, but the sleek shape of her head was haloed in the sun-light, a radiant haze of black fuzz escaping the pomade's discipline in the heat and the washwater's steam. Althea gazed at the line of perspiration beading the girl's upper lip, the two dark weeping rows that trickled from her temple, ran down the side of her cheek, and disappeared below her ear, where the jagged ends of coarse hair stuck out at the nape of her neck. The after-rain light bounced off the gray porch planks, picked up and il-luminated in iridescence each particle and cell. Light played on the curve of her cheek, the broad plane of her nose and forehead; receded beneath the swell of her lower lip; disappeared entirely in the hollow beneath her eye, as if soaked in by the skin. As if the skin might receive light or throw light back as it chose.

Althea became suddenly acutely aware of Graceful's color. Not the classifying tint that declared one of them to be mulatto or black or high yellow or quadroon, not the general darkness that simply said to Althea's mind *colored*—but the precise hue, the very tone Althea's skillful eyes would have scanned and evaluated in matching furniture and draperies. Graceful's skin was a perfect, pure walnut brown: the same deep, rich, true-brown color as Althea's polished dining-room table.

Surprised, vaguely disoriented—and what, after all, had she come to tell the girl? what task had she come to lay out?—Althea watched the two perfect-brown hands reach into the water and pull up one of Franklin's white dress shirts, slowly twist it into a knot, wring it, and begin to feed the shirttail into the rollers' clenched grip. She realized that Graceful was left-handed. The recognition disturbed her, and she tried at once to dismiss it. The fact was irrelevant. A simple, insignificant, inconsequential little actuality—but a fact nevertheless, one she'd failed to note before, one which she could not ever go back to un-knowing, any more than she could un-know the fact that the girl had a last name. Althea's last name. The last name of her father, and her father's father. The dread began to rise in her, and Althea stepped through the doorway onto the porch.

Graceful looked up at her, apparently unsurprised. She did not quit turning the wringer handle. There was a long moment when only the creaking sound of the rollers, the metallic grinding of the iron crank filled the hot, dank air beneath the porch roof. Then the end of the flattened shirtcuff slid between the rollers into Graceful's upturned palm and she bent slightly to lay the shirt among the wet clothes in the tub. She stood straight again, her face in no way expectant.

What? Althea's mind scrambled to remember what she'd come for; her eyes swept the porch, and she spied the wicker basket beside the door, piled high with wet colored clothes. "What's that basket doing sitting there?" she said. Instantly there was a comforting return of order, a grounded sense of things as they should be. "You think those clothes are going to run out and hang themselves on the line?"

The girl made no answer.

"They'll sour in this heat wadded up that way, don't you know that?"

Still the girl was silent. She returned Althea's gaze without expression.

"Don't you know enough to hang one load before you start another?" Althea took in a deep, righteous breath. "Don't tell me you're stupid on top of everything else. That clothesline won't hold all the colored clothes and the sheets at the same time. You haven't got the sense God gave a green goose. What in the world was I thinking of," she said, glaring at the new, brightly galvanized washer, "to have Franklin buy that Eden when I could be sending my laundry out like every other sensible white woman, instead of pretending I've got a girl with enough brains to do a load of wash. Put those clothes on the line this minute. Just stop right now. Stop!"

And Graceful, who'd begun feeding a new sheet into the rollers, stopped turning the handle. The side of her face registered nothing. She dried her hands on her cotton shift, and as she did so, her head lifted slightly; there was the habitual upward tilt of her chin, a barely discernible shifting of weight in her shoulders, but Althea saw it, saw within the gesture what she expected to see: the sullen, resentful look of Negro pride. A clean, terrible rage flared in her.

"I know what you're up to," she spat. "Don't think I don't. It'll be straight up dark night before the laundry's finished, you won't have time for the mending, the waxing, nor much of anything else. You're so afraid you're going to have to do a little work around here. Take the whole day to do a little laundry, maybe you won't have to do anything but cook supper, is that right?"

Without a word the girl sidestepped the washer, walked the length of the porch. She paused at the door a moment before she bent and lifted the clothes basket, hoisted it to her left hip. Still she did not turn to face Althea. The spring twanged loudly as she pushed on the screen, nearly covering her words, spoken in a flat tone just at the range of hearing. "Man come while ago." She pushed through the door, negotiated the steps with the heavy basket resting on her outslung hipbone. Just before starting across the yard she spoke again, the words delivered in the same flat, even voice. "He's sitting in the front room." She turned then, looked up through the fine wire mesh at Althea, her highslanted brown face still without expression, without comment or judgment. "I aks him if he want me to come fetch you," she said, "but he say he'd rather just wait." She turned away to stride barefoot across the sparsely covered, shaded-out yard.

Man come while ago. Althea's heart raced, and within her chest she felt the rush of blood and heat. She ought to slap that girl, the rude, unmannered thing, saying *Man come,* when the term was *gentleman. White gentleman.* But in fact Althea's flare of anger was already extinguished, replaced by a deep, secret pleasure; she wanted to laugh out loud. It was Jim Dee, of course. Who else would it be? There was no reason for anyone—any gentleman, that is—to come calling to see her rather than Franklin. But, good Lord, didn't he have any better sense than to come in the middle of the day, when the girl or any of the neighbors had to see? Althea's hands flew up to remove the sunhat, the tips of her fingers feeling for stray hairs fallen loose from her chignon as she turned toward the kitchen.

In an instant she became aware of the brown smears on the front of her gardening dress, her run-over-at-the-heels, mud-caked shoes, the sweaty, outdoor smell rising from her whole being. Dear God. Her thoughts were displaced by the sense of urgency, but it was clear, well defined now, voluptuous with pleasure: she tiptoed into the back hall, glanced at the parlor doorway to make sure he wasn't standing there, and, seeing no one, she slipped into the foyer, around the newel, and up the staircase, heading directly for the bathroom, where she turned the thick milky cross on the hot-water faucet hard to the right. A rush of rusty water pounded fullforce into the porcelain tub. Althea didn't wait for it to clear but plugged the stopper into the drain and let the tub fill while she retrieved her wrapper and fresh undergarments from her room.

As she bathed, she called up the image she'd been unable to find the night before: the sunburned face on the far side of the parlor, the unblinking hazel eyes. She hadn't seen him since then, a year ago, at the end of last summer, when he'd come to the house with that rowdy bunch of wildcatters Franklin had invited, drillers, tool pushers, a few strictly lease men, roving about the room with their too-soon-dry shotglasses twirling in their coarse fingers and their loose mouths dropping hints, boasts, joking insults. Althea had smiled as she wandered among them offering tiny ham sandwiches, pouring white mule from the cut-glass decanter, reaching up to light Franklin's stogie, but her eyes were every minute on her husband's partner as he paced the damask confines of the room. The same behavior she loathed in the others seemed in Jim Dee a mark of his tense, masculine nature, and she'd watched carefully to see if he might nod his head toward the side porch to tell her to slip away and meet him. He did not. But once, as she'd stood near the mantel, her hand placed on the cool marble while her husband held her about the waist with one loosely draped paw, Althea had caught Jim's restless glance: he stared at her blankly, refusing to know her; but then his eyes stayed, unblinking, and he'd held her glance, and held it, until she didn't understand what the look meant, and then he'd held it longer, until she could not help but know its meaning: he wanted her, still. As he'd wanted her from the beginning. Seven years nearly. From the first minute he saw her, she told herself, smiling, as she stepped, dribbling rose-scented water, from the clawfoot tub.

For a year she'd nursed the memory of that long gaze; a thousand times and more she'd relived it, burnished it, carried the image beyond remembrance into a dream where she withdrew her waist from her husband's grasp, slipped out of the room and met her lover on the darkened porch: a fantasy revisited so often as to have become firm as memory—more so, for Althea's memory was filled with great blank spaces bordered by fabricated images from her many stories told. She hurried to the bedroom, re-brushed and pinned her hair, put on a simple and elegant gray silk afternoon dress. Only for a moment did she pause to examine herself in the dresser mirror. Flushed with heat and excitement, her cheeks moist and eyes sparkling, her lips red where she'd touched them with rouge—it was only the faintest hint, he'd never know—yes, she looked beautiful. She turned from the glass, pleased, and swept out of the bedroom. Slowly, with tremendous elegance and grace, she descended the stairs, one slender hand lightly touching the cherry banister. At the base of the stairs she paused for a deep, calming breath before she entered the parlor.

The man sitting in the high-backed chair did not bother to stand when she entered the room but merely gazed up at her in silence. In direct contrast to the thick, tawny hair and light hazel eyes she'd expected, this person was dark-headed, sloe-eyed: a stranger, someone unknown to her, although his thin face was uncomfortably familiar. He wore dirty denim pants and a cotton shirt with the sleeves rolled to the elbows, the collar open, and he appeared to be quite young, perhaps no more than eighteen or nineteen, although he slouched against the velvet with a kind of weary contempt unlikely for a young man. The man—or boy—whatever he was (she had to admit the aptness of Graceful's wording: this was no gentleman, even if he was white)—continued to stare at her in insolent silence, until at last Althea said, "Yes? What is it?" She thought she saw him smile slightly.

"You don't know me, I guess."

Her gaze ran down the length of him in a haughty, appraising glance. "No," she said, a clipped word of dismissal. She was ready to order him and his filthy clothes immediately off her beautiful maroon velvet chair, but the strange insolence of the fellow somehow prevented her from speaking.

"Look close," he said.

And she did, taking in the slouching length of him, seeing that the white shirt was in fact clean, as were the lean forearms, the two swarthy hands splayed on the arms of the chair. She saw that the dark blotches on the denim pants were not filth but well-laundered oil stains. He was an oilfield worker, of course: a roustabout, from the looks of him. It wasn't Althea he wished to see, but Franklin. Relieved, she glanced at the face then, but the fellow stared boldly at her, and her relief stopped cold. His gaze swept the room, returned to Althea's face in languid contempt for the parlor, its furnishings, Althea herself. He arose from the chair and came toward her in a slow saunter.

Althea stepped back, ready to shout for Graceful or to rush out the front door if necessary, but the fellow paused a few feet from her, turned with casual deliberateness toward the mirror over the mantel, and looked at himself. Althea followed his gaze, looked first at the young man's reflection, then her own, then caught his eyes where they returned her likeness: sloe-brown eyes beneath arched brows in a mildly masculine, distinctly younger replica of her own thin, beautiful features. His faint smirk widened to a grin. "Good to see you again, Sister."

She stared back without blinking, her expression unnaturally still. Her fingers came up, touched the cameo at her throat; her hand retreated to her side again. The movement of her lips did not disturb the placid surface when she said in a low voice, "I'm afraid you'll have to leave."

The grin dropped from the other's face. He continued to stare at her until Althea herself broke the locked gaze, turned in a whisper of silk to float across the room and seat herself on the divan. She smoothed the skirt beneath her as she tilted slightly sideways on the wine-colored velvet, ankles crossed, her slender calves revealed. It was the very image of the gesture she'd dreamed for Jim Dee as she'd donned the gray silk, though she had no recollection now of the fantasy.

"If you have business with my husband—"

She stopped herself. The last thing she wanted was for this person to speak to Franklin. She could think of nothing then except to repeat the phrase, more harshly this time, with such authority he couldn't possibly disobey: "I'm afraid you'll have to leave."

The young man strolled to the armchair, dropped into it, and crossed his denimed legs almost primly at the knee. "I'm afraid not," he said. There followed a brief silence wherein Althea, furious at her own helplessness, glared at the creature and calculated how much time she might have to get rid of him before Franklin came home, and how she might manipulate Graceful into secrecy without making herself vulnerable to the girl's loathsome, mute opinion.

"Well?" she said at last. "Speak."

"This is sure some warm welcome after— What's it been? Fifteen? Sixteen years? I can't remember. Ma told me, but some things I just can't seem to remember. It's other things," he said slowly, the dark eyes unblinking, "I can't seem to forget."

A highpitched whine sang in Althea's ears. Teeth clamped, chin rigid, one muscle spasming along her jawline, she waited.

"Of course, I was so little, I didn't even remember what you looked like. Now I do, though, sure." The eyes appraised her, then dismissed her, or dismissed something within her, and turned with a kind of lazy derision to survey the room. "You've done well by yourself. Of course, Ma told us that. She harped on that quite a bit." His eyes completed their tour of the parlor, returned to gaze steadily at Althea. "Looks like she was right."

"What . . ." She couldn't get her voice to work properly. "What do you want?" This last was almost a whisper, but the words grated harsh and clear in the airless room.

"Oh, I don't know." He stretched his long arms over his head, clasping them behind his neck, the grin broad now, delighted. "A bite to eat, maybe? That'd be a place to start. The girl offered a cup of coffee, but, now, a man who hasn't eaten in a couple of days, he don't want coffee, he wants meat and bread." He barked a short laugh into the air. "Meat. Bread. You remember those Snake Indians down around Iron Post? Couldn't speak a word of English but they knew them two words. Meat. Bread. Learned how to beg before they learned how to walk." He unclasped his hands from his neck and leaned forward slightly, hunkered toward her. "You remember? Sister?"

And Althea did remember, the image swimming to the surface of her disciplined mind: the two Creek children standing at the back door with their crusted hands out, their mouths chanting in singsong, *meat, bread,* over and over, and then the back door itself, five long rough-cedar slabs tacked together, and the barn behind the house, the manure-dappled feedlot, and behind it the prairie rolling away north and east and west, and the sky arching blue, impenetrable, rising forever. She could see the house then, or feel it, sense its frailness on the breast of prairie: two stories of slapped-together post oak and cedar, and the wind whistling through the whitewashed slats, and at last then, as if everything were conspiring to force the one image and its meaning upon her, she saw again in her mind's eye the flax-colored dress, soiled with blood, lying crumpled in a corner of the barnyard, trampled beneath sharp small hooves. Althea saw her young and naked self, bone thin, arms crossed before her in the cool darkness of the crib's depths, and a voice calling outside, several voices crying the same word again and again, the sound rolling across the prairie with the harsh, spitting wind.

"Letha? Sister? You're not going to faint, are you?"

The voice was amused, artificially concerned. When Althea's sight cleared she saw the person, young man, stranger, whatever he was (her mind would not allow her to say brother), half prepared to rise: boots flat to the carpet, hands stiff on the armchair, the insolence gone now, though not the sardonic amusement. She saw that his hair was not so much dark of its own properties as blackened by hair oil; saw that his swarthy complexion had been burnt so by the sun.

"I told Estaleen you'd faint when you saw me. You going to prove me right?" He watched her a moment, then settled back against the velvet, the white smile flickering in the dark face. "Naw, you're not going to faint. You're too mean and tough for that. That's one thing they always told me: Letha's tough as a hickory stick. I can remember that from before I could crawl."

"Tell me what you want."

"I told you already, a bite to eat. That's the first thing. I'm famished. Stomach feels like an old shriveled up twist of jerky. You're not too mean to feed me, are you? I don't want to have to go back and tell them that."

Without a word or change of expression, Althea stood and left the parlor. Sedately she crossed the foyer into the library, moved through the dining room and kitchen, and on to the back porch. Graceful stood at the washer, turning the wringer handle and gazing out through the screen as if no earth-shattering interval had passed. Althea's voice was quite calm when she said, "Please stop that now and come in and fix the gentleman some dinner. You can finish later." She didn't wait for her instructions to be acknowledged but turned immediately and headed back to the parlor. She stood in the archway and spoke in the same controlled manner. "You may have a seat in the dining room. I've told the girl to prepare dinner. I don't feel well, and if you'll excuse me, I'm going upstairs to lie down." She turned toward the staircase but stopped, frozen, when the voice sang out.

"Letha!"

Loudly. Too loudly. It could be heard on the street probably. Could be heard all the way through the house to the back porch.

"Cut it out now," the voice said. "You can quit the high-and-mighty act, you're not fooling your own flesh and blood. I've come to stay awhile. You might as well have your niggergirl fix me a bed."

On that muggy Thursday evening, when Cleotha Whiteside stepped out her back door to toss washwater and saw the sun sinking behind the refineries west of town, her sense of another day's passing set a ponderous urgency in her bosom. She slopped the water onto a row of marigolds and zinnias beside the step, turned and went back into the house with the same unhurried determination that marked all her movements, but within her chest a cold weight squeezed her breath. She took off her apron, hung it on a nail beside the door as she passed through the small kitchen into the middle room, where she retrieved her hat from a knob atop the dresser, donning it and pinning it in one motion as she went on into the front room. Her youngest child, William, lay belly-down on the linoleum with his chin on his crossed hands, gazing out through the screen door.

"What's the matter with you, boy?" Cleotha stepped to the mirror beside the door frame and adjusted her hat with all seeming mindfulness on the wavery image inside the glass, though her full attention was on the nine-year-old sprawled, too still and far too quiet, on the floor. She could hear children's voices laughing, hollering, as they played farther up the street.

"Nothin," the boy said. He did not take his chin off his hands to say the word; the top of his head rose and fell with the two syllables.

"If nothing's the matter, I think I know somebody better get his young behind up off the floor."

The boy didn't move, did not raise his eyes to his mother, and in Cleotha's chest there was a further tightening of the stricture that had come on her at sight of the reddening western sky. *Not now, Lord,* she thought, *don't give me trouble with this boy now. I got all I can.* And she began to hum a low, sweet melody, her rhythm of movement slowing as she turned to face her son. "Willie, get up from there now. You know how to act better than that. If you're not going to play out, you go see what you can put yourself useful about. Miss Clay give y'all any homework yet?"

The boy dared not be quite sullen with his mother, though still he didn't lift his head, and his voice was barely audible when he pushed himself away from the linoleum and sat up. "Yes, ma'am."

"Time I get home I want to see every bit of it done and you washed up for bed. I want to see your tomorrow-clothes laid out and your today-clothes on the line and a clean glass in the dishpan where you finished your cornbread and sweetmilk and washed up after yourself."

"Where you going?"

"That's for me to know and you to wonder about. Jewell and LaVona going to be here soon. You go on and do like I say." Cleotha turned to the screen door, her chest dense with worry and a familiar sensation, a kind of perpetual heartsickness she felt for this boy, her last child, the one most tender, who took all the world at its ought-to-be, not as it was. As she pushed through the screen she paused, looked over her shoulder, said, "You sure, now, you took that letter to the right house? The lady say it's the right place where Graceful stay?"

The boy shrugged, gazing past his mother to the street. "She say she going to give it to Graceful," he said softly, his mind apparently not on his words but on the children's voices drifting farther north.

Cleotha watched him a moment. "All right, son," she said at last. "That's fine. You mind what I said, now." She turned to go, stopped one last time; without glancing back at him, she said, "Dip you up a bowl of peaches after supper, if you want. Don't forget to wash the bowl out." She went on down the steps.

As she made her way south, the rusty light bled away slowly, turning amber, and yellow, until it had faded to a wan greenish twilight by the time she reached Archer, where tinkling music came from the east, mingled with laughter and soft voices floating on the patinaed air. Cleotha turned toward the candescent lights and gasoline fumes along Greenwood Avenue, though her purpose was not to immerse herself in that rich smoke-and-food-and-music-filled atmosphere but to slip into the redbrick building halfway up the block which housed the *Star* office and speak to a certain young man who operated the linotype machine there. As she moved along the street, her mind taken with her silent worries, she saw the young man in her mind's eye: his skin near as black as the ink on the tiny letters he tapped into place with his long, deft fingers; his broad, white, beauteous grin and infinite politeness. He was a good boy, or he knew himself to be a good boy, and Cleotha did not trust him. Nevertheless, it was to Hedgemon Jackson she'd gone with her request to compose the letter to Graceful, one that would make sure Graceful came home quick but, hopefully, wouldn't frighten her.

Now Cleotha doubted the content of the letter, and with doubt came fear and the old suspicions slipping around her, worn and familiar as an old housedress. He'd written no telling what; she had not dictated, hadn't wanted the boy to know the details of her private trouble, and so she'd left the nature of the emergency unspoken, had not even used that word—*emergency*—by no means, but had only asked could he write a note to Graceful to say someone wanted to see her uptown. A letter had been the best way, surely. A telegram was too dear, and in any case would've scared her, and Cleotha would not even dream of telephoning to a whitelady's house. She'd had to have somebody write that letter. Surely she'd done the right thing.

The lone unsure place in Cleotha Whiteside's front to the world was this old secret sore of not knowing how to read and write. It drove her in a thousand ways: drove her to push her children to work harder, study more, learn plenty, so they might someday be something in the world besides a bootblack and a housemaid on the southside; drove her to use her other gifts to their greatest strengths and beyond, so that she not only sang in the Macedonia First Baptist Church choir in her clear, mellifluous alto but offered that same gift as gospel solo almost weekly, and even led choir practice now and again when Brother Goodlow had to be out of town. Her natural-born skill with numbers had become so practiced she could figure in her head any quantity of the box dinners she sold to the pipeline layers along Dirty Butter Creek and make change in an instant without picking up a pencil or a paper sack to figure on, and without ever making a mistake. From her childhood in the old Chickasaw Nation she'd craved to learn how to read and write, but her mother's death when she was seven, and her father's disappearance a year later (whether by choice or violence or accident, none knew: he'd simply ridden off on a horse one afternoon and never come back), had left her a child orphan with a brother to raise, and she'd given up what hope she might have had for schooling.

For years she'd thought the time would come later, someday, when she would learn to decipher writing, but never had that someday come. At last she'd made up her mind at the age of twenty-seven, exactly during the birth of her fourth child, that she was too old to master such a complex code, and afterwards abandoned all longing in that direction. But Cleotha had stayed vigilant in seeing to it that her offspring attack the written word particularly well. And they *could* write, all five of her living children, beautifully—they each had a beautiful handwrite, every one of their teachers said so—and she had two girls still at home who could write anything you'd want to ask them. But Cleotha hadn't called on Jewell or LaVona because she hadn't wanted to scare them or get their nervous selves stirred up and giddy, how they were apt to do. Now, turning onto Greenwood Avenue, the light and noise coming almost as a blast of air against her face, Cleotha thought she might have made a mistake in judgment (a rare admission, even to the silence of her own opinion): maybe she should have gone down to whitetown and fetched her daughter herself.

Cleotha moved up the block, stopped at the glass window marked with gold scratches, which she knew declared, somewhere within the myriad slashes and humps and crosses and curlicues, the motto and title of Greenwood's renowned Negro weekly, *The Tulsa Star*. No light came from within, but she knew the boy's typesetting duties kept him there late, and she pulled the door open and went in. The sweetish odor of ink and newsprint swelled around her when she entered. She passed through the front office, where the shape of a large desk announced itself among the shadows, and eased toward the back, where she could see a slit of light slicing across the wood floor from beneath a closed door. She knocked once, twice, pulled the door open.

A large brown man stood at the back of the room, where the huge metal presses ground a thunderous, relentless *ka-lack ka-lack ka-lack,* and neither he nor the boy was aware of her. Hedgemon swayed before the linotype machine, a complicated iron monstrosity of wheels and trays and black gears, hitting the keys so rapidly it was hard to believe there was purpose or design to his dancing fingers. His eyes scanned the sheet of scratches tacked to the wall in front of him as his long, quick fingers played the huge keys that snapped the tiny letters into straight lines in the metal tray, to make words, to make meaning, to translate to the whole of the colored community the thoughts and opinions of Mr. A. J. Smitherman, editor, and the news. Cleotha paused a moment in renewed satisfaction as she recalled why she'd chosen Hedgemon Jackson to write that letter to Graceful. His skill with those bits of metal made him a translator, she thought: inside that long-limbed dancing body, the boy was entirely fluent in both languages, gliding effortlessly from written to spoken and back again in the same way Cleotha's father had translated without pause between the white traders and the old fullbloods at Tishomingo when she was a child. Her confidence restored, Cleotha pushed forward into the room to find out just precisely what meaning the boy had translated in his backtilted handwrite onto that blue page.

"Hedgemon," she said flatly.

The boy jumped, looked at her, and his expression was such a wash of guilt and quick, knowledgeable fear, as if he'd been found out about something, followed almost instantly by that wide, beautiful grin as he nodded and reached behind himself to untie his leather apron, that Cleotha instantly remembered why she distrusted him, and her own fears and nameless insecurities rushed back. But the woman was indomitable in any pursuit once she'd set out on it.

"Come out here now," she said over the sound of the clacking presses, "I got a bone to pick with you."

And she turned and went back into the dark hallway and all the way to the front of the building, where she stood at the window. Across the street the show had let out at the Dreamland, and a stream of beautifully dressed men and women emerged from the theater, blinking their eyes, laughing and talking, but it seemed to Cleotha that she could feel the tension through the glass, their laughter a cover-up for their nervous dread: it didn't matter in Greenwood that it was a whiteboy last weekend the people in Tulsa had lynched.

"Anything wrong, Miz Whiteside?" Hedgemon said behind her. "Ma'am?"

"What sort of story you put in that letter? That letter to Graceful?"

"What? Why, just what you told me, ma'am, just could she come home, somebody's waiting to see her. That's all. Just only what you said."

"Whose name did you sign to it?"

"Whose?"

"I'm asking you what name you put on it." She turned to look up at the young man, whose black skin receded to near invisibility in the darkness of the newspaper office, but whose eyes and unwilled smile flashed brightly in the reflected light from the street.

"Why, just . . . I just signed it, you know."

"Sign it what?"

"Uh . . . my name. I just sign Hedgemon T. Jackson, just, you know . . . my name. Is something wrong?"

"What makes you think my daughter is going to pay one bit of attention to anything Hedgemon T. Jackson got to say on any subject?" Cleotha said, disgusted, turning back to the window as the stream of folks from the Dreamland bled onto Greenwood Avenue, merged with the grander river of movement on the street. Several automobiles cranked to life. A slow wail from a cornet rose, crescendoed, died away up north somewhere. She wondered if she might still make her way—might dare to make her way—across the Frisco tracks into whitetown this late of an evening.

"I didn't mean to think nothing, ma'am," Hedgemon said, his voice soft. "You requested me to make that letter, I just . . ." The hushed words died away, drowned in the *ka-lack ka-lack* from the back room and the lively, muffled streetsounds seeping through the glass.

"That's all right. It's all right." She didn't mean to make the boy feel low; there was just too much worry in her mind.

"I put it in there you the one say to write it."

"What's that?" She turned to look up at him again. *He must be over six feet tall,* she thought. *I believe he's taller than T.J.*

"I mean, I didn't act like *I* was the one telling her to come home, I put it right there on the page, 'Your mother Mrs. Ernest Whiteside request the honor of your presence'—like that."

"Oh, Lord." Cleotha couldn't feel any satisfaction one way or another. If the boy had made the letter so garbled with his high-toned newspaper talk to where her daughter couldn't make out its meaning, well, that was one problem, and if he'd done the job right and Graceful still hadn't come—and this was Thursday evening, maid's night out; there hadn't ought to be the excuse she couldn't get off from working—why, there was something different, and worse, to worry about. Cleotha's mind was so disturbed now, just filled to the brim and flowing over, that she rejected both possibilities. She simply dropped the issue of the letter altogether and veered onto another track. "What time the cars quit running?"

"Ma'am?" The boy appeared to be fading back into the darkness of the office. "Oh. I don't believe I'd take a streetcar yonder this time of evening."

"I don't believe I would either, if I could help it."

"I don't know. Sure don't. I never took no streetcar this time of night. I never took no streetcar yonder anyhow, not since I was eleven." He was, indeed, moving backward, gliding on agile feet toward the slant of light from the pressroom. "She'll be here tomorrow morning, you watch. Or right now, I bet she's home right now, while you come over to Greenwood."

Cleotha could make out nothing but the tall, gangly shape of the boy, his warm, invisible presence.

"Tell Graceful I said hello when you see her," his voice said. "I didn't make out like it was me looking to see her, I truly didn't, but you could tell her from me I'd be proud . . ." A brief pause. "You didn't say who it was . . ." He hesitated long enough for Cleotha to offer the answer if she was willing, not so long as to seem to be expecting. "I just left it blank, that part, about who it was wanting to see her." The voice was muted, whether from secrecy or shame, she couldn't tell; she could hardly hear him. "But you could let her know Hedgemon Jackson be proud to see her." And he turned, pulled the door open quickly, and disappeared into the brightly lit *ka-lack ka-lack ka-lack.*

Cleotha stood in the dark office a moment longer, pondering the two sounds she'd heard in the boy's voice, understanding two facts about Hedgemon Jackson she'd never dreamed of, any more than she'd imagined his inky, dancing life had anything to do with her or her family: one, that the boy was, and probably had been for a long time, in love with Graceful, and two, that he was a terrible coward.

But Hedgemon Jackson disappeared from Cleotha's reckoning as quickly as she walked out the *Star* office door. She trundled swiftly south along the avenue, weaving among the highly dressed folks making their evening promenade, skirting the clot of youngsters knotted up in front of the confectionery, her senses deluged with the glut of sights and odors and cacophonous voices, and her thoughts circling in their worn, familiar rhythm. As the deep trouble arose, she would receive it and worry it a while before she'd think to speak a word or two to the Lord to take it in His hands. A moment later it would roll to the surface again. In her mind's eye she could see him: T.J.'s thin profile in the kitchen, his face fretted with worry, frowning with that old pettish fretsomeness he'd carried from the womb, but the lines worn deeper, more serious, as he stood in the square of moonlight, saying softly, No, Mama, don't turn on the light. Just spoon me up a bowl of them beans, that's all I want. T.J. home, in her kitchen, three nights ago, and now gone again. *Oh, my Lord, take and keep him,* she prayed in her mind's silence. *Take and keep him, oh, my Lord, help my son.*

Cleotha stopped at the corner of Greenwood and Archer and looked south. She could see electric lights twinkling in the buildings of downtown, twelve and fourteen stories tall, some of them, and dark and silent, unlike the swirl of light and noise behind her on the street. The railroad tracks, too, were silent, hardly visible in the blackness a hundred yards away. She willed her feet to keep walking into that darkness, but they carried her no farther. The darkness was a wall of white, and she could not enter. For a moment she pondered the changes inside herself that had brought her to see in such a manner: the wall stood invisible and solid on the south side of the tracks; she saw it not with her eyes but with a tender, feeling place on the whole front of her, and there was a terrible mystery in how it could look so blank and dark, and yet feel like the heat of fire burning in the distance against her skin. *This belongs to Ernest,* she thought. *He pass along plenty things to me besides our children, and one thing he pass is how he grew up to dread whitefolks. Him and the whitefolks both have passed Ernest's way of seeing on to me.*

She gazed south, willing herself forward, thinking of her daughter Graceful and her deep-in-trouble older son. She was a woman of strength, of courage, of unassailable will for herself and her children, but Cleotha Whiteside could not bring herself to leave the light and noise and melodic voices behind her and cross the street, the train tracks, and penetrate that invisible dark border.

I believe that boy's probably right, she said to herself. *Graceful's probably sitting in the front room this minute. Let me just go on home and see. If she don't come tonight, I'll go down there myself in the morning. I'll go in the morning.*

And the woman turned heavily and began walking west toward Elgin Avenue, unable to admit to her own mind that the dark wall of white was stronger than her desire on this evening to bring her daughter home.

Boldly, in cunning, he'd hidden himself within the lynch mob. In secret now—although, he considered, with no less cunning—he hid himself in his sister's house. It was all the same. Fools who searched in the concealed places might hunt uselessly forever; as for himself, he'd settled in his mind long ago that the most obvious was the very place the majority of idiots forgot to look. Japheth smiled as he smoothed open the *Tulsa Daily World,* scanned the headlines, sipped coffee from a fine china cup.

BELTON LYNCHING PROBE CONTINUES
Reward Offered for Arrest of Leaders of Orderly Mob
Witnesses to Be Asked to Tell All They Know

In amused satisfaction he read that hundreds of "witnesses" were being summoned by the grand jury to name the lynch-law leaders. One eyebrow arched delicately as he scanned the paragraph declaring that Belton's missing partner was still at large, though there were rumors he'd been spotted in Springfield, Missouri; in El Paso; across the border in Juárez. *Fools,* Japheth's mind said. His lips curled.

Among the oft-changing traits of Japheth Whiteside's nature there abided only two constants: an unshakable certainty in his own immunity from punishment, and constant, overriding contempt. Five nights ago, when white men stood in the dark at Orcutt Lake, smoking and drinking and cursing, with their hat brims pulled low and their boots propped on Ford fenders, Japheth had stood among them. When one said, Jesus Christ, a man don't have to do nothing to get away with murder in this country, and spat, and wiped the lip of the bottle before swigging and passing the flat flask to the next man, Japheth had said, Ain't it the damn truth, and spat, drank a long swallow, passed the flask in the darkness, wiped his own lips. Later, when they dragged Roy Belton from his cell, jabbing their gun barrels in his ribs and beating and cursing him, Japheth stood at the back of the crowd, watching Belton's eyes to see what fear would do to him, but with his own head bowed, hat brim tugged forward, so that the condemned man's eyes might not meet his.

Within the snaking line of automobiles crawling away from the city, he'd crouched on the running board of the second-to-lead car with his arm thrust through the open window, holding to the armrest with strong, clamped fingers, reveling in the feel of the cool nightwind, thick with a storm coming, gliding over his face. On the black, pitted road east of Red Fork, with the woman beside him and a thousand voices crying for rope (Rope! Rope! Rope! Rope! repeated pondlike in the darkness), his cry had joined the chorus. And when the body was cut down and the mob scrambled for bits of cloth from Roy Belton's death clothes, Japheth had been not first or last but one among many who ripped the soiled cotton from his partner's purpling, cooling body on the dark road. Even as he'd joined the scrabbling mob, he had scorned them in silent derision. No less so now, as he breakfasted in his sister's sun-splashed dining room almost a week later, did he sneer in his soul at the city's mind, turned already, and with great vehemence, against itself. He shook the paper out, reached for a buttered biscuit, devoured half in one bite, placed it carefully on the edge of the saucer before he thumbed to page 37, "In the Oil Fields," to read carefully the day's oil report.

A tall, thick man with coarse blond hair came into the dining room as Japheth was rubbing the last biscuit facedown in molasses. The man stood at the far end of the table and watched him smear the biscuit in the circle of brown syrup flecked with yellow. Japheth glanced up once but made no acknowledgment as he raised the dripping mound to his lips and finished it in two swift bites, wiped his hands and mouth neatly, tossed the linen napkin on top of the swirl of molasses and leftover yolk in his plate.

He pushed back from the table and reached for his coffee, sipped it as he gazed up at Franklin's perplexed, handsome face.

"Have a seat," Japheth said at last, cordially, as if it were his own polished Windsor chair he indicated, his own fine walnut table and steaming china pot of coffee, and Franklin the uninvited guest. "Girl cooks up a good biscuit, don't she?" He took another genteel sip. "Can't say a lot for her coffee, though." He dipped his head for a third small sip, a slight frown darkening his smooth features. "I've drunk better creekwater." Suddenly he smiled broadly, an effect both disarming and chilling. "I'm going to have to guess Sister didn't say a word to you. Is that right?"

Franklin turned without speaking, went out into the library. The smile instantly disappeared from the young man's face. He listened to the dull metallic uncradling of the telephone receiver, the throat being cleared, the authoritative voice say, "Osage six, four nine four," and, in the pause following, the nervous tapping of fingers on the oak desk where the phone stood.

"Miss Greyson," the voice said. A slight curl returned to Japheth's lips.

Another short pause, and then: "Sylvia, listen, ring up Jim Logan and tell him I'll be a little late but I'll be there. Tell him not to get up on his high horse, I'll *be* there, tell him to wait. Now, hurry up on that because he gets out before the damn chickens, and then phone L.O. and Steve Parsens, tell them I'll get in touch with them on Monday. No, no. Just I'll get in touch Monday. I don't have time this morning. I'll ring up from Bristow. Yes. Three or four o'clock, I think, at the latest. All right." There was the thick, muted click as the receiver returned home.

By the time Franklin came back into the dining room, Japheth had transformed his appearance: Where arrogance had cocked the dark head ceilingward as he'd smirked at Franklin from his seat at the table, now he stood diffidently beside the chair with head slightly bowed. Where mockery had crooked the little finger of the long, thin hand holding the china cup, now both hands were clasped humbly before him, and the contempt that had bled through his smile had simply vanished. The young man gaped at Franklin almost stupidly, puplike, as if he cared for nothing more than a kind word, a bone off the table.

"I'm Letha's brother," he said. "I didn't mean to shock you while ago, I thought she would've told you I was here."

"Letha."

"Oh, I mean Sister. We used to call her Letha sometimes. We all had a nickname. Althea, of course I mean. I thought she would've told you."

The young man came forward with his hand stretched out, and Franklin instinctively took the limp fingers in his thick grasp. He looked around the room a moment, as if the answer to his confusion might be found in a corner, or in one of the still-life prints framed on the papered wall. His gaze returned finally to the face before him, which, indeed, bore a troubling resemblance to Althea's, and he said at last, "Well. I guess Gracie took care of you. She does cook up a flaky biscuit, you're right there." And then, vaguely, "You ought to taste her fried pies."

As if her misspoken name were an actor's cue, Graceful entered the dining room through the deep passageway from the kitchen, her arms laden with the silver tray bearing chafing dishes, her features hardened into a carved mask, and yet grinding beneath with a silent, barely controlled fury.

"Ah, here we are!" Franklin boomed, and pulled a chair out at the opposite end of the table from his usual place, where biscuit crumbs and spots of congealed gravy marred the white cloth all around Japheth's plate. It's unlikely he'd have noticed the girl's anger under any circumstance, but in his present state of disturbance he had no ability to see anything except his arriving eggs and meat and gravy, which could as well have been walking through the door of their own volition. He welcomed the familiar forms of silver tray and covered dishes, grateful for the fact they gave him immediate direction. "Thank you, Gracie," he said heartily as the dish of eggs thunked onto the table. "Listen, I wouldn't bother with breakfast for Mrs. Dedmeyer this morning, I don't believe she'll be down. She took one of her sick headaches last night." He glanced at Japheth. "She gets these sick headaches, put her right in the bed."

He waited for a murmur of concern from the one who claimed to be Althea's brother, but when none was forthcoming, he turned his glance back to Graceful as she moved to the sideboard for clean plates and silver. He continued, unseeing, to watch her as she set the place before him, snapped open the napkin, uncovered the lidded dishes with slow, forced violence. Graceful finished her work, turned without letting her eyes pass over either man, and went back into the kitchen.

"Well." Franklin seated himself, scooped a slithery fried egg onto his plate. "It's probably that sick headache. They just flatten her sometimes. They make her so sick." He ate quickly, hardly chewing. "She has to lay in the dark for two and three days." He glanced up at the stranger, who continued to stand, gazing down at him from Franklin's own place at the head of the table. "I know that's why she forgot to mention you'd come to visit." This explanation seemed offered as much to himself as to the stranger, but why his wife had forgotten to tell him, ever, that she had a brother at all, Franklin searched out no excuse for, even for his own mind. "I'll just . . ." And he didn't know what he would do. He filtered his thoughts for his next sure purpose, but, finding none, he went back to eating rapidly. In a moment he said, "I'll let her know you've had your breakfast. You need anything?" The young man was silent. Franklin couldn't see his face clearly for the brilliant slash of orange light coming through the French doors. "Well, if you need anything, just tell the girl. She'll see to it."

"You're in the oil business."

Franklin stared at him. Why wouldn't the fellow sit down, or move some kind of way so that Franklin didn't have to crane his neck so, squint up through the sunlight to see him? "Have a seat. Have a seat," he said at last, in exact unconscious imitation of the other's first words to him.

"Got any openings for an ace tool dresser?"

"Well, I . . ." Franklin chewed a piece of steak, pondering. "It could be. . . ." He reached for the gravy spoon. "Might be possible."

"No!" His wife's voice jumped hard behind him.

Althea stood sheathed in pale blue in the alcove between library and dining room. Light played and refracted on the silk hem of her dressing gown, though her face remained in shadow. She posed, quite motionless, her hair loose on her shoulders. "You know Jim won't have anybody but Ben Koop on his rig," she said. Her voice was strong, certain, only slightly taut. She raised a hand to her face, let it fall to her side once more.

"The lady's right," Franklin said with a forced laugh. "My partner's pretty particular about picking his toolie. Not that they all aren't, but Jim's one driller you can't even discuss it with. . . ." And his words faded, clipped by his wife's judgment and his own ever-present reluctance to share a word about his business. Abruptly he stood, stepped toward the archway. "Here you are, my darling, how's your headache? My goodness, I had no idea. I already told Grace not to fix you any breakfast, but I'll just step to it and have her put the eggs on. Are you better? Do you feel like you could eat a bite of something?"

"Morning, Sister."

Althea leveled her eyes on the stranger a cold instant, then swept her gaze past in apparent unconcern as she floated into the room and seated herself on the east side of the table, between the two men, with her back to the light.

"Is your headache gone?" Franklin asked.

She gave her husband a weak smile.

"Graceful!" Franklin called, and again as if on cue—or as if she'd been waiting just out of sight beyond the passageway—the girl immediately appeared.

"Eggs and grits for Mrs. Dedmeyer. Grits, dear?"

Althea nodded.

"Grits," Franklin repeated. "And bacon?"

The nod again.

"Bacon. Not too crisp," Franklin directed, never taking his frowning gaze from his wife's face. "Guess you'd better whip up another little batch of biscuits if there's none left. Can you eat a biscuit, dear?"

There was an instant's hesitation before Althea nodded.

"All right. Biscuits. No gravy. No gravy, right, dear?"

She nodded again.

"And a little glass of sweetmilk to coat her stomach. You ought to take a glass of sweetmilk before you have your coffee, darling. Dr. Taylor said that."

As if she'd always been of the most agreeable and compliant nature, Althea smiled meekly, nodded yet again.

Had any of the three seated at the table looked up, they would have seen in the sculpted brown face a rage beyond their reckoning, a choked, suppressed fury. But even Althea, who was obsessively aware of Graceful's mien and presence at almost every moment, did not raise her eyes; she continued staring across the table at her husband. While Franklin spoke, Graceful looked at each of the white people in turn, ending with the profile of the one who slouched in the master chair, an amused, careless curl at his lips as he gazed at his sister. Though Graceful's expression remained unchanged, there was a sudden quick flaring of her nostrils, a deepening of the clenched line at her jaw. She turned, even as Franklin continued his instructions, and went back into the kitchen.

" . . . fresh cream for her coffee, and a little dab of that plum jelly," Franklin said. "You'll save room for biscuits and jelly, won't you? You will once you get a taste of this new batch of Grace—" He glanced up then, but seeing Graceful's back disappearing in the passageway, he dropped his gaze seamlessly to Japheth. "She loves wild-plum jelly, the sourer the better."

"Yes," Japheth said. "I know."

Althea's glance swerved to him, snapped back to her husband at once, and remained there. "Darling," she said, and the sound in the word was so natural that even Franklin didn't consider that she hadn't called him by any endearment for many years, "didn't you say that today was the day you were going to take me downtown?"

"She used to climb those scraggly sand plums down at the river, pick off the hard, bitter little fruits before they'd turned orange nearly, eat them till her mouth puckered."

"I really do need to go to Renberg's and pick up a few things."

"Well, to tell you the truth, dear—"

"And I wanted to stop in at Seidenbach's." Althea swept over her husband's words in a rush. "They're having a new fall-suit sale, I could use a good fall suit, I really could."

"Ma used to whip the daylights out of her when she caught her, said her mouth was going to shrivel up like an old lady's."

"And then I wanted to look in at Vandevers. You know, L.O. and Nona are having this silly masquerade ball in honor of that new strike. I guess he told you." Althea's eyes glittered, the long line of her neck arched beautifully as she tilted her head toward her husband. "Nona was here yesterday, she couldn't say a word about much else besides L.O.'s strike and that disgusting lynching—"

"Shrivel up like an old lady's! Isn't that what Ma used to say?"

Althea held her glazed stare on Franklin's face. "The vain thing carried on for an hour, you know how it is when Nona gets wound up about something." She released a brittle laugh.

"Chased her into the middle of Sand Creek with the hickory switch, that's how they used to tell it."

Franklin looked at the two faces across from him, one pale, one darkened nut-brown by the sun, and yet as alike as is possible in two born of the same parents a decade apart and of different sexes. Their kinship was undeniable, though he would have sworn with his dying breath that his wife was the only child of aged parents who'd been killed in a trolley accident at Kansas City when she was fifteen. The abhorrence and fear he'd felt at first sight of this stranger at his table now bled from the stranger to Althea. The thought came to him that in almost sixteen years of marriage he had never, in any way, known his wife. Immediately he stood, came around the table toward her with his voice fixed in a forced tenderness, saying, "Of course I'll take you to town, certainly—but with your headache and all, don't you think we should wait till tomorrow?"

"I'm fine," she said, and smiled up at him.

He reached to feel her brow. "Of course, dear. If that's what you want."

"I thought you had to meet your partner in Bristow this morning," Japheth said.

Althea immediately flinched away from Franklin's hand, darted her eyes across the table, quickly back up to her husband, then to the mirror above the sideboard on the opposite wall.

"Damn," Franklin said. "Damn." He glanced at the mantel clock. "Too late to catch him. Sweetheart," he said, touching her shoulder, "I can't cancel it now, he'll be sitting at that depot till next Tuesday, and red hot to boot. Jim's got something—" He stopped abruptly. Not even to soothe his wife could Franklin bring himself to reveal his business. "I'm sorry, darling." He caressed her shoulder. "Tomorrow. I'll take you right down first thing in the morning."

Althea reached beneath her hair, touched the pulse at the side of her neck, let her hand drop to her lap again; then she folded both hands and placed them before her on the cloth.

"Damn!" Franklin exploded. "Where's that girl with your breakfast? Graceful!" He rushed toward the passageway. "Gracie!" His voice came from the depths of the kitchen. "Grace!"

The one at the end of the table began to chuckle softly. There were only the two of them in the room then, and the unvoiced history. "You don't have any choice, Aletha. I'm here now, I can't help it if you don't like it." He paused, an ear cocked toward the kitchen, leaned over and whispered, "She's gone."

Immediately Franklin came back into the dining room. "She's gone." He turned his perplexed face to Althea. "I don't know where she went. She never even started the biscuits."

"Gone," Althea echoed, her voice hollow. She stood quickly and hurried through the kitchen into the back hall, jerked open the maid's-room door. The rope that stretched across the corner in lieu of a closet showed only two bare wooden coat-hangers. The sheet had been stripped from the narrow cot. The pine shelf below the mirror was empty of brush, comb, blue jar of pomade, though the pomade's spiced scent permeated the tiny cubicle, sweet, petroleum-laden, almost medicinal. Althea swept her gaze again and again around the room, as if she might have overlooked Graceful's solid form in that cramped six-by-eight-foot space. The scent was so strong, it seemed the girl must be somehow present. A weak fury passed over Althea, kin to the inexplicable rages that had ravaged her in recent days, but tempered by fear, muted by recognition of her own helplessness, and the understanding that, in some way she could not comprehend, for reasons unknown to her, she needed the girl.

"Darling." Franklin stood in the dim hallway. Behind him she saw her brother's sylphlike form outlined against the bright kitchen door. "Why don't you go upstairs and lie down. I'll fix you a bite of something, and then let me run down to Bristow and take care of this business. Soon as I get back I'll call Sutphen and see about him sending us a new girl. First thing in the morning. We'll have you some help here in no time. I don't know what got into that girl." He shook his head, looking over Althea's shoulder into the empty cubicle. "I thought we had a pretty fair hand in her. I thought she might stay awhile."

"Don't worry about Sister." Japheth had his arms braced against the jamb, his legs spread slightly, so that the reedy figure formed an X, blocking the door. "I'll make her some breakfast. You wouldn't credit it, but I'm a pretty fair cook myself. I can stir up a flapjack and fry bacon, anyhow." Even with the light behind him, the white smile showed in his dark face. "I learned that in California. You like a good flapjack, Sister?"

"No! No. Really. I wouldn't care for anything, thank you. I'll . . . I think I'll just go upstairs and lie down." She moved quickly along the dark hall to the front of the house, paused a moment in the foyer. "Dearest!" she called back. "Will you come up in a minute?" She didn't wait for an answer but disappeared in a swirl of blue silk up the stairs.

Franklin glanced at the fellow, who remained as yet nameless to him. The other stepped to the side with an elegant gesture, his back pressed to the doorjamb, inviting him into the kitchen. Franklin turned at once and followed his wife. When he entered the bedroom he found her, not lying down, as he'd expected, with the shades drawn and a cool cloth pressed to her eyelids, but pacing dramatically from window to wardrobe to vanity dresser.

"Out!" she said. "I want him out of here!" She turned on her husband as if the presence of the one downstairs were entirely at Franklin's invitation and insistence. "This morning!" she cried, her face twisted. "This instant!"

"Darling—"

"Don't *darling* me!" And then, in a lower register: "Don't you dare . . . one more minute . . . give me that God-blessed fake worried look." She whirled and walked to the window.

Franklin stared at his wife's back a moment, then he turned and left the room.

She waited. A scattering of morning sparrows twittered in the backyard. The sun had eased south with the coming autumn; yellow light burnished the lace curtains at her window, but summer would not release its muggy hold, and already the heat was rising. Her upper lip began to bead with perspiration. Translucent threads of moisture slid slowly at her blanched temples. She was completely motionless, even her eyes were set, unblinking as a deathmask, staring without sight at the bunched pleat of lace curtain. Only the threads and beads of sweat, the slow rise and fall of breast betrayed life in the still figure at the window. But within, hidden from the fixed surface, Althea's mind tumbled with swirling images: a tremendous tongue lolling from a cave of mouth, a thin trickle of red water, and above it a black woman's face swiveling toward her, shocked, and then shouting, and ever returning, relentless, the floating, sinister image of the flax-colored dress, smeared with blood.

She turned to rush out of the bedroom as Franklin came through the door. He was frowning, and it was not the familiar frown of tender concern. Althea stopped short in the middle of the room, her hands clasped at her breast in an unconscious gesture of supplication.

"What the devil's going on in this house?"

"What?"

"You tell me what. What the hell is that fellow doing here? If he's your brother, how is it I never heard about him? And if he's not your brother, who in God's name is he, and where'd he get off to now?"

"I don't know," she whispered. "Franklin. I don't know. He's gone?"

"I looked all through the house, out in the yard. He's gone the same as the girl is. I want to know what the deuce this is all about." His eyes were more demanding than at any time in their married life together, and Althea met them for only an instant before she dropped her glance to the carpet. Immediately she recognized her mistake; she looked up.

"You're the man of this house, aren't you? Whose job is it—"

"Don't pull that," he said. The forcefulness of Franklin's authority with men, with anyone connected to his worklife, settled, for the first time, on Althea. "Sit," he said, indicating with a nod the dressing stool. She did so. "Talk."

Althea opened her mouth, closed it again. His eyes would not turn away from her. She began almost literally to squirm under their demand; she twisted about on the vanity stool, plucked at the silk gown across her knee. "Franklin . . ." she said, and stopped again. "Really . . . I . . ."

She had nothing to say. There was nothing she could say that would not collapse the carefully built structure of lies she'd raised over many years, as a bottom ace pulled from a house of cards will tumble the whole house. She willed her husband gone, prayed he would go on to the office, or just go, completely, leave her alone, disappear from the face of the earth, so that she might not have to deal with his stupid, incessant questions.

"Who is he, Thea?"

"Nobody," she whispered.

"Yes." Franklin walked over and took her by the wrist, not roughly, not threatening violence, but with cold authority. "He's somebody. Talk."

Her mind flew through new lies, a new tale beginning to weave its elaborate intricacies—an old friend? no, not friend, enemy, an old enemy of her brother's—but no! Dear God, there was too much confusion, she needed time, an hour or two alone, to weave a new history. "Franklin, please. My head. I have this blinding headache. I can't . . ." She rubbed her temple with her free hand, her other limp in his grasp. Franklin watched her a moment, and then he released her hand, which dropped heavily to her lap. In silence he turned to leave.

"Where are you going?"

He stopped. Her eyes were wide open, the fear showing plain in them, and for an instant the old tenderness pulled at him. His voice was milder when he said, "Bristow. I told you, I got to go meet Jim. We'll talk when I get home this evening. Or tomorrow. Late as it is, I might have to stay the night." He gave her another piercing look, though there was slightly less demand in it. "We'll finish about this in the morning." And he started toward the door.

"Wait!"

In the very moment before, she'd wished him off the face of the earth, but now Althea understood she would be alone in the house—alone without Graceful, alone with Japheth if, as she suspected, he was only hiding in some rock-slitted, lizardly way—or else just alone entirely, with only herself and her many terrible thoughts and the many cruel mirrors and that restless wanting, wanting, that wanted nothing, that could find nothing to want. Jim! Yes. Jim Dee was in Bristow. She had wanted Jim Dee. For some long time she had.

"Franklin, please."

He turned to look at her. She had not even the strength to wheedle, to manipulate or charm him, as she'd charmed men for many years. She said simply, meeting his eyes, "Take me with you. I'll rest on the train a little and then I'll drink a cup of tea. I'll explain all this, it's very simple really. I'm just too tired right now, my head hurts. Franklin? Let me go with you. Please. I don't want to stay here."

The jitney lurched, and Graceful bumped hard against the large woman beside her. She murmured an apology but the woman stared out the window as if she hadn't heard. Graceful followed the big woman's gaze, staring likewise through the smudged glass at the crowded downtown street. Whitefolks moved along the sidewalk in stiff, henlike struts, nodding to one another, or bobbed ahead to angle across the stream of passersby into a doorway. Across from the Drexel building bootblacks knelt before their wooden boxes, snapping blackened rags over smooth cordovan, or stood at attention, offering their services—Shine, mister? Shine?—to whitemen passing in new worsted autumn suits and gray fedoras. Everywhere along the avenue was a jagged rush of hat brims and angled shoulders. Graceful watched a man in a seersucker suit dart into Renberg's, and her belly cramped. *Some of these whitemen right here on the street was there,* she thought. She couldn't bear to look at them, and she refocused her gaze to the other passengers in Mr. Berry's jitney. The inside of the bus was silent, though the street sounds poured through the open windows. *That lynching's working on them,* Graceful thought. *On me.*

She kept her gaze trained on the nearby women riding with their shopping baskets in their laps, the one lone brightskinned fellow asleep near the front, his naked head bouncing against the seatback. Every few blocks the driver would pause at the corner to receive or discharge another Negro passenger. As she watched the women's faces, the hard sickness in Graceful's chest began to ease. Their features, clothes, sizes were all different, and yet, gazing at the curled and processed hair, the multiple shades of brown and black and coppery skin glistening in the heat, the weary or closed expressions, Graceful had the feeling that the women were every one kin to her, close kin, like aunts. Like near blood to her own mother. She felt safe among them. In another moment she put her head against the seat, closed her eyes, and allowed the wrapped-around feeling to go on and ease her, and presently, rocked by the motion of the motorbus, and in spite of the fumes and noise and sudden pitching starts and stops, she descended toward the wafting images of sleep.

Her mother's face swam forward, and then her brother's face, T.J., whom she hadn't seen in a year and a half. An old longing welled in Graceful, a deep, familiar ache. Within the halfwaking dream, the narrow face of her mistress appeared. The pale jaw opened, and from its depths came the tortured scream of a claw-caught rabbit: the chilling hunt-cry of a redshouldered hawk. Graceful jerked awake, sat forward, gasping. Her vision darkened, and she felt again the whiteman's breath behind her neck, as she'd felt it in the early morning darkness, ripped awake by the smell and feel of him, his breath first, and then the length of him, hard bone and metal, pressing down against her back while she lay facedown upon the cot. She couldn't breathe. She couldn't see. The close depths of the motorbus, which moments before had comforted her, now seemed to suffocate her. In a garbled rush she cried out, "Next block!" and the driver nodded. Graceful reached for the rolled quilt that pressed against her knee. "Let me out, please!" When the jitney paused, the big woman beside her turned sideways to allow Graceful to climb out.

Standing on the hot brick street, she realized she'd not come far enough: she was still in whitetown. On the edge, yes, the northern perimeter, but not yet home. She began to walk toward the tracks a half-mile distant. The small frame houses grew cheaper and shoddier, the whitechildren in the dirt yards blonder and thinner as she hurried north with the awkward bedroll beneath her arm. The morning sun burned the side of her neck and shoulder. Sweat beaded her lip. She felt the sharp pulse in her chest, thrumming in fury, as she tried to justify how she could have mixed biscuits, fried up steaks, stirred gravy, served them, served them on the silver platter, oh Lord. The sickening rage surged again, the revulsion, and she paused, lowered the rolled quilt, kept it clean of street dirt by balancing it on her shoe top while she took off her maid's apron, shoved it beneath her arm. The muffled feel of something inside the starched cotton, the faint, almost inaudible crackle of paper, spoke to her, but she ignored it as she walked on, face lifted, shoulders low. Just as she never knew what showed on her face before Mrs. Dedmeyer, or what the whitewoman thought she saw, Graceful didn't know that her surface presented an image far different from what she felt: her bearing was serene, almost haughtily dignified as she glided evenly along the rough-cobbled street. Whitewomen stared at her from their scraggly yards, but she paid no attention to them or their pale and squawly children, caught as she was in the clamp of fear and rage and the urgent need to get home.

She stepped high over the Frisco tracks like crossing over Jordan and turned with relief toward Elgin, welcoming the familiar square of Booker T. Washington High School, the sights and sounds of the men working in the brickyard, the smells wafting from Mrs. Jenks' laundry and the confectionery. But as she climbed toward her mother's house, she began to walk faster and faster, until she was nearly running. From three blocks away she saw that the front door on the yellow shotgun house was closed. Her mother's door was never closed in warm weather. Graceful understood for the first time that something was wrong. She rushed up the steps, knowing, before she tried the handle, that the door was stayed on the inside by the block of wood turned crossways on its nail. Without pause she dropped her bundle, hurried down the steps and around to the back, where the door was also locked, she knew, by the long metal key her mother used on the rare occasions when she closed up the house: the key her mama always carried away with her, hidden in her bosom on a gray string tied around her neck.

The door rattled in its frame as Graceful twisted the knob, jiggled it, pushed on the wood without hope or expectation. Standing on the cinderblock step, Graceful looked around the narrow yard, past the privy and the smokehouse, toward Standpipe Hill, and she thought of the letter from Hedgemon. She'd dismissed it, of course, hadn't even finished trying to make sense of it, crazy as Hedgemon wrote. Hedgemon. That fool. Even as she'd scanned the swirly script in the maid's room, she had dismissed it as a love letter from the too-black longlegged boy who'd taken to following her home from church a year ago and had not ceased his gangling pursuit of her since. She'd crumpled the page and crammed it back into the blue envelope, jammed the envelope in her apron pocket when Mrs. Dedmeyer shouted at her from the kitchen to come wipe up the muddy porch floor.

Hedgemon Jackson had been the least of her concerns yesterday. Now, though, praying for a sign from somewhere, and the letter having jumped into her mind like an answer, she shook out the apron and pulled the envelope from the pocket, unsheathed the smeared page.

> *To all interested parties, let these presents hereby be made known:*
>
> *Whereas it has been declared and forthwith articulated that upon the First instant of the Ninth part in the area known as Brickyard Hill at a location five blocks north longitude of the Avenue known as Archer there abides on the street called North Elgin an interested party whose express wish is stated to be in a conversant condition with one Miss Graceful Angel Whiteside for the express purpose of which is not revealed to this your humble servant and scribner Hedgemon T. Jackson, Esq., therefore, the honor of said lady's presence is forthwith invited and duly requested to appear at her earliest convenience in the home of Mrs. Ernest Whiteside, her mother.*
>
> *Signed and witnessed this Thirty-First day of August in the Year of Our Lord 1920.*
>
> *Yours, most truly,*
> *Hedgemon T. Jackson, Esquire.*

Graceful's eyes traced the backslanted scrawl time and time again. Never could she get the words to make sense to her, but she saw now what she hadn't read on first glance: her mother's name. She could think of nothing except to go talk to him, find out what her mother's name was doing on the page, what foolishness the boy had been up to, and dear Lord let it be some kind of foolishness, let Hedgemon Jackson know where her mama was gone. Within moments Graceful was hurrying toward Deep Greenwood, the crumpled letter bleeding blue into her perspiring palm. Her apron lay forgotten on the cinderblock step with the envelope beneath it, and her bedroll, partially open, spilled its thin contents onto her mother's empty front porch.

Mr. Smitherman leaned against the slats in his oak chair, his forehead wreathed in a green eyeshade, his eyes ringed in dark circles, his smooth amber-colored face frowning as he stared up at her. An uncapped fountain pen rotated in his hand. Graceful stood uncertainly outside the low gate that separated the editor's domain from the rest of the *Star* office.

"Graceful Whiteside," she repeated. "Miz Cleotha's daughter. You remember me, sir?"

"No, miss," Mr. Smitherman said after a moment. "I don't believe I do." He continued looking at her, his expectant expression clearly lined with impatience.

"Hedgemon?" she said finally. "Is he working today, sir?"

Slowly Mr. Smitherman capped the fountain pen and placed it carefully in the center of the page on the desk before him. His voice was clipped when he said, "I'm afraid he's no longer in my employ."

Graceful stared at the editor, waiting for him to say something more, waiting for him to say he was joking, or that he'd misunderstood her, because she couldn't think of the *Tulsa Star* without Hedgemon Jackson any more than she could imagine the newspaper without Mr. Smitherman composing all the articles himself.

"Hedgemon Jackson, I mean, sir."

"Mr. Jackson handed in his notice yesterday."

Graceful stood a moment longer in silence, intimidated by Mr. Smitherman's respectable presence. But it seemed impossible. Hedgemon had been working for Mr. Smitherman since he was big enough to run errands; he lived and breathed that job, everybody said it, and about the only time Hedgemon Jackson couldn't be found hanging around the *Star* office was on Sundays, when the building was locked shut. It was unbelievable that he would just now up and quit. At last Graceful drew her courage around her, and she said softly, "I wonder if you could tell me where I could find him."

"Bigheart," Mr. Smitherman said instantly, and the word might have been a mild curse. "Mr. Jackson has gone to Bigheart, as I understand it, to engage in a business opportunity there." The editor rubbed his forefingers against his eyes beneath the lenses of his glasses. He straightened then, having clearly dismissed her, and picked up his pen, uncapped it, looked several moments at the writing on the paper before him, and then began to add words.

Graceful waited outside the gate. Bigheart. She tried to remember just where was Bigheart. She thought to ask Mr. Smitherman if the interurban ran there, and then instantly dismissed the notion. It didn't matter if it did, Bigheart was too far for her to go track down Hedgemon Jackson, she didn't have time to track down Hedgemon Jackson, because she had to find her mother, her sisters and brother, right away. Something was bad wrong. Still she kept staring at the editor, waiting for him to tell her something, explain something, but Mr. Smitherman scribbled words following words as fast as his pen could dance across the paper, and he didn't look up again, and in another few minutes she turned and wandered back out to the street.

There were only two places her mother regularly went and took all her children with her, and one was to church, which wasn't likely at ten o'clock on a Friday morning, and the other was to her brother Delroy's house, up on Latimer Street. Yes, Uncle Delroy. Of course. She'd go quick and ring Uncle Delroy's garage. She glanced up and down the street, trying to think where she could call from. State law forbade any colored person from talking in a white phone booth, and city law made it illegal for Negroes to operate pay telephones inside the Tulsa city limits; phone booths for colored folks were few and far between, and expensive. Graceful hurried back along the avenue and into the *Star* office again.

Mr. Smitherman nodded toward the phone on the wall opposite the little gate and went on scribbling with hardly a glance at her. She cupped the earpiece tight to her ear, listening to the exchange ring and ring and ring until the operator came on at last and said, "Your party doesn't answer." Graceful rang off and stood facing the wall, telling herself that Uncle Delroy just hadn't opened yet, he'd be at work in a few minutes. But she knew her mother's brother opened the doors to the old livery stable that served as repair center for half the motor machines in Greenwood at seven o'clock every morning. Uncle Delroy was not a man to sleep late, to open late, to change the habits of his workday life, ever. The only time she could remember Uncle Delroy's garage being closed on a weekday was for her father's funeral. The fear in Graceful notched higher. She didn't know what to do. She couldn't think. She stared a long time at the whorls and lines in the oak grain of the telephone inches from her face before she realized Mr. Smitherman was speaking to her.

" . . . something I can do for you, miss, I'll be pleased to render my services, but if not, I'm . . . I'm going to have to ask you to leave."

Graceful turned around then and, seeing the editor as if for the first time, realized that he was a man so weary he looked about ready to weep. A slender, lightskinned man with a high, smooth forehead, Mr. Smitherman seemed to have grown older, thinner, in his big oaken chair. He took his glasses off and set them on the unfinished page on his desk, breathed in deeply once, said, "Miss Whiteside, your Hedgemon Jackson knocked on my door last night and told me he was departing my employ, after almost six years' service—at nearly midnight, Miss Whiteside, and without a minute's notice, this week's paper not even half set, and just now, in the wake of these lynchings requiring our most stringent and calming efforts. I've been up all night trying to teach my pressman to run the linotype. I haven't been to bed, my newspaper has not been put to bed, I haven't written my editorial, which effort I'm in the process of undertaking, and which, if you'll pardon my saying, is the most urgent piece in this publication needed to keep hearts and minds calm in our community before even worse happens. Now, if I can do something to help you, please tell me, and if not, will you be so kind as to leave me in peace so that I can finish my work."

She stared at him.

"Oklahoma shook hands with the state of Georgia last weekend, Miss Whiteside, as you may know." Mr. Smitherman stopped, scritched a few words on the paper. "Two lynchings and a letter from the governor to report, these are not yet common occurrences in the state of Oklahoma, but they're in critical danger of becoming so."

"Two?"

Mr. Smitherman frowned. "Where you been, child?"

"Working," Graceful whispered. "I been working." The dread poured through her. If it was two, one was black; it was always going to be thirty blackfolks for every one whiteman. She waited for Mr. Smitherman to tell her what she already knew.

"Don't you know they lynched a colored man at Oklahoma City last Sunday?"

"Sunday." She could only repeat him.

"Twenty-four hours, Miss Whiteside. Two men lynched within twenty-four hours in our illustrious state: a Saturday-night lynching in Tulsa matched Sunday evening in Oklahoma City. A white lynching matched with a black one quick as they could find a loose nigger. Lest anybody get the notion lynch-law justice is going to be applied equally among the races, observe carefully, Miss Whiteside: they'll find another Negro killed before the week's out. I'd stake my life on it."

Graceful's mind raced. Oklahoma City. What had Oklahoma City to do with her? "Who was it?" she said.

"A colored boy caught in the wrong place at the wrong time. Who else would it be?" His tone softened. "Everett Candler was his name. He was from Arcadia, as I understand it." The editor remained silent a moment, and then he picked up his eyeglasses, twined them around his ears, uncapped his pen. "That's all I can tell you, Miss Whiteside. I'm in receipt of a letter from Governor Robertson on the subject, and am at present composing both response and commentary, which you may read in tomorrow's edition, should you be so gracious as to allow me to get on with my work." He waited for the girl to leave, but Graceful made no move.

The instant she'd heard the name Arcadia, her mind screamed, *T.J.!* She couldn't breathe. Her brother had gone to visit a cousin in that community a year and a half ago, and he hadn't come home since. Sometimes he wrote to his mother, and Graceful or one of her sisters would be asked to read the letter to Cleotha, over and over, until the daughters knew the words by heart and would begin to quote them from memory while their mother stared straight ahead, her face so still with grieving that the girls, seeing her, would look down at the page again, unable to bear her expression. Slowly the name filtered into her mind. Candler? Graceful didn't know any Everett Candler, that was not a name she'd ever seen in one of her brother's letters. She began once again to breathe.

The wooden door at the back of the office opened, releasing into the room the sharp odor of heated newsprint and fresh ink. A huge brown-skinned man poked his head through, said, "Mr. Smitherman, I almost got done with page four. You want me to go back and try and work some on page one?" His glance passed incuriously over Graceful, and then abruptly swept back to her again, and Graceful, looking at the man but seeing in her mind's eye only the face of her older brother, didn't at first realize he was staring at her.

"That's all right, Lawrence," Mr. Smitherman said. "I'll be in in a minute." He frowned down at the paper on his desk. With one hand he kneaded his forehead beneath the visor, and the visor rose and fell in rhythm. It seemed he'd forgotten her, or at least dismissed her. Graceful wanted to ask him more, but she was too intimidated by Mr. Smitherman's frowning concentration, by his exhaustion, his revered place in the community, and in any case she'd suddenly become aware of the man staring at her from the back. She turned and went out of the *Star* office to stand, uncertain, confused, on Greenwood Avenue again.

It was late morning now, and the street was fully alive with activity. A few doors down Mr. Thompson came out to sweep the walk in front of his drugstore. Across the street a boy was changing the letters on the Dreamland Theater marquee. Mr. Berry's jitney passed her, going south now, and all along the street vehicles were passing, belching gasoline fumes and noise, and amidst the Model T's and touring cars were delivery wagons drawn by blindered drays and shining new delivery trucks, and one battered Nash truck careening recklessly down the avenue, which she realized within seconds was her Uncle Delroy's. It seemed like that snubnosed truck had been flying toward her down Greenwood forever, and Graceful stepped to the curb to flag it down.

The truck continued past her, but she saw her baby brother, William, jumping around and waving at her from inside the cab, and the truck, almost to Archer now, suddenly stopped and began to back up against the traffic. Willie waved at her wildly. She darted across Greenwood, dancing between wagons and cars, and before she'd reached the curb, Uncle Delroy stuck his head out the open window and shouted back at her, "'M'on, girl, get in!"

Her little brother scooted over to make room, and the instant she closed the door, Delroy ground into first gear and started down the street. His face was a smooth mask, motionless and intent. William, caught between excitement and his wordless understanding of how serious was the situation, bounced lightly on the seat, turning his head to look up at his uncle, and then his sister, and back to his uncle again.

"Where's Mama?" Graceful said.

Delroy turned onto Archer, squealing the rubber tires around the corner, and, as if continuing a prior conversation, said, "She's down there already." He shifted into second and sped up, heading west. Graceful watched the side of her uncle's face. His profile was a leaner, younger replica of her mother's, in which bled through the Anglo features of a forgotten white grandfather, but Delroy was much darker than Mama, almost black, and his very leanness and the tight nap of his hair spoke of Senegal. *He sure do look like T.J.,* Graceful thought, her heart catching on the old comparison that was standard in the family: the two lean, loose-jointed men so alike in their faces, their movements. Unconsciously she glanced down at William to see if he'd yet begun to turn lean; but, no, her baby brother carried his same round face and thick thighs; he would be sturdy-built. His soft features were most like their father's, and Graceful's heart caught on that recognition, too. Ernest Whiteside had been dead seven years, and it might as well have been seventeen for all the presence he still held in the household: a framed studio photograph on the parlor table showing a round, handsome man in a suit and bow tie, with a stern, serious expression. And yet, for Graceful, who remembered him better than the younger children—and maybe for T.J., too, she thought—her father was a smiling man who brought gifts home from his travels as a Pullman porter and tugged the children onto his lap and teased them and sneaked up on Mama when she was cooking in the kitchen and grabbed her in his big arms and hugged her from behind.

"Your mama gone down last night," Delroy said. He stared fiercely through the windscreen and did not offer any further explanation. She wanted him to say he had carried Mama out to the pipeline field with her box lunches early this morning. She wanted him to laugh big once and say, What you doing on the street, girl, ain't you suppose to be working? She wanted a reasonable and lighthearted explanation for her little brother to be fidgeting in the seat beside her; for her mama and sisters being gone from the house on Elgin; for her uncle not being at work in his garage. Graceful waited for the words she knew would never come and watched through the side window as they crossed the trolley tracks and turned west toward Sand Springs. *For sure we not going up by Dirty Butter Creek,* she thought.

"Where's LaVona and Jewell?" she said.

Delroy nodded, as if that told her something.

"Uncle Delroy, what is it? What happened?" Her voice was barely audible above the roaring motor, and yet the sound in it was nearly a scream.

Delroy hunched forward, his hands gripping the steering wheel high and tight. "Nothing to speak of, honey. Just . . . your mama had to go see about some business at Arcadia yesterday evening. She ask me to bring Willie this morning and come on." He glanced down at the boy, met Graceful's eyes, and his face when he turned back to watch the road was so furious and veiled that she would ask nothing further.

She felt her little brother's eyes on her and, looking down, saw him smiling slantwise up at her with the shy grin that could so easily split his face and endear him to any witness to it. "You get that letter?" William said. She saw him trying to be grown-up and sober, but he was just too proud.

"You the one brung that letter?" Graceful said, and the boy nodded, smiling. Her mind flew through adjustments, dropping Hedgemon Jackson as the deliverer of the strange missive and putting her baby brother in his place. *Why?* she thought, and then, suddenly: *What'd I do with it?* She didn't have the page with her; she carried no pocketbook, had no pockets in her skirt, had left her apron somewhere. *I must of dropped it by Mr. Smitherman,* she thought. *Lord, no telling what he'll think.* Aloud she said, "Come all that way by yourself? My Lord, you going to be grown and gone before I get a chance to turn around."

William ducked his head. The grin spread farther across his face.

"Who give it to you, Willie?"

"Mama," he said, surprised, the grin disappearing, the look on his face asking, Who else would it be? A fleeting confusion passed over his soft round features, and then the beginnings of fear. His eyes darted swiftly between his uncle and sister once more, trying to decipher how he was supposed to act, how to feel, and Graceful quickly said, "Well, of *course,* Mama give it to you. I just wondered did one of my snoopy sisters write it, didn't look like they handwrite to me."

"I don't know," William said, and the beautiful grin was entirely replaced now with the closed sullenness that was the boy's defense against his impulse to take blame for every trouble. Seeing the change in him, and feeling her own fear rising as her uncle continued west past the shacks at the edge of Sand Springs, Graceful reached down and rubbed the back of her brother's head; she took small, playful handfuls of nap in her fingers and tugged gently, said, "I don't know what to think, you so grown up you taking the trolley all that way by yourself. You're going to be driving a Ford motorcar here in a little bit. Uncle Delroy, you going to teach this boy how to drive?" She touched the smooth cheek, where the smile was beginning to crack again. "Somebody have to teach him," she said. "Can't me or Mama do it, and I wouldn't trust LaVona to teach him how to fly-swat!" She laughed, and though her voice was edged in fear, the boy laughed with her, and their uncle joined them as they continued west on the rutted road.

E yes closed, head pressed against the seatback, Althea surrendered to the jolting, forward-propelled motion, the railcar's rude lurch and sway. From time to time she would allow her lashes to part slightly, and she'd cast a hidden glance at her husband, or turn slitted eyes to the right, where a golden blur raced past the smeared window. With every mile ratcheting backward, dread and a quavering excitement settled more deeply in her belly. She hadn't been to Creek County since the last morning she'd boarded the train in Bristow in 1904. She hadn't seen Jim Dee in over a year. She tried to conjure the image of him staring at her from the far side of the parlor, the dozen or more men milling about the room between them; she searched for the dream and could not find it. She couldn't even recall in any clear way what her husband's partner looked like.

The train whistle blew a mournful warning as they neared the Kellyville crossing, and the cry filled Althea with sharp, unexpected longing. An unwilled sound, a near whimper, escaped her lips.

"What is it?" Franklin said. She could feel his eyes on her. "Althea?" The tone was without threat, but he never called her by her full name, not since the first weeks of courting. The word frightened her. She would not open her eyes.

"Thea, I want you to sit up now. Talk to me."

She forced herself to breathe slowly, feigning sleep, but he touched her arm, and when she didn't respond he lifted her wrist and shook it.

"Stop!" she snapped, and sat up, frowning. "Lord God, it's hot." She fanned her face with her open hand. Franklin's eyes were steady on her. "What?" she said.

"I believe you're rested now. Talk."

"About what?"

But he only stared at her.

"Oh, that . . . that boy . . . Well. He's . . . Please, Franklin. My head . . ."

"Talk."

Why wouldn't he leave her alone? Her mind was void of creative thought, and this, this grimy railcar was so miserably hot, the leather seat was sticky, the window filthy. . . .

"He's your brother, I know that. I can see that with my own eyes. I want to know how come I never heard of him."

Althea opened her mouth, took a breath, and then just stopped. Not a word came to her, not an image. "Yes," she said at last. "He is."

Her husband remained silent.

"I never told you because . . . Oh, for God's sake, Franklin, I was ashamed! Ashamed of him, them, all of them! What do you think?" She turned to glare out the greasy window. The train gained speed. Jaws clenched, she watched the folds of yellow prairie give way to a snarled clutch of post oak and blackjack, open to rolling grassland again. Had Franklin pressed her then, he could have received not only the answers he was seeking, but much more: an entire history, dark and long secret, and staggeringly different from all he believed he knew about her. But he didn't ask; he simply watched her with cold, unfamiliar precision, as if she were a stranger, and in another moment she put her head back against the seat once more, closed her eyes.

Franklin traced the long curve of his wife's neck, crossed faintly with palely etched lines; he examined the slope of her jaw, the perfectly arched brows, frowning slightly, the tiny whorls of fine black hair at her temples, where the dark tresses began and mounded thickly in a loose chignon toward the crown. As Althea's face slackened toward sleep, the harsh lines softened and her features eased themselves into the appearance of innocence, and he saw her as he'd first seen her in the Raglands' foyer: a young girl stepping away from her cotton wrap, dismissing it to the arms of the housemaid as regally as if it had been fur. She'd glanced at him shyly, her hair clasped to one side with a sprig of mistletoe, her lips and cheeks white with cold. Never had he seen anything like her pale avian beauty, stunning in one so young and frail and unformed. And then she'd come fully around and stared directly into his eyes for an instant, secretly bold, before turning to Joe Ragland to smile and offer her hand. Franklin had fallen in love in that moment. Never in the many difficult years since had that infatuation failed. The old tenderness did battle now with the morning's suspicion and anger; he tried to shrug it away, but the pull was too strong, and he rode swaying with the emotions rolling over him in alternating waves of warmth and cold doubt.

She moaned in her sleep, a low, gritted groaning, and then the little sound came again, clearly now a whimper, animallike in its helplessness and terror. Her hands convulsed in her lap, and her lips moved, trying to form words, though all that escaped was the low moaning. Franklin reached out and brushed the back of his knuckles against her cheekbone. Her hands came up before her throat, clenched, batting the air, and she said distinctly, "No, no, Franklin, get back! There's a snake on me!" She sat forward. "What?" she said. She looked at him, not seeming to see him, then her eyes swept the inside of the railcar, the row of seatbacks in front of her; she twisted to look behind, where a few passengers were beginning to gather their belongings. Her breath cut the air in short, sharp gasps. Franklin could hear it above the rush of iron wheels. "Where is he?" she whispered.

"Who?" Franklin touched her. "It's just a dream, Thea. You were sleeping."

Althea leaned back, allowed him to stroke her, grateful for the fleshy reality of his thick palm on her forehead. Dear God. She tried to retrace the dream, what had terrified her so, but the curtain had dropped, and she was left only with the recollection of a dark, focused terror: fear of someone or something, as if a hidden presence were watching her from inside the car; she couldn't bring herself to turn and look, but shrank further into the seat, tried to make herself small beneath Franklin's hand. The locomotive began very gradually to slow, and the more the train slowed, the more terrible the burn of fear rose in her; she closed her eyes entirely against it.

The whistle sounded, not mournful now but shrieking, a terrified warning. The brakes groaned beneath the car and then began their high-pitched piggish squealing as the locomotive rolled into the station. Althea sat up, shrugged Franklin's palm away. Her eyes were wide as she stared at him, the pupils so swollen her gaze was nearly black. A little boy in a ragged suitcoat raced up the aisle, followed by a woman with a bawling infant in one arm, a battered valise in the other, and two crying toddlers stumbling after. Franklin started to rise, but Althea's hand on his arm stopped him. Still she didn't turn her eyes from his.

"We're here," he said. He pulled away, stood and put his hat on, reached up to retrieve his case from overhead. Althea didn't move. Franklin picked up her cloth purse and blue silk traveling bonnet, extended his palm to her. As though coming fully awake at last, Althea suddenly grasped the hand and scrambled quickly to the aisle, rushed toward the front of the car, and then stopped in the open door at the top of the steps, confounded by the neat redbrick depot trimmed in white. For a moment she forgot where she was. She saw the word BRISTOW etched in bold white letters above the façade; the word seemed to float up from a long-ago dream. A tawny head separated itself from the little clutch of waiting passengers and began to move toward them. Althea's mind cleared then, and she remembered.

He sauntered hatless toward the platform in denim britches and a shortsleeved khaki shirt open at the throat. Even in the relaxed stroll there was an undercurrent of impatience, so that it seemed he kept glancing at a timepiece, though he wore neither fob nor wristwatch. Althea watched him with the same black intensity with which she'd watched her husband, as if she were drowning and the only thing that might save her was the other's face. But, though she expected and longed to feel the old tremble of excitement, she felt only dullness and a kind of empty wonder at how much older he looked. Not some little bit older, not just a year older, but shockingly so, his face more wind and sun scarred, the squint lines at the corners of his eyes etched deeper, the once faint dusting of freckles now distinct and particulate as paint. All she could think of was why in heaven's name didn't he wear a hat.

Jim Dee's eyes lifted and met hers. He didn't blink, smile, offer recognition in any way; his gaze passed on, casually, as he strolled toward them, and it was only by how his pace slowed that she knew he was surprised to see her. He shook Franklin's outstretched hand, nodded at her, turned with hardly a word of greeting and began to walk toward a battered tin lizzie parked at the curb. Althea hurried along, her arm clinging so tightly to Franklin's and the rush in her step so urgent that her husband looked at her in surprise as she pulled him along.

Franklin tried to help her into the front of the open car, but Althea shook her head and climbed into the rumble seat in the back as Jim Dee moved to the front of the old Ford to crank. Hunkered in the narrow space, Althea watched the few remaining passengers milling about the platform. A couple of roustabouts in stained pants lounged in the shadow of the depot wall, smoking handrolled cigarettes. On the wooden bench facing the tracks an old Indian man sat erect and motionless in a tan suit-coat and a broadbrimmed black hat. The woman with the three crying youngsters came to the curb and climbed awkwardly with them into a battered spring-wagon, where a farmer in overalls held the reins to an old dray and did not offer a hand to help. The whistle screamed, the brakes hissed their released steam, the Frisco engine grumbled to a louder pitch. Althea watched the train grind out of the station, gaining speed, until she heard the whistle in the distance, not shrieking now but lonesome, moaning, as the Frisco roared on toward Oklahoma City. Still she couldn't shake the sense of a malevolent presence behind her, and she shrank into the well, pressing her spine against the cracked leather binding.

As they drove south on Main Street, Althea stared at the three-story Laurel Hotel, the new pharmacy, and Stone's Hardware & Furniture lining the brick-paved street that had been, on the November morning she'd last seen it, a mud thoroughfare sentineled by slapped-together wooden falsefronts and plank sidewalks. She tried to listen to what the men were saying, but her mind wasn't calm enough to take in the words, had she even been able to hear them clearly over the popping motor and rhythmic thumps of the rubber tires as they bumped along the brick street. At the edge of town Jim Dee pushed the Ford to its limit, speeding up to nearly thirty miles an hour, so that Franklin had to cram his boater down on his head to keep it from being blown off. The men yelled over the sound of wind and motor, and the wind caught their words and lifted them above the battered turtlehull and blew them north over the prairie. Althea put one hand over her eyes, the other to the top of her head, as the wind beat her chignon to pieces.

Within a mile of town the pavement gave out, and the Ford bucked and jolted so fiercely Althea bit the inside of her jaw. The lizzie backfired once and slowed, grumbling, to a more reasonable gait as the road turned to gritty, wagon-rutted dust. Althea's eyes swept the treeless fields on either side, the salmon-and-ochre-and-olive-colored ditches, where the soft earth, raineaten into pastel furrows, clotted around buffalograss; she raised her gaze to the horizon again. There were no houses, no fences, no manmarks of any kind but for the dirt road itself and, far off on the eastern horizon, a black pumpjack like a rocking horse dipping rhythmically toward the earth to drink, lifting its face skyward again. This was the landscape of her deepest memory, and she couldn't bear to look at it, and could not bear not to look.

After a very long time, what seemed to Althea several hours in the noise and wind and sun, though it was perhaps less than two, the Model T slowed to a near stop, and Jim Dee turned the wheel hard to the right, nursed the front tires over an impossible dirt hump. The chassis shuddered as the back wheels followed and the car thumped to the ground, and Althea bit her jaw again, and the motor, vibrating in union with the chassis, backfired once and died a belching death. Jim Dee cursed and got out to crank. Althea combed her fingers through her snarled tresses, trying to tuck the windblown hairs back inside the hopeless chignon. She could feel the grit in her mouth and the salty irontaste of blood, could feel the oppressively fine dust coating her face and hands and neck. *Lord God,* she said to herself, *I thought I left this damn stuff.* The motor coughed to life, and soon they were driving west on a surface that could not be called road, could hardly be called a blazed trail, and the Ford moved in the salmon dust at a near crawl.

The prairie was thick with blooming milkweed and blackeyed susans and joe-pye, and the track held straight across it, though the way was pitted and rough, nearly invisible in places. But Althea felt somehow protected by the path's absolute uselessness, and she began to relax a little with the Ford's altered rhythm, which was wagon rhythm, which was the slow, creaking rhythm of an ancient stockdrawn cart. She settled back into the seat. The wind no longer struck her but stroked her, so that she could breathe now, she could see, without the windbeat hairs flaying her eyes. She raised her face to the sky—cloudless, crystalline, almost turquoise in its autumn turning—and for an instant her heart lifted. The sun beat on her skin, and she didn't fear its burning. Something old in her tried to awaken, some hard pushed-away memory of space and light, and her chest swelled and she breathed in a sensation very kin to joy. She touched Franklin's arm. "Darling?"

He turned to her, his face showing nothing of surprise at the word.

"Oh, you know, I didn't bring a parasol. I didn't think."

Instantly Franklin turned to his partner. "Jim, can't we put the top up on this thing?"

"No!" Althea couldn't bear the thought of being enclosed in the cramped seat. "No, dear, I just meant . . ." She smiled at him sheepishly, and she could feel how the wind and sun had brought red to her cheeks, and she believed it made her beautiful. She could never have dreamed how badly the dust jaundiced her complexion, how the wild tousle of her hair made her look disheveled and confused, made her look poor. "Oh, this silly thing is just useless." She slapped the small neat blue traveling bonnet in her lap. "It won't do a bit to protect me." She saw something in her husband's face, some new emotion, unrecognizable to her, but since she had no pattern to gauge it by, she dismissed it. "Couldn't I borrow your hat? Just a little something to keep that old sun off me, I'll be burnt crisp in a minute."

Franklin removed his straw boater and handed it to her. She grinned impishly as she put the hat on. In times past, Althea could have snatched a gentleman's hat and placed it on her own head, tilted her face to the side, and flirted from beneath her lashes, and the effect would have been daring, rakish, so that it made that gentleman laugh with pleasure. Now she only looked foolish. Franklin turned away, began to speak in a loud voice to Jim Logan; he didn't glance at his wife again.

Althea listened to the men's voices, lulled by the comforting, deep-throated rumble. Once, she looked behind and believed she saw the dust of an automobile or perhaps a wagon following, but the prairie rose and fell here in great folds, and the dust's source was hidden behind a pleat of land. Even as she watched, the smoking column disappeared, a fading dustdevil, and Althea forgot it as the dirt track began to be closed in on either side by a thick tangle of oak and hickory. The prairie disappeared. The sky receded; there was no breeze at all, only the close swelter of humidity. The darkness was so abrupt it was as if they'd entered a tunnel. The path began to meander, reptilish, undulating, and the Model T kicked and groaned and rattled as the pitted ruts became deeper. Althea thought she could smell riverdank and mud. *It can't be the Deep Fork,* she thought. Surely they hadn't come that far south. Or had they? Her perception of how far they'd come was confused, she had lost all sense of direction, all knowledge of land and distance. She touched Franklin's shoulder. He glanced at her as if a fly had landed on him, some faint distraction; he returned his attention immediately to Jim Dee.

"All right," he said, "let's say the field proves, how do we know you got the right Indian?" he said.

"I'm telling you, I looked it up six ways from Sunday, the courthouse in Sapulpa, went to Okmulgee and checked the rolls myself. She's not Creek anyhow, she's a freedwoman, but the allotment's hers, it ain't her husband's."

"It's unbelievable." Franklin shook his head.

"Believe it," Jim Dee said.

Althea shoved Franklin's shoulder. "What are we doing? We're going to get mired down in here. Franklin, you can't drive down in here!" Her voice was shrill with panic. "These old creekbottoms are quicksand! They sink to the middle of the earth. We'll get stuck to the hub in a minute! The mud goes down, it goes down—" Her throat clamped closed. She looked up at the entwined oaks pressing into the path; the impenetrable tangle would weave closed behind them, they'd never find their way out. "Dear God." She heard the whisper and only dimly realized it came from her own lips. In the front seat both men sat, half turned, staring at her. She realized that the engine no longer coughed and sputtered. A windless silence, dense as cottonbatting, held the earth, the tangled woods. Then, far off, she heard a crow call. As if at a signal, the timbers erupted in a high, urgent din, a thousand million insects crying hard against the coming winter.

"What the devil's the matter with you?" Franklin said. "You are really . . ." But Franklin's voice trailed away. He looked at his wife in silence. Abruptly he reached over the side window and opened his door from the outside. "Come on, Jim, let's go have a look at this thing. I'm afraid Thea's not feeling well, I better get her back to town."

"Where are you going? Franklin, wait!"

But the two men disappeared into the tangled scrub, and she was left alone, surrounded by the clutching tree branches and chirring insects. She couldn't see where they'd gone, so dense was the undergrowth, but she knew the water was off to her left somewhere. She could smell it, the rank mud of the Deep Fork bottoms, and she nearly choked in her terror. She scrambled over the seat, over the shut door, fell sprawling when her skirt caught on the door handle, and got up instantly, rushed toward the thicket of sumac and ivy and ancient blackberry brambles, crying, "Franklin! Franklin! Help me! Dear God, please help!" She heard the low murmur of their voices, but she couldn't see them; she couldn't reach them. The briars snagged her skirt and held her, the low branches of the jackoaks crossed in front of her, black and roughscaled, hard as pig-iron clothed in dry, olivedun leaves; they stabbed earthward like fencespikes, forbidding her, but on she went, driven by her terror, pushing through the tough branches as through a wall of fire, holding her arms before her face.

When she burst through the growth to the slick bank, her face was bleeding in long scratchlike swells; the backs of her hands were lacerated from the clutch of blackjack twigs, the sting of berry thorns. Her husband's face told her at once that she hadn't cried aloud: she could not have made her way screaming, as she'd thought she did, for he was surprised to see her. Both men were surprised. The other thing she understood was the meaning of the look on Franklin's face. This time its substance was unmistakable: he was embarrassed by her. She'd made him ashamed. She saw herself: a ridiculous-looking woman, bedraggled, dirty, foolishly frightened. The image was intolerable to her, beyond endurance. She could not hold it in her mind and live.

"What do you mean," she snapped, "letting me sit and swelter in that blessed car till the mosquitoes carry me off?" She hated her own voice and the words coming from her mouth, hated the hunch in her shoulders and the twisted sneer of her lips. "I could suffocate, I could get eaten by a panther, little you'd care! Either one of you!" She turned her glare to include Jim Logan, fingered her snarled hair in upward combings. "Y'all've got the manners of a pulpwood hauler, leaving me out in the heat and weather like that!" And now she turned her glare entirely on her husband, and the more she hated her own soul and bearing, the more scathing was the loathing she poured out upon him. "You are really beyond belief. I can't dream you'd carry me out into the absolute bojacks and walk off."

"I'm sorry, Thea. We'll be through here in a minute."

"Take me back to town. This instant!"

"In a minute."

She stared at him. Never did Franklin resist her outright demand, she couldn't remember his ever having done so, and yet now he didn't even bother to look at her but turned away, dismissing her, and Althea, more amazed than angered, was thrown off balance. She wanted to whirl on her heel and storm back to the car to sit in wounded silence until he came to her, but her instincts told her that to stumble back into the brambles would make her look not outraged and injured but buffoonish. And she did not want to be alone.

Moving over to stand at the edge of a canebrake, she began to brush the dirt off her dress; she wiped her fingers beneath her eyes, rubbed her cheeks one at a time against her sleeve, pushed and fingered her hair. She longed for a brush or a comb, a mirror to tell her how she looked. She didn't raise her eyes to the men. The same instinct that told her when to leave or enter a room, which tight or sweeping gesture to use, when to blink and smile and when to hold another's glance, told her now that to look at either of them was death. She, who believed masculine regard to be the most telling and perfect mirror, dreaded to see in her husband's eyes, in Jim Dee's eyes, the truth. Turning away, she combed and picked and brushed at herself, silent, absorbed in her grooming as a cat. But her fear was gone now, gone even was the shame that had followed it, all swept into disappearance by the quick and blaming rage, and now even the rage was gone: she wanted only to be still awhile. She wanted a bath, a nice quiet room, a clean dressing gown, perhaps a nap.

"There's no producing field anywhere closer than Depew." Franklin's tone was musing, calculating, though he clearly expected comment. Jim Dee said nothing. Their eyes held steady, very studiedly and frowning, on the water. Althea peered down at the river, murky with washed-in silt, oozing slowly past the bank in olive swirls and eddies. In complete silence, in a dark place within, Althea recognized the clay-contained, viscous waters of the Deep Fork, and in the same instant dismissed it, shut off all recollection. Click. She raised her gaze to the grapevines trailing from the overhanging branches across the river. The insect din rose and fell in the undergrowth. She slapped a mosquito whining at her neck.

"Heard last week Gypsy Oil finally quit drilling on the Yargee lease," Franklin murmured. "That's not a mile from where we're standing. Good anticline, too, not some low, boggy bottom. Twenty dusters, a bunch of teasers, one little nine-barrel-a-day producer." Both men continued to stare at the sluggish place below the cutbank. Althea followed their gaze, the fear trying to snatch at her, until at last she saw what they were seeing: a thin rainbow film upon the water. She saw the exposed roots of a dead cottonwood reaching from the bank. The gnarled wood was covered in a thick greenish ooze. She smelled it now, sweetish, mechanical: the earth-bowel smell of raw crude. Slowly the meaning began to filter clear to her. She looked at Franklin with a sudden surge of hope.

"One thing I know," he said, "it hasn't been this easy in a lot of years." Wonder mingled with the skepticism in his voice. He knelt on the bank and dipped a hand into the water, then raised up, rubbing his thumb and forefinger in an oily circle. "Last time I heard somebody found a seep was back in Fourteen or Fifteen. I thought this whole country'd been gone over with a finetoothed comb." He looked hard at his partner. "You're a hundred percent sure that old freedwoman still holds the claim?"

Jim Dee stared unblinking at the water. His expression was distant, trancelike, his thick brows rising in an odd little frown; his lips, the same tawny color as his skin, pressed together almost primly.

Franklin turned back to the river. "If there is another big strike coming," he said slowly, the wonder and barely kept delight overswelling the doubt in his voice, "another Glenn Pool, another Cushing Field, under this useless prairie, I don't know why this wouldn't be it right here." He knelt and scooped a palm of water, cupped it before him reverentially, let it trickle back to the oily bank. Suddenly he turned his face up and grinned broadly at the late-afternoon sky. "Why the hell wouldn't it!" Franklin got to his feet then and began to pace the clearing. "First thing," he said, "we better get out to that old lady's before somebody else comes nosing around. We've got time for that before dark. I believe we do." He glanced up to gauge the sun's position. "Yes, all right, that's fine. Now . . ." Althea could see his mind flying, calculating, but Jim Dee suddenly came out of his reverie, and without a word turned and walked downstream. "Jim! Where are you going?" Franklin was caught in mid-stride, mid-sentence.

Jim Dee continued to pick his way through the brambles. He spoke over his shoulder. "Y'all each find another way out of here. Don't go back the way you come. We don't want to leave any sign of a trail." His khaki shoulders disappeared in the tangled growth.

In the back of the roaring, bouncing Ford motoring toward Bristow, Althea struggled to listen to the men talk. The task made her tired. Their words—*paraffin base, asphalt content, bentonite clay,* and on and on— were so much gobbling in her ears, and she could not keep her mind on the sound, much less the words' meaning. There was only one thing she cared to know anyway: was it the big strike? Somehow she knew it was, or she knew that Franklin believed it to be. Never had she seen his face so animated and open, his voice so free of the infernal cautiousness that dogged him. Her husband's belief brought her a new and thrilling excitement. Suddenly the horrors of the past week, her fears and sense of dislocation and the terrible emptiness, were lifted away. Of course. *This* was what she wanted. To be rich as the Murphys were rich, the J. Paul Gettys, the Josh Cosdens, the Gilcreases, the Marlands, the Sinclairs. And it was almost in hand. The first well hadn't been spudded in yet—the lease, in fact, from what she understood, had not been secured—but such details weren't important. Franklin believed, that was what mattered. And Jim Dee did.

Althea watched him through the hairs flying about her eyes. He was no longer scowling, taciturn, but yelling excitedly at Franklin in his near-foreign tongue—*depth of sand, degrees of gravity, syncline, anticline, cavey formation*—words that thrilled her with a sense of his capable nature. She saw that the excitement was as great in him as it was in Franklin, as uncluttered with doubt, and she kept her eyes on him, willing that the old feeling would return, until her senses began to fill at last with the look and scent of him, and she ceased to find his weatherscarred skin distasteful but saw the squint lines and rough texture as masculine, romantic. Her eyes traced the curl of his hair behind his sunburned ear, the skin on his neck rippling in leathery folds as he turned to Franklin, and she surrendered to the old daydreams as if they—or, rather, the man himself—had returned to her from a great distance. But even this she could not hold for long, and soon she turned to her husband, graced him for an instant with a benevolent thought for his caretaking, rushed past him to the new visions that sustained her.

She sat turning the straw boater over and over in her hands, her own silk bonnet forgotten, trampled in the floorboard beneath her feet. Not that she was mindful of her husband's property; she only fiddled with it as one strokes a buckeye thoughtlessly picked up from the ground. Her mind's eye was on herself descending a long staircase in a diaphanous ballgown the color of lit smoke; she saw heads turning toward her in desire, others bending to murmur in awe and envy. Immediately her home on South Carson was shabby in her own eyes, and she built for herself and her husband a mansion as grand as that L.O. Murphy had built for Nona, as grand as any on Black Gold Row, grander, with many more bedrooms, more imported marble, more artworks hung in more galleries, more gold inlay and silk drapery and Italian Renaissance fresco displayed in better taste.

As the Model T picked up speed on the open prairie, Althea's vision of herself transformed. Now she was a gracious philanthropist, broadly renowned in Saint Louis, Kansas City, New Orleans: far beyond Oklahoma's dusty borders. She saw herself moving tenderly along a row of iron beds in a dreary orphanage, and as she passed, the little pinched white faces darkened, became Indian for a time, and then colored, and Althea gently touched the little dark hands reaching through the iron bars, for her largess as patron and benefactor knew no prejudice, just as it knew no bounds.

She was lost in this new vision when the automobile began to slow, the engine popping, and Althea coughed as the boiling dust suddenly caught up with and surrounded the abruptly slowing Ford. Through the coppery haze she could see his lean figure standing in the dirt track with legs akimbo and his two arms stretched laconically overhead, reaching up and outward, a lanky X. The black fear swelled over her. She'd known. Of course she'd known. It was all completely recollected, and yet strange, like the familiar, unplaceable sense of a present moment relived from the past, already seen. He had followed, hidden in the railcar, a wagon, on the bouncing gate of a sputtering truck, and part of the time walking, and all the time she'd felt it; somewhere within herself, she had known.

The two men in the front seat said nothing as Japheth sauntered toward them, smiling as if it were the most normal thing in the world to be found standing on a dirt track at nearly sunset in the middle of nowhere.

"Evening, fellas. Could you give a man a lift?" His smile widened as he reached for the handle on the passenger's side.

Franklin turned to his wife for guidance or explanation, but she only stared back at him, mute. He glanced at his partner then, whose face was baffled, suspicious. Franklin blurted sort of helplessly, "Jim, this is Althea's brother. . . ." He still didn't know the fellow's name.

L ooks to me like I ought to known them. Their faces ought to been so burnt in my mind I couldn't help it, or hers ought to been, but I didn't think a thing, only what in the world is that noisy stinking tooloud horse-less carriage doing, come boiling up the road and into my yard scaring the daylights out my chickens. But I ought to known, and I can't quit thinking on that, still yet, all these years later, because before ever I heard that rattly old Model T coming, before I seen the dust on the horizon even, Bluford's dogs had already set in to howl.

The yellowhair fellow climbed out the seat first, come walking so nice toward me across the yard. The other dogs kept barking, but old Bone slunk up wagtail at him and try to lick his hand, and see, now, that too caught me off guard, because what I seen in that yellowhair gentleman and what Bone seen might of been the truth on that one day out of his life only, but I do know it for true: that whiteman didn't mean me no harm. I wasn't in the least afraid.

Let me tell you something my daddy used to tell me. He'd always say, One thing Indians got over colored is they don't fear the whiteman. My daddy'd say, An Indian'll go on and die before he let the whiteman make a slave of him, and that is on account of he ain't afraid. My daddy had a powerful respect towards Indians on account of that one issue. You never going to see the KuKlux after the Indian, he'd say, because you can't scare an Indian to make him act like you want to, you can't do nothing but kill him. Well, I have seen Indians scared of whitefolks, but it ain't in the same way. Indians I've known—and I count my two husbands among them— they don't carry the same kind of wicked in their souls, and so they don't have any way to fathom how downright evil whitefolks can be. They don't even have words in their language for how whitefolks act. I'm not saying you won't find a bad Indian, because you sure will—murderous as a rattler if he want to be, and jealous-hearted, Lord God, it's a disgrace how jealous-hearted and wicked some of them can be to each other. But they're not wicked the same way as whitefolks.

All right, I'll tell it to you like this: to me, what I think, at the beginning of the world the whiteman got caught in a stickyball of stuff, just gummed on the material world like he glued to it with pine-tar, and he get greedy, let greed swell up and suck him in till it won't turn him loose, and that's one of the things make him to act so evil. The Holy Word say that, just exactly: The love of money is the root of all evil. You heard that all your life, I guess. What else make somebody want to own all the land on the whole earth if it ain't greed? I know greed ain't the only kind of evil, but it is sure one that do make people act a terrible sneaking lowdown kind of vicious, and I never seen a greedy fullblood in my life, except only some of them greedy for whiskey, and that's howcome them not to be afraid of whitefolks in the same kind of way. I tell you something else, too: the reason they used to have their black slaves to parley with whitefolks in the old days is because blackfolks do understand that particular kind of evil, because they got that same room in their own souls. I can't trouble myself about what you want to hear or you don't want to hear. You ask me to tell the truth, long as I can open my mouth, that's what I'm going to speak. How you think I know it if I'm not telling it on myself?

But look here: if you're a person able to know evil, if you been given the means to recognize evil, and it come walking across the yard at you, then, if you got any bit of sense in the world, you better be afraid. And right yonder on that day, I wasn't. I'd seen enough from whitefolks by that time to respect how much harm they can do you, some of them—this was 1920, remember. The nightriders was having a big time in Oklahoma right then. They'd lynched a man at Oklahoma City not a week before, and I sure enough did know about it—we didn't have telephones, no way to get around but a plowmule if we was lucky and our own two feets if we wasn't, which was most of us, but word got around fast back then. We known about the Holdenville lynching—that happened that same year—Sable Merryweather come walking over the field to tell me about it when that man wasn't two hours dead. So you'd think I'd been more cautious when a carload of whitefolks come rumbling up in my yard, even allowing I didn't sense a thing evil in that yellowhair fellow but only just the color of his skin.

But, no, I'm going to stand on my porch and look at him walking crost my yard, I just nod at him, say, How do, mister. Nice evening. Y'all lost?

He say, No, ma'am, I don't believe so.

I only had a whiteman call me ma'am twice in my life, and both times it was nothing but trouble follow after, and that was the first time, and, yes, I got skittish then, finally—but I should of been way more than skittish. I should of been protecting myself. I should of seen them and known them from the first minute they driven up in my yard. Probably I couldn't even tell you when he and she climbed out the car and come over, because I's standing there talking to that Mister Dedmeyer, or I ought to say listening, because he the one do all the talking, and that's what else I mean about being off my guard. He talk all around everything—the weather, which that evening wasn't nothing but average, just hot and humid. He say, Look yonder at that sunset, which was pretty-looking, yes, but just normal for any sunset got clouds building in the west, big bank of thunderheads rising yonder toward Depew. He talk about Bluford's dogs and reach his hand down till they every one hush except Tennie. She slink off out by the privy and snarl and growl from the back side of it till that car finally drive on out the yard, and Bluford, he always did say that's the smartest dog he know anything about, and I ought to taken one look at Tennie and shut my ears clean up to that man.

I don't know howcome me to stand there and listen. You got to act like you listening, sure, but I had learnt the trick long before then how to open my ears just enough to nod at the right place, make them think I's listening, keep my ears shut enough I'm not going to start to believe something I know better, which if you listen hard at them they can sure make you do. I have seen that, more than a few times. You listen much to whitefolks, you'll be believing no telling what. And, see, that's just what happen.

Oh, you think the devil of greed can't get you, but let me tell you something: the devil can shape hisself anyhow he want. If you hadn't steeled yourself with prayer and smoke and right thinking, he's going to jump up and snatch you out before you know what you're about. He can make hisself look like a nice yellowhair whiteman don't mean you a bit of harm, and it might be that whiteman don't mean you anything but just to set you in the middle of the road so he can drive over you on his way to getting whatever little bit of something you got. And it weren't a little bit of something, it were a lot of something, which I didn't know, but if I'd been listening to hear only what-all I ought to known and not what-all that man want me to believe, I might could've stopped what was coming right then.

Lord God.

You picture it. Three whitemens and a whitewoman dressed up like sixty and covered in roaddust, stand around in a colored woman's yard saying ma'am and talking so particular and polite, and that colored woman just go right along with them. You think I didn't know they want something out of me? You think I believe they drive fourteen miles from the nearest whitetown to pass the time of day? What make me act like a fool with no better sense than to spill out her business? I been studying the answer to that question a long time.

Afterwhile Mister Dedmeyer start in talking some words I do not comprehend, all letters and numbers, but he say two things I known completely, *Deep Fork* and *allotment.* You put them two together, you know just what he's talking about. My allotment run in a little narrow strip right down to that river, and the rest of it was just nothing but scrub and underbrush, what the U.S. government give me for my portion when they tuck up all the land. Bluford carried me yonder once to see it. I looked at that worthless land, say to myself, They want to give us freedmen what the Indians won't take. They aim us to sit on a piece of land you can't give to nobody but the sorriest old white trash or a fool. I just shake my head, we come on back to our little place at Iron Post, and me and Bluford just go on living just how we was. Probably him and me never thought another word about it, not even when all these mixedbloods from here to Sapulpa been driving around in new motorcars they bought with lease money, because me and Bluford, the two of us together, we known better than that. But he's dead. My Bluford's dead, and looks like he taken ever lick of sense we had between us right into the grave with him.

Whiteman talking about my allotment, and me there on the porch, I opens my ears to every last word. He say four hundred dollars, I hears four hundred dollars. He say twenty years, I hears twenty years. He say fair percentage, I hears fair. I hears *fair.* You see what I mean? I hears it, and *believes* it, and you tell me when ever on this earth whitefolks intend fair with colored or Indian. Tell me when ever they even know what the word mean. And look at me yonder, I'm going to stand there and say,

Yessuh, oh, yes, massah, where you want me to sign? Which is not the words I told them, but it might as well been. What I said was, Yes, that do sound like my land. And, No, sir, I never leased out the mineral rights. Far as I know, nobody ever come and asked.

You see how the minute I let my ears open, that just shut my eyes blind. Still I didn't recognize her or him either one, not even when he start to talk Indian. Oh, yes, that one. One I ought to seen for a snake if I seen anything, the devil's own progeny, which these own two hands helped birth into the world, Lord forgive me, that very one: he stand there and talk Creek to me. And he ain't going to talk nice like Mister Dedmeyer about sunsets and yard dogs and fair percentage, he set right in to talk about Bluford, am I sure he's dead or didn't he maybe just go off and leave me, and how many children we got and was we married 'cording to whitelaw or just Indian, do Bluford have any children from a Creek woman, and things which he got no business to know, and I don't begin to answer but just shut my mouth tight, won't say another word to any of them, Creek or English neither one.

They don't know what he's saying, them other two whitemens don't, but they see he's saying something make me start crawfishing, and they both of them step in front of him, and I mean quick, get in between the two of us and talk English hard and fast as they can talk. I bet you that yellowhair say ma'am fifty times if he say it once, and the other one, the frowny lighthair, he tumble his own words out, say, We going to bring you a contract first thing in the morning, cash money on signing, give you half soon as you put your mark on the paper. Say, Tomorrow morning you going to get two hundred dollars right in your hand.

And look at me there, I'm going to stand there and keep listening, let that he-devil and his sister do deals with me right in my yard. Don't matter if it was the other two talking, it was them two behind it, and I should of known it from the beginning. Truth.

Maybe I can't fault myself I didn't know him, but I should of known her, I don't care if it was twenty years nearly since I seen her. She stare at me like she's trying to place me, got a queer, baffledy look on her face, every once in a while she kind of brush the air in front of her, like gnats are flying—but me, I got my greedy mind on what I'm going to do with a little money, and I never pay any attention to that whitewoman, not till they start on off across the yard again and I see her scrawny backside, just how she turn and walk away floating, like she's in a trance. My heart give a little jump then, there's a little minute's recognition, and I just wouldn't see it, I wouldn't listen, because I got my mind on how they going to come back tomorrow and bring me two hundred dollars for nothing but just sign a paper, and in my mind all I'm thinking is, I ain't seen two hundred dollars put together in one place my whole life.

T hey were an odd quartet: the beautifully dressed husband and wife and the two roughnecks seated contrapuntally at the back table, the dark brother and sister opposite one another, the two fair-haired men facing each other across the white cloth, arguing in hushed voices. Their steaks lay nearly untouched in their bloody juices—all but Franklin's, which was now only ravaged bits of meat and fat close to the bone. Their coffee had been served. The Negro waiter, uncertain whether to offer dessert, would start toward the table to remove the plates and, seeing one or another take a desultory bite, would immediately retreat to stand at attention near the kitchen doorway again. But the hunger that radiated from the table was unsated, for the powerful appetites had nothing to do with food.

The brother gazed at his own reflection in the large gilt mirror on the back wall, observing that glee was a hard thing for a man to keep to himself. *Even when a fellow remembers not to smile,* Japheth mused, *it's hard to hide the glow in the eyes and the complexion.* He shifted his gaze to his sister's face. Althea wouldn't meet him but stared, glittery and attentive, at the two partners hunched toward one another.

"I'm telling you we've got to get back out there first thing!" Franklin rasped. He struggled to keep his voice down, although an interested listener could have picked up that the partners had scouted a promising location, as well as the even more attractive fact that they hadn't yet secured the lease. Bristow, of course, was an oil town: interested listeners lurked everywhere. "Drive me out to the old lady's cabin first," he whispered; "then you can go track down Ben Koop."

"He's way the hell and gone up to Osage country, take me a day and a half to get there."

"Can't you reach him by phone?"

Jim Dee didn't bother to dignify that with an answer.

"Take the train, then. I'll drive your old Ford."

"You tend to your business, I'll tend to mine."

"You know damn well we've got nothing until we've got her mark. What do you expect me to do, walk?" Franklin ran his hands through his thick hair, blonder than the partner's, his face ruddier: a beefy, thickened version of the other. He leaned over his plate, spoke slowly. "There's no goddamn train to Iron Post."

He's the more ruthless of the two, Japheth thought. *And the softer.* His gaze drifted to Jim Logan, who sat silent now, sullen and restless, one leg jittering beneath the table as he knifed butter onto a dinner roll so furiously the soft bread turned doughy and mangled. Few pleasures gave Japheth more satisfaction than perusing another's secret nature, and he sipped his coffee as he studied the partner. *This one,* he said to himself, amused, realizing the similarity for the first time, *is very much like the very famous, very late Roy Belton.*

The memory flashed: his own ex-partner standing on the dark road with the hijacked cabdriver on the ground before him, and yes, it'd been Roy Belton's rash anger, his restless, withholding silences, his fidgety nature that had pushed him to fire the pistol twice, stupidly, in Homer Nida's belly—enough to kill the cabbie, not enough to kill him quick. The hack driver had taken four long, stupid days to die, long enough to name his hijackers, so of course they'd caught Belton in Nowata and brought him to the Tulsa jail, from which the good citizens had taken him and carried him out to that same spot on the Red Fork road, and lynched him. *I told him and told him,* Japheth said to himself, *a fellow's got to learn how to hold his temper.*

His attention returned to the two men. Japheth had an unerring sense for the concealed lives of others, a kind of second sight that allowed him to know what people tried to keep hidden, and he saw that the husband was hiding something now. Not ambition; not the merciless depths he'd go to in order to satisfy that craving: those were excellent traits in a good oilman. What Franklin Dedmeyer strove to keep secret was his smallness, the pinched parsimony that derived from that ambition. It wasn't money Franklin was tight with, but information, and that was a characteristic despised among insiders in the business of oil. Even now he was keeping certain facts from his partner, which was part, Japheth saw—although only part—of the other's long resentment. He took another sip of coffee, savoring for a moment his developing knowledge. The smile broadened behind the fragile rim of china cup as his gaze returned to his sister. *And you, my dear, are so filled with secrets as to be a transparency to me. I know your little tawdry wants, and to what lengths you'll go to satisfy them. I know your unpitying nature and where you've come from, which, above everything, you'd like to keep hidden.* As if feeling his eyes on her face, Althea turned to him, and instantly looked away—but not before Japheth saw the fear there, and this gave him the greatest pleasure of all.

"I don't care!" Franklin burst out. "Can't you hear a word I'm saying? It can't wait till Monday!" He glanced at the full dining room behind him, fought to bring his voice under control. "We've got to fix things with the old lady first," he hissed, "take care of the rest next week." He sat back, sawed off a bit of steak. "All right, it's settled, then," he said, though his partner's scowl declared that it was far from settled. "Darling," he said with his mouth full, "I think you'd better take the early train tomorrow. We're going to be driving those old rutty roads again, I don't want to leave you sitting in the car. You won't want to wait around the hotel all day."

"The girl's gone, Franklin. You said you'd get me a new one. I can't stay in that house by myself. You know that."

Franklin turned for the first time and looked directly at his wife.

"Take me home. Please." The light from the chandelier cast a muted radiance that scooped gentle hollows beneath her cheekbones and flattered her pale face. Althea held herself very still.

Japheth watched in grudging admiration as she dipped into a well deep within herself and came up changed. She didn't modify a flicker of her expression, didn't blink or blush or draw herself tall in the chair, but everything transformed about her, and Japheth saw himself vanish from her thoughts, a sheet drawn across him, a curtain.

"Get me a new girl," she said in a flat, firm voice, "then you can come back next week if you have to."

"This can't wait till next week."

"Yes," Althea said. "It can."

She looked boldly, almost seductively at her husband, and then, with equal boldness, cast her dark, glittering eyes on his partner. "Let Jim take care of the lease business," she said. "He can handle that. Jim Dee's capable of handling all kinds of things." She held the driller's gaze. "Aren't you, Jim?" The words were a direct, heated challenge.

Japheth saw the hunger rise over the partner's bronzed, fissured face. *Ah, of course,* he thought. *He's had her, hasn't he?* His irritation at having missed that obvious twist for so many hours was soon overswept by unspeakable delight. *Oh, the fool.*

"Tell him," Althea said. The clink of crystal and the soft murmur of conversation at the nearby tables died away. The attention of the other diners, the waiters, even the mustachioed owner greeting guests near the front, all turned toward the four strangers at the back table. Perhaps it was the abrupt hush of the table's urgent, low conversation, or maybe it was only Althea herself, who'd called forth the vehemence of desire and will that had since her youth made all eyes fly to her. When it flared in her, as now, she was an unsurpassably beautiful woman. The sensation of many eyes watching caused her cheeks to flush with titillation; she lifted her head so that her face might better catch the chandelier's golden light. "Jim?" she said. One eyebrow arched gorgeously.

"Yes. Tell him, Jim," Japheth said. The partner flicked a frown in his direction, and Japheth met it, took a very long, slow sip of water.

"No," Franklin said. "There's nothing for Jim to tell me." His voice was low, controlled. "You take the early train tomorrow and I'll be on directly. Tuesday afternoon maybe, if everything goes well." Franklin's gaze passed from his wife to his partner, back again. "You won't be alone long."

Japheth saw at first only that the man was torn; he couldn't tell what divided him, and he wanted sneeringly to believe it was cowardice that made Franklin turn away. For a moment he was perplexed by the husband's stillness, the slow, calm measure of his voice. It was only when Franklin settled his gaze solely and intently on his partner and went on with his veiled words about the lease that it came clear to Japheth what the stillness meant: in this single day's time Franklin Dedmeyer had passed from a man who kept his marriage and his business obsessions as separate as if they belonged to two distinct lives, to a man troubled by the two worlds' encroachments on one another, to this single moment of division when each weighed in the balance. Franklin's lust for oil had won out. He would rather turn away from the wife than the potential of the big strike.

But Althea drove heedlessly on. She had seen in the driller's unblinking hazel eyes that her desirability still held, and in the rush of that certainty, she interrupted her husband, leaning toward him and touching his arm, speaking in a throaty purr: "If you just have to do it all yourself, then let Jim Dee see me home. He can do that as well as anything, don't you think?"

The look Franklin turned on her was so cold, so entirely unaffected, that she pulled back, abashed. Of the world's many chaotic possibilities, the only one inconceivable to Althea was the loss of her husband's devotion. She could more nearly imagine the prairie around the hotel crumbling and sinking to ashes.

"I need Jim here," he said curtly, and then, as if realizing the presumptuousness of the *I* when they were supposed to be equal partners, he added, "We can't make a move without him. He's got to get the equipment lined up, got to start hauling out to the site."

"Oh, *we* can't, can't we?" Jim Dee's tone was ominously mild. "What time would you like to leave in the morning, ma'am?"

Franklin rolled right over it; he spoke low, forehead tilted. "If that new supply-and-tool here in Bristow won't give you a price on casing, go on over to Conroy's in Sapulpa." He knew very well what would claim the driller's attention. "Conroy played us fair on the Gobeddy hole. And when you find Ben Koop, have him see if he can't lay his hands on a Fort Worth spudder."

"I told you already, that formation's too cavey. We can't machine dig. We're going to have to build a rig."

"It can't be better than six hundred—"

"I said we're going to have to build a rig."

There was a beat of silence before Franklin nodded, letting the tension bleed away. "Of course. You're the driller."

"I am."

"Well. I'll get out to the old lady's cabin at dawn tomorrow—"

"I'm not riding in that low class commuter railcar by myself, Franklin! I absolutely am not!"

Franklin skimmed his wife briefly, and then his glance fell absently on Japheth, who returned it with steady gaze. "Your . . . brother can see you home." The word still hesitated on his tongue, tinged with disbelief. Blood rose instantly in Althea's face and her eyes widened; there was a small flutter of her fingers at her throat, but the gesture was lost on her husband, who turned back, very casually, to press the point about the spudder. "Of course a rig's a lot of time, a lot of money, Jim," he offered gingerly. "We know that's bound to be a shallow sand—"

The partner's frown quickly darkened.

Now! Japheth surged forward, elbows on the table. "I'll be glad to take Sister to Tulsa, if that's the first order of business. I mean, if that's what you want. But I was just thinking: if you're tied up all day on lease business, and if Mr. Logan here is in Sapulpa . . . or wherever . . ." Japheth smiled. "Why then, who's"—his voice dropped low, conspiratorial—"going to stay down on the Deep Fork, protect that seep from some other 'catter nosing around?"

"Hssht!" Jim Dee's voice grated to a whisper. "I've been scouting a week, nobody's seen or heard me. Nobody knows a thing but us right here at this table."

Japheth turned slightly and glanced over his shoulder at the attentive dining room, where dozens of pairs of eyes dropped their gaze quickly to numerous white tablecloths, and the seized-up murmur of conversation coughed a time or two, then purred into a steady low rumble once more. The partners looked at each other.

"I told you. . . ." Franklin's voice trailed away. Of course, it was a good idea to have somebody at the location around the clock until the lease was filed. The sooner the better, before word got out. Franklin shrugged, his thoughts already scrambling toward how he was going to snatch up leases on the land all around the old lady's allotment—not in the name of Delo Petroleum Corporation, but for himself. It was the very bit of secrecy Japheth had detected, though he'd missed its meaning, and he didn't see it now. His attention was on Jim Dee.

"What do you say, Mr. Logan?" Japheth arched one brow in precise, insinuating imitation of his sister. "Unless you'd rather do it yourself?" Something passed between the two, the dark brother and the scowling, sunburned partner, a grudging, instant complicity, made up of equal parts knowledge and loathing.

"Might be a good idea," Jim Dee said finally. "At that."

"Yes, all right," Franklin said. "Better get down there first thing. I'll take you on my way out. We'll haul in some camp supplies tomor—"

"Franklin! Take me home!"

"If you're going to make a fuss, Thea, just stay here at the hotel. We ought to be clear enough I can take you back on the train Monday evening."

"Why, sure, Sister," Japheth said. "You can stay here in Bristow, do a little visiting," and he threw the word away; he might as well have said *a little knitting* or *shopping*. Neither of the men caught the hidden meaning, just as they'd failed to hear the brother in the cramped back seat, whispering as they bumped over the brick streets of the town, *And there's Dorcas's house, that little shack on the corner. That's her oldest boy hanging on the gate. She moved up in Sixteen, right after Jody. You won't see Estaleen, she lives over on Choctaw with Katie. She don't hardly ever come out now since that damn flu took her so bad, but she's dying to see you. She told me so herself.*

Suddenly Althea yearned to escape to the room upstairs, with its beautiful brass fixtures on the sink opposite the bed, its lace canopy and fine rug. She would stay there, she thought, in their room at the Laurel Hotel; she'd simply wait for Franklin each evening. But, no, the thought of sitting in the small room, away from sun and light and air, was impossible to her, she couldn't do it, and in any case, Japheth would be here, always, lurking around corners, skulking along the carpet runners in the hall.

There was only one force on earth that could have convinced Althea to willingly be alone, to travel alone, stay in her large and empty house on South Carson alone, and it was sitting across the linen cloth from her, smirking, sweeping his eyes once around the room to say, See, Sister? You thought it was all in the past, but, no, it's here in the town of Bristow. If you walk down a sidewalk tomorrow, if you go into one of these nice new brick stores, you can't help but find it. Or it will find you. She met her brother's eyes for only an instant before she turned away, knowing that in the morning she would take the train to Tulsa, alone.

Althea watched her husband and his partner as they argued; she appeared to be listening, but her eyes were black and vacant. She didn't speak again. After a long time she brought herself to glance across the table. Her brother still sat back, draped languidly in the chair, but his eyes followed the men avidly, ravenously, as a starving cur watches a flock of crows feasting, waiting for its opportunity to rush in among them and snatch away the kill.

The truck snaked through the low hills on wagon trails gone wash-boardy from rain, over dozens of swollen creekbeds on rumbling board bridges, and sometimes straight across the water at rocky fords. Several times Delroy stopped to add water to the radiator or to pour gaso-line into the side tank from the orange can bouncing in the truckbed; other times he had to climb down from the cab and pull the long timbers off the pile of tarps in the back and use them to pry the tires free from mud. At each of those pauses Graceful would stand down to stretch her legs, and William would scramble out behind her and dance around in the open land, looking up, or run off chasing after a jackrabbit, until Del-roy called them to come, and they'd slam the truck doors and drive on, along the rutted and muddy roads, along dustbitten cowtracks, past blackened oilfields steepled with derricks, and green-ripened cornfields, golden wheatfields, red arroyos cut deep in the earth.

At dusk Delroy did not stop; when daylight came again, they were still driving. They skirted the boom towns and farm towns—the white towns—though Delroy bought gasoline at a station near Shamrock, re-filled the orange can. In the afternoon they stopped at a little colored store outside Kendrick and bought sardines and cheese and crackers. They ate their dinner, washed down with tepid water from a jar, as they continued west toward the glaring sun, the sky vast with light, brilliant with fuchsia and orange-vermilion at sunset, fading to mauve, to plum, to purple, and at last blueblack from horizon to horizon, and jeweled with stars.

It was after midnight when they stopped in the yard of a house whose outline was only a darker blackness against the black sky. Wan yellow light shone somewhere in the back. Graceful woke her little brother and walked him, still half asleep, toward the porch. She knew where they were—Uncle Delroy had spoken softly over the sleeping boy's head to tell her—though not yet why. Only that her mama had said come. Bring the boy and some blankets in the truck, and come. Go by the whitelady's house and fetch Graceful, drive as long and hard as it takes, all night if need be, and come, here, to this rickety frame house on the rolling prairie six miles north of Arcadia.

The door opened, and Mama's powerful shape stood outlined in the faint light. Graceful rushed forward, so that William stumbled and nearly fell to the porch floor, and Mama said, "Hush! Hush, now." She grabbed them, pulled them into the house. And then Mama was rasping in the dark at the end of the porch, a harsh sound completely unlike her normal voice, and the edge in it cracked ice in Graceful's bones. William swayed in a groggy stupor beside her. Graceful couldn't make out Mama's words, but in a moment she heard Uncle Delroy's truck start up, too loud in the yard silence, and drive around toward the back, and in another minute her mother's hands came hard around her shoulders, pulling her so tight Graceful's arm was crushed against her brother's bony skull. Mama began to whisper again, not harsh now but murmured, and it took a minute for Graceful to understand that her mother was praying. At last Mama's fierce grip loosened, and she heaved in a long breath. Graceful heard the ragged sob in it, and the fear she'd held away from herself for so many hours flooded over her. But Mama's voice was strong, military, when she said, "Y'all keep quiet, everybody sleeping. Come on back here to the back."

Through the dark room, their footsteps creaking on the raw flooring, the walls sour, and the room filled, Graceful could hear now, with the soft mouthbreathing sounds of people sleeping. She held her brother's hand, felt her way toward the crack of light at the back. Mama's fingers were tight on her shoulder. The sour smell grew stronger as they went into the back room, a kitchen, where a kerosene lantern, trimmed so low as to hardly keep burning, sat on the oilcloth-covered table. The room was hot and close, and the odor was overpowering, familiar, and yet strange, as if it had once been something good that had transformed itself, and degraded as it changed. It made Graceful sick to her stomach. She looked to the stovetop, saw a big skillet and her mama's covered stockpot cooking there, but the sour odor didn't come from that direction. It seemed to seep from the walls of the ratty kitchen, and the floor.

"Sit," Mama said, and then before they'd had time to obey she looked hard at the boy, said, "William, when's the last time you washed them hands? Get up here to the sink. You too, girl. I just brought that water in fresh." And she turned immediately to the cookstove, opened the firebox as if she meant to put in more wood, though the iron stove radiated heat, and the room was sweltering. Graceful thought she'd be sick all over the cracked linoleum if she didn't get some air. She stepped to the door and would have pulled it open if her mother's voice hadn't snapped hard behind her, "No!"

"Mama, it stinks in here!"

"I don't care. You'll get used to it. Get over here and help your brother, we got to eat now. We got to get Delroy some supper and then he got to rest." Cleotha wrung a wet rag into the dishwater, began to slap at the rough board countertop, wiping it down. She glanced over her shoulder, said in a voice that matched the look on her face, "I don't want to have to say it again."

Graceful moved as in a dream to the tin basin at the end of the counter; she picked up a yellowed piece of lye soap, motioned the sleepy William to come over, took her brother's limp hands in hers, and dunked them in the pan. The whole time she watched her mother. The expression, the voice: Graceful had seen it before. Seven years ago. When she was twelve. She'd come home from school one afternoon to find her mother transformed, as now, from a strict, good-humored woman to a harsh disciplinarian who barked orders and had not a smile or a bit of softness about her, and that time, like this, the conversion was sudden and complete, and it marked the end of something, a change in their lives that was irrevocable, permanent, and she'd known on that day by the sign of her mother's behavior, long hours before she was told, that her father was dead.

A welling began to rise in Graceful's throat and chest, and she scrubbed her little brother's hands with the lye soap till he said, "That's good, that's good enough!" The boy was wide awake now, and afraid. She tried to make her voice light when she said, "Rinse off, then. And hurry up so Mama can fix you a plate." She began to rub the harsh soap furiously between her palms.

A tapping came at the back door, and her heart jumped, and she heard her mother release a little jumpy sound—*Oh!*—and Willie shoved himself up against her, silent. *What are we acting so scared for? What is it we afraid of?* And yet she knew, because there was only one thing to cause such silent, quaking fear. She wanted to snuff the lantern, prayed for her trembling baby brother to stay hushed. The tapping came again, a light tick behind the cardboard covering the door window. Her mother started across the kitchen, and Graceful whispered loudly, "Mama! No!"

In the slight moment before her mother reached the door, Graceful passed from fear to resentment that Mama had snapped at her when she'd started to open the door and now was going on and performing that very act herself. Cleotha lifted a corner of the cardboard to peer out, then quickly slid back the iron bolt, turned the wood block, fiddled with the skeleton key in the slot below the knob. Graceful thought, *I never saw any blackfolks' house locked up such a way in my life.*

Her mother cracked the door a bit before pulling it open wide enough to admit Delroy, who slipped in lean and quick. Mama slapped the bolt back in place. "They all right?"

"Hungry." Delroy sat heavily in a cane chair at the table.

"I'll send something out in a minute. Got to get you fed first, you got to have some rest."

"I'm not tired," he said; indeed, his hands were restless at the table, fiddling with the saltcellar and the butter crock, his long ashy fingers touching the tin base of the lantern, now and again reaching out to flick at a speck on the dingy oilcloth. But his shoulders slumped, and his head dipped toward the table as his sister thumped and clanged softly over by the stove.

"You tired all right." Cleotha set a bowl of turnip greens in front of him. "Eat now."

Delroy fished up a chunk of fatback with two fingers (and Graceful thought, *How come she don't tell him to wash his hands?*), wolfed it in one bite, and had nearly finished the bowl before Cleotha put the cornbread and the hoppin'john on the table. "Y'all come eat," she said, and William came and sat obediently, bent his head over the bowl she put in front of him. But Graceful knew she'd vomit if she had to eat anything in that sour, overheated atmosphere, though Mama's hoppin'john was her favorite food on earth. *What she got to lift the lid on that pot of greens for, she going to make us all puke.* Her indignation at being treated as her mother's child swelled, joined with a deep long-ago resentment, and she thought, *This is no way to act. Why she got to act so mean every time somebody die?* Her mind cried out: *T.J.!* The dark welling began, and she saw her brother in the hands of a white mob, white faces hooting with laughter as that one had laughed while he pushed her face into the pillow so she couldn't scream, couldn't breathe. . . . She felt herself begin to descend, the room going dark and turning, and the sour smell smothering her as she went down, but her mother's arms came around her and lifted her.

"Delroy! Clear off that chair!"

Her mother's shout came from a great distance, but the sound was sweet to her, and the strength of her mother's arms around her was firm. The hard ridge of wood came against her legs, and she sank into the spongy cane bottom as the sickness swirled over her, made a great roaring in her ears, and the wretched nausea swelled; she opened her mouth, helpless against it, and vomited fish and putrid cheese all over the table. She heard Willie yelp, heard her sister Jewell cry out, "Mama! Help her!" and she thought, *How did Jewell get here, too?* before she began to sink toward the tabletop, because she needed to lie down, she needed to put her head down. Mama's hands gripped her, held her face, and brushed it with a dry cloth; she could hear the voices going on, many voices talking, but she leaned the weight of her face against her mother, let her heavy, leaden head rest in her mother's hands.

"Ooh, Mama, she making it stink worse!" LaVona's high, prissy voice came from the front-room doorway. She stood barefoot, on tiptoe, her hair springing in a thousand directions, her little slanty eyes big as coins. Beside her, Jewell's legs were long and thin beneath a white cotton gown. Graceful thought, *My Lord, they getting tall.* She tried to sit up, but her head was too heavy, and she leaned against Mama, felt her face wiped again with the dry cloth, and realized it was Mama's apron; then the shame came on her, more sickening than the body sickness. "Oh, Mama, I'm sorry." She pulled away. "I'm sorry, I'm so sorry, Mama." She wanted to stand up and go to the water basin, but her lap was soiled with vomit. She started to cry.

"Hush!" Mama's hands were tender, but her voice was the harsh, exacting voice that stood no argument, no sniveling, no weakness of any kind, and instantly Graceful quit. She pulled away, picked up her maid's skirt in both hands as she stood and walked shakily toward the dishpan on the counter. It was then she first saw the little faces behind her sisters, peeping out of the dark door to the front room.

She couldn't tell how many of them there were, maybe half a dozen, little smudgy faces that blended with the darkness. Their eyes showed round and scared in alternating heights from way-little to pretty-big, and then a bitty one in a dirty gown came toddling out and went to Jewell and put its hands up to be lifted. Graceful couldn't tell if it was a boychild or a girlchild; its unplaited hair was a puff of soft, radiant fuzz all over its head.

The child said, "Hold you! Hold you!" and tugged at Jewell's nightgown, and Jewell bent and picked the child up and lodged it on her skinny hip, and Graceful could see the knobs of breasts on her sister's narrow chest. She felt suddenly that there was a whole world she didn't know, that her family had gone on and had itself, its family life, which was the only life, without her. While she was working at the whitefolks', her sister Jewell had got big enough to have titties and LaVona was more sassy-mouthed than ever and getting tall and Willie was grown up enough to ride the trolley, and Mama had changed again, had gone hard-edged and gruff again, and a whole batch of little children appeared here from nowhere. They all knew what she did not know, and her grief at not knowing was as hard as her fears about T.J., as ferocious, even, as her secret rage and shame, though the grief didn't come in crushing waves, as that other, but held her as fog does, dense and thick. She cleaned herself with the sour dishrag while her mother wiped the table and barked orders. The girls tried to hustle the many strange children back to bed, but the little one on Jewell's hip started bawling, and another one, a boy of maybe four or five, skipped under LaVona's outstretched arm and came on into the kitchen, stood with his hands on his hips, and announced like a big man, "We hungry!"

Before Graceful had finished washing, the whole bunch was in the kitchen, and her mother was allowing what she'd never allowed in her own household, which was a mess of children eating from bowls and cups with their fingers, not at the table with a proper blessing and a clean napkin, but scattered all about the room like a bunch of slave children, eating standing up and squatting on the floor and just anyhow. There were seven of them, five boys and a girl, plus the little one on Jewell's hip. Graceful watched them gobble their food like wormy pups, and her wonder was equally at her mother as at the youngsters, for Mama dipped up the hoppin'john and handed it around and did not say to the children, wash your hands, sit up to the table now, use a napkin, wipe yo nasty mouth. The children's nightshirts were filthy with old dried food, they had blackeyed peas and rice smeared all over their little bug-eyed faces, and Graceful thought, *They're not ours, that's why. She don't care how they act.*

"Hurry up," Mama said, and it took a second for Graceful to realize her mother was talking to her. "Take this in yonder and put it on." Mama shoved something at her, and in a minute Graceful found herself in the dark front room, where she could make out an old springy double bed in one corner, three or four pallets spread around. She dropped her smelly uniform on the floor and put on her mother's good white going-to-church dress.

When she stepped back into the kitchen, her mother was setting a small wooden crate by the door.

"Mama!" LaVona's thin voice squeaked from the corner. "You're not gone let her th'ow up all over your church dress?" Cleotha ignored her, motioned Graceful to come over, pulled her close, and said, "What make you to get sick like that?"

"This whole place stinks, Mama."

Her mother looked hard at her a minute. "You over it?"

Graceful nodded. Cleotha continued to peer at her in silence, then, finally, she said in a low whisper, "I want you to take this to them yonder in the storm cellar. Listen good at the door once you get outside, you got to make sure there's nobody around. It's out to the side of the barn." Graceful looked down. In the crate were some tin cups, spoons, a cracked blue crockery bowl, her mother's steel stockpot with the lid on, a greasy slab of something wrapped in newspaper.

"What barn, Mama? Storm cellar?"

"Barn's right up behind the house, if you go out the door and walk straight you can't help but go to it. Then feel your way easy around to the side—" Cleotha suddenly turned to the room, said to her brother nodding at the table, "Delroy, go lay down on the bed and sleep. You got to get some rest."

"Mama, that's where me and Jewell sleep—!" LaVona started, but Cleotha looked at her and the girl piped down, went back to feeding a little one with a big spoon. Jewell was trying to edge over to where Graceful stood, but Cleotha gave her a hard look, too, and the girl stopped, bent to wipe the face of the little mannish boy. "Go in and rest," Cleotha said again. Delroy scraped his chair back from the table and went into the dark room.

"Somebody going to be sick all over somebody's church dress," LaVona muttered to the child she was feeding. "Somebody won't have nothing nice to wear to church."

"I wouldn't worry about that, missy. You not going to be there anyhow, you're going to be right in this house minding these children. Hurry up and finish with that mess and get these kids in the bed."

LaVona cut her eyes at her mother, said nothing more.

"Mama, what happen . . ." But Graceful let the words fade away. She shut her lips tight, lifted her head, stood silent while her mother whispered at her to sneak quiet, quiet across that yard, listen hard at the door, because if somebody was outside watching they might follow her and find them.

"Find who, Mama?"

"Hush!" And then, in a barely voiced whisper, "T.J. and them."

"Tee—? You mean T.J.—? Ow! Mama!"

Her mother's pinch was brutal. "When you going to get some sense?" The whisper was fierce with exasperation. She suddenly began pulling Graceful by the arm into the front room. In the dark Cleotha whispered at her eldest daughter, her fingers tight on Graceful's arm, her mouth close to the girl's ear. "If there ever been a time in your life you need to quit asking questions, this black morning right now is it. Hear me? I need you to pay some attention. Keep your mouth quiet and pay attention. T.J. and that trashy girl he got mixed up with and her mama are all out in the storm cellar, and now that's the only time I'm going to say it. If the whitefolks find them, they bound to be lynched same as that girl's brother last week." Her whisper went harsher, lower. "They're not the only ones in danger. If that mob come in here and find Delroy, they liable to take him. I don't know but what they'd take you or me. We got to act calm. We got to act like we don't know nothing but just we taking care of these children, we don't know where their mama's gone. Because Delroy got to sleep awhile, we got to let him get some rest. This is the most dangerous time, the most dangerous, and I need you to be your grown self and not some girl going to puke and pass out over smelling a little spilt sourmash. Not some girl going to open her loose lips and say what them in the next room don't need to know. Your sisters too young to keep their face right if whitefolks ask them a question. But you're not." She paused, let her words sink in a moment, and when she continued her voice was softer. "I got to depend on you, Graceful. You my grown girl I got to depend on. How come you didn't come home the minute Willie brung you that letter?"

"Mama, I didn't know—"

"Nevermind. Hush. Listen. You got to carry that food quiet. I wouldn't even send it, but they haven't eat since yesterday, probably won't get another chance till way up tomorrow evening. Now, listen. That cellar door face this way. Knock soft, three quick taps, then wait a little bit, then two more. All right? What'd I say?"

"Three quick taps, wait, then two more."

"And go quiet."

"Go quiet."

Her mother's mouth drew away, and Graceful felt the coarse palm on her forehead. "You're still warm."

"I'm all right, Mama."

"Go on, then. Mind everything I said. And Graceful . . . be careful."

When her mother let out her breath there was again the ragged, dry, unspent sob in it. Graceful, already moving toward the lit kitchen, heard it, and something turned over in her, like a stone plate turned upside down.

Mama's white dress flowed around her, too big and floating, lifting its hem in the nightbreeze. The young moon was hardly a fingernail paring, but the white dress on the crowblack land took the little light and shimmered it back to the night. The crate was heavy in her arms, thumped against her thigh. Twice Graceful paused to listen, but all she heard was the wind soughing, a million night crickets singing, the alien sound of her own breath. Her eyes adjusted to the darkness, and she gazed out across the shadowed land, imagining a white mob hidden in the folds, secreted in the moonshade below the clumps of cedars.

She saw the lump of hill to the side of the barn and made her way toward it, set the crate down. Three soft taps on the tin-and-wood door set into the mound, pause, two more. Silence. She bent over and hoisted the door with both hands, laid it open. The sour smell poured out through the opening, along with the thick odor of mildew, the dank sweet scent of dirt. Graceful waited almost politely, as if at a stranger's front door. "T.J.?" she whispered. "It's me." The adjustment her eyes had made to the moonlight was no good now: the rectangle in the mound of earth was ink black, impenetrable. "T.J.? It's Graceful. I got some food here for y'all but I ain't comin—"

"Where at?" Her brother's voice came from below, and she could have wept for gladness, though the rasp in T.J.'s throat was uglier even than Mama's.

"Here," and she lifted the crate down toward the opening. "Easy, it's heavy." She felt the weight relieved from her.

"In or out, but shut that door!"

She did not want to descend to that hole in the earth, but neither did she want to go back to the reeking kitchen and her mother's hard face and closed mouth. She knew Mama was not going to tell her what she wanted to know. She felt her way onto the top step, stood breathing deeply of the night air.

"Shut the door!"

Graceful reached over for the cumbersome door, pulled it up from the mounded earth in an arc, lowering it over her head as she went down into a dark beyond any darkness. She heard scrabbling sounds below, like rats, a few soft murmured words, the rushed, gulping sounds of eating. Graceful stood as near the top of the ladder as her height would allow, clinging to a dank wooden slat.

"You coming down or you just going to hang there?"

How could he see her in such pitch? And then she realized T.J. was not seeing her but sensing her, as a blind man does.

"Ain't y'all got any light down there?"

"Not at night. Leaks around the door. It's nasty down here, Graceful, why don't you go on back to the house?" She heard more hushed whispering.

"I'm coming down." Slowly she felt her way down the ladder, stood at the foot of it. The dark seemed not an absence but a presence, solid, odoriferous. The rank smell must be sourmash, like Mama said. Her brother's voice came from the back, very low, but distinct. "Delroy get some rest?"

"He's sleeping right now."

T.J. didn't speak again, but she could sense his satisfaction with the answer. Suddenly it clicked into place that Delroy was to carry her brother away from here in the truck; that was the purpose of the tarps in the back, why everybody was so worried about the state of Uncle Delroy's rest. Before she thought, she said, "Where's he going to take you?"

"You don't need to know that. Mama don't need to know."

"Why, T.J.? How come the whitefolks looking for you?"

"Hush!" The small, foul space was quiet a long time. She heard the soft scrabbling sounds come toward her across the dirt floor. T.J. whispered close beside her, "It's better you don't know nothing."

She was silent. After a long while, she said, "You're my brother, T.J."

T.J. let out a slow breath of air, and when he spoke his voice was so low she had to strain to hear him. "On account of what I seen."

"What was it?"

"You don't need to know that either. It's for your own good, Graceful. What you don't know, can't nobody make you tell."

"They don't care what a nigger see. It's not something you seen. Why they named you, T.J.? What they name you for?"

"I told you to hush."

"Everybody's been telling me to hush. Everybody treating me like I'm four years old, like I ain't got good sense."

"Everybody who?"

"Mama. You and Mama. You're my brother, T.J.! Tell me what it is."

"I didn't do nothing. I tried to save my friend's life. Nothing." He was silent awhile, and then he sighed slightly, as if he were tired of the whole subject. "I didn't set out to kill no whiteman. It just happen."

When Graceful set the crate on the worn linoleum, her mother took one look at her and instantly turned away. *What?* Graceful thought. *What'd I do now?* But she knew. She had asked questions, and T.J. had told, and now the truth was burned on her, right into her skin, her face, her eyes sharp with fear. Well, maybe she couldn't hide it from Mama, but she could hide it from whitefolks. She knew that she could. Jewell was sitting at the table, bleary-eyed, her chin in one hand. Mama snapped, "All right, Graceful's here now. You happy? Go on in yonder and get yourself some sleep, we got a big day tomorrow."

"Mama?" Jewell said sleepily. "I'll stay with the children. You can let LaVona go to church."

"Take you and LaVona both to mind that many wild children."

"Me and Graceful can do it." Jewell smiled hopefully at her sister.

"We'll see. You go on and get in the bed."

Jewell came and hugged Graceful, hard and quick. *She's the sweetest one,* Graceful thought. *She the best of any of us.* Little Jewell, the peacemaker, who was no longer little but tall and thin, like T.J. As Graceful hugged her sister's long boniness, she thought, *I know one thing, I'm not going back to work for whitefolks. I'm not leaving them no more.* The tail of Jewell's nightgown had hardly disappeared through the doorway when Mama came at her, whispering hard, "What'd I tell you? What did I say? Answer me!" Her mother's face was such a fury that Graceful was afraid to speak. "What you got to go and ask him questions for?" Mama turned, sank into a chair at the table. Graceful watched in terror as her mother sagged, trembling, with her face in her hands.

But when Cleotha looked up, long minutes later, her face was clear of emotion, masklike, stony. She stood, moved purposefully toward the cookstove. "Go wake up Delroy. Quiet, now. I don't want them children getting up again." She turned, held her daughter's eyes a moment, looked away finally, across the kitchen, to some blank and empty space on the wall. "I guess you're going to have to go with them." Cleotha snatched the tin percolator off the stovetop and in the same motion went to the bucket, began to dipper water into the pot.

The sky had begun to lighten in the east by the time Delroy turned his Nash truck out of the yard. Graceful looked back once, but the sight of the black shack in the gray dawn and her mother alone on the bowed porch was too hard, and she quickly turned front, stared through the windscreen. Her uncle seemed to be still half dopey with sleep, though she'd watched him drink down three cups of scalding coffee, standing at the stove blinking and yawning, before he'd gone out to prepare the truck.

Neither of them talked as they drove north across the bucking land. To the right the sky began to glow rose-colored, brightening to coral at the line of the earth. Straight up above arched a teal, gleaming vault, but in the west the heavens stayed indigo, lit here and there with a few winking stars. The toenail moon hung suspended, spurs up, very high in the turquoise sky, and Graceful saw now the shadow above it, the black, dense orb snugged against the gleaming crescent. *Old moon sleeping in the new moon's arms,* she said to herself, repeating Grandma Whiteside's old saying, and suddenly she was overwhelmed with a wash of grief that made her shudder, made her want to weep and wail from some lost place, made her long to cry out. The feeling was new to her and at the same time familiar. She shut her mind against the future. Shut her mind to everything but what was in front of her eyes, beneath her body, what her senses received.

The truck shook and shivered and rumbled over the humped hills.

Again and again they hit bumps hard enough to jar her teeth, make her thrust out her arm and brace herself against the dash. She thought, *My Lord, that must be some terrible ride in the back.* She wanted to turn and look down into the truckbed, see if they were still covered. She wanted to ask Delroy to slow down some, it was too rough for them back yonder, and she wanted to urge him to hurry up, hurry, and she listened to the chugging of the motor, watched the world turning light, said nothing at all.

As the day opened they began to see wagons coming toward them filled to the tailgates with fine-dressed Negroes on their way to Sunday morning worship, and Graceful would gaze at them with that same new-old feeling, while Delroy lifted one hand from the steering wheel in greeting. But when whitefolks passed in their motorcars or wagons, she'd hold herself as still as she could in the bumping truck, hardly breathing, and she would turn her face away. Every white farmer in overalls lumbering along with his family in a spring-wagon, every elegant whitelady with a filmy tied-on hat beside a smirking whiteman speeding by in a roadster filled Graceful with dread and loathing, with the cold beginnings of hatred, and a fierce, driven protectiveness for T.J. and the other two hidden under the mildewed tarps in the back.

It was full morning by the time they reached a town. Delroy still had not spoken, and Graceful asked him nothing, and it was only because she saw the building on the horizon and the sign before it etched with scrolled letters that read LANGSTON UNIVERSITY that she understood where they were. She thought, *Oh, sure, now, this is a good idea—Langston! Six hundred blackfolks going to school in this town. T.J. and them'll disappear here like nothing.* But Delroy drove straight past, and on through the all-black town, or it was supposed to be a black town, but the streets were empty. The fear stirred in Graceful. She stared hard at the frame houses shuttered against the heat, the closed stores on Main Street, the cinderblock church, which was silent on Sunday morning, the big front door shut, and she prayed that any minute Delroy would stop at a good place, a safe place, but Uncle Delroy did not stop. Her tongue tried a dozen times to ask where they were going, where were all the people, but her mother's angry face kept coming to her, saying, You got to keep your mouth quiet and not ask questions, girl. And then her mind's eye saw the silhouette of a colored boy hanging from a tree.

They drove east now, into the brilliant sun, and the only words that passed in the truck cab were when Delroy asked for the water jar or to be handed a piece of cornbread, and once Graceful asked in embarrassment could he stop a minute by that clump of cottonwoods yonder. The tense unbroken silence was not the only way the trip was different from the drive out to Arcadia, as the absence of Willie's smiling face wasn't all, or the fact they were traveling in a different part of the state. For Graceful the journey was a lifetime's worth of different. All that she'd held away from herself before was now fully present. What was known could not be unknown; what had happened could not be pushed away.

Every time they neared a white town, the nausea and fear would come hard on her, and her hands would begin to quiver so that she'd have to jam them against the seat to keep Delroy from seeing. She'd bite her lip, stare at her lap in order to not look at their stores, their houses, their white faces coming from church; she wouldn't lift her head until they were driving in the open land again, so different from what they'd driven through on the way to Arcadia. Every time the truck shuddered to the top of a rise, she could see the red dirt road descending, and rising again in the distance, miles of faded prairie sloping down, and then up, and then down again, in all directions, like ridges in a giant washboard big enough for God. But always they continued east, and at the top of one rise, Graceful suddenly thought with relief, *Why, we're going home to Tulsa! Yes. We just going by a different road, that's all. Mama'll be coming soon. Quick as she get those kids took care of, she'll come.* From that moment, satisfied with the answer she'd made up in her own mind, Graceful felt her fear and sickness begin to ease, and she allowed her unasked questions to float through the open truck window and out across the undulating prairie with the hot wind.

Late in the afternoon, Delroy turned off the dirt track, drove down into a caney creekbottom way back off the road. He set the brake, killed the motor, groaned a little as he climbed down and moved off toward the rear of the truck. Graceful sat gazing discreetly ahead until she heard the thundery sound of the big tarp being pulled off the back; she turned to watch T.J. jump down and stretch, take a sip from the water jar Delroy held out to him. It was the first time Graceful had seen the two women. She stared first at the mother, who grunted when T.J. helped her climb down. The woman was much older than Graceful had expected, considering how young the children in the house were: saggy-bosomed and heavy, her skin ashy as she moved stiff-limbed off into the brush. And then Graceful turned her eyes to T.J.'s girlfriend, and her breath caught. *Lord God, I bet she's not a year older than Jewell.*

The girl stood beside the truck in a sleeveless cotton shift almost the same color as the dirt beneath her bare feet, a sort of soft, washed-out red. Her skin was coppery, her unprocessed hair the dull color of an old penny, and Graceful could see that she was too thin, her arms like a child's arms, her knobby neckbone protruding from the scoop of neckline like a chicken neck, though she had big buttocks that stuck out firm and high beneath the faded cotton. She kept her face turned every minute toward T.J., even when he disappeared into the bushes, and when he came back, his eyes darting about restlessly, his flared nostrils sensing the air, she touched him on the arm as he passed. But T.J. ignored her, as if her touch were no more than the brush of a mothwing. The girl turned once, feeling Graceful's eyes on her, smiled up quickly, and as quickly turned away. She was a little frog-eyed, Graceful thought, but pretty. When her mother came back from the canebrake, the girl darted off the way the woman had come, and Graceful thought, *What is T.J. doing messing with a young switchtail like that?*

At once she was ashamed. The girl's brother had been lynched. That woman's son. Graceful had been hearing about lynchings all her life; she'd never known a family it had happened to. She watched in a kind of humble fascination as the mother leaned against the tailgate, her face deadened, her natty hair matted and sticking up at the back of her head. Looking at the woman's ruined face, Graceful felt the cold nausea welling up again, and the hatred. Again her mind saw the boy hanging, hands tied behind his back, his body slowly turning, but it was T.J.'s face she saw on the lynched body, and despite herself she had to look over to make sure that he was really standing there, alive, on the dirt ground. Yes, it was T.J., her living, breathing brother T.J., bending secretively toward Delroy, speaking low and urgent as their uncle hoisted the orange can.

Graceful could tell by how high Delroy held it that the can was almost empty. *We'll have to stop and buy some.* Her belly clenched at the thought of driving into a white filling station. *Maybe we got enough to get to Tulsa.* Her brother and her uncle spoke without expression, first one, a beat of silence, then the other. There'd always been that closeness between them, like Delroy was T.J.'s brother instead of Mama's, though he was fifteen years older than T.J. and had taken care of him since T.J. was a little child. Delroy nodded at something T.J. said—a quick, slight dip of his forehead—and they met eyes an instant, then turned away; in that passing was too much knowledge and a flat, closed understanding, and Graceful craved to know what they were saying. Though she knew they'd hush as soon as she got out of the truck, she shoved the door open, jumped down to the ground.

Uncle Delroy was screwing the cap on the big can as he walked toward the rear of the truck. The moment and its knowledge, whatever it was, had already passed. T.J. looked up impatiently. "Better hurry." He turned to help the mother climb up. Graceful watched as the woman pulled herself onto the tailgate, though there was such bled-out despair in the woman's face that she wanted to turn away, as she'd turned her eyes from her own mother while she read the letters from T.J. This mother was as unlike Mama as it was possible to be, but Graceful felt, watching her, that they shared grief from the same source. The only difference was, in Mama grief turned brittle hard; it made this woman soft as an old shoe. The girl appeared from the undergrowth then, sidled up behind T.J., reached a fluttery hand out to touch him.

"Get in the truck," T.J. told her.

She kept her round eyes on him, watching him in mute, hopeless expectation, though what she expected Graceful couldn't tell.

"Y'all want to eat something?" Graceful said, as if that had been her intention for getting out of the truck, but T.J. spoke before the others could answer. "We'll eat when we get there." He hopped up on the tailgate, reached a hand down. The girl, obedient and shy-acting, took it and climbed into the bed. She hesitated, said softly, "Can't we leave it off now? I can't breathe, T.J., feel like I'm going to choke to death." Her voice was as fluttery and mothlike as her fingers. T.J. didn't answer, but moved front and settled himself on the pile of rags and blankets against the cab as if he'd been traveling this way, hiding this way, his whole life long. The mother, with her despairing face, lay down beside him, and then the girl came and curled up on the other side, and T.J. glanced around, reached above the girl's head and picked up a yard-long piece of blackjack from a hidden fold of blanket, grasped it by one end like a club. He nodded at Delroy and lay back flat, the oak limb cradled across his chest. Graceful watched the girl's face, the still terror on it as the tarp came up and buried her, how she put a hand up over her head to make air space.

Moving on leaden feet toward the cab, Graceful tried to push her own terror down, hold it tight in her gullet, since she could not shove it away. She stood with her hand on the handle, taking big gulping breaths, before she climbed in. Delroy looked hard at her when she banged the door shut. "You all right?" he said.

"Fine."

He shoved the big gearshift into reverse and began to back up.

By the time they drove into the familiar eastern scrub-oak hills, it was almost dark. She worried that they'd run out of fuel, because Delroy didn't stop again. What if they ran out of gas by a sundown town? There were so many towns with green laws, you'd never know if you were in one. Most were marked with signs at the edge: *No Negroes Allowed Within These City Limits Between The Hours of Sunset and Sunrise*—or sometimes just plain NO NIGGERS AFTER DARK—and she knew that Uncle Delroy knew the worst ones, Henryetta and Norman, the towns every colored person had heard of; she knew he'd never drive within miles of those towns at twilight. But there were so many small towns, Delroy might not even know he was by one, and anyhow every Oklahoma town was dangerous after dark, mixed or white, if it was colored people driving. The only safe towns were the black towns. Graceful thought sleepily, *Maybe he fixing to stop at Redbird or someplace, get some more gas.*

The sky was full-dark when they turned north again, and still Delroy drove on. Graceful slept before she knew she'd done so, and it was only by her head bumping against the side glass, knocking her awake, that she realized she'd slept. She worried now that Delroy would fall asleep driving, crash them into a ditch, but her exhaustion was so complete that before she knew it she'd dropped off again. She didn't dream, or if she did, she didn't know it, for the sleep was a velvety black warmth of nothing wrapped around her, and then she'd be thumped awake again, and before she could come fully to consciousness, the fear would be there.

The last time she was knocked awake, she thought for sure she must be dreaming. She blinked at the thousand winking lights rising up out of the darkness, and she thought that all the stars had been shaken down from heaven and landed in stacks on the plains. And then the stink came to her, and the sound, and the great mechanical sense of it, and she saw small figures of men moving about in the lights, but most of all it was the fetid smell that was so familiar, and she knew what she was looking at was not a dream but the lights on a tremendous bank of oil refineries. *Maybe we're back in Tulsa,* she thought, trying to wake up, trying to get some sensible thoughts in her head. *That must be the refineries by the river.* But Delroy kept driving toward them, and Graceful didn't see the dotted skyline of Tulsa on the far side, didn't see the Arkansas River or any familiar mark, but just the great stacks of belching, smoking, stinking vats and chimneys amidst the steel girders, and men moving about, working in the brilliant white light spreading out on the dark prairie, miles from any city, miles from any reasonable place on earth.

Delroy turned off the road, and in another moment the truck's head-lamps revealed the tangled growth of another creekbottom, though this one was not caney and willowy, as the last had been, but clotted with scrub oak and sumac, matted with thick vines snaking through the under-growth, looping down from tree limbs, crawling over limestone boulders made distinct and strange in the refineries' glow. When Delroy cut the motor, he sat so long with his head on his arms draped over the steering wheel that Graceful began to get scared; it reminded her too much of Mama at the table, and after a while, her tremored voice rising with the sounds of the nightcreatures scrabbling and chirring all around the truck, she said softly, "Uncle Delroy? We going to sleep here?"

Delroy snapped his head up so fast Graceful jumped back. "No." He looked around, took a long, deep breath. "No, honey." He blew the air out, hard. "We're not there yet. Listen, you're going to have to stay here with them. I'll be back quick as I can get here." His voice was hollow, dreamlike. He lifted his hand twice before he could get it connected with the door handle, and then he pushed the squeaking door open in slow motion; his movements were thick, lugubrious, like he was dreamwalking, moving underwater. He disappeared slowly into the darkness at the back of the truck. She could hear him talking to T.J., heard the gas can scrape on the metal truckbed, although she didn't hear the tarp being pulled off. She sat very still, listening, her heart beating hard, but Delroy left so qui-etly she never knew when he walked off.

The only sound was her own blood and the ceaseless chorus of crick-ets. The air was ruddy with reflected light from the refineries, hidden be-yond the treetops, though the stink and the low hum told her they were not far away. The moon hadn't risen, or she couldn't see it yet, but the truck was so wrapped around with undergrowth and the pinkish glow was so strange that she couldn't tell if it was getting close to morning. *Maybe they getting some sleep now,* she thought. *At least we're not bumping around all over creation.* It didn't come clear to her in words that the one she hoped was sleeping was the whispery too-skinny girl who felt herself buried alive beneath the tarp. Graceful stretched out across the seat to try and sleep, but each time she'd start to drift she would see white faces at the window, white hands reaching to snatch the truck door open, and she'd jerk full awake, her heart pounding. She got up, rolled the windows up tighter, lay back down, sweating. She felt naked. She wished she had a big chunk of blackjack, like T.J., something to protect herself besides her own quaking, shivering silence.

And then, later—how much later she didn't know, though it seemed hours—she thought she heard footfalls, somewhere out in the woods. She held her breath, tried to listen through the din of insects, and then, yes, she was sure of it: someone was coming through the undergrowth, snapping twigs. There was a low whispering sound, though she couldn't make out if it was leaves rustling or murmured voices. She slid off the seat into the dirty floorboard, hating the white dress of her mother because it was so visible, glowing like moonflowers in the dark. Her frenzied hands scrabbled around the truck floor, but there was only the empty water jar to protect her, the sorghum tin of uneaten biscuits and fatback. When the dark head loomed over the window she gripped the glass jar tight in both hands. She couldn't make out the features but she knew it was a black man. It wasn't Delroy. The man's palms came up to cup his face, and he peered into the truck, trying to make out what he was seeing. There was another voice behind him, and she heard the tarp being pulled off the back. The one at the window said something, deep and soft-inflected, muffled through the closed glass, and Graceful's breath released, and she thought she'd weep or shout or something, she didn't know what she might do. Never could she have dreamed she'd be so glad to hear the soft-slurred voice of Hedgemon Jackson saying her name outside in the dark.

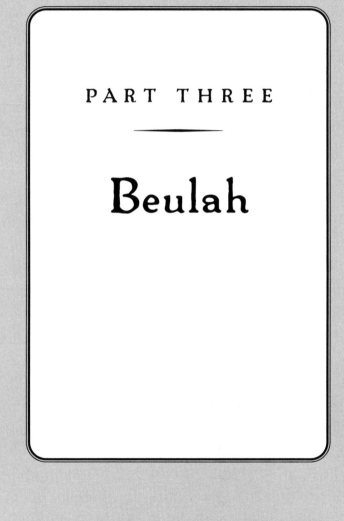

PART THREE

Beulah

Arcadia
Sunday
September 5, 1920

That church was too small for such a gathering, just a little slapped-together clapboard country church on a rise of prairie north of town. But on that Sunday morning it was swelled to full and beyond full, people standing in rows at the windows, swatting flies, looking in. There was one white face. A tiny songbird-looking whitewoman with a smile pasted on her face like it had been grown there. She must have arrived early, because she was sitting at the end of a row, halfway to the front. Folks had to step over her to get to the seats in the middle, but she never moved over, never quit smiling. There was little to smile at. You could taste the grief in that room like bad air. What you could taste even more bitter than that was the anger. Maybe she thought smiling would help something.

They'd buried the boy on Tuesday, the day after they cut him down—buried him alongside his father—so it wasn't the funeral that had folks lined up seven deep at the windows and front door. The pastor called it a memorial service, but I believe folks from that community and those of us from around Luther knew pretty well Reverend Shew didn't intend to offer a memorial to that family of moonshiners; he had something else in mind. People rode the train from Taft and Rentiesville, drove down from Langston, came from Boley and Bookertee and Redbird, all the old colored towns. Some of them must have started out the evening before to get there by morning. What they thought that service was going to be I can't tell you.

I heard a few of them milling around in the yard early, before Sunday School, murmuring against the Reverend, why had he called it on a Sunday morning at regular divine worship time, because folks had to miss their own service. But I thought it was shrewd of the Reverend: what other time does it look innocuous for so many colored people to be traveling together except Sunday morning going to church? They came in flatbed wagons and walking and driving new Chandlers and Model T Fords, started before daylight, and they kept coming on late into the morning. Folks quit murmuring afterwhile, because every time there came a new wagon, muleheels kicking up dust, we could feel it, every person in that church and outside it could: we knew something powerful was taking place.

I will tell you something. That wasn't the last time colored folks from all over Oklahoma came together in the wake of such trouble, but to my mind, as far as I know, that was the first. And I will tell you something else: Reverend Shew was one of the cleverest men I've ever witnessed. He was a small-church country preacher, but he had an extremely subtle mind. I admired him sufficiently that, had it not been for the fact that the drive from Luther was twelve miles, which, in those days, took several hours in bad weather on the kinds of roads we had to drive, and had I not belonged to our AME church from a child, I would have joined his little Mount Zion Baptist congregation. He had my respect to that degree.

He began the service in a completely ordinary manner, sitting very simply in his chair behind the pulpit with his fingertips together, his head bowed. If a person didn't happen to see the dignitaries in dark suits seated on the front pews, he could almost imagine this was a regular Baptist Sunday-morning worship service, or the last service of a revival, maybe, to account for all the people standing along the walls and the back and outside. The choir came from the rear of the sanctuary in customary processional, moving up the aisles in their white robes, clapping and singing "Marching Up to Zion." They were small— no more than a half dozen women on each side, and three men—but as they climbed the podium the congregation joined voice, and there began some clapping, a little shouting, but the Reverend was not ready to rouse us yet, and he stood and came forward, and everybody drew quiet while he offered a prayer to the Holy Spirit to pour out His mighty presence on our service here this morning, and then he went back very simply, sat down again, and bowed his head.

Here, now, I'll offer evidence of the subtlety of that pastor's mind, for I've no doubt that he selected the hymns just as he selected the passage of Scripture for his text and the hour of gathering and the very list of men seated in the front pews. A woman in the choir stood and sang alone, without accompaniment. She had on a worn housedress, which was strange there among us, white gloves, a little white lace cap on her head. She started out slow, singing the shaped notes, and in such glorious voice that the bosom of the entire congregation swelled: "I Been 'Buked, Lord, I Been Scorned." She moved from that old spiritual right into "Beulah Land" like it was an extension of the same song. When she came to the chorus the choir joined in, and in another beat the whole of that congregation, from youngest to eldest, was singing, "Ain't going to stop till I get there, I got a home in Beulah Land," and there was much shouting and clapping, because it is, you know, our story. But the Reverend Shew was not done with us yet.

At a sign from him, the soloist bowed her head, went silent a moment, and the clapping dropped away. When she lifted her face and began again, her voice had slid from the joy of Beulah to a great lowbelly sorrow, and she sang "Were You There When They Crucified My Lord?" so slow and sacred no one thought to join voice with her, and when she came to the part that sings, "Were you there when they hung him to the tree? Oh, sometimes it causes me to tremble," we were all, I believe, every one, trembling. The woman—I never did know her name, she was not from around here, but, my Lord, she had a glorious voice— she swung from sorrow right on into "Victory In Jesus," and the whole of the congregation once more lifted voice and sang till we about raised the shingles off that little church, and it was the whole story, wasn't it? In that precise and telling order. The Reverend had reminded us of the whole story, and still no one had mentioned the word lynching. It was the loudest word in that sanctuary, not a soul had whispered it with their lips.

Now he stepped to the pulpit himself, and very slowly he began to sing, "Lord, sometimes there is trouble in my life." The man had such a power that none joined him for several moments, until the sound began to roll in through the open windows. The preacher sang out, "Trouble in my life," and the response, "Some-t-i-i-imes," came from without like the echo of thunder, low and deep, from the throats of the men standing outside. How many there were I had no idea then, but the sound was a great rumbling, a great power, and in a moment the women's voices joined in. Think of it. Oh, I see it in my mind's eye to this day, I hear it, I remember: that small clapboard church on the rolling prairie, and the day sweltering, burning as this land burns in early September, the earth so hot the colors are bled from it, switchgrass fading to beige, and the sky white with heat, the red dirt itself fading, gone sifting coral and salmon, flour-soft, and around this little country church the sound is rising, swelling in waves like the heat rising toward heaven. Men and women in rows at the windows, women in blue and red and yellow dresses, in silk hats, and the men in straw dress-hats, white suitcoats, cream-colored jackets, brown faces bleeding sweat, and their mouths open, the sound rising, and the yard trampled, wagons and buggies and motorcars lining that red-dust road, and our voices within the sanctuary joined with them outside, joined as one voice. And the Reverend led us on. "Jesus, He will fix it," he sang, and the voices answered, "After whi-i-ile," and a great shout went up from that place, the seat of the Lord, the Lord's house: "Jesus, He will fix it, afterwhile," a shout not of anger but of faith, and that is the gift the Great God of Zion did give us.

From the corner of my eye I could see the little whitewoman trembling, smiling and trembling. An usher came forward and gave her a hymnal, and you would have thought that poor woman's face could not crack any wider, but it did. She smiled up at the usher and opened the book just anywhere and looked at it, still smiling, but she didn't sing. I'd seen her mouthing the words to "Victory In Jesus," which showed her to be a Christian, or at least somebody who went to church, but she did not sing this hymn with us.

We sang a good long time, long enough for the Spirit to begin its work, to still our thoughts and our anger and even the old grief finally, and that of course is what the Reverend intended, because he knew we could not hear him till our minds were still and the Spirit moving among us. He meant us to be receptive before the Lord. It took a long time. When he led us down to quiet finally and began to pray, we were ready.

"Blessed Father, look down on Your children here this morning. We're hurting, Lord, our hearts are broken, and You know that, Lord."

Throughout the congregation the people murmured, "Yes, Jesus. Yes, Lord."

"Your word tells us there's a balm in Gilead, Lord."

"Oh, yes, Lord."

"We just ask You to pour Your balm out upon us this morning."

"Thank you, Jesus."

"We ask You to heal our hearts, Lord, lead us in Your path of righteousness."

"Yes, God."

"That we might do Your will, Lord. In the name of Your Son Jesus we pray. Amen."

He opened the Book then. "Would y'all turn with me this morning to the sixty-first chapter of Isaiah." There was the sifting, shuffling sound as Bibles were opened and leafed through. "Isaiah sixty-one, the first verse." Very calm, very slow he started. "'The Spirit of the Lord God is upon me,'" he read, "'because the Lord hath anointed me to preach good tidings unto the meek; he hath sent me to bind up the brokenhearted, to proclaim liberty to the captives, and the opening of the prison to them that are bound.'" He paused, looked up at us. "Y'all hear the Word of the Lord this morning?" he said. "'Bind up the brokenhearted.' Are we brokenhearted here this morning?"

And from the whole of the congregation went up a mighty "Amen!"

"What do the Lord say He's going to do for the brokenhearted? Bind us up, amen?"

The people answered, "Amen."

"Do the Lord say He's going to proclaim liberty to the captives?"

"Yes, Lord!"

"Do the Lord say He's going to open the prison to them that are bound?"

"Praise Jesus!"

He looked at us very quiet for a minute, and then he read on. "'To proclaim the acceptable year of the Lord, and the day of vengeance of our God, to comfort all that mourn.'" He repeated very slowly: "'The day . . . of vengeance . . . of . . . our . . . God.'" Looked up at us. "Whose vengeance He going to proclaim?"

"God's vengeance!"

"Do He say He's going to proclaim the people's vengeance?"

"No, Lord."

"Say He's going to proclaim *God's* vengeance, amen?"

"Amen!"

"And here in the third verse: 'To appoint unto them that mourn in Zion'— Lord, listen to it—'them that mourn in Zion'! Are we mourning in Zion?"

"Yes, Lord!"

"Is the Lord going to comfort us?"

"Amen! Praise God. Thank you, Jesus. Yes, Lord."

"'To give unto them beauty for ashes'—y'all hear it?—'beauty for ashes'— amen?—'the oil of joy for mourning, the garment of praise for the spirit of heaviness.' The Lord is not going to leave us alone in our mourning. He is not going to abandon us in our grief. He's going to exchange the oil of joy for our mourning, don't He say that? Going to give us a garment of praise for our low-down spirit of heaviness, amen?"

"Amen!"

"Now, why is He going to do that? Because He loves us, yes. Because He don't want to see His children eating their hearts out in grief and rage."

"Yes, Lord!"

"But you look here at the third verse. He is going to give us beauty for ashes. Why? 'That they might be called trees of righteousness, the planting of the Lord.' The planting of the *Lord*, do you hear it? 'That he might be glorified.' Let us pray. Lord Jesus, make us Your planting here this morning. You promise to bind up our broken hearts, Lord, we trust You on that."

"Yes, Lord."

"You going to ease our hearts with that oil of joy, Lord."

"Oh, yes, Lord."

"We know You are able."

"Thank you, Jesus."

"But, Lord, we asking You now, Lord, to show us how to be a planting for You, Lord. Show us how we going to be trees of righteousness for You, Lord, that Your will might be done through our right doing, Lord, our right doing and our faith, Lord. Amen."

"Amen."

And then the Reverend Shew stood quiet with his head bowed for so long that the congregation inside and outside began to get restless. All over the sanctuary people had their cardboard fans going, moving the hot air. We all were perspiring, we all were waiting, and though the Spirit had just a minute ago been moving among us, now people began to shift in the pews, stirring, because the heat seemed to rise in Brother Shew's silence.

It was in that uncomfortable quiet that I realized that the family of Everett Candler was not among us. I looked all around. No passel of children, no widowed grieving mother. I craned my neck to look behind, though they wouldn't, of course, have been seated in the rear of the sanctuary; they'd have been on the front pew, right directly before the altar. Rather, the first three pews across the front of the church were filled with dignitaries in dark suits; they were not craning their necks, as the rest of us were, looking around; they sat very still, facing forward. But the family of the lynched boy was not there.

The Reverend raised his head after a long time, he laid his eyes on us, stood behind the pulpit in his white robe with the two gold crosses embroidered on each breast, stood so very still, his face that high, clean, copper color, so perfectly still you could see the peace on it, you could see what surrender he'd done made with his Lord. He said, "I want y'all to open your Bibles one more time to Isaiah, the sixty-second chapter, the fourth verse. Isaiah sixty-two, four. Y'all got it?" For the first time he turned and acknowledged the faces crowded at the windows. "Y'all got it out there? Isaiah sixty-two, four. All right now, I want you to read it with me."

And the sound went up in a low rumbling.

"'Thou shalt no more be termed Forsaken; neither shall thy land any more be termed Desolate: but thou shalt be called Hephzibah, and thy land Beulah: for the Lord delighteth in thee, and thy land shall be married.'"

The Reverend closed his Bible, and all over the sanctuary you could hear little thuds as many Bibles shut. "We all know what happened last Sunday. Not a soul here don't know that one more time one of our sons been taken out by a white mob and lynched."

The hard murmur began to rise among us, and you could feel that house ready to be exhorted to rage. We wanted to be. I believe that's what most of us had come for, whether we knew it or not. But the Reverend put his hand up, he eased us down again; he had something different on his mind.

"Now, there's lots of rumors been flying all around our communities, too many rumors. Here in a little bit I'm going to ask Mr. Roscoe Dunjee to come up and relate the truth to us, tell us all the facts he knows as a newspaperman and a member of the governor's Race Relations Committee, and as one colored citizen that have the acquaintanceship and the ear of Governor Robertson. Mr. Dunjee is going to tell us what did happen, what's going to happen, and all of that. We going to settle some of these wild rumors."

A murmur of approval went up, a few scattered amens.

"But I want us to listen to the Word of the Lord here a minute longer. The Word say our land is going to be called Beulah, isn't that right? That's what we read here this morning. And God knows we've been dreaming about the Promised Land a long time, amen? And what do the Lord tell us? Again and again He says, I'm going to deliver My people. He says, I'm going to lead My people to a land of milk and honey, amen? Are we the Lord's people here this morning? Amen. Amen. And if we the Lord's people because we are faithful to Him, will He not do as He promised? Amen. And now there are some among us, I'm going to say maybe even most among us, who came right here to this Territory believing we getting to the Promised Land at last, amen? And what do we find when we get here? Find out things in Oklahoma aren't much different from Memphis and Mississippi, from Arkansas and Texas and all those other places we come from, am I right? I hear some mighty amens. So what are we going to think now? Do we suppose to think the Lord been fooling us? Why would the Lord want to fool His people? Well, what are y'all thinking? Maybe it wasn't the Lord fooling us, but just us fooling ourselves. Maybe we the fools."

He paused a minute. That little church got so quiet. All the amens and the Yes, Jesuses just disappeared from the air. The Reverend looked down at them on the front pews and said softly, "Brethren? Would y'all stand?"

They stood as one man. Then, in the next beat, they turned around and looked at us. The Reverend said, "You look here among us. Do we have a bunch of fools gathered here this morning?"

The Reverend gave us a long time to look at them. In the center stood Mr. Roscoe Dunjee, editor of the *Black Dispatch* out of Oklahoma City, and on one side of him stood Mr. Smitherman from the *Tulsa Star,* and on the other Mayor D.J. Turner of Boley. I recognized the mayors of Taft and Rentiesville, several ministers, a number of doctors, our grand master of the Knights of Pythias, Dr.

Wickham, a half-dozen editors of colored newspapers from all over the state. At the end of one row stood attorney I. H. Spears, and next to him, in great dignity, President Marquess of Langston University. They stood there, men in their prime mostly, and of every color known to the Negro race, looking out at us, and we knew they were lawyers and educators, business leaders, writers, doctors of philosophy and medicine and the Word. They were our leaders, the very cream of our colored leaders. The Reverend waited for us to comprehend.

I cannot speak for others, but as for myself, that moment settled something deep in me. I understood we were gathered for a purpose not like any gathering of our people before. We had come together not to memorialize, not to grieve, or to give vent to that old powerless wrath. We had come to *do* something, come to make something, create a new way among us: there was change coming. I did not know what kind of change, but something powerful. Something unspoken before in this land.

"The Lord don't lie," the Reverend said softly. "If we come here believing, then we got to go on believing." He held his peace yet a while, and the deep understanding ran through the sanctuary. "Thank you, brethren," he said finally. "Y'all can be seated."

And the men sat down again.

Reverend Shew stepped out from behind the pulpit, came front and stood at the very lip of the podium. "From the time our people came in chains to this America," he began quietly, "we been waiting. The Lord promised He was going to lead us, and He did lead us. Right here to Beulah. Right here to the Promised Land, and we making something here, amen? In Tulsa and Oklahoma City, in Langston and Boley, in that old Creek town Muskogee and that good colored town of Taft and all over this state, we are making something, can I get a witness? Amen. Amen. We come here, we say we going to build us a home Over in Beulah, like the old spiritual says. Did we build us our home? Amen. Built us some strong black towns, some fine businesses, a powerful Negro university, and come to find out, what? The whiteman's no different in this land. No different in this land. They're going to make laws to have us to live separate from them—that's going to be the first laws they make soon as they become a state. They don't want to allow us to ride in the same railcar with them, they don't want us to use their same telephone booths. Well, that's all right, isn't it? We're going to go on and live our own lives. But here now, come to find out they're going to write up a grandfather clause like they got all over the South, say we can't vote unless our slave grandfathers voted. But we just going to put our good lawyers on that one—amen, Brother Spears?—going to get the U.S. Supreme Court to turn over that one, we going to go on and live our own lives.

"But now, here, come to find out, they going to lynch this young man Everett Candler Sunday evening, like they're lynching black men in Georgia and Alabama and Chicago, Illinois. Whoa now. Whoa, now. We can't go on and live our own lives in the light of that, can we? What kind of land is this? This the land of milk and honey? How we going to believe that when they come in the night and snatch up our sons and take them out on a dark road and murder them? They lynched Everett on Sunday, but what do we find out they did on Saturday night in Tulsa? The very night before, at the other end of the state, they gone and lynched one of their own."

We began to murmur amongst ourselves.

"Is this the land the good Lord promised us?"

The murmured fury was rising.

"Listen here, now. I'm here to tell you something: yes, it is."

We all got quiet again.

"What is it the Word tell us? 'Thou shalt no more be termed Forsaken.' Hear it? We going to be called Forsaken no longer. Praise God. Our land is going to be called Beulah. Why? Because the Lord delighteth in us, the Word says. And what does that name mean, Beulah? We talk about Way Over in Beulah like it's the heavenly hereafter, but I'm here to tell you Beulah is a real place, it is right here on this earth we going to quit being called Forsaken. It is here our land is going to be called Beulah, the Book says that, and what does Beulah mean, brothers and sisters? It means *married*. What do the Lord mean to tell us, *married*? Just this: we married to the whiteman. Oh, no, now, I don't want to hear y'all grumbling. What else is it? They were our captors to start with, yes, now they our doctors and lawyers and newspaper writers, they the opposite to us and the same as us, and we are *married* to them. But let me tell you something else, brothers and sisters. The whiteman is married to the Negro just as well. Y'all know it? Amen. And there's no place the whiteman knows it like he know it in Beulah. That's why they make Jim Crow laws hard and fast as they can make them. That's why the Klan rising up so bad in this state. They know it in the truth of their hearts, and those that don't know it yet, we're here to teach them. Amen?"

"Amen!"

"Whiteman might think he'd sho like to get a divorce from us. We might think we sho like to do the same. Lots of blackfolk saying they don't want nothing to do with the whiteman, and Lord knows we feel like that. We'd like to not ever have to deal with him anymore. We come here to this land, we think maybe we going to be allowed to do that, but we find out last Sunday night that's not going to be the case. We got to deal with the whiteman. We got to *deal* with the whiteman here in Beulah. Amen?"

"Amen!"

"We don't know what the Lord's after, but let me tell you this: He is after something, and He aim it to be right here in *this* America. He aim *us* to be right here in this America. Brother Garvey up in New York, he's saying we all got to go back to Africa together, but I mean to tell you something this morning: what God hath joined together, can't *no* man put asunder. Oh, yes, I hear you: Preacher, that weren't God put our people in them slave ships. The whiteman done that. You right. You right. But listen here. The Lord God is a mighty God, y'all believe it? He can bring ten plagues on top of Pharaoh, am I right? He can part the Red Sea waters, lead His children safe over on dry land. Great God of Zion can do anything He want. He can allow anything He want. He can *stop* anything He want. How come He don't stop the hand of these whitemens lynching our children? Last year in Chicago, how come He didn't stop them going yonder to the South Side and burning down our houses and killing us like lambs to the slaughter? This very year, fifty-three black men already been lynched in America. That's the truth in this country. That's the truth. I want to ask you something: could the Lord stop these whitemen's hands if He wanted? What? Y'all mighty silent out there. Any believers here this morning? Can I get some amens from some believers here this morning?"

"Amen!"

"Is the Lord God a mighty God?"

"Amen."

"Then could the Lord *stop* them if He wanted?"

"Amen."

"Amen. Amen. Now, I don't believe the Lord *want* these things to happen, but He sure do *allow* them to happen, and we here to ask ourselves this morning: why?"

The Reverend got quiet then, looking out at us, letting us ask that question of ourselves. Like we hadn't asked it a thousand times, a hundred thousand times over, and never come up with any answer but the pure mystery of evil, the plain old wickedness in whitemen's souls. And still the Reverend was silent, so that we went from asking it of ourselves, to asking God. Like we hadn't asked it of Him, too, a hundred thousand times for every black man and woman and child dead.

Very softly the Reverend said, "What do He want from us? What does the Book say: 'that they might be called trees of righteousness': that they might be *the planting of the Lord.* Would y'all bow your heads.

"Almighty Father, we're gathered here this morning to look and see how we might be a planting for You. This is Your Word, Lord, and Your promise. You know what's in our hearts, Lord, like You know what's in the hearts of them that have done this terrible thing. Like You know the hearts and minds of all Christians and all non-Christians alike, Lord, white and black, red and yellow, all over this world, Lord, just like You know the instant any little sparrow fall. You have not turned Your face away from it. You know what have happened and what is going to happen, Lord, and we know You going to see us through. We know You are able.

"But now, Father, we asking You to send Your Holy Ghost Spirit here among us. You promised to send us a Comforter, and we need to be comforted here this morning. We asking Your Presence among us, because, Lord, we got to face some hard things. In a minute Brother Dunjee is going to stand up and relate some terrible things to us, some hard truths we going to hurt to hear, some facts going to fill us up with hatred, make us wrathful in Your sight, Lord, and we know if we angry we can't be Your tree of righteousness. If our hearts are full of hatred we can't be Your planting. But, Lord, we can't save our own selves from anger. It's too hard, Father. It is too hard. They killing our sons, Lord."

"Yes, Jesus."

"They killing our daughters."

"Oh, help us."

"We in the sieve of Satan, Lord, he is testing us mightily, and like Job we want to know why. We asking ourselves that question. We asking You, Lord. Why? How long You going to suffer them to do like this here in this country? How long? Almighty Father, we need You to come here among us to save us from anger. Hold back our hearts from hatred, Lord, that we may be Thy planting. That Thy will might be done, Lord, on earth as it is in heaven. In Jesus' holy name we pray. Amen."

The Reverend raised his head and looked down at the front pews, said, "Mr. Dunjee?"

Now, Mr. Roscoe Dunjee was a very handsome, very dignified man, slender in his physique, but he had a mighty power in his presence, and he came and stood to the side of the pulpit, put his hand out to touch it as if it might keep him steady. That church grew completely silent, and all out in the churchyard and beyond—how far distant, I do not know: perhaps far across the prairie—there was silence: no murmuring or shuffles, no sound even of the dense air being stirred by cardboard fans. I have never heard such a silence. It was as if a glass bell had been placed over us by a great hand, and inside that bell the absence of sound was complete.

Mr. Dunjee cleared his throat, said, "Folks, we all know what happened, in its essence. We know young Everett Candler, nineteen years old, was taken from the Oklahoma County jail by several whitemen posing as officers. We know he was given up by the jailer without a struggle, and that he was driven to a dirt road ten miles southwest of the city and strung up by the neck. We know that when the young man's body was located the next day it was found to be desecrated by two gunshot wounds to the forehead as well. He'd been hung to a tree. His right eye was wide open. The pupil, a dull, unnatural color, seemed to gaze upon the world. His left eye was closed. One shot had been placed in the center, the other in the right center of his forehead." The editor paused a moment. The church held its breath, waiting. "The gunshots were perhaps a final *coup de grâce*," Mr. Dunjee said, "for the young man died by hanging. His tongue protruded from his mouth and hung over his lower lip. His hands and feet were tied. He wore a filthy suit of white ducking made red with his own blood. Those are the facts of the lynching."

Brother Dunjee seemed to sink a little then, grow smaller, as if he felt sick. His formal manner changed. "We tried to stop them," he said. He took a white handkerchief from his breast pocket, dabbed it on his forehead. "When word came that the boy had been taken, the whole of the Oklahoma City Negro community joined together to prevent that lynching. We gathered on East Second Street. Many of you here this morning were there. We had a caravan of automobiles ready to head out in any direction, had we only known what direction to go." He paused, looking out at us, and he spoke so low we had to strain to hear him. "When we found the lynching site the next day, that grass was hardly trampled. There could not have been more than a half-dozen of them at the killing. We were almost a thousand. And, citizens, I want you to know, we were powerless to stop it. Powerless. Probably by the time we started to gather on Second Street the boy was dead. I don't need to tell you, ladies and gentlemen, that the time to stop a lynching is before the Negro man is taken, not hours later!"

I heard a kind of low rumbling from without, and I thought at first it was far-off heat lightning, the way it will sometimes send its murmurs across the prairie, and then I knew it to be crowd sound, murmured words in men's voices passed back from the open windows to the farthest edges of the gathering. I thought, All our kept anger will burst forth now.

"Now, ladies and gentlemen." Brother Dunjee raised his voice. "One of the many rumors that have gone round this terrible week is that the mother and sister of Everett Candler were also arrested and taken to the county jail at Oklahoma City. The Reverend has asked me to dispel that rumor, and I can and will. Last Monday evening, I must tell you, the Negro community in Oklahoma City, stirred up as it was and filled with wrath, came near to unleashing its own mob violence because of that tale. We'd heard that those two innocent women were incarcerated in the very cell from which the boy had been taken. We heard that another white mob was gathering to storm the jail and lynch mother and sister, to 'finish the job,' as it was said. Remembering, as we all do, the lynching of Marie Scott in Wagoner six years ago, we had no doubt that the women, too, would be lynched if they could be found. We'd been too late for the Candler boy, but we would not be too late for the women, we were determined—*determined,* ladies and gentlemen, on that! Many hundreds of us gathered, fully prepared if need be to march on the Oklahoma County jail. We sent a delegation to Sheriff Johnson to ask entrance, that we might see for ourselves if the women were there. It took the personal intervention of Governor Robertson, but we were at last allowed to enter and look around the jail, and we were able to satisfy ourselves that the Candler women were not there, so let me lay that particular rumor to rest."

I thought the editor would tell us then what had become of the Candler family, why they were not here at the declared memorial service for their son, but he did not. "We are gathered today for several reasons," he went on. "We're here to mourn Everett Candler, another of our black sons dead at the hands of a white mob. But we are here to do more than that. We must this day speak the unspeakable. We got to tell not just what happened to Everett Candler but what happened to a whiteboy in Tulsa Saturday evening. We got to tell what is happening not only in Oklahoma but in our neighbor Texas almost weekly, what is happening daily in Georgia and Alabama and Illinois and Missouri and Mississippi, throughout this nation. We are here to tell it, and to shout, as God is our witness: No more! No more!"

"No more!" came a cry from the crowd. "No more! Amen! That's right!"

"We don't want to go to that dark place, brothers and sisters. We don't want to tell again how our sons are taken from jail cells, how they are pulled from railcars and automobiles and their own beds, how they are chased by bloodhounds through canebrakes and swamps. We don't want to describe how they're tortured and hung, how their bodies are wrapped in chains and dragged behind cars through our communities. How they are literally butchered alive, or riddled with a thousand bullets, or slowly roasted to death, crying out to their Maker and their torturers to deliver them. How their bodies are mutilated, their fingers and toes snipped off, lips and ears sliced from their heads while they are yet living, their parts severed and forced in their mouths, or kept as souvenirs in jars of alcohol on white storekeepers' counters—"

Mr. Dunjee stopped then. The complete and utter silence had returned. He passed his handkerchief over his face.

"Yes," he said, after a long time. "It is unspeakable. What they do is unspeakable. Too horrible for us to remember. Too horrifying to forget. We don't want to say the words. As a newspaperman, as an informed Negro citizen, I know what they do, what they have done, as you all know it. My soul is outraged, folks, as your souls are outraged. My heart is cold, knifed through, it is sick. I can't stand here before you and describe it any longer, the words are too terrible to say out loud. But I will declare to you this: the only way to stop the cataclysm of lynchings in this nation, this apocalypse that has fallen on our people, is to bring these white mobs to justice!"

"Amen!" said the people. "That's right! Yes, Lord."

I glanced at the little whitewoman then, unconsciously. It was not that I thought of her but that she seemed merely to appear in my line of sight. My inner eye was in a place of horror, and it took a moment to realize I was seeing the woman's face. The smile had at last been wiped from it. Her skin was a sickly yellow, her lips were thin and clamped, though whether in disbelief or judgment or nausea it was impossible to say. Her chest was heaving. She seemed to have shrunk into herself even smaller, as if she'd soon sink away into the pew.

"You cannot stop a mob's fury in the midst of it," Mr. Dunjee continued. "They rage with impunity. They seize battering rams and break down jail walls. Once they've made up their minds to lynch a Negro, there is no human force that can stop them. Their own people cannot stop them—and, yes, there are decent whitemen who try, men of conscience who will stand against them, but I tell you, brothers and sisters, decent whitefolks are not a force powerful enough to stop the bloodlust of a raging mob. One year ago, just last September, the very mayor of Omaha, Nebraska, died at the hands of a lynch mob when he tried to hold them back from taking a Negro prisoner—their own elected mayor! There have been others who died trying to stop them, and we thank God for the ones who will stand against them, but they can't do no good.

"That was a throng of two thousand men, women, and children in Tulsa last Saturday night, and it is told that the Tulsa police directed traffic at the site! That's the kind of crowd gathered in Tulsa to watch the life wrung from the neck of one of their own! If they will gather by the thousands to lynch one of their own race, if they will bring their wives and children to watch the festivities and scramble like hounds for snippets of the rope that choked the life from a whiteman, fight like snarling curs for little shreds of that whiteman's clothes, tell me, ladies and gentlemen, what can we hope for? What can the black man expect in this Oklahoma? Governor Robertson has called for full investigations on both these lynchings, he's calling aloud to bring the mobsters to justice, but I want to ask you, can we get redress from the law in Oklahoma? Who do you think is going to convene a grand jury to investigate the lynching of Everett Candler? Why, none other than Oklahoma County Attorney Cargill—the very man who had that boy brought from Arcadia to his own jurisdiction, where the sheriff was in sympathy with his views—in sympathy, folks! Yes, I will say it! And for what reason? For the *crime of being a black man in the vicinity of the killing of a white man!* For such 'crime' that young man was lynched!"

The low, angry hum began to swell out toward the windows.

"Now, I can make a prediction, ladies and gentlemen, I can tell you just as well as a gypsy what's going to come of that investigation: the conclusion is going to be brought forth and declared to the world that Everett Candler met his death 'at the hands of parties unknown'!"

The rumbling gave rise to angry voices, saying, "Yes, Lord. That's how they do!"

"Always it is declared following another outrage that none of the participants was recognized; always it is the same old story: 'death at the hands of parties unknown.' I tell you, ladies and gentlemen, these parties are known!"

"They known! That's right, brother! Amen!"

"And we may begin with the sheriff of Oklahoma County, for who else is responsible for the safekeeping of a prisoner in the county jail? Now, one of our purposes here this morning is to form a second delegation, one made up of our most learned and articulate men, gleaned from the Negro communities all over Oklahoma. We are going to go directly to the governor's office tomorrow morning—"

Brother Dunjee stopped then, as did all the low, rumbling words of anger rising throughout the congregation, for the little whitewoman had stood up from her place at the end of the pew, and she opened her mouth and held it open as an ugly, featherless baby bird does.

"People," she managed at last. Her voice was faint, screaky. "People, I . . . I . . ."

We were silent. We waited. She was perhaps sixty, though she may have been younger, a frail, pale, gray-headed lady with eyeglasses and bony arms protruding from silk sleeves. Her dress was stylish in an old-fashioned manner, and she had a cameo pin at her throat. No trace of the embarrassed smile remained. Her face was twisted with pain. She looked as though she might faint. At last she found her voice again. "I just wanted to say to you, that . . . I feel . . . terribly . . . sorry. I'm just so . . . so sorry. . . ." Her thin voice trailed away. She looked baffled, helpless, and it came to me that she had practiced over and over what she would say to us, and then, at the moment's unfolding, she'd gone blind, gone mute and mindless. At last she turned and made her way back along the aisle toward the door. An elderly Negro in a chauffeur's uniform slipped out of the pew behind her and followed. The people parted, watched in silence as the whitewoman walked out the open sanctuary door, the old man limping to catch up with her. After some time we heard an automobile motor start up in the distance.

Brother Dunjee did not speak again. None spoke, and yet there was not the silence as before. There was sound among us, coming from us, and yet it was not whispers and murmurs, not the hum of anger or the low, bitter rumbling. It was a kind of rustling, almost like the sough of wind. I'm not certain I can say what it was, but I do know this: the swell of our wrath was halted in its rise by that whitelady standing up to speak. Not her few useless words. The most well-spoken words of regret from a whiteperson could not have assuaged our fury that morning, and it was not, by any means, a fact that our anger had bled away. Quite the opposite. There were many of us whose ire was made worse by her presence, by her very presumption to speak. There were some who hated that whitewoman and her garbled "I'm sorry" with a horrible hatred, and I could feel that around me, too.

But there were others whose anger was tempered by embarrassment for the lady's clotted tongue; some, perhaps, who grudgingly admired her courage to come among us. There were yet others, I believe, who felt compassion for her pathetic cry, or thought her sorrow genuine, if thin, innocent of the hard sources of true grief. No doubt there were even a few who were thrilled at the woman's coming, as there will always be some among us who suck up to whitefolks and curry their favor and believe that a whiteperson's good attention is better than God's. As for Brother Dunjee himself, I believe he was simply thrown off stride. The climax, the crescendo of his speechmaking had been ripped from him, and he had to regather himself.

We were thrown out of unity. Yes. That is what it was. We had been, as a crowd sometimes is, of one mind, one heart rising, as we listened to Mr. Dunjee's furious, articulate, truthful words—and that whitelady threw us wide from each other. She scattered us from one mind to many hundreds, made us pause to ponder or feel or think, and what had been building was in this way dispersed.

I was not angry then—I cannot say to this day what was within me, other than my curiosity at that strange soughing sound—but now, when I think back to all that happened afterward, I get angry. Because she may indeed have felt sorry, but regret is not repentance, and that is what we have not seen in Beulah, repentance that owns its part—that is, like the Word tells us, at once sorrow and self-knowledge and a changing of the mind. I saw no mind changed that morning. And yet, if that whitewoman, whom I had never seen before and have never seen since, had not come among us with her few choked words that came from sentiment and meant nothing, stopped nothing, but altered everything—if she had not appeared, the thing that was building among us would have come to its full power.

Many times I have asked myself what would have happened if she had not come, if we had remained, as we were that morning, of one mind. But we'd been scattered, and the oppression of the day's heat began to press upon us, for it was almost noon now, and still no one spoke. Mr. Dunjee stood mopping his brow with his handkerchief as that strange sound, that disjointed murmur, like the fitful whispers of a dry wind in tall grass, passed among us, and then, after a long time, the big woman in the faded housedress stood up in the choirbox and began to sing "There Is a Balm in Gilead."

In a few moments Reverend Shew joined his voice with hers as he got slowly to his feet and came front; he stood just a little behind Roscoe Dunjee, and I saw him reach out and place a hand on the editor's shoulder. In another few moments Brother Dunjee also began to sing, and then we all began, and as the other hymn had swelled from the outside of that little church inward, now the sound arose from the front of the sanctuary and undulated slowly backward and out the windows and beyond, and it was way long out on the prairie, I'm certain, before it stopped its swell.

F or two nights Althea prowled the rooms of her house in darkness, her terror growing more horrible with each tick of the mantel clock in the dining room, each hour chimed by the grandfather clock in the front hall. She napped fitfully Sunday afternoon on the fainting couch in the parlor, only to waken at dusk with the fright unabated, tindered now with a vague guilt and the sight of her face in the hall mirror: puffy, creased, with queer paisley lines swirled on her cheek from the imprint of the silk brocade. Monday dawn found her sitting sideways on her still-made bed as gray light swelled through the lace curtains to reveal the image in the mahogany mirror. The puffiness was gone now; the woman in the mirror looked simply haggard, aged, hawklike and bony. She was nearly mad with fear.

Abruptly she stood in the sullen light and went to the dresser. She sat down to brush her hair, savagely twisted it into a tight knot, arose and crossed the room, flung open the door to the wardrobe. Within moments she was dressed, had locked the door behind her, and was moving swiftly and with great purpose down the front walk. Carefully she trained her eyes front, that she might not by accident catch a glimpse of the ravaged rose garden in the side yard. She'd reached Fifteenth Street before she realized that she didn't know how to get to Little Africa. The recognition gave her only an instant's pause. It was north, wasn't it? That's how they

called it: Little Africa, niggertown, North Tulsa. That was all she had to
know. She stepped off the curb, crossed Fifteenth Street, walking north.

The obvious solution, of course, would have been to go right to Bill
Sutphen's office, order up a new girl, and tell him to make certain she arrived by early dark. But Althea didn't want another girl; she wanted
Graceful. It was her sudden recognition of that fact which had driven her
up from the bed, out into the silent, dawn streets. She could not have, under direct questioning, said why. She might have answered, Why, the girl
knows how to cook bacon just how I like it, or some such pointless answer. The truth was hidden from Althea's conscious mind: that she felt
her soul bound to the girl who bore her own birth name—the one who'd
seen her terror and rage in the dark foyer, who had witnessed and turned
away in silence, and so had become watcher and knower and silent, secret
judge. Althea understood only that the urgency she felt to have Graceful
back in the house on South Carson was as compelling as any of her many
little driven hungers, and as easily remedied. Never did it enter her mind
that the girl might refuse.

She walked so fast that in less than half an hour she'd reached the edge
of downtown. The city of Tulsa seemed to rise up and close behind her as
she entered. Though there'd been milk trucks and delivery wagons stirring in the residential area when she'd left it, not a vehicle, not a pedes-
trian broke the silence of downtown. The sun had risen in the east, but the
many-storied buildings held her in shadow, the brick walls on either side
echoed her footfalls. Once, she glimpsed herself in a department store
window, and the image, so ghostlike and faded, made her breath catch,
her already tense jaw clench harder. She rushed forward, cursing silently
her kid leather shoes with their too-high heels, the impractical, narrow-at-
the-knee hobble skirt that limited her stride.

When she emerged at last from downtown, stood panting and sweating
on the street, looking north toward the community on the far side of the
tracks, she didn't realize she was looking at Little Africa. Never had she
formed an image of the place clear enough for her mind to give shape to it,
any more than she'd given thought to a last name for Graceful, a family, a
house. The sunlit buildings gleamed like a distant city across a river.
She'd heard stories of sporting houses and pool halls, choc joints and
gambling holes in North Tulsa, of course, though she believed those
places would be closed this time of morning and she could walk quickly
through the shacks and shanties till she found the girl. The business district coming awake before her was too well appointed and prosperous for

Althea to imagine that such a place could be Tulsa's niggertown, and, staring at it, she thought only, with an inward groan and another silent curse for her shoes, of how much farther she still had to go. With gritted teeth, and limping slightly from the blisters coming on both heels, she walked toward the tracks.

She stopped just south of the crossing. Across the iron rails dozens of brick and stone and wooden buildings lined the streets, with printed signs overhead that declared them to be pharmacies and rooming houses, cafés and grocery stores, but the groceryman in his white apron sweeping the walk in front of the green awning was a colored man. The woman setting out a sandwich board in front of the café was colored. The men driving the delivery wagons were, and a man in a straw boater and bow tie driving an elegant roadster, and the bunches of young people, male and female, teasing one another and joking loudly at the trolley stop. The several women walking fast, holding tight to their children's hands, were colored, and the children were colored, and the ones in motorcars and strolling along the sidewalk and opening doors to barbershops and drugstores and newsstands and moving everywhere as far as her eyes could see.

Althea felt faint. Her disoriented sense returned in full measure: this world was unbehaved, unreal, without proper order. She would have turned and fled, had she been able to move. But Althea's feet were burning fire, not only the blistered heels now but the very soles burning, as if the brick street beneath scorched up through the leather; she could smell the scent of her own perspiration, could feel it trickling between her breasts, down her sides beneath the charmeuse middy she was wearing. A girl in a maid's uniform came toward her, paused almost imperceptibly on the far side of the tracks, and then crossed them, stepping carefully over the wooden planks raised in the roadway to meet the rails. The girl moved decorously to the other side of the street, her head tucked properly, so that she might not stare at the strange whitewoman standing on the street in an ostrich-feathered hat and silk dress clothes, sweating and glaring.

Althea followed the girl with her eyes, took a step as if to go after her, and winced as pain shot from her blistered feet. She stood a moment longer, tears coursing down her face from the shock, though she made no sound, and her features did not scrunch with the look of crying. She seemed as unaware of the tears as she would have been of a stray eyelash on her cheek or a flick of lipstick on a tooth: she needed a mirror, or another human, to tell her that her face was marked by them. She stared north across the Frisco tracks once again.

Several of the Negroes moving along the avenue had become aware of her. She felt their scrutiny pass over her, taking in everything about her and registering nothing in that invisible manner they had, and the heat of resentment rushed over her, followed instantly by a deep, instinctive swelling of pride. Althea in that moment claimed inheritance to her mother's defiance of pain. She squared her shoulders, lifted her chin, began to walk toward the railroad tracks again. She did not limp. She didn't wince. She glided over the tracks effortlessly, unaware, even as she traversed it, that she was passing an invisible, inviolable boundary. A woman as self-absorbed as Althea held freedoms others might never win. By the time she reached the intersection she could hear the trolley bell clanging as the car crested the hill, coming south, carrying bootblacks and porters to their jobs on the southside, and motorcars were spewing fumes in all directions, and the bustle and movement had risen to full morning peak.

She walked on, and she would not look in the faces of the Negro people as she passed them; nor did they appear to look at her, but went on about their business of opening shop for the day or walking to work or standing on a street corner awaiting the jitney, but she felt eyes following her, could feel their stares burning into her back, and she moved forward briskly, with great purpose, as if she knew exactly where she was going, what she intended to do. The more swiftly she walked, the more a sense of panic began to push her, drive her, and though it was she who was moving, to her sleep-deprived and fearsick brain it seemed that the hundreds of dark faces were sweeping past her, rolling over her like a black sea tumbling and cresting in waves, and she rushed north, deep into the heart of Greenwood, because she felt herself drowning and knew only to keep moving, keep moving, before the sea swept her under.

"Ma'am?" a voice called out behind her.

Althea stopped, caught by something soft in the voice; she turned to find a black woman in a flowered dress, her hair pressed and fingerwaved tight to her skull, standing, broom in hand, beside an open door, above which ran a brightly lettered marquee that said BRYANT'S DRUG STORE. "You want a bandage or anything, ma'am," the woman said, "we got everything right here." Her glance dropped, and Althea's eyes followed, and she saw for the first time the spots of blood that had begun to seep through the bone-colored leather of her shoes. "You welcome to come in and rest you feets awhile," the woman said.

Althea stared blankly at her feet as if they were foreign objects entirely unrelated to her, then she turned vaguely and continued up the street, slower now, the sense of aimless panic still upon her, but subdued. She saw a glass-fronted brick building ahead, neat and square, the gold lettering on the window declaring in bold, crisp letters that the building was occupied by THE TULSA STAR, Fearless Exponent of Right and Justice, Oklahoma's Largest Circulation Weekly, and though she'd never heard of the newspaper, she thought with a great shudder of relief that she was safe: she'd passed through the raging sea to the far and sacred shore. Nearly running now, she rushed toward the glass door, pulled it open, stepped in.

She was met by a sweetish, clean metallic odor, and complete silence.

She stood very still, listening, but all she heard were the harsh little barks of her own breath. Her knees were trembling; her throat was dry as ashes. The desk area to her left was empty, and the door at the back of the room was shut tight, but a telephone on the wall just outside the gate gave her a renewed burst of relief. As soon as she'd found a sip of water and had retrieved her breath and voice, she would phone Franklin to come get her. A surge of secret gladness swelled in her: this, surely, was reason enough to call him back from Bristow. Her mind was instantly fuming with words of blame for her husband, the damned selfish fool, forcing her to stay alone, making her live that nightmare in niggertown. The pain in her feet sprang awake, burning, searing, so excruciating she thought she would faint.

"Help?" she called thinly. "Can somebody help me? Please?"

In the silence she heard automobiles rumbling on the street, the sounds of voices muffled through the glass, a fruit seller calling out "A-a-a-apples! Pe-e-eaches!" as he drove his wagon slowly past, fading away north. She would not turn to look out the window but made her way gingerly to the low gate, pushed it open, limped to the chair behind the desk and lowered herself to it. She pulled the hatpin from its nest of ostrich feathers, removed the hat, and set it carefully to the side, then lowered her head to her hands on the desk.

"Might I be of some assistance, madam?" The voice was clipped, harshly intoned.

Althea jerked her head up from her hands. She hadn't heard him come in. Had she fallen asleep? The light was behind him where he stood on the far side of the desk, and she couldn't make out his features. She saw only that he was a thin dapper-looking gentleman, wearing a brown derby and a chocolate-brown suit. A vaguely familiar scent of cologne wafted over her, clashing with the rich smell of coffee and warm bread from the paper sack he carried, and Althea's mouth, previously dry enough to spit cotton, suddenly filled with horrid-tasting water, and she recalled that she hadn't eaten since she'd breakfasted alone at the hotel in Bristow two days before. She could have nearly snatched the sack out of the man's hand.

"Oh," she said, "oh," and she blinked up at the man, tried to smile. She thought of how dreadful she must look, and she reached to straighten her chignon; but the knot was as tight and neat as she'd pinned it earlier. She smiled beautifully at the gentleman, glancing up from beneath her lashes. "Oh, thank God you've come! You've no idea what I've just been through!"

The man was silent.

Althea waited a beat longer than her instincts wanted for the man to begin his solicitous murmuring, but finally, when no sounds of concern were forthcoming, she leaned back against the oak slats and smiled again, wearily. "If I could trouble you for a tiny sip of water, sir? Just a cool drop to wet my throat?" She spoke in tight, short syllables, hardly exhaled, for the taste in her mouth was wicked as old pig-iron, and she did not want to push the gentleman away with her breath. "I . . . I . . ." And she cleared her throat lightly behind her hand, looked with such tender longing at the paper sack the fellow held that she couldn't imagine him denying her an instant longer. Still the man stood over her, silent.

She sat forward, and her tense fingers moved unconsciously to her throat. How dare he stand there like a nincompoop, staring at her, when she was obviously in such distress. "I've been chased, sir!" she burst out at last, forgetting her coquetry, her rank breath, hair, sweat.

"Indeed," the man said, slowly.

"Yes. Indeed!" she said, and her fingers moved to the back of her head, swept upward, swept upward again, pressed the snug hairpins in tighter. Who was this rude fellow? Why, she'd have Franklin on him in a whip-stitch. "A sea of them, sir! A big bunch of niggers chased me up the street, I thought I'd never escape! I saw your open door, your sign," and she waved her hand at the backward gold lettering on the plate glass. "I thought, Oh, thank God, thank God, and I . . . I . . . came in . . . to . . ." What the devil was the matter with the man? He ought to go to the telephone this instant, call the sheriff, call *some*one, for God's sake.

Mindless anger flashed though her, and Althea started to rise, ready to come around the desk, though whether to slap him or to leave she could not have said, but instantly she shrieked in pain. Quickly the man stepped away from her. Althea, collapsing into the chair, gasping , staring down at her feet, did not see the man's eyes dart swiftly about the office, out to the street—nor could she have recognized the fear and fury in that racing glance had she seen it; for never could she have known how meticulously this man had worked for fifteen years to defeat just this sort of situation. Althea wept, and her tears were conscious and fullflowing, her face was twisted, mounting toward hysteria as she stared at the puffy white flesh, engorged now with fluid, swelling out over the tops of her kid shoes, the iron-red blood at her heels drying in blotches on the outside of the leather.

Had Albert Smitherman been anywhere but the womb of his own office in the heart of Deep Greenwood, probably he would have, despite his long habit of controlled dignity, turned to run. No Negro knew any better than he the dangers of a whitewoman's screams. But Tulsa's Greenwood was the last safe place, the haven he'd searched for since leaving the South as a younger man: a world separate from the white world, a prosperous and autonomous place entirely of blackfolks' making. If he could not be safe here, there was no safe place anywhere. He watched the weeping woman in a kind of raging despair, for, as his thoughts said to him, the troubles with whitefolks must reach to the ends of the earth: if you won't go among them, they will come to you. What good would it do to run?

"Help me," the woman whimpered, and she looked up at him, her face ugly with weeping. She was hunched forward in the desk chair, her skirt pulled up, revealing the pale flesh of her thighs. She held the beige silk off her knees, as if that were where the pain hurt her, though he could see the bloody swellings of her feet now, lightly touching the wood floor. Smitherman looked at her a moment. In silence he set the sack on the desk and turned and exited the little gate; he walked toward the door at the back of the office, went inside, and closed the door behind him.

Althea sobbed and sobbed. After the man left she didn't try to stop, for there was no need of vanity now, and she gave herself up to it, wailing as she bent to pull the leather away from her blistered heels. She sobbed harder as she peeled off the kid shoes, seeing the misshapen feet, the swollen flesh, the opened wounds oozing blood; she surrendered to a great wash of self-pity, for of course it was Franklin's fault that she'd come away in a stupor at dawn without stockings. The weeping was delicious, a great release, like the hysteria that had swept the girl in the pen with the red calf twenty years before. But as Althea wept, something began to change in her. The bottoms of her feet were lacerated, the fragile skin burning as if it had been held against hot coals, and something in that searing pain in the most tender place seemed to lay her open, cut her and make her raw and new with pain; the hurt radiated on flaming nerves upward through her flesh to her life's soul: burning it clean, leaving her with no core, nothing true of herself but these bleeding strips of her own mortal flesh. In terror Althea tried to pull back, control the surrender, but it was too late.

The editor returned from the back room to find the woman prostrate across his desk, her shoulders rising and falling in great shudders, the feathered hat clutched and crumpled in one hand, as she beat her forehead rhythmically against the bare wood. His sack of bread and coffee lay on the floor, leaking a dark pool.

He stood without moving, only watching, and the cup of water he'd brought for her trembled in his hand as his mind whirled with a thousand riotous thoughts, all of them leading directly to danger. Was it possible she'd really been chased? He thought of the rising outrage here, the anger kindled by the back-to-back lynchings. Yesterday's gathering at Arcadia had been calm enough, had reinforced the resolve of Oklahoma's black communities to meet the malignity with law and intelligence; still, there was a lawless element in the colored population of Tulsa, just as there was in the white; there were dope-runners and bootleggers and gamblers, and any number of Negro soldiers who'd come home from Europe bold and fearless, unwilling to submit to the old lynch law's reign of fear—and if a reckless and stupid whitewoman had made a liaison, had come north to meet her lover within days of these lynchings, and instead, having met a loose, half-lit gathering . . . ? No, it was impossible. Impossible. But . . . what could explain such a paroxysm of pain and hysteria in the woman? How to account for her bloody feet? With sudden relief, he thought, *Maybe she isn't white.* Certainly he'd known colored women as fairskinned as this one. But no, he thought, looking at her shaking shoulders. This was a whitewoman. His instincts told him unerringly she was white.

When the pressman Lawrence came in a half-hour later, Smitherman still stood outside the gate, staring at the woman, the cup of lukewarm water yet in his hand. The woman no longer sobbed, no longer beat her head; she lay quiet across the desk. She might nearly have been dead, so still was she, and Lawrence turned his eyes from the woman to his boss and back again, trying to see what this strange scene might mean. He couldn't see yet that the woman was white.

Smitherman didn't change expression or glance up, seemed in fact not to have noticed the other come in, but, as if arrested in mid-motion and suddenly released by this new presence, he went on to the gate and swung it open, stepped in, and set the cup on the filing cabinet behind the desk. He picked up the coffee-soaked sack and held it away from himself. "Lawrence," he said, his eyes on the woman's back, "go over to Frankfort and get Dr. Blanchard. Tell him to come as soon as he can."

The woman moaned slightly, rolled her head to the side, and Lawrence, seeing her race then, backed out the door as fast as he could move and turned to run down the street.

She couldn't imagine where she was, or who were these men standing around. She lay on her back, blinking up at the three masculine faces. The brown one she dismissed instantly, as completely as if it were a dog's face, for it was colored and therefore not truly a man's face, and so she allowed her gaze to pass between the other two as she tried to remember where she was. The man in the brown derby seemed familiar, though she couldn't place him, and who the other might be, she had no idea. The men did not speak but continued staring at her. She made a move to sit up. No hand reached to help her. Surprised, she pushed herself upright and sat dizzily on the edge of the desk, and as she did so the three moved away from her in a ragged half-moon, the colored man farthest, halfway out the gate, and she thought bizarrely she must have come down with a contagious disease. The pain in her bandaged feet began to throb then, and she remembered.

She looked at the white gauze taped around her heels, glanced up at the sallow man in the derby, whom she recognized now as the one who'd come in earlier, then she cast her eye to the tall, handsome fellow who stood beside him in a vested herringbone suit and silk tie. She tried to smile. Still the men looked at her in silence. The sallow man stepped forward and handed her a cup of water, and as he did so, the familiar scent wafted over her once more; this time she recognized it. It wasn't cologne she smelled on him but the faint odor of pomade: the same blue pomade that permeated her maid's room on South Carson. She understood in a slow dawning that the man was colored.

"I'd recommend having those dressings changed tomorrow, or the day after," said the other. "They're going to suppurate rather severely." Her gaze turned to him. He was indeed handsome, dark-eyed and delicately mustached, his tawny cheeks shaved smooth and his black hair slicked straight at the sides, trimmed precisely to meet the immaculate white collar at his neck. He, too, was a Negro. The shock came to Althea first as a seeping, like the slow swell of floodwater beneath a doorsill, followed by the deluge.

"Is there . . . ?" The man hesitated. "Would there be somebody you'd like us to telephone?"

Althea hardly heard him. Her senses buzzed, every instinct in chaos. She dropped her gaze to the floor. Not that light-complected blacks were an uncommon sight: Nona Murphy's yardboy was redheaded as a new penny, with queer green eyes and dark freckles on his coppery skin—though the boy's features were thickly Negroid, his rust-colored hair appropriately nappy; a person had no embarrassing trouble knowing he was colored. But it wasn't the humiliation of having mistaken these two for white; it was the fact that they looked and spoke so much like—well, there was no other word, was there?—like gentlemen. She'd never in her life been at a loss for how to behave in the presence of gentlemen, and yet . . . these were colored men. Weren't they? She couldn't look up. The very sight of them tossed her instincts into turmoil, tilted her mind and her will completely askew.

"Madam?"

She resisted the impulse to reach up and fix her hair. After a moment she shifted her gaze to the men's shoes a few yards away. The handsome man in the herringbone suit wore brown-and-white oxfords, polished to a high sheen. The silence grew longer. She could hear the darky by the gate breathing, and she ached to glance up at him; she'd know how to feel looking at him—imperious, superior, slightly fearful if she'd been alone with him, for he certainly qualified as a big buck nigger—but she couldn't bring herself to raise her eyes. Why didn't one of them say something, for pity's sake?

The gulf that separated Althea from the three men was so deep, so wide, that none of them could see it. The men shared one desire: to get this whitewoman out of the newspaper office, out of Greenwood, and back to wherever she belonged quickly and quietly, without bringing the wrath of white Tulsa—the wrath of the whole of American race history—down on their community. Oklahoma was dry as touchwood in the wake of the two lynchings. A whitewoman's fear, malice, hysteria could ignite it in an instant. The editor was the only one who gave even vague credence to her claim that she'd been chased; he told himself it was because he'd seen the depth of her nervous frenzy, but in truth his credulity belonged to the kind of rage he'd witnessed following other lynchings. The other two knew she lied, knew it mattered not that she lied, because a lie was the same as the truth from a whitewoman.

Althea herself—shaken and confused, stripped of her most familiar presumptions, and yet inescapably, irredeemably white—couldn't imagine that the silence in the room was born of fear; she believed it must be the silence of judgment. *Nigger judgment*, she said to herself, and a weak swelling of outrage pushed through her, followed by deflation. She was too sick, too tired. Aching and flayed raw as she was, she longed for a mirror.

"Do you have—?" She stopped herself. Dear God, she couldn't ask these colored men for the powder room.

"Yes? Madam?" It was the sallow man who spoke.

No, not sallow, Althea thought. *High yellow.* "Nothing," she mumbled. Lost, she simply sipped the warm, acrid water, kept her eyes unseeing in the middle distance at the level of the men's neatly pressed and creased trouser knees.

At length a peculiar sigh escaped from the editor, and he said softly to the man beside him, "I wonder if we might send her back in your car?" But the doctor shook his head fiercely. Immediately Smitherman understood. The only permissible way a Negro could be seen driving a whitewoman would be as chauffeur: Dr. Blanchard would have to borrow a chauffeur's uniform, seat the woman in the rear of his new Maxwell touring car and himself in front as liveried driver. Even lightskinned as he was, it was the only safe way. Not even the doctor's desire to get the woman out of Greenwood could make him humiliate himself in this manner.

The silence stretched longer, stretched beyond confusion and discomfort to a kind of absurdity. Althea had a terrible impulse to laugh, but she bit the inside corners of her lips and managed to choke it off. Still she did not raise her head.

"Madam?" Again it was the voice of the sallow man. "May I ask for what purpose you've come to our community? Perhaps we can be of service. Are you . . . were you looking for someone?"

"Oh—" Althea glanced up. "Why, yes. I am." Like spinning cylinders suddenly locked into place, the proper positionings in the world returned to her. Of course. She'd come to fetch Graceful. That was all. Her face lifted. "My maid, Graceful," she said calmly, and she smoothed the front of her skirt. "The goose ran off last Friday, God knows why. I'd simply dismiss her, except I need . . . I expect her to stay the month, at least. Till the end of September. Or October. She's already been paid." She reached up to smooth her hair as the lie slipped serenely off her tongue. "Would you know where I could find her?" she asked, as if the more than eight thousand souls in Greenwood ought, by the simple fact of their shared race, to know one another.

"What did you say her name was?" This from the handsome man, and Althea stifled the impulse to smile at him the same way she'd choked off the urge to laugh, by biting down on the inside corners of her mouth. The effect gave her an odd look, a kind of flirtatious primness that pursed her unrouged lips.

"Graceful," she said. "I don't—I don't know her last name."

"Whiteside?" The sallow man's voice was thin, the inflection rising.

"What?"

"It isn't Graceful Whiteside you're looking for?"

The brown man beside the gate released a low, wondering sound, "Un-huh," very softly.

"Well, yes. I guess. Graceful. Graceful isn't common, is it? The name?"

"By coincidence, she was just here." The editor's voice was tinged with a kind of irritated curiosity. He seemed to be speaking exclusively to the doctor now, as if Althea were an uninterested party, or a child. "Last week. When was that, Lawrence? That girl asking for Hedgemon?"

"Next day after Hedgemon quit, Mr. Smitherman. She come that next morning."

"That'd be Friday."

"Friday. Yes, sir."

"Do you know the family, where the girl stays?"

"No, sir. I wouldn't know." The pressman glanced at the whitewoman, and quickly away.

Smitherman took a step toward the desk where Althea still sat, but almost at once he stopped. "There was a letter," he said vaguely. Then, as if coming to himself, "If you'll permit me, madam, that drawer there," and he motioned toward the desk drawer partially covered by her skirt. "Miss Whiteside left a letter behind. I found it on the floor some while after she'd gone, and put it in the drawer for safekeeping. Perhaps there's an address?"

A renewed hope surged in him, a sense that this jeopardous circumstance would be rendered harmless more quickly and easily than he'd thought. But the woman made no move to clear the way for him, and he would not come within such intimate distance of her—the drawer was just below her thigh—and so the editor stood awkwardly, an old fury rising, certain that the whitewoman was purposely trying to confound him. Althea, for her part, was numbed by the very mention of the letter, for it seemed that it was that blasted letter—oh, she had no doubt it was the same one, brought by the little colored boy less than a week ago—that was the cause of all her disturbance and turmoil and grief: the same letter that had been the beginning of chaos, Japheth coming, the old memories and recognitions. She remained motionless on the desk, staring straight ahead.

The doctor saw Smitherman's hesitation and at once stepped forward. Blanchard had passed as white when he was a young man in Milwaukee, and this secret of his own history, assiduously kept, had left him thoroughly unintimidated by white skin, though acutely distrustful. "Madam?" he said and gestured at the long drawer, and Althea rather automatically turned to the side so that he might open it. Dr. Blanchard shuffled through the many papers and clippings and pencil stubs and envelopes; he glanced up once, but the editor didn't come forward to guide him. At last he picked out the crumpled thin sheet smeared with ink, opened it, and read through it quickly. Lawrence edged forward a few steps from his post by the gate. The doctor handed the page to Althea. She didn't open it but merely clutched it, creasing the center, as she had the pale blue envelope the boy brought. Her curiosity was strong, but her fear was stronger, and she was made still by her terror that the letter held some secret which would open the abyss so wide and inescapable she could not help falling in. In another moment Dr. Blanchard discreetly took the page from her hand and read it aloud in his crisp voice:

"'To all interested parties, let these presents hereby be made known:

"'Whereas it has been declared and forthwith articulated that upon the First instant of the Ninth part in the area known as Brickyard Hill at a location five blocks north longitude of the Avenue known as Archer there abides on the street called North Elgin—'"

Althea began laughing.

"'—an interested party whose express wish is stated to be in a conversant condition with one Miss Graceful Angel Whiteside for the express purpose of which is not revealed—'"

The peals of laughter made it impossible to continue. The men stared at her, and she tried to say something but collapsed back into laughter, her shoulders and chest shaking, her face twisted, the peals pitched toward hysteria. The editor and pressman began to grow angry, for Lawrence be-

lieved she was laughing at his friend, Smitherman believed she was laughing at his race. The doctor frowned as he watched the rising hysteria, and
he tried to think how he might calm the woman without touching her; his
mind quickly inventoried his black bag for a sedative.

"No, it's nothing! Nothing!" Althea managed at last, squeezing the
words through her chopped breaths that were like sobs, and in fact tears
were streaming down her face and she didn't quite know if she was crying
now or laughing; her belly ached, the muscles cramped along her sides
and her jawline, and she couldn't catch her breath. The laughter was kin
to the earlier weeping, it came from the same place inside her, and yet it
was different, filled with relief as it was, and a strange, ineffable joy. Oh,
see, it was nothing. Just a stupid letter to a stupid colored girl, it had nothing to do with her. Nothing. Althea reached up to wipe the wetness from
her cheeks, sighing deeply, shuddering. She felt herself seared clean once
more, and she forgot what she wanted. "Ohhh," she said, and sighed
heavily again.

"If you like, madam," said Smitherman, his voice taut with dignity, "we
can send Lawrence over to Elgin to see if we can locate this Miss Whiteside and let her know you'd like to speak with her. We can telephone
someone for you, someone to come see you home. We'll ask Miss Whiteside to contact you, as soon as we find her. Would that be all right?"

Althea gazed at him. A small sound escaped her, a little voiced exhalation that was almost a whimper. "Oh, I'd better go."

Immediately the editor went to the telephone and lifted the ear cup as
he turned the crank in a brisk black whir; he looked back with lifted
brows. "The number, madam?"

"No. My God. No. There's no one to telephone. He's out in the bojacks,
they both are." Her eyes cast about the office, seeking. "They're down
at . . . No, don't you see? There's nobody home!" She looked at the editor,
hardly seeming to see him. "That's what I mean. Graceful. I really need to
find Graceful. I can't go home without her. Where is she? You'll . . . you'll
have to take me over there. To Graceful's . . . To that house."

The party in the Maxwell was a peculiar vision never before seen in
Greenwood: the two well-dressed and dignified businessmen in the front
seat, the pallid whitewoman in silk and ostrich feathers in the back, and
the big-shouldered workingman walking swiftly beside the open touring
car as it moved slowly west along Archer, turned north, climbing the hill

at hardly two miles an hour, past the shoemaker's and the photographer's and Williams Confectionery, continuing on past the high school and the brickyard and a row of shotgun houses to the area, five blocks north, where the smaller frame houses gave way to brick homes of the stout Craftsman design. Dr. Blanchard eased the car to the side of the street and parked it. Althea stared at the fine brick houses and the several small Negro children in the yards who'd paused in their play to stare back at her. Lawrence stood gazing across to the west side of the street, at a certain narrow yellow-painted house nestled between the larger, porched homes on either side. The front door of the house was closed. A lump of quilt lay on the wooden porch, beside the door.

Smitherman saw the look on the pressman's face and instantly grasped, not through a succession of deductive thoughts but in an instant's revelation, that this was the Whiteside girl's house; he saw, too, that Lawrence had known it all along, just as he knew more than he'd told about the girl's appearance in the *Star* office on Friday, and that any further information was to be gleaned from the big man through great difficulty, or not at all. The editor followed his gaze. The house was empty—not abandoned, as if someone had moved out, but vacant of human souls. Something more than the shut door in the bright morning made him know it, something blank and distant in its affect. Like the face of a blind man, he thought. Or, no, not like the blind, for there'd be active listening and sensing there: more like the emptiness in the face of the dead. The half-drawn shades were like the drooping lids of the recently departed.

Still, there was nothing to do but continue. Reluctantly he got out of the Maxwell and started across the street. He glanced back once at Blanchard, but the doctor sat stiffly behind the steering wheel, hands gripped as if the car were yet moving, his eyes straight ahead, his immaculate boater cocked at a precise angle, his head high, neck stiff above the starched collar. Smitherman's eyes fell on the whitewoman in the back seat, and the urgency he felt to get her out of Greenwood rushed upon him, and he turned away, continued at a brisker pace over the worn path across the yard and up onto the porch. He picked up the bedroll and held it fastidiously away from himself as, without hope, he rapped on the wooden door. He didn't knock long, for he knew there'd be no answer, but turned and motioned Lawrence to come up on the porch. The pressman ambled slowly across the road, obviously disinclined. Smitherman gestured for him to hurry up, and at last came down off the porch and met him halfway across the yard, told him to go around and try the back, and could he move a little faster, please, they had work to get back to, a news-paper to get out.

And then the editor stood alone in the yard, holding the rolled-up quilt away from his clean suit. He gazed south at the buildings of downtown Tulsa, thinking that this was a broad view here at the top of Brickyard Hill. People spoke of Standpipe as being the dominant hill in the area, and it was, of course, and white people owned it. But one could stand here and see most of Greenwood, could see all of that other city, Tulsa, the one they called the Magic City, across the Frisco tracks. His gaze swept the hori-zon, turning in a slow circle, across the tops of the buildings in Green-wood, taking in the delicate spires of the white churches downtown, the erect peaks of the brick skyscrapers, the stolid squares of the grand hotels, all the buildings oil had built; he allowed his gaze to drift to the right, pass over the smoking, stinking refineries on the banks of the Arkansas River, and settle at last on the low humping hills beyond. The hills seemed al-most a gentle barricade between Tulsa and the western rolling prairies, and the editor pondered a moment how whitemen had succeeded in tak-ing the riches from beneath the earth, secreted yonder, without bringing the soil and muck of it to their glistening city. The imagery worked on him, and his thoughts began to form the cadences of written language: an editorial was shaping itself in his mind, perhaps an essay.

"Mr. Smitherman, they's nobody back at the back."

The editor was startled, lost as he was in his reverie, though Lawrence had spoken softly, his head tucked low, one arm held diffidently behind him. Smitherman looked at him for such a long time without speaking that at last Lawrence brought his hand front and said, "I found this," and held out the white apron, the crumpled blue envelope pressed against it with his thumb. Smitherman took them and started across the street, ig-noring the several neighbor women who'd emerged from kitchens and parlors and bedrooms to the nearby front porches, as he ignored the questioning look on Blanchard's face, as he ignored above all, most stu-diously, the ashen face of the whitewoman in the back seat of the car, though, had he looked at Althea, the expression he'd have seen there would have been unfathomable to him. Perhaps no one could have named that expression, or the truth it told of what was inside her.

Fear, yes, but fear had been with her all her life. She had tried to make it an ally, or at least she'd learned long ago to court danger so that the thrill of fright might titillate her senses, make them acutely present, and so subsume that greater fear: the dark one, unnamed and unnameable, that threatened always to engulf her. In some ways her face was like that of a combatant in defeat, yielding without humility, in hopeless, angry surrender—and yet that wasn't all. What made the woman's expression such a puzzle was the absolute, accepting wonder there. In the same way that the mind, witnessing something intolerable—the earth exploding, a head severed from its body—will at first deny and then at last make its adjustment and close around what an instant before had been unthinkable, so Althea's mind had opened to accept a reality as unimaginable to her as one where men walk on water. She sat in the Maxwell with her feet seared, her soles burning, and watched the black man who looked like a white man moving swiftly and irritatedly across the street, holding in one hand the thin quilt Graceful had carried into Althea's kitchen, wrapped tightly around her small cache of toiletries and clothes, the first morning she'd come to work, three months before. The man's other hand pressed the blue envelope against Graceful's apron, as the big Negro's brown hand had pressed it so when he'd brought it forth from behind his back, as the little colored boy's hand had pulled that same smeared blue envelope from his threadbare shirtfront, and Althea had known, in ways far beyond her small and selfish comprehension, that something irrevocable had begun.

Trancelike, she watched Smitherman open the car door, toss the bedroll and apron and the fluttering envelope onto the leather upholstery before seating himself quickly. "Madam, if you'd care to leave a note, I'll see that Miss Whiteside gets it." Althea nodded. But she didn't reach out to take the small leatherbound notebook and stub of pencil he tried to hand back to her. She got out of the Maxwell and limped on her bandaged feet across the road. The several women on the neighboring porches stared in silence at the shoeless, footbandaged whitewoman who mounted Cleotha Whiteside's front steps, went right up to the house, and did not even pretend to knock, but turned the knob and hobbled in through the unlocked door.

"Graceful?" Althea called out. The parlor was dim, the two front windows darkened by the half-drawn shades. She could see straight through to the closed back door. The smell in the house was the odor of a house well lived in and well cooked in, shut up for days. Slowly she crept forward, and as her eyes adjusted to the lowered light, the character of the room revealed itself, and she looked closely at the objects as if they were displays in a museum.

There was about the room an immaculate, almost painful neatness. A braided rug lay in a precise circle in the center, and the linoleum surrounding it was shining with wax, its mottled green-and-white surface patterned with large red flowered swirls, and the curtains at the windows and front door, too, were spattered with flowers. Against the far wall stood a horsehair divan, the back and arms draped with large white crocheted doilies, like threaded snowflakes, and next to the divan was a polished table, also dotted with doilies, starched to lacy, intricate coils, each cradling a framed photograph from which stared one or several Negro faces. Beside the little gas heater a leather hassock crouched before a green armchair, and on the wall above hung a framed print of the Last Supper. Althea's eyes passed over the picture. Jesus leaned on one arm in the middle of the long row of disciples, looking sorrowfully at Judas, the Betrayer, as he sneaked guiltily out the door. *It could've been any of them,* she thought oddly. *Any one of them could have betrayed Him.*

But Althea's gaze did not linger with the colorless faces at the Last Supper but kept returning again and again to the photographs with dark faces; then she raised her eyes to the corner above the divan, where the walls met. A darkwood treasure shelf was wedged there, holding on its various shelves a china teacup and saucer, a porcelain cat, the figurine of a blond angel with folded hands and wings, its pale painted face bowed in prayer, and a large, elegant, gold-embossed frame, from which gazed the broad, smiling face of a black man. Within Althea a kind of dull queasiness began to arise, a nauseous sense of familiarity conjoined with otherness, as if something ordinary were suddenly wedded before one's eyes to another thing very foreign and strange. She heard footsteps on the porch but didn't answer the voice that called to her, "Madam?"

On she went, into the middle room, where a trundle bed huddled against one wall, an iron bedstead against the other; she hurried past the dressing table, into the kitchen, brighter than the front of the house, with its bright yellow curtains and yellow walls. Upon the counter sat a basin of soured dishwater, floating with scum, as though someone had washed up swiftly and neglected to finish the task of emptying the pan.

"Graceful?" she said again, softly, almost in a whisper. She stepped to the door and turned the knob, but the door was locked. She jiggled it absentmindedly a moment before turning back to the room, her eyes sweeping over the pump at the sink, the icebox standing in a little pool of meltwater from the overflowing reservoir, the dried-out dishrag draped on the back of a chair, the several plates and cups turned upside down on a dishtowel spread open on the counter. Looking up, she saw at the other end of the house the sallow man on the porch at the front door. He held his face to the screen, his hands cupped on either side to see into the dim interior. In one of his hands the blue envelope stuck out, clamped between two fingers. She believed that he saw her, but he would not come in.

"Madam?" he called. And when she didn't move or answer, he held up the envelope and the letter with it, wagged them in the air. "This letter is from my linotype operator! I know the boy's handwriting!" He paused for response. "My pressman knows where he's staying. Madam? We'll send a telegram to Hedgemon Jackson at Bigheart, he'll know where your Miss Whiteside is."

"Yes," Althea said, or she believed that she said, though the man still stood with his hands cupped around his eyes, peering in the door. She moved toward him. In the next room she paused. The narrow room was cramped with the two small bedsteads, a cheap wood-veneer vanity dresser, a painted chifforobe standing by the window, its door gapped open to reveal two limp cotton dresses on wooden hangers. Against the lamp on top of the chifforobe was propped a cardboard-framed photograph of a little bunch of colored children lined up in front of a log country school. It was winter in the picture, for the branches of the trees in the background were bare, although the children were in shirtsleeves. They stared straight out of the picture, unsmiling. Graceful stood at the end of one row, tall and gangly, and yet her highboned face was soft with the softness of late childhood, her hair radiating in a dozen ribboned braids. She, too, stared soberly out of the cardboard frame, as self-consciously serious as the other little darky children. Little darky children. The strange pressure began to rise in Althea's chest.

On the vanity stood another elaborately framed studio photograph, like those in the front room. Where did they go to have such photographs made? What studio made such elegant, formal portraits of colored people? How could they afford them? The vision of Negroes arranging themselves so formally, with such dignity and presumption, in a photographer's studio dug at Althea's chest. In this picture the broadfaced man posed in a Pullman uniform, standing with his hand on the shoulder of a beautifully dressed colored woman seated with a white-gowned colored baby on her lap. At her side stood a thin, solemn boy of perhaps seven, and a little gap-toothed pickaninny, the only smiling face in the picture, beaming out at the camera from behind her mother's voluminous skirt. Though the child was round-cheeked, grinning through missing front milkteeth, Althea recognized Graceful. In gold lettering at the bottom of the frame were the words:

MR. & MRS. ERNEST WHITESIDE & FAMILY

J. H. Hooker Photographers
Tulsa, Oklahoma, 1907

The feeling in Althea's chest as she stared at the words was not a pressure now but a dark rush, a burning that surged from her core through her face muscles to the top of her head. She had no words for it. The closest she could have named it would have been to cry out that she'd been left out of everything: something huge, significant, of infinite importance had been going on in the world, and no one had told her. How could this child be here in this picture? This impish round-cheeked colored child with black slanted eyes that were Graceful's eyes, who had had a life, a history, a family. They had lived out in the country, Graceful had gone to school, she had plaited her hair, her mother had plaited her hair in those many tight corkscrew braids, she had worn gingham, she had worn muslin, she had worn floursack dresses. Within Althea a new impulse was rising, a kind of secret maternal swelling she believed she had long ago cut away from herself, and the recognition was too terrible to receive, a betrayal, and she turned away from the picture.

On her surface Althea moved as she'd always moved. She could not let the thing opening inside her show. Not even to coloreds. Especially not to coloreds. She hobbled toward the front of the house. The man at the door stepped back to allow her to come out, but Althea stopped in the center of the front room, stood quite still, closed her eyes and smelled for a moment the smell of the house, the familiar, ancient odors of old food and floorwax, and dust.

"Madam?"

Would the man never shut up? She opened her eyes. He stood back from the screen, leaning forward from the waist, peering inside, as if he dared not contaminate himself.

"Are you . . . ? Will you come out now?"

His amber face frowned with worry, and something else, some other emotion she didn't identify. Without speaking, she moved toward the screen, and he retreated farther, to the end of the porch. The pain in her feet was horribly awake now, and she limped out of the house, down the front steps, feeling the eyes of the colored women on the nearby porches, and the eyes of the big brown man beside the car, and the light-skinned handsome man behind the wheel of the Maxwell, and she made her way across the street without looking at any of them, got into the back seat, and said, with implacable authority, "Take me home."

F our miles east of Bigheart the patched and dingy U.S. Army tent
stood, flaps closed, seemingly abandoned, beside a nameless feeder
creek. There were few signs around the tentsite, hardly any footscuffs on
the creekbank, but at certain hours smoke could be seen rising from a
crude pipe at the rear of the shelter. On the days that it rained, the smoke
stood in the air above the tent, motionless, making the scene look like a
photogravure. If you kept watch at dawn, you could see a tall Negro slip
out of the tent and make for the nearby footpath, or, again, on a bright
morning, you might see a young girl, delicate as red gossamer, lift her face
as she emerged from the closed tent, look up toward the sun, and dart
quickly toward the bushes behind the tent.

Of the five people living cramped together inside the tent, only two
ever went into town. Hedgemon Jackson walked to work before daylight,
came home after dark. The uncle, Delroy, had been gone for over a
month, so it was T.J., the fugitive, who determined that his sister Graceful
should be the one sent to buy supplies in Bigheart, just as it was T.J. who
bossed, directed, allowed or disallowed everything the three females did.

Her brother's bullying was something Graceful had never seen before;
it seemed to have appeared all at once, in the moment of his emergence
from beneath the mildewed tarp. As the women sneaked from the back of
the truck into the shelter, T.J. had stood in the tent doorway, holding the

flap open, looking at the Nash truck nosed to the creek like a spent horse caked in mud and red road dust. Delroy had been standing on the bank beside it, staring dazedly over the hood toward the water, when T.J. said with quick, sure authority, "After you get rested, go fetch Mama, carry her and the girls home. I don't want them riding that dirty Jim Crow car again." And Delroy had nodded without protest, as if T.J. were the uncle and himself the young pup, although he'd slept a full day first, his loud snores scraping the very tree limbs above the tent, before he got back in the truck and headed out again.

To Graceful it seemed that the hours her brother spent in the black smelly cellar, and later, beneath the tarp, had completed the metamorphosis that had been coming his whole life. He'd always been tense, fretsome, a little too serious, but now he was transfigured into a new form of himself, harder, with no trace left of his old humor, no tenderness, or at least none that showed through the new impenetrable shell. *Everything done happen*, she said to herself. *What he been fretting about all these years already come to pass, he don't need to fret anymore.*

Still, she'd find her back rising when he told her to come inside now, somebody liable to see her, each time he caught her standing at the tent door. He ordered his poor fluttery girlfriend and her mother around with such rough thoughtlessness that Graceful found herself defending them, at least in her own mind if not to T.J.'s face. The girl, Elberta, kept her eyes on T.J. every minute, watching him with that hopeless expectancy, but it was Mrs. Candler who most touched Graceful's heart. The woman sat day after day on the army cot, her breasts heaving slowly beneath the dirty bodice of her dress, the great crescent sweatstains beneath her arms getting larger, her face blind. The only time she moved off the cot was when T.J. told her to do something; then she'd obediently get up and go do what he said. It wasn't only the woman's son who was dead but her husband, too, killed in a shootout, not lynched, but it was still whitefolks that killed him. *T.J. act like he's the only one know about trouble,* Graceful thought. *He ought to ask that woman right there.* She would glare at her brother when he told her to wash this or clean that. Though she knew that he bullied them, in part, because there was no man-work to do, she would lift her chin at him and say, "Wash it your own self." T.J. didn't argue with her but would instantly turn and snap at one of the other two to do it. Sometimes, he'd fly into a wordless rage, pace up and down the dirt floor from tent-wall to tent-wall, but there was no place for him to go.

He don't like nobody to give him any sass, she thought as she picked her way along the main street in Bigheart, trying to keep the mud off her mother's white dress. *That's how come him to send me to do the shopping, just to get me out his face.* An automobile beeped its nasal horn behind her, and Graceful jumped up onto the board sidewalk, but a little white-boy came barreling along the planks, and she stepped down into the road-way again. Bigheart was a boomtown, sprawling, filthy, wild as Kiefer or Whizbang, composed of hundreds of tents and makeshift shelters, slap-dash stores rigged together from tin and wood and canvas, haphazard rows of clapboard buildings fingering outward for miles from the old trading center. In the middle of Main Street an oilwell pumped midst the perpetual din of honking horns and rumbling timber wagons. The place had been a quiet Osage settlement before Josh Cosden opened his re-fineries here in 1909 and produced the first boom, then took his operation to Tulsa and created the first bust. But the town was exploding again with a new boom from the fast-growing Barnsdall refineries that had replaced Cosden's, and now—as if to make sure the old Osage village erased all memory of its former self—from L.O. Murphy's tremendous strike a few miles north of town. The muck and noise and sheer man-ness of the streets had at first frightened Graceful, but it had all grown so familiar that today she moved calmly along the unpaved street, sidestepping the mudholes, skirting the muledroppings, as deftly as if she'd been doing it all her life.

Her reaction to the white faces was not so easy to get used to. There were a few colored folks and quite a few Indians on the streets, but the town was mostly white, mostly men, mostly all in their high young prime, and they didn't frighten her so much as fill her with that familiar nauseous loathing. Primarily it was the shouting roustabouts and the muleteam drivers who set the bad feeling on her, although she felt nearly as ill watch-ing the whitelady in the mercantile measure out her little purchases of beans and saltmeat. She couldn't look white people in the face, so sick did they make her with cramped, useless rage. She kept her gaze lowered as she hurried along the board sidewalk, and when she sensed one of them coming toward her she gave such a wide berth that she spent more time in the muddy streets than on the wooden planks.

"That pretty dress of yours about to get ruined," a soft, deep voice said. "You better quit jumping around in mudholes like that."

Looking up, she found Hedgemon Jackson in his blue cap and blue uniform walking backward, away from her, on the plank walk. He had a big leather satchel at his side, and he smiled, walking slower, his eyes skat-ing over her head to glance up the street, then back down to Graceful standing on tiptoe in the mud. He looked so tall and familiar, with his wide white smile, and his eyelashes long as a girl's, curling up, and his awkwardly long, endlessly moving legs, that she smiled back against her will. Hedgemon's retreating steps went even slower, until he stopped completely, though his restless legs shifted weight side to side as he shoved the satchel on its long strap around to his back, then front, then back again.

"Where you going?"

"Nowhere," Graceful said. "Just yonder." She nodded toward the wooden falsefront of the mercantile a few doors down. "Thought I might buy us some very delicious beefsteak and Irish potatoes for our supper, get us some storebought cake for dessert."

"How about you get a nice angelcake?" Hedgemon's smile widened. "Hadn't had any angelcake in years."

She looked to see if he was making a joke about her middle name, but his grin was innocent. "I guess I could," she said. "Serve it up with some good fatback."

"Mmm-mmm, hadn't had good fatback in years either." He had pretty teeth, big white straight teeth, and when he smiled like that his lips couldn't close around them.

"You welcome to come eat with us, we're going to have plenty brown beans to go with that fatback and angelcake."

"Oh, I might. If somebody don't give me a better invitation." He glanced around the street again, back down to Graceful. "You going to be here long?"

"No longer than I can help it."

Already he was moving away. "I got to go deliver these, quick," Hedgemon said, "but I'll be right back. I'll walk you home a ways." His gaze flicked up the street. "Past the bawdy tent, anyhow." He looked down at her, not smiling now. "Just wait here when you finish? I'll walk you back?" It was almost a pleading, and he was suddenly the too-eager black boy who'd followed her home from church so many Sundays. Graceful shrugged, her own smile fading. But Hedgemon's grin flashed again, and he turned and ran.

She watched him go around the poor-looking whitemen crowded in front of an oil company office, past several women in hats and hobble skirts making their way along the board walk, and though it was nobody but just Hedgemon Jackson leaving her standing on the street, Graceful felt bereft. Slowly she stepped up onto the planks, turned toward the mercantile again, but she'd forgotten to protect herself and immediately she bumped into a whiteman coming out of the tool supply. "Whoa there, little heifer!" The man grabbed her around the waist, laughing, and the smell in his mouth was the same as the pit of the cellar, the same as the rank walls of the kitchen from which Everett Candler had been taken and hung.

She twisted free and ran into the alley beside the store, leaned back against the tarpapered wall, gulping air, heaving. She heard the man laughing in the street, as the whiteman had laughed when he pushed himself down on her spine in the tiny maid's room, laughed as he held her head down while he rubbed his skinny hard thing on her, rutted against her nightgown, rutted against her backside, pushing her face into the pillow so she couldn't scream, couldn't breathe, pushed her down harder, until she thought she would die, until the whiteman quit laughing and only rutted against her in silence, pushed himself, pushed himself, and Graceful convulsed at the memory of the devil whiteman brother groaning against her head while his nasty seed came in a hot and then cool and then cold mucousy blob, and in the alley beside the supply store Graceful bent at the waist and vomited in the dirt, over and over, until she could heave no more.

It took a long time for the shaking to slow enough that she could lift the front of her skirt to wipe her face, longer still before she could force herself to go back out to the street. But when she stood in the mercantile a few moments later, holding herself motionless in the center of the sawdust-covered floor, keeping her hands in plain sight so that the whitelady behind the counter, with her thin pressed lips and her lank hair and her washed-out squinty suspicious eyes, might have no cause to accuse her, the sickness came on Graceful again. The whitelady weighed out the cornmeal, the brown beans and pale, hard kernels of hominy, in pursed silence, and Graceful saw the woman's thumb on the scale, but she could say nothing, she was allowed to say nothing, and suddenly she turned in fury and walked out of the store. *I'll come back tomorrow,* she told herself, *Berta soaking the beans already, we got enough for one more night. We don't need coffee. T.J. can do without his coffee one more morning.* Though she dreaded her brother's wordless snapping rage, she dreaded whitefolks more, and Graceful turned east and hurried as fast as she could through the street, past the tents and clapboard buildings, heedless of the mud splashing her mother's dress, because it was ruined now anyhow, had been ruined a long time ago, she didn't know why she bothered to try to keep the mud off. She heard him calling behind her.

"Graceful? Graceful!"

And she was glad, just glad, to turn and see Hedgemon Jackson trotting up, breathing hard, the satchel bouncing at his side. Hedgemon's wide smile was gone, and his dancing nervousness; he stood panting in his blue messenger-boy uniform, staring hard at her.

"Where's your beefsteaks and angelcake?" he said at last between breaths, trying to renew the joke, but his face was serious. Graceful didn't answer. "Graceful? Something happen?"

She shook her head.

"You run out of money? I got money. Here, I can give you some money." But Graceful turned her face away. "Is it . . . T.J.'s trouble?" Again she shook her head. "What?"

She didn't even shake her head this time. She wouldn't look at him. The terrible taste in her mouth made her ashamed. They turned and walked in silence, on the plank walk now, where Hedgemon led her, and he took her arm as they passed the brothel tent, the saloon that operated openly in spite of the law, and walked on to the edge of town, where the planks surrendered entirely to the muddy roadbed. Still they didn't speak. As they drew near the stinking vats and smokestacks of the refineries lining Bird Creek, Hedgemon stopped. "I can't go all the way out there," he said. "I got to get back to the telegraph office."

Graceful looked at him from behind a stone mask.

He grinned. "I sure didn't expect to be no messenger boy when I moved up here from Greenwood. They told me I could learn the telegraph machine easy as I learned the linotype, but when I got here they had a whiteman on the key. They said I could run the wires around town, out to the refineries and camps." He was silent a moment. "Think that might have been a mistake, I think I should have stayed working for Mr. Smitherman." He waited for her to say something. "Well," he said, "a man can't go back, can he?" There was another beat of silence. "Graceful, what is it?"

She didn't want to look at Hedgemon's asking face. She turned her gaze to the ground. There were spatters on the toes of her worn shoes, her muddy maid's shoes, which looked so stupid with Mama's dress. There were spatters on the hem of the dress, too—new, ugly spatters from where she'd been sick, mixed in with the splatters of mud. Shame burned in her at the sight. There was no way to wash herself clean, no way to wash Mama's dress, nothing to wear while she washed it, and no place private to wash. Suddenly she missed her mother with a pain that was all-engulfing, too huge and agonizing to allow room for anything but itself.

They hadn't heard from Mama, and T.J. said they couldn't send word to her, they'd just have to wait for Delroy. Uncle Delroy would soon come in his truck to bring news from Mama. Maybe he'd bring Mama herself. The thought gave Graceful sudden hope, and she lifted her face. "You know when Delroy's coming?" But Hedgemon shook his head. She thought then of something she'd been meaning to ask first chance she got to talk to Hedgemon out from under T.J.'s frown. "Hedgemon? How did Delroy find you that night? That first night we come here in the truck?"

His shining black eyes darted up the road toward the creek, back again toward town. "I don't know if I'm supposed to say."

She waited.

"He knew before y'all come," Hedgemon said finally. "Delroy the one give me that cot. He didn't tell you that?"

"Neither one of them tell me nothing."

"It was Delroy come by with T.J.—"

"T.J.? In Tulsa?"

Hedgemon looked pained, as if he knew he was telling what he knew better than to tell. But he kept talking, his bright gaze tracing every inch of roadway and refinery smokestack and tacked-together shack within see-ing distance. "The two of them came by late, pretty late. Well, it was Del-roy knocked at the window, but T.J. was in the truck. They picked me up and we went driving, they didn't tell me anything except T.J. need a place to hide. I didn't ask questions. That was right after. . . ." He glanced down at her. "The lynchings. Just a few days after. I didn't ask." His gaze went back to tracing the roadway. "It was my idea to come to Bigheart, on account of my cousin Terence live here, he's the one told me about that telegraph job. That suppose-to-be job. Delroy carried me up here. He help me to set the tent. They didn't tell you?" And then, vaguely, when she didn't answer, "I don't know why it matters. It don't matter."

"If T.J. was already in Tulsa, how come we had to drive all that way to get him? How come Mama to go to that nasty house way out in the mid-dle of nowhere?"

"I don't know about your mama." Hedgemon shrugged. "T.J. went back to get the girl."

Graceful made a little sound, half recognition, half contempt. *He sure don't act much glad to have her now he got her.*

"What?"

"Nothing."

"Graceful? Listen, I got to get back."

Graceful lowered her head, made no move to go. Laughter spilled down the street from the saloon; grumbling wagons and oilfield trucks rolled by; a pumpjack across the road hissed and squeaked its grinding, monotonous complaint; but between the two of them there was silence. At last Hedgemon said, as if it were the most normal thing to think about, the most logical next subject, "You hear anything from Carl Little?"

She looked up, surprised. "What make you to ask that?"

"Oh, nothing. I was seeing him around a lot, and then next thing I know I hadn't seen him in a while."

"Last I heard he's living in Memphis. I don't know. I ain't seen him since he got out of the army."

"Oh." His smile was starting to creep back. "I thought y'all . . . I thought maybe you'd know . . . Oh, well. Yeah." The smile was broadly back on Hedgemon's face now. "I got to go but I'll . . . I'll see you tonight. Okay? Okay?" Though she didn't answer he grinned anyway, and turned and began to run fast toward town.

Graceful stood a long time before she could make herself walk on, across the timbered bridge over Bird Creek, over brown water slick with crude, reeking with refinery runoff, and on east toward the camp. Carl Little's name woke up the old ache in her, not because of who he was—she hadn't seen or thought of him since before she went to work at the Dedmeyers'—but because the sound of his name, the soft, ticking syllables, called up a whole lifetime in Greenwood, a world where she and her family fit smooth as dovetail joints, and she'd had a sweetheart and lived in a nice yellow house and walked to Booker T. Washington High School in the mornings with her friends, and white people were a distant, unfathomable power, like fickle gods—unappeasable maybe, but far enough off to be forgotten most of the time. It was too hard to think about the past, and there was no perceivable future to swing her thoughts to, only the dull, cloistered present, the closed tent and the two sad women and her testy, bullying brother.

A dozen times she'd opened her mouth to ask him what they were going to do, where they were going to go, but that hard crust on him and her mother's warnings about asking questions wouldn't let her speak. Her biggest fear, the one barely whispered in her own mind, was that T.J. didn't have a plan. That they were just going to stay in the dank U.S. Army tent till the clothes rotted off their shoulders and T.J.'s little cache of money ran out, till Hedgemon Jackson got tired of having his salary go to buy beans and saltmeat for four people not even kin to him and kicked them all out, and then what? She'd tried to tell herself that they would soon go to live in one of the colored towns, Taft or Boley, Redbird maybe. Go live as they had lived when she was little, far out in the country, among their own. But if that's where they were going, why didn't they do it in the first place, instead of coming to this stinking, roiling whitefolks boom-town? It made no sense. *T.J. got a plan*, she tried to tell herself. *Sure he do.*

In a few moments Graceful turned off the road and began to wade through Indiangrass and big bluestem tall as her waist. The amber seed-heads nodded in the morning sunlight; the air flicked with flying grasshoppers, black-and-yellow wings buzzing as they sailed over the plumed heads. Here the land was not yet blackened and fouled with the mess of taking oil from the earth, the air wasn't rank with the stench of alchemy but sweet with goldenrod and compass plant, and in the open grassland Graceful walked fast toward the line of trees scrawling off on the horizon to the north. She dreaded that khaki square of tent worse than a prison, but there was nothing else to do but go back. *He's going to be mad enough anyhow, might as well get it over.*

Inside the tent the kerosene lantern smoked and stank on the crate, its wick needing to be trimmed, globe needing to be cleaned, and the feeble light threw shadows on the three sitting so still, Mrs. Candler in her usual blankfaced dream on the army cot, her daughter useless and listless be-side her. T.J. crouched in his same place against the back wall with that stupid chunk of blackjack in his hand, and yet he didn't even glance up when she came in. It was as if they were waiting—for what? Someone to come, some outside occurrence to change things. *They act like they still hiding in the dark in that cellar*, Graceful thought. *In their minds they still laying down underneath Delroy's tarp.* The only variation she could de-tect since she'd left was that the tent's odor of mildewed canvas and un-washed bodies, of kerosene and cooked pinto beans and dirt had swelled in the morning sun, and the stink and the despair swept her as bad as the sick feeling from whitefolks, and suddenly she was just so mad.

"How long y'all aim to sit around here in the dark?"

All three pairs of eyes looked up at her.

"Somebody come along and see this tent," she said, "if they looking for you, they going to find you." She glared directly at her brother, her chin lifted. "Crouching in here in the dark ain't going to stop them. Keeping these tentsides rolled down ain't going to stop them. Holding on to that little switch of blackjack ain't."

T.J. looked at her in silence. He didn't make a move to get up.

"What are we going to do, T.J.? We can't sit here in the dark till we rot like last year's sweet potatoes."

"Hush."

"Don't tell me to hush. Tell me what we're going to do."

"I'll tell you when I know it myself."

"I tell you what I'm going to do," she said, and she came on into the center of the dim square, stood looking down at all of them. "I'm going back to Tulsa."

"No, you're not."

"I am, T.J., I am! I can't stand this."

"What are you going to tell them when they come around Mama's yard looking for me?"

"How you know they looking for you? Maybe they're not. I haven't heard anything about they're looking for a colored boy. You know they always blare that all over the white papers, and I've never seen it. I would of seen it, T.J. I'm the one goes into town."

"Hush your mouth."

"I won't."

"You don't know a thing about it."

"Tell me, then. I want to know how come I got to live like a mole in a hole without a way to wash or eat nice or fix my hair, no way to see that pretty day outside without you going to stand behind me and tell me to get back in here in the dark. Tell me!"

"Keep on, girl. Didn't get yourself in enough mess asking what you got no business knowing."

"Then let me go. Let me take the train to Tulsa."

"You're not a prisoner here."

"Oh, sure I'm not, only every time I go to the bushes you like to have a fit till I get back, you so scared somebody going to see me, and we way out in the middle of nowhere!"

"You don't know when whitefolks going to show up, they're hunting oil over every inch of this country."

"What did we come here for, then? This was stupid, it's a stupid place to hide from whitefolks, in the big middle of their faces!"

"We're not going to stay here, we going on soon as Delroy get back from Tulsa."

"When's that going to be? When!"

"Hush your loose mouth!" T.J. made a move as if to rise from the damp earth, and Graceful felt herself flinch and pull back, afraid of his anger, and she thought in despair, *We like dogs in a pen, we going to tear each other up.* But her brother settled back on his haunches, said softly, "You get that coffee?"

"No." Her face lifted. "I didn't get no coffee. I didn't get none of they filthy whitefolks' nothing." She waited for his anger, but it didn't come. He remained silent in his coiled crouch. She glanced over at the Candlers. The mother stared at the dirt floor, unblinking, as if she were deaf to them. The girl had one hand on her mother's knee; the fingers of her other hand tugged restlessly at the ratty quilt on the cot, pulled and twisted a bit of leaking batting into a little corkscrew mound. She'd plaited her hair since the morning. Already Graceful's anger was bleeding away. "Whitefolks make me want to puke," she said. And then, softer, "I'll get your coffee in the morning, T.J. I'm sorry. I'll go back tomorrow." And she turned and went out of the tent.

She heard the girl scrabbling out behind her. Immediately Graceful headed toward the path beside the water. She wanted Berta to think she was going off to do her personal business and not follow. She didn't feel like dealing with the faint mothy creature in any way. Graceful went at a steady pace, pushing the vines and sumac out of her way, but the girl came along, and Graceful went a little faster, but the girl would not be discouraged. So Graceful stopped. She waited in the tangled growth for Berta to catch up.

"Where you goin?"

"Where do it look like?"

"I wanted to talk to you a minute."

"You talking."

"I just wanted to tell you, he don't mean to be mean, he just . . ." Her breathy voice fluttered off into the air, soft and trembly as her gestures. She gazed up at Graceful from sienna eyes round as marbles, not froggy enough to be ugly, only enough to make her look scared every minute. "He don't normally act like that."

"You don't got to tell me about my own brother."

"No, I didn't mean . . . There's somethin else. Can't we sit someplace and talk?" Berta looked back along the path, and Graceful, torn by the same tug of sorry she'd felt at the girl's terror when the tarp came up over her head, now felt her resistance go, draining away as her anger had done. *She just a child,* Graceful thought. Her old mantle of calmness returned to her; the stillness rose up into her face, slowed and gentled her gestures. "Down there." She nodded at an uprooted cottonwood on its side on the bank; it was grown up with ivy and brambles, but the trunk lay bare above the tangles, skinned free of bark by years of weather, and the two made their way to it, sat down looking at the water. The creek was so high from the recent rains it pulled at the tangle of sumac and riverwillows on the bank.

"I'm listening," Graceful said. The girl met her gaze for only an instant before she turned her face away. Her copper features began to twist and purse and bend themselves, and she started to cry.

Graceful watched in silence. Every few moments the girl seemed to descend to a new circle of grief, spiraling deeper, so that her weeping became progressively more ragged, more wrenching, more uncontrollable. After a long while, Graceful put her arm across the girl's shoulder. Berta covered her face and collapsed into long voiced sobs, close to wails, not hysterical but horrible, and from a place so deep and ancient it didn't seem possible they could belong to her young self but must be wrenched up through her body from the soil beneath her feet. She began to blubber between the sobs, the words mauled and broken.

"I— don't—know—what I'm going to do! I can't—" And she put her head down in her lap until the sobs quieted enough that she could squeeze more words out. "They was running around the house, like that, outside, outside, man shot him through the back, my daddy just fell down in the yard and there was so much bl— bl— bl— bloood." She pulled her shift up to wipe her face. "They couldn't even get his tongue back in his mouth! Graceful, they bury my brother with his tongue hanging out and my mama gone and lost her mind, they say whitefolks fixing to come take us to jail, me and Mama, we had to go down in the cellar, but I think she lost her mind on account of the children, she's afraid we never going to see the children, and T.J.—" And now the sobs returned fully, and Graceful just let her bawl.

"He act so *mean*! And, oh, Graceful, Graceful, he don't want me no more! I can't even get him to look at me, we was going to get married, he said we'd get married, he say he'll carry me to Tulsa, we going to get us a house, and he, he promise he'll quit running liquor, because that's what killed my daddy, but he don't want me, and I—I—" She held her hand cupped over her nose and mouth, stared at Graceful with those huge eyes, gulping air, trying to control herself. Finally, she managed to calm the sobs enough to say, "Will you tell him for me?"

"Tell him what?"

But the girl started crying again, and Graceful knew. She was swept with anger at her brother, and it seemed to go such a long way back, to him leaving home even, going off from the family and staying gone and getting himself into no telling what kind of business, and then he'd come sneaking back in the middle of the night to get Delroy to risk his neck for him, get Hedgemon to fix a place for him, get Mama to come clean up his mess, just barrel on getting everybody in trouble, most of all his own self—most of all this girl. Graceful couldn't keep the anger from her voice when she said, "How old are you?"

Between sobs Berta said, "Fifteen."

"How far gone?"

"I don't know," she said, hiccuping.

"Then how you know it?"

"On account of—I keep getting sick, that's how my mama do. Any time she going to have another baby, we all know it 'cause she be so sick in the morning she have to lay in the bed. I don't eat, but sometime I be sick anyhow. I'm scared to tell T.J., on account of how he act. He didn't use to act so." She lifted her face, pleading with Graceful to believe her. "He treat me good. He so sweet. T.J. sweeter to me than any boy ever been. Now he act like I got poison or something. . . ." And her breathy voice faded away; she turned to gaze out over the water. When she went on, her voice was dull, the words shaken from time to time with a jagged sob, as if she were retelling a bad dream. "I didn't think I'd see him again. T.J. run away the minute it happen. It happen so fast. We all just sitting down to breakfast when the whitemen come, they talk so quiet and normal, we didn't know nothing, I didn't, I didn't even know they was sheriffs till way after, but it was just in a minute everybody start shooting and T.J. come running from the barn, I seen him running, my daddy and that whiteman chasing each other around the house, around and around outside the house, they come by the back door three times. They kilt my daddy right at the corner of the house, whiteman shoot him, and T.J. shoot the whiteman, but them others already got hold of Everett and start to beat him, and me and Mama run upstairs with the children."

Graceful's stomach pitched. She didn't want to hear those words. *T.J. shoot the whiteman.* She didn't want to think of the terrible truth she'd closed her mind to since the night in the storm cellar at Arcadia: the unspoken reason they all had to live in a cramped tent outside Bigheart, the reason her brother had changed into a gaunt, harsh, bullying man who crouched in a corner with a chunk of blackjack. Hiding from whitefolks. T.J. had to hide; they all had to hide. Whitefolks would lynch him if they caught him, because whitefolks would do anything. Anything. Graceful was knifed through with hurt for her brother, pitying, fearful; the pain was followed, as she stared at the swollen-eyed, hiccuping girl, by an impossible dawning.

"I didn't see where T.J. went," Berta said. "Time I go to look for him, he was just gone." She repeated with a kind of low wonder, "I didn't think I was ever going to see him again. But he come back for me. He come back, and now he act so mad." She paused, gazing at the roiling creek. "I say to myself he's going to be glad when I tell him, he'll quit being mad. But how am I going to tell him if he won't look at me?" She drew quiet again. Somewhere in the open land behind them a flock of crows cawed. When Berta went on, her tone was oddly reasonable, explanatory, like a child imitating its mama. "T.J. wasn't mean when he first come back, though. He didn't start to be mean till we gone down in the cellar, it was all them nights in the cellar, they 'bout make us all crazy." And then, as if to correct herself: "He's not *mean.*" She looked up. "He's just rough."

Graceful kept staring at the girl as if she were listening, but she only half heard. Her mind had turned away from her brother, turned in on herself, her own body, the floating sense of fullness and the cold nausea she had thought to be hatred, which was not hatred only. She blinked when Elberta repeated her name, and she realized the girl had said it several times.

"Graceful? Could you?"

"What?"

"Tell him. You the only one can talk to him. He won't even answer me, he won't look at me, but you're his sister." And the girl went on in her whispery voice, absorbed in her own woes, so that she could not recognize the look on the other's face. "I'm not going to tell my mama, not ever going to tell my mama. She don't need more trouble. She'll kill me anyhow, she been warning me my whole life." Berta began to cry again, not the deep sobs of grief as earlier, but the self-pitying, frightened tears of a young girl in trouble, and she reached over and took Graceful's hand, held it tight between her own. "I been wanting and wanting to aks you. You a sweet lady. Please? I'll do whatever you want. You want me to fix your hair? I can fix hair good, everybody in Arcadia come to me to fix their hair for them, sometime."

"Yes." Graceful said. "Go on back, now. Leave me be awhile. I'll talk to him." Without speaking the girl leaned over and hugged her hard; she was thin and bony as Jewell or LaVona, a wisp of a child with hard, swelling breasts beneath her shift of brick-colored cotton, and when she pulled back she swiped her forearm across her face to wipe the tears. She smiled as if her troubles were all over, jumped up from the old tree and darted lightly up to the footpath.

For a long time Graceful sat without moving; she couldn't see anything. She couldn't think. The unfolding knowledge blocked out the external world of afternoon light and humming air, blocked her inner world as well, the mind's round of thought and plan. She sat motionless, feeling her body, knowing that it was true. After a while she got up from the cottonwood and made her way to the water's edge. She could hear the crows in the distant field. Trembling, she stepped to the little roaring creek.

The water ran fast near the banks, but out in the middle the current was slower, a thick, powerful flow pulling branches and broken sticks downstream. She had no thoughts; there was no past or future, only the demanding *now* of the body, and so she received with her body, slowly, in a rising swell, the full knowledge of her condition. The thing was inside her. She could no more resist it than those sticks in the water could resist being carried downstream. Dizzy, afraid she might fall, she lowered herself to the bank, sat on the muddy ground in her mother's dress. She sat for a long time, without tears, without thinking, her face buried in her hands, letting the truth enter: she carried a white child, a half white child, from that devil. *What am I going to do?*

No answer came. In another moment she got to her knees, palmed creekwater into her mouth, spit it back, again and again. The water tasted of earth, dank and darkly sweet, and she swallowed a little before she splashed her face with it. She stood and began to undo the buttons down the front of her dress; she took off the dress and knelt again in her thin chemise to wash it. With both hands she scrubbed the white cotton against a rock, rubbed without soap the spots of mud and vomit, taking big handfuls of skirt and rubbing one against the other, wringing the material out again and again, the dirty water raining down onto the bank. When she shook the dress out she saw that the material was no longer white but a light tannic color. But the soiled spots were gone. Gathering the sopping dress in her arms she climbed toward the path; she didn't turn onto it but kept on straight through the undergrowth, clutching her mother's dress tight in her hands. She made her way from the tangled creekbottom straight out to the open land.

The dress made a billowy tea-colored tent on the tops of the big bluestem when she spread it to dry, and she sat down beside it, the tall grasses coming up over her head, sheltering her, hiding her, and she sat so for a long time, trying to think. Once, she reached inside the scooped neck of her chemise, touched her changed breasts, felt the heat and the swollen tenderness, felt again the floating sense of fullness in her, as if the air were displaced each moment by the turning of her head. How could she not have known? *On account of T.J.*, she thought, *so much trouble.* And then, *Lord, help me. What am I going to do?* She had to get home to Greenwood, that was all. She had to go to Mama. Immediately the cold nausea swept her. Mama would take one look and she would know. Mama would see what that devil did, how he did it; she would suffer the scent and grunt and feel, she would know all of it, and Graceful could not bear to think of looking in her mother's eyes and seeing the knowledge there. *After*, she thought. *When it's gone. Then I'll go home.* She wouldn't let her mind say what she meant by the word *gone*.

Elberta was outside the tent, pacing up and down in the clearing. As soon as she saw Graceful she came running, breathless, saying, "Where you been, where you been? We been looking everywhere! T.J.'s about to have a fit! Hedgemon, he, Hedgemon—" And she stopped, out of breath, her excitement and fear choking off the words.

"What? Something happen to Hedgemon?"

"He come in over an hour ago! We been looking for you! They gone back to the creek, they both about to decide you was drownded but I knew you wasn't because you promised you'd tell him, oh, Graceful, you won't forget, will you? You ain't going to back out?"

"An hour?" She glanced at the sky. "What's Hedgemon doing back so early?"

"He come to tell you! Whiteman looking for you! Right in town, he say a whiteman come right to his office, aks for you by name!" And Berta's big eyes grew even bigger as T.J. and Hedgemon appeared from the brush, walking fast toward them. "Where you been?" T.J.'s fury was not cold and fretsome now, but hot, focused entirely on his sister.

"Nowhere. I washed my dress." Graceful's chin lifted. "I couldn't be sitting around here in my underdrawers while I'm waiting for it to dry."

T.J. strode past her toward the tent, where Mrs. Candler's face was framed in the V of the entrance; as T.J. got nearer, the woman shrank back, and in another instant the despairing face in the entryway disappeared. T.J. ducked inside, and Elberta followed him. Graceful didn't look at Hedgemon.

"What kind of whiteman?" she said.

"I don't know. Just a whiteman."

"What does he look like?" She stood with her back to him, facing the water. "What color hair?"

"I don't know. Just look like a whiteman. I don't remember what color hair. He had a hat on."

After a moment Graceful said, "Did he say what he want?"

"He just ask for you."

"Me personal?"

"You personal. Except he didn't say your last name, but it couldn't be nobody else, could it? Man was sitting at the telegraph office when I got back. Mr. Belcannon say, Gentleman in yonder want to see you. He'd asked for me by name. Both names. First and last. Mr. Belcannon told me that."

"He didn't say nothing about T.J.?"

"He only ask me if I know you. Or, no, he say"—Hedgemon twined his voice up into his nose—"'I understand you're acquainted with a young woman named Graceful. I understand you might possibly acquaint me with her whereabouts.'" Hedgemon mimicked whitefolks' talk perfectly, but Graceful was too sick to laugh. She walked away.

"Graceful, what is it? I thought all this time . . ."

But she was already across the clearing, standing in front of the tent, breathing deeply, the nausea rising as she faced the closed flaps. Hedgemon came up behind her. "You going to go?" he said.

"I got to ask T.J." She couldn't force herself to enter that dark interior.

"Man say he'll give me twenty dollars if I can tell him how to find you. Said he'll be at the Gusher Hotel, if I come tell him where you're at, he'll give me twenty dollars cash."

When Graceful shot him a glance, Hedgemon said quickly, "I don't aim to take it, that's not what I meant! I'm just telling you how bad he wants to find you!"

"T.J.!" she yelled. "Come out! I got to talk to you!"

Immediately T.J. ducked out of the doorway, the piece of blackjack in his hand, and here came the mothgirl fluttering after him. Graceful's heart ripped with how bad her brother was changed, his face thin as a flint, and murderous hard. *They're killing us,* she thought, *every way they can.*

"What do you want me to do?" she said.

"How come a whiteman looking for you?"

"I don't know, T.J. I don't even know who it is."

"You going to go see?"

"That's what I'm asking. Tell me what to do."

But her brother turned his gaunt face to the water, staring in silence, staring hard, as if he saw something there too terrible to allow him to speak; his face was grim, ashy, like an old man's face, but it was rigid with fury, stupefied with fear. Graceful couldn't bear it. "Say something!" she cried. "You been bossing my every living breath for weeks now! Tell me what to do!"

"I don't know!" he exploded. But the spell was broken, the vision, whatever it was he'd seen. "If you don't go," he said in a moment, staring at her, "they're liable to come out here looking for Hedgemon." T.J.'s gaze was steady on her. "If you go yonder, you fixing to tell them? You going to show it in your face?"

"I ain't going to tell nobody nothing."

He stared at her a minute longer. "You better go, then. Find out what it is. Maybe—maybe Mama sent word." But neither he nor any of them believed it. Graceful stood silent a moment. She looked around the campsite vaguely, but there was nothing to gather; she had no handbag, no apron. "Come on," she told Hedgemon. "You might's well get your twenty dollars." When he started to protest, she walked out of the clearing, calling back over her shoulder, "Take it, Hedgemon. Buy a nice angelcake, bring it back for supper."

She heard quick, light footsteps behind her, and she kept going, but the girl's fingers brushed her elbow, and the breathy voice pleaded behind her, "Graceful? Graceful, you won't forget?"

She turned to snap at the girl to go back. The pouchy lids of Berta's round eyes were swollen with crying; her whole face was swollen. "Shhhh," Graceful said. "Go on, now. Quit your worrying. I'll be back before dark."

"You going to tell him tonight?"

"Sure."

"You promise?"

Looking over the girl's shoulder, Graceful saw her brother's bent back disappearing into the tent. Her gaze returned to Berta's face. "I promise," she said.

They walked fast toward the hotel, and Hedgemon held her by the elbow and wouldn't let her step down in the mud; he guided her between the whitefolks crowding the plank walks so deftly that nobody could have accused them of being uppity. The town was even more swarming because it was just four o'clock and the refinery shifts were changing. With every step Graceful grew more sickened, more frightened, but Hedgemon Jackson negotiated the crowds as if he'd been doing it all his life. When they stood in front of the brick façade of the Gusher Hotel, he put both hands on Graceful's shoulders and deposited her by the front window, next to a reeking brown-spattered spittoon, saying, "Keep your face down, don't look up at anybody, if they ask you anything wag your head, don't look up and don't talk."

Graceful watched through the window as Hedgemon entered the lobby in his messenger-boy uniform and spoke deferentially to the man at the desk, ducking his head, one of his hands on his leather satchel as if he had a wire to deliver. *He sure learnt quick how to shuffle his feet in front of whitefolks,* she thought miserably, *considering he been working for Mr. Smitherman his whole life.*

The man at the desk nodded toward the lobby, and Hedgemon started toward the big leather chairs facing one another around a low polished table. Graceful saw him then, Mr. Dedmeyer, sitting in one of the chairs with his gray fedora propped on one crossed knee, a newspaper before him, held wide in both hands. Her heart bucked up, gagged her, as if it would be the very thing she'd finally vomit out from herself, and her pulse beat hard in her throat, deep in her chest. Every muscle in her legs tensed to run. But it was already too late. Mr. Dedmeyer was lowering the newspaper, raising his gaze to the window as if he felt her eyes on him; immediately he bounded from the chair and started toward the door. Graceful began to walk away very fast, but she didn't run, and when she heard him calling after her, she slowed down.

"Gracie! There you are! Graceful!"

Whitefolks in the street were staring at her. She stopped, turned around. Mr. Dedmeyer hurried toward her, and Hedgemon was behind him, both of them rushing up to her. Mr. Dedmeyer's face was burnt red from the sun, how whitefolks get, and he was beaming at her, happy to see her, obviously relieved. She couldn't understand this at all. She looked down at the roughcut planks below her feet. The sickness was rising. The world had gone crazy.

"Thank goodness! We've been hunting all over! I was about to give up."

She was so confounded she could only stare at her feet while Mr. Dedmeyer went on about he was sorry if they'd insulted her some way, he wouldn't for the world want to do that, he knew Mrs. Dedmeyer acted a little nervous sometimes, a little flighty, but really she'd never for the world want to offend Graceful, she appreciated Graceful, she really did; in fact, she'd be tickled to learn he'd finally tracked her down. *How?* Graceful looked up. *Do he know about T.J.?* But she could tell nothing from Mr. Dedmeyer's expression.

He paused to clear his throat, and when he went on, his voice was hesitant, almost secretive. "I know Mrs. Dedmeyer acts a little vexed sometimes. It's those sick headaches, they just torture her, but really, you know . . . uh . . . we . . . I was hoping . . ." He stood with his hat in his hands, his blond head cocked to the side; he seemed to look up at her from beneath his eyebrows like a shamed dog, and Graceful was so bewildered she dropped her gaze again. Everything was too unnatural, too strange to comprehend.

"You could take the early train in the morning. I'll leave a ticket for you at the window. I've got to go back this evening, but you can take the colored car tomorrow morning. You'll come?"

Slowly she realized what Mr. Dedmeyer was saying. "You want me to come back to work?"

"Yes. Didn't I say that? If it's about money, we could, I'm sure we could make a better arrangement, say . . . twenty-five a week?"

Graceful stared at him. Twenty-five dollars a week? Nobody paid their live-in servants that much money, not even the richest oil people. *Black-folks be lined up six deep every morning,* she thought, staring at him, *jumping to go to work in whitefolks' kitchens. Dedmeyers don't need my particular self to scrub their floors.* She tried to read in the man's face if this was a trick to get to T.J. But Mr. Dedmeyer's face was blank and open, though he did frown a little as he stood watching her. Graceful's mind swirled; she wanted to walk away, but there were white people everywhere, in the streets, all up and down the sidewalks.

"Mr. Dedmeyer, I can't come to work for y'all."

"But . . . but . . ." Then his eyes narrowed with suspicion. "I don't know what you're thinking," he said, although she could tell he believed he knew just exactly what she was thinking. "But twenty-five is my absolute top offer. That's as good a dollar as any Nigra servant's going to bring anywhere in Oklahoma. What's the matter with you?"

She hadn't even the will to be angry at that slithery word whitefolks used when they were too ignorant to recognize their own scorn. Graceful's mind was fully consumed by two facts warring within her: one, she knew she had to go back to work for whitefolks—she had to, because there was nowhere else to work, and she was not going to go home to Greenwood, not yet. The Dedmeyers wanted her. Mr. Dedmeyer was here looking for her, they would pay her, pay her good, and she would not have to stay in the dark tent with Hedgemon's eyes watching, T.J.'s eyes watching, while her belly got big. The other thing she knew was that as long as she lived and breathed she would never go back to the house where that man was. That devil whiteman brother.

"I can't stand here all night." Mr. Dedmeyer's voice was exasperated, a little frantic. "Are you coming or not? I need to know so I can tell Mrs. Dedmeyer. She's most . . . anxious to have you back."

"How many folks I got to be cooking for?"

"Why, two, of course." The man looked at her, puzzled at first, and then relieved. "Why, you thought— No, no, it's just the two of us. I'm surprised at you, Gracie. Trying to hold me up for more money, thinking you're going to have to do a little more work. At twenty-five a week you shouldn't care if it's two or two hundred. Now, come, tell me you'll take the train in the morning. I'll leave your fare at the station, all right?" His impatience was showing. "All right?"

Graceful nodded.

"First train out with a colored car. Go check at the station this evening to find out the time. You'll do that?"

Hedgemon stood behind him, a head taller, his face so serious.

"Yes?" Mr. Dedmeyer said.

"Yes." Her voice was barely audible, but Mr. Dedmeyer turned immediately and started back to the hotel. Graceful pulled her gaze away from Hedgemon, called out, "Mr. Dedmeyer!" The man paused, frowning as if his patience were at last stretched too thin. "Hedgemon brung me." Mr. Dedmeyer's frown deepened. But Graceful would not be swayed. She said, "Hedgemon's the one come got me. Like you wanted." Her face lifted, lips tight around her teeth. Without a word, Dedmeyer took a money clip from his pocket, released a folding bill from its clasp, held it out to Hedgemon, who looked to Graceful for direction. Her tone was harsh, exacting, when she answered in a voice that was like the changed voice of her mother: "Take it."

Money got such a power, even if a person don't have it but only think it, that invisible force going to change them, the way hunger do. But money power is not what I'm talking about. I'm speaking of the earth's own black blood, and that power don't come because oil turn into money. Listen. Oil got its own power. That power come from under the earth.

Bluford's mother told me. Way back when whitemens first come into this country with these pounding machines, boom, boom, boom, pounding holes in the world to go deep and open up a shaft for that power to get loose, she told me, You pray, daughter, pray plenty. A terrible time coming. These whitemens don't know what they doing. The earth's bleeding now, a terrible time is going to come. Bluford's mother passed over before the worst happen, but many a day she smoked us with cedar, prayed over us, me and Bluford and Cunsah and Joy. She told us, not for a warning to try and stop it, because you can't stop it once it let loose—I tell you, there are forces we can't even begin to dream—but Bluford's mother want us to prepare ourselves for what's coming, because she have the power to see.

You think I prepare myself like she ask me? Well, I tried. I did try. But somehow the Lord didn't give me the eyes to see then. Or maybe it's because I'm too much colored and not enough Indian, I don't know. But let me tell you, unless you been witness to it, you can't imagine what oil will do to people. You can't picture how a man will sell his soul to get timbers to make a hole because he believe he smell oil flowing under the earth. How it will turn a town mean as seven devils in a heartbeat. Yes. The very minute oil spouts up near a town, in that very instant that town's heart going to corrupt. Oil have the power to bloom a new Sodom overnight on the prairie, same place yesterday nothing but switchgrass stood. It'll turn a man so wicked he'll kill little children to get hold of their lease rights. I tell you, honey, God have made plenty mysteries under the sun, but the single biggest mystification I ever see is what I seen unleashed yonder from my own native dirt. But it took me too long to know what it was.

First time I gone down to the Deep Fork I stared right at it, but I couldn't see. I can tell you very well what put the mud on my eyes: nothing but old plain greed. Now, that's money-power mixed up with oil-power, Lord, Lord, it's a terrible force. It'll snatch you out quick as Satan, you never even feel it because you got a mind telling you lies right inside your own head. Them whitemens never did bring me my two hundred dollars, never brung me no paper to sign, so I took a notion they change their mind, and what I say to myself is, I'll just go down yonder to that allotment, see if I can't find out what make them to come around so interested one evening and then never darken my dooryard again. But what I really wanted, I want to see if I can find where that oil's at so I'll know where to show some other whiteman so *he* can bring me two hundred dollars.

I get Bluford's nephew Istidji to carry me down there. Istidji just a boy then but he's a good driver, and he come in the wagon, we start out from Iron Post way up in the morning. What I got on my mind, I'm going to look over every acre of that useless scrubland, see if I can't find me a medicine weep—that's what they used to call it. Indians used oil for all kind of medicine on account of its power, a lot of us did, and they known from a long time back about these places oil seep out the ground. I couldn't figure how I's going to be able to look over that whole allotment, but the way it turned out wasn't any need to worry over that, because before we reached halfway to the river we could hear it. Istidji's little horses like to had a fit, he couldn't hold them, finally had to get down and talk Indian to them, grab their faces and make them settle down. Sound like the most terrible popping, but loud and completely regular, like this: *Bang. Bang. Bang. Bang. Bang.* Like a heartbeat, like God's thunder heartbeat—or, no, not God's: it's something else, something else—making a hole in the world.

We drived down toward the water, and you talk about power—we seen power that day, yes, Lord! They have built this big wheel, like a

wagon wheel, only that wheel ten feet tall maybe, and it have a belt going around it, run around and around in this huge whipping circle like a
rolling snake, and I seen that! I seen it but I couldn't see. That belt turning so
fast you know if you get close it's going to snatch your arm off like snapping
a twig, and it is whipping around that wheel, running from the big wheel
over to a little wheel, and this wheel in a wheel is what's giving the power to
the big wooden machine, tall as a hickory tree, pounding a hole straight
down into the Lord's earth. But you think I know what it is I'm seeing?

Listen. Right there before me is these two signs: Big Snake show itself
in that belt looping, Ezekiel's prophecy show itself in the wheel in the
wheel. No, you wouldn't know anything 'bout the Big Snake. I ain't going
to talk about that. They don't like us to talk about it. But surely you know
God's Holy Word? You don't know that old verse? Where Ezekiel tell
God's children he seen a wheel in a wheel by the river Chebar? Ezekiel
seen the heavens open, God's terrible messenger come down, and he tell
us right then the spirit of the living creature is in that wheel in a wheel by
the river Chebar—but me and Istidji, we on the Deep Fork, and I ain't
looking for God's sign because I got my mind on two hundred dollars,
make me blind as a cob. Or, no, I do see, but all I recognize in it is plain
old whiteman's power, the same as these big steam engines on railroad
trains, same as motorcars and aeroplanes, whatever they want to make,
because whitefolks got a strain in them make them have to get hold of
natural power and hook it up short, bend it to their will. I don't believe
whitefolks is the only ones God made to be that way, but around here
they the only ones act like it. And these two whitemens here, they sure
enough got hold of some power, and they working it, yes Lord.

The redhair is one whiteman I never laid eyes on, but you can tell by
how hardknotted his arms is, how he jump and scramble, he's one of
these little rooster men works without pause from kin to can't, no matter
what. The lighthair one I don't know yet, I don't recognize him, he's in the
grip of that power, make him look changed, and he is working like crazy,
same as the redhair, dodging in and out around that stick beating a hole
in the earth, they both keeping out the way of that rocking arm on the
hickory tree and that belt whipping, them wheels turning, and even if it's
just two men working, they making as much stir as a beehive. Act like
they believe God's fixing to strike them dead if they stop or slow down,
they don't have time to talk to a old colored woman and a Indian boy in
a wagon—and I think maybeso they haven't seen us yet. That power scare

me, scare Istidji's horses, scare the boy himself, and we all know this is not a good place. But still yet I do not have the sense to tell the boy to turn his wagon around and carry us home.

The pounding stop. The two mens don't stop, only the pounding, and they go to clinking and clanking with big tools, and that's when I finally see who that lighthair one is. Mister Logan. The very one stand in my yard and tell me he's going to bring me two hundred dollars. But here is how oil got such a power: it make this whiteman's whole face to change. He don't look a bit like that man in my yard two weeks past. That man was fidgety maybe, but he talked polite. This man look like he'll snatch the veins out your throat with his teeth if you cross him. The redhair walk off for something, and Mister Logan take over beating that steel bar at the forge. Lord God, he beat it, beat it with that sledgehammer big as a stone.

He lift his head one time, he got the hammer raised up and he look right in my eyes, and believe it, he don't see me. Not that he don't re-member me—I mean, he don't see. You know how a earthworm got no eyes for anything but the very soil it crawl in and out of? This man's the same: he got eyes only for the earth, except his eyes are not for the earth-skin, how a farmer see, but for the blood and bones under it: he sees down to the rocks and water and that power in its deepest part. Because nature call to nature. Fire speak to fire, earth to earth, iron to iron. That's so. And oil been calling a long time to something in the spirit of this lighthair man Logan—but what I don't know is: oil taint me, too. There's never been no deep-earth nature in me, my nature is for the two crossovers, the coming-in and the going-out, but this is how I'm telling you the degree of oil's power. It's going to call out to a person and claim them, even if that one never had a nature for it before. Mister Logan put his head down and go back to pounding with the big hammer, but this been enough to make me get down from the wagon. You see how it work on me? That invisible, that fast. Same as money's power: the *idea* have power in your mind.

Here in a minute the redhair man come back carrying a long metal pole, and him and Mister Logan put the steel mouth back on, and here go the rocking arm, the wheel in a wheel, the whole force winding up again, starting, *bang, bang, bang, bang,* and in a bit the redhair notice me stand-ing by the wagon, he shout something to the lighthair, and Logan look up then, he see me now. First thing he do is swivel his head and look hard at the dark one yonder by the little wood shack.

Yes. That one. He been back there the whole time. You see how greed make me blind? I never seen him before that moment, nor yet did I know him, except to know he's the one talked Creek to me and asked me questions in my yard. He push off from the shack wall and slink over to talk to Logan and right away they having words. But the lighthair Logan, he's the bossman, and he's so busy arguing with the dark one that the little redhair rooster man can't keep up with the rocking arm, and pretty soon they all three shouting, but you can't hear what they saying because that machine going *Bang. Bang. Bang. Bang.* But I know they talking about me. I know.

Well, it is not long till the redhair walk back and turn off the engine, and everything grind down so quiet it is like you gone deaf. We all of us looking at each other, three whitemens and me and Istidji and his little horses and the two mules they got hobbled yonder by that shack. The dark one start toward us, but Mister Logan say something to him and he stop. Then Logan himself come over, and he is not saying ma'am nor anything like it, just stop maybe twenty footpaces in front of me, say, What do you want?

Two hundred dollars, I say. Lord, Lordy, them words just pop out my mouth.

Next month. Didn't he tell you next month?

Who tell me?

But he don't answer, he just turn and glare at the dark one again. Sure enough, now, that one is going to come over. My blood feel like it want to turn solid inside me, to watch him gliding toward the wagon, and still I don't know him. I smell the water in the river behind him, yonder where the trees mark its path, and it come to me right then to remember everything Bluford's mother told me about the Big Snake, how it will part the Deep Fork waters, rise up huge, and if you look at it, just look upon it once, it will capture you, carry you down, hold you forever like a soul thief. Maybe Istidji thinking about the Big Snake, too, because he whisper to me in Creek language, Let's go!, because Creeks and Seminoles, Euchees, all the Indians around here know about the Big Snake, they respect it, they won't mess with it, because it is a terrible force, but listen: this new force being unleashed from under the earth is way more powerful than that. I seen it. I witnessed it, I watch it come up and spew its power and rain down destruction. Not that day, later, but it have started that day, and I took my own part, Lord help me, I did.

One thing I know now, if we going to unleash it, we going to be the ones receive its sorrow. And we have done. We still receiving. You look at what happen since it get loose, look at Tulsa, look at the whole earth gone to war with itself, not once but twice, three times, we *all* warring each other, who set that to work? God? You think God do it? Or Satan? Or man? I'll answer you: none of them. That force do it. That power is what make humans capable to do it. How is the whole earth going to war itself without oil? God's the one create the power, yes, but He bury that force deep where we can't get to it. Don't that make you think we not supposed to get to it? God didn't open up them holes in the world and unleash that power for a hundred years. Man done that, and it is not Satan's power he unleash, though some will tell you so. It's not human evil, either, though it is surely enlarged by man's sin, nursed with sin till it get to be so powerful it want to tear the world asunder. The name of one sin that gorge that force like a baby: greed.

The dark one slink toward me, he don't stop twenty foot back like the lighthair, he got to come right up in my face, say, Next month. I told you next month already, what's the matter with you?

When you told me that?

You must be sick. You sick? He lean in so close to me I can feel his breath on me, but the breath got no smell. Oh, that make me shrink back. You losing your memory? he say.

I got my memory. My memory say this man here—I lift my chin at the lighthair. Stand in my yard and tell me he's going to bring me two hundred dollars next morning, that's the last I hear or see any of you peoples.

Mister Logan come close then, but he ain't studying me, he's mad at the dark one, and they take in to arguing. I go back and climb up in the wagon. Istidji getting more and more scared. He don't know what they're saying, he don't speak good English, but he knows we in the presence of danger, and he's looking at me, wanting me to tell him to turn the horses and go. Me, I'm scared too, but not scared enough. I speak good English. I know what they're saying. They trying to talk around it, but I know. Mister Logan say, I thought you said you fixed it, and the dark one say, I did, I'm telling you I did, can I help it if a old crazy niggerlady can't remember from one day to the next? And Logan say, Don't be lying to me, it's one thing I can't stand is a liar. And the dark one say, You ain't been lied to and you ain't going to be. And Logan say, What's she doing here, then? And the dark one say, I told you, she's crazy. And Logan say, Crazy, my foot, did you fix it or not? And the dark one turn and glare at me, say, I fixed it all right, but looks like I'm going to have to fix it again.

What I see is, they two have made a bargain together—not like they joined up to be partners, but more the way Judas and the Pharisees made their deal together. And I see another thing: these two don't neither one trust the other. They both thinking the other one fixing to cut him in the back any minute. And I see that this bargain is about me—or not me, but about that allotment I drawed for being the daughter of a freedwoman on the Muskogee Creek Indian rolls. You not going to believe what come out my mouth. I don't know where it come from unless the devil slip his fork-tongue in my mouth, because I jumps up and hollers, You whitemens, listen! Listen to me here! I am Iola Bloodgood Bullet Tiger, and this is my allotment! You hear me? This is my land! Y'all got no right upon it.

That sure quiet their mouths. They both turn eyes to me now, black eyes on the dark one, greenbrown eyes on the lighthair, a thousand thoughts flitting between them, and every one of those thoughts a danger, a murderous danger. I see it, but the greed devil got hold of me, and I just keep on. You got no right to be drilling holes here, I tells them, without you pay me my money. Two hundred down, two hundred when the oil come. You don't give me my two hundred dollars, I'm not going to sign that piece of paper you asking!

Oh, Mister Logan shoot eyes at the dark one when I say that.

I'm going right up to Bristow this evening, I hollers, tell the sheriff I got trespassers on my allotment cutting up my land with their oil-drilling machine!

Them two whitemens stand yonder and stare at me, and for that minute they're fearful, I can see it, and I feel the power, what it is to have hold over somebody. Oh, Lord. I ought to been praying like I never pray in my life, but I can't think to pray any more than I can think to get away from that place, let them keep what-all they aim to unleash from under the earth. I stay in the presence of that power while it get loose, get big enough, while it roll up and come catch me, make me to stand there in the wagon bold as anything, say, You whitemens hear me? I'm going up and get the Bristow sheriff to come run y'all off.

We hear you, the dark one whisper. But you hear us, old woman. If you got a lick of sense in that woolly head of yours, you ain't going to do that.

He start to walk toward the wagon, but Istidji slap up his little horses then, he ain't going to wait on me to tell him, and he drive that wagon out of that clearing, fast. I don't try to stop him, because my mind so full of greed. That power already own me. You don't think so? Look here:

I wake up next morning at Iron Post, and I forgets to pray. You understand? I *forget* the Lord.

I don't feed the dogs, don't do anything but sit on the porch thinking. Old Bone laying under my chair, I can hear his tail lift off the wood, come down again, thump. Afterwhile, thump. The other dogs scratching around in the yard, whining, they hungry, except that Tennie dog, I think she's gone off somewhere, but I ain't studying no yard dogs, I got my mind on what I'm fixing to do about this situation. You think I don't know better? Bluford's mother teach me. I ought to been smoking my house with cedar and sage and tobacco, I ought to prayed unceasing for the Holy Spirit to come breathe on me. No, sir, I'm going to sit on my porch without any sign of protection, sit there waiting, until that dark one come driving up in my yard. I'm not a bit surprised to see him. I known one of them would come.

He climb out that old car and come stand with a foot on my porch step. It's pretty late in the morning, the sun's already high. He got a piece of paper. Just a white piece of paper with writing on it. Ain't it strange how much power whitemens put in a piece of paper? Someplace there's a paper say that worthless swatch of Deep Fork bottom belong to me, another piece somewhere say all this land in Oklahoma belongs to Indian people as long as the waters run. Just depends on which piece of paper you paying attention to—or which piece they intend you to pay attention to: which one they want you to sign. Who give power to that white piece of paper? Nobody but the whitemens themselves. But this dark one act different than yesterday by the river. Look different, too, he duck his head, talk nice, talk polite. He say, I believe we had us a little misunderstanding yesterday. I come to fix it with you.

I wait on him. I hear Tennie now, growling; she's right here under the porch.

He smile up real big at me, say, I come to settle.

You got my two hundred dollars? I ask him.

That's what I come to tell you. We had to use that for drilling equipment, but soon as my brother-in-law gets back from Tulsa, we'll bring you your money.

He make a move like he's fixing to come up the steps, and I can hear thumping and scrambling then, Tennie wiggle out from under the porch, growling like she mean business, and the dark one stop. Smile up at me so polite, say, You can call your dog off. I'm just looking to conduct a little friendly business.

I ain't signing nothing, I say, till I get my money. Take me for a fool if you want to, I got better sense than that.

Everything on his face change then. He can't hide it, no matter how much he smile and duck his head. He start in talking low, say, If you're not a fool or crazy, maybe you remember what happened to Mary Big Pond and her family.

I don't answer.

What was it happened to Moses Wolf? he say. You remember Ada Harjo and them six children?

Of course I remember. We all hear about it, same as we hear about a lynching, every time they put dynamite under somebody's house and blow it to smidgins. That's one of they favorite tricks. Ada Harjo was the worst, every one of her little childrens was killed. Most times they'll give a warning, because they don't so much want to kill somebody as threaten them, make a freedman or a Indian sign that white piece of paper. A lot of times they'll get somebody drunk, get the mark that way. Some other time they just kill us, sign the lease paper theyself. But listen, I know all this, and I look at the dark whiteman, and I am not afraid. Greed got no fear but fear of losing what it crave. I look at the dark one, stare straight at him, say, I'm not Ada Harjo. I'm Iola Bloodgood Bullet Tiger.

You can see what pass over him: he just mad at first, for me to sass him, that's how he think, I got a big gall to sass him. Then he get madder, because he see I'm not fixing to lay down and do what he tell me. Whatever he have writ up on that paper for me to sign is going to have to wait a little longer. Then I see a flick of fear pass over, because he see something in me. What it is I can't tell you, but it's inside me, he's not just mad now for how I cross him. I'm still sitting in my chair. I never did stand up. Tennie growling steady now behind him, she's getting louder and louder, got her lips pulled back, showing her teeth.

The dark one step down off the step, slow and easy, start easing himself backwards across the yard. I'll be back in the morning, he whisper. We'll talk.

PART FOUR

Oil

Tulsa
Saturday
October 30, 1920

T he orchestra began to play at seven-thirty, long before the invita-
tional hour etched in gold baroque letters on silver paper and sent
a month earlier by Nona Murphy to all the best homes in Tulsa. It was
L.O. himself, rushing through the ballroom in white tie and tails as he attended to several last-minute calamities, who motioned the maestro to the
edge of the stage, shouting, "Good Lord, man, I didn't bring y'all down
from Kansas City to sit around and drink coffee! Play something, for
chrissake!" before he hurried off to his quarters to don a magnificent
floorlength Sioux headdress for the party. The seventy-five borrowed Negro servants finished their preparations to the sounds of "Hungarian Fan-
tasie" and "I'll Build a World in the Heart of a Rose." Relieved of the
gentleman's bullying direction, many of them allowed themselves to nod
and move in time to the orchestra's rhythms, although the nine regular
mansion employees didn't so much as pause to tap a foot as they rushed
about trying to get everything done.

When L.O. came back downstairs at half past eight, the first thing he
did was to fling open the solarium doors and dash through the salon into
the great chandeliered ballroom, tux tails and eagle feathers flying, shouting, "Crank it up, boys, I want 'em to hear you clean up to Skiatook!"
Again and again he exhorted the bandleader to crank it up, so that by the
time the earliest guests began to arrive the piercing tones of clarinet and

trumpet could be heard a mile away above the continuous rumble of automobile engines. Each time the twin carved oak doors with their twin brass lion's-head knockers opened to receive a new party of masqueraders, the sweetish strains of harp and violin, undergirded by tympani, swelled out of the Murphy mansion and drifted along the five-acre lawn of imported Kentucky bluegrass sod, to float west into the darkness over the Arkansas River.

It had been the talk of the town for a month, this upcoming masquerade ball at the Murphy mansion, and it wasn't only Tulsa oil society that had made moves to wrangle an invitation: the famous baron of Ponca City, E.W. Marland, had made certain he was on the list, as had the relatively unsociable Mr. and Mrs. Frank Phillips from the little city of Bartlesville, fifty miles north. But of the several city-states oil had spawned in eastern Oklahoma, none was more self-created, self-defined, self-obsessed than Tulsa—the Magic City, it called itself—and the Murphy masquerade was the premier event of the Tulsa season. Everyone who was anyone, and many nobodies, had donned elegant costumes and headed out in their Pierce-Arrows and Rolls-Royces to make an appearance at the newest and grandest (if perhaps not the most tasteful) mansion on Black Gold Row.

For a state as young as this one—hardly thirteen years old in 1920—Oklahoma had an extraordinarily mythic sense of its own character, and its many exotic selves could be recognized each time the liveried doormen swung wide the oaken doors. In pairs and little clutches, and sometimes singly, the mix of aviators and ballerinas, rodeo stars and bandit queens, pioneers, divas, dance-hall girls, baseball players, an inordinate number of outlaws, and too many cowboys and Indians to count entered bowing and gasping, laughing, depositing their mink wraps and silk capes in the arms of the several Negro servants who stood at attention in the front hall.

By ten o'clock the ballroom was aswirl with caped men and masked women, and the crowd was forced to spill from the terrazzo dance floor onto the open terrace at the rear of the ballroom, into the salon to the north, the formal dining room to the south, the large entry hall facing west. It would have taken a discerning eye to pick out from the crowd the lone Southern belle in the pink ballgown standing in the salon archway, gazing intently from behind her silver mask at the front doors. She stood as close to the marble wall as the wire hoops beneath her skirt would allow, an open fan before her lips, her beautifully coifed head slightly bowed. Each time the doors opened, her face would lift and she'd watch L.O. dash forward to kiss a can-can girl or slap a lawman on the back, his bulky head dwarfed by the huge war bonnet of black-tipped white eagle feathers that swept from his brow all the way to the tiled floor. When at last she'd discovered the identities of the newly arriving masqueraders— or at least determined to her satisfaction who they were not—her head would again bow, up would come the silk fan, and the belle would retreat from the swirling crowd once more. It's likely that none but her closest intimates would have recognized her, for Althea Dedmeyer was very changed. She stood motionless in the archway, and from a distance it appeared to be diffidence that bowed the dark head, modesty that lifted the silk fan. If one were to draw nearer, though, look closely, pierce the shadows behind the silver mask, one would discover a glazed stare not so much of fear but of a woman who, beyond all reasonableness and expectation, found herself trapped.

Shrinking from the press of revelers, Althea turned her caged stare to the many Negro servants passing busily through the ballroom, or allowed it to wander past the sea of masked faces on the dance floor, through the open French doors, to the terrace, where her husband stood outside smoking with several other men in the torchlight. She could just see the puffy silk edge of his white sleeve. But, no, it was not Franklin she hunted. Her gaze wandered toward the front hall just as Josh Cosden entered with his new wife. Cosden was the man who'd clinched Tulsa's place as oil capital when he'd moved his refineries down from Bigheart, but this wasn't the only reason Tulsa called him the Prince of Petroleum: he was an extraordinarily fetching man, blond, debonair, movie-star handsome. Tonight he was costumed as a flamenco dancer. Althea watched him sweep into the ballroom with his hand on the bare arm of his new wife. The wife, too, was dressed as a Spanish dancer, a black lace mantilla crowning her head, a red rose in one hand, and in the other a small jeweled mask on a stick, which now and again she held up to her face. Althea stepped back to the wall as they passed. The hooped skirt belled out in front of her in a ridiculous manner, and she had to step away again. She opened her painted silk fan in front of her lips, forced her gaze past the Cosdens to the foyer, where the wildcatter Tom Slick suddenly rushed in looking as tousled as a roustabout in the field; he hadn't a sign of a costume about him. Behind Slick sauntered a thickset pair in matching Harlequin outfits, and then another couple, their heads poised beneath tremendously large white powdered wigs, their faces hidden behind gold-trimmed masks, he in a tailed waistcoat, she in a wide, magnificently hooped skirt. Althea turned away. Near the dining-room doorway a man in blackface suddenly dropped to one knee, strummed his banjo, and burst into song, and the little party in front of him laughed and applauded.

"You'll never guess who that is." Althea, startled, turned to find Nona Murphy in a fringed white buckskin dress and feathered headdress smiling up at her. Nona was barefoot—a shocking, bold stroke—and thus half a head shorter than Althea. She wore no mask. Her ordinarily pale skin was stained a deep copper color; her green eyes were lined in kohl. Two perfectly drawn brows arched teasingly beneath the intricately beaded headband. "So? Who do you guess?"

Althea glanced across the floor at the plinking minstrel, but Nona laughed, "No, silly!" She flitted her smile over the crowded ballroom, allowed it to settle on the couple laboring toward the dance floor beneath the huge powdered wigs. "That's none other than E. W. Marland and his adopted *daughter,* who is also, by the way, his wife's niece, but *his* constant companion. The girl never leaves his side, but the wife, eh? Where is she?" The sly face tilted up at Althea.

"I wouldn't know," Althea murmured, though she was hardly aware of what she was saying; she passed her eyes over the crowd in search of a different face: the brown, closed mask that revealed nothing.

"I declare." Nona clicked her tongue. "Tom and Belle Gilcrease look like they're having a nasty fight. Is she supposed to be Carrie Nation, you reckon? Oh. No. Silly me. She's trying to be a suffragette. In honor of the vote Tuesday. That'll be something, won't it? Voting for a president? Of course, L.O. said he'd spank me if I tried to register, but"—her voice dropped to a whisper—"what L.O. don't know could fill a liberry. Oh, but, now, who's that bank robber coming in?"

Althea blinked, tried to concentrate. She couldn't see who Nona was talking about, only the polyglot mix of disguises, some masked, some not, several who could hardly be considered to be in costume at all. It occurred to her that Nona had intentionally led some to dress one way, some another, for the perverse satisfactions of her own twisted mind.

"Oh, look." Nona grasped Althea's arm. "Yonder's Chief Bacon Rind." The Indian man entering did not pause beside the liveried servants in the foyer but passed immediately through the arch into the ballroom: erect, heavyset, dignified to the point of austerity, he wore a suitcoat and a beaded amulet, gold looped earrings, a headdress not of feathers but of some kind of sleek fur shaped like a brimless top-hat perched on the crown of his head; he was followed by a short, roundfaced woman in a blanket. "That Indian's rich as Croesus," Nona whispered. "He's got a Pierce-Arrow for every day of the week and two for Sunday. L.O. had to invite him. Oh, watch this, watch this!" And she pulled Althea's arm in excitement as L.O. strode toward the Osage man with both hands outstretched, the feathered war bonnet sweeping behind him like duckwings, and his big voice booming, "There you are, Chief! Welcome. Welcome!"

The image of the white man masquerading as Indian rushing up to the Indian dressed as Indian—who wasn't in costume but, like the wildcatter Tom Slick, simply dressed as himself—was so odd that Althea opened her mouth to say something. But Nona was already gliding away from her, tripping delicately on her bare feet across the room to join her husband. The fringed skirt hardly covered her calves, and her legs, too, had been stained chestnut. She was not wearing stockings. Althea watched them, the whitebuckskinned white hosts chatting with the two Osages, who even still did not seem very Indian to Althea, because to her Indian meant poor, meant dirty, meant two blackhaired blackeyed children holding out crusted hands at the back door, chanting, "Meat. Bread. Meat. Bread." The recollection made her dizzy, made her afraid she might swoon. She stepped out into the center of the ballroom, rushed toward the terrace, the hoopskirt belling and swaying awkwardly, her callused feet spooned into tiny lace-up shoes.

She stopped just inside the French doors, put a hand down to still the bobbing skirt, held herself near the wall as she tried to catch her husband's eye. Franklin stood in the center of a dozen or so men, all of them hatless and coatless in the crisp air, their fingers clutching fat cigars, their shotglasses in the torchlight glowing with bootleg bourbon. Franklin was holding forth loudly, good-naturedly, and the others were listening. His silk shirt was open at the throat, a black one-eyed mask pushed up and riding his forehead. Franklin said something, and the others laughed, and Franklin laughed loudest of all. Althea longed to step out into that cold torchlit darkness, but the terrace was a gentlemen's domain, a woman could not simply walk out there. She turned toward the ballroom as if that had been her intention all along—to view the masquerade from this vantage point—and it was then, finally, that she saw Graceful, in a black maid's uniform and white apron, carrying a tray of hors d'oeuvres across the room. The sight of Graceful's face instantly calmed her. She had an impulse to move toward her, though she didn't give in to it but merely folded her fan and slipped it into a secret pocket of her dress. Graceful had been here since yesterday, as had the majority of the best servants from the best homes in Tulsa, installed at Nona's clever behest inside the immense buffbrick mansion to prepare for the Murphys' party. Althea watched the solid black-and-white form moving through the costumed dancers: the brown face backtilted, more perfectly concealing than any of the gilded masks on the white people in the room. The girl's visage was hard, and yet Althea thought her features seemed somehow softened. How was it possible that Graceful's face was at once softer and harder? Had it been like that when she came back from Bigheart? Althea couldn't remember. An image began to push in on her—the girl standing on the porch in a cotton shift, turning the crank of the Eden washing machine— and then another picture, not of Graceful but of herself—sitting up in the bed in the gray light of early morning, the sheet pulled over her knees as she stared with swollen eyes at her own image in the mahogany mirror. The long-submerged source trembled close to the surface. She turned blindly and started toward the hallway that led to the powder room.

"Ah, here you are, my darling!" Franklin's big paw came around her waist and stopped her; she could feel his warmth through the boned corset. He bent to deposit a kiss on her forehead. "You look so beautiful," he nearly shouted, though his words were barely distinguishable above the orchestra. For an instant she leaned against him.

"Dance with me," she said. Her voice was flat, loud. Her voice had nothing to do with the pleading inside her: the words sounded like a command.

But Franklin was flushed with bourbon and the heady rush of his own happy secrets. He grinned down at his wife, his forehead tilted. "And why wouldn't I want to dance with the most beautiful woman in the room?" he shouted. "Madame?" He bowed at the waist, took his wife's hand, and escorted her to the dance floor.

Althea allowed her arms, ribcage, cinched waist to go limp as he led her in a waltz; she followed her husband's feet as if bound to them, glad for the music and the motion as Franklin whirled her around the floor. For a time her thoughts were hushed; her mind filled only with the music's three-four rhythm, the swirling crescendo of harp and violin, the sweeping movements of her own body. But then the orchestra swung into a fox-trot, the clarinets chortling, the snare drum rattling a complicated tempo, and Althea tried to perform the alternating gaits in her tiny lace-up shoes, but her mind was distracted, she couldn't rely on her body's memory, and she suddenly dropped her hand from her husband's shoulder, turned and walked off the floor.

"Thea! What's the matter? Darling—" Franklin trailed after her, but Althea hurried across the ballroom, weaving through the crush of quick-stepping guests; she made her way swiftly into the formal dining room, which served now as libation room for the boldly flowing illegal liquor, where dozens of men stood about talking business in deep-pitched, urgent clutches of threes and fours as they sipped champagne punch from crystal goblets. At one end of the room an elderly Negro stood at attention behind the long table, where a gold-rimmed crystal punchbowl sat squarely on a French-lace tablecloth.

The room shut silent the instant she entered. Althea ignored the men who glanced up as she passed, and the men in turn, seeing the husband rushing along behind the woman, quickly looked away. The room began to thicken again with the low rumbling of male voices. Althea made her way to the table, the great bell of her skirt bumping against masculine knees; she barked at the servant, "Two, please." No tremor of expression flickered over the dark face. The old man ladled champagne punch into two gold-rimmed goblets, handed them to her as if it were the most common thing in the world for a lady to demand liquor. Althea turned to Franklin rushing up behind her, stared at him as she held out one of the goblets, put her lips to the rim of the other, and drank. "We're celebrating, aren't we?" she said quickly, as Franklin started to speak. "One ought to have champagne to celebrate, I thought. Don't you think?"

"Are you all right?" He tilted his head toward her, frowning, and she suppressed the impulse to click her tongue, turn away. Her face felt brittle, but she smiled at him.

"I'm fine. Why wouldn't I be fine? It's a party, after all. Besides, this masquerade is nothing." She swept her hand airily over the crowded room, and in the same glance and gesture indicated the glittering ballroom beyond the arch. "Nothing! It's a little pale tea party compared to the ball we're going to give when the Tiger well comes in!" She took another sip from the goblet. "Nothing!" she said again. Her voice was faint, a bare whisper, but she smiled ravishingly at her husband. As she turned to have the glass refilled she caught sight of her own image in the mirror above the mantel: it was not the horror from her upstairs bedroom that gazed back at her, but an exquisite silver-masked creature in a diaphanous pink ballgown, surrounded by sleek anonymous masculine faces.

Whether it was the effect of that image or only the rapid soothing of the champagne, Althea felt herself suffused with warmth, her limbs relaxing with a slow, delicious ease, her thoughts focused and calm. She returned her smile to her husband, but Franklin had already turned his attention to the many magnates in the room. She watched him sip his drink as he eyed the other oilmen. He'd lost weight in the past month camped out on the Deep Fork; he was less fleshy than he'd been in years, less soft-looking, and for an instant she admired the rakish tilt of his head, the newly revealed line in the thrust of his jaw. Franklin's lean face, his tanned skin, the unruly golden hair springing out around the black line of the silk eyepatch riding his forehead all made it seem that this was not the man she'd lived with for nearly sixteen years, but a new man, mysterious, hard-edged, perhaps even a little dangerous.

"I'm damned," he said.

"What?"

"That's Harry Sinclair right there, talking to Bill Skelly. That's him. Damn."

She followed his gaze to the two tuxedoed men standing near the mantel, and it took her an instant to realize that the two stood out precisely because they were not in costume. Casting about the room, she saw that several of the men were in black tie and tails.

"You believe it? Here comes J. Paul." Franklin nodded at a hawk-nosed man coming through the door in a white silk tuxedo. "Son of a gun lives in London, don't tell me he's come back to Tulsa for L.O.'s stinking party. I don't think so. Something's up." He pulled the one-eyed mask off, tucked it in his waist sash. He drank deeply of the champagne punch and murmured something else, but Althea, sipping her own drink, did not listen. Her inner eye turned to imagining the party they'd give a year from now, the mansion she'd have Franklin build. She tipped her head, gazed up at the vaulted, frescoed ceiling, inlaid with platinum and gold, the magnificent Waterford chandelier pendulous in the center. She skimmed her eyes over the displays of Italian art on the walls—beatific blond angels; pale, big-bosomed women lying prone in filmy gowns within fantastically ornate frames—trying to imagine for herself and her future mansion a new style, a singular identity, when the Tiger well should come in. But Althea had passed a threshold. She couldn't call up an imagined future, couldn't see anything with her mind's eye; she saw only the very real crush of masqueraders around her, the Sheffield silver-plated sconces on the oak-paneled walls, the gilt mirrors, the dozens of fainting half-clad women reclining in rococo frames. Her dreams failed. Perspiration slicked the buckram on the mask against her face. She felt closed in, claustrophobic. Abruptly she turned to have her goblet refilled just as Graceful came through the service doorway.

The girl's shoulders were slightly bowed under the weight of the tremendous silver tray she carried, filled with dozens of the heavy crystal goblets. Althea, standing by the table with the empty chalice held out in midair, felt her hand lift slightly when the old Negro took the goblet away. She stared at Graceful from behind her mask, a secret, attentive, trapped stare, while the girl thunked the goblets one at a time onto the table, slowly, methodically, as if it were the most significant task in the world and she had the rest of her life in which to do it.

An image came to Althea suddenly, not in mirrored reflection or daydream but in clear recollection: a vision of herself sobbing, shrieking, prostrate across the desk in the newspaper office in Greenwood. Other images followed unbidden, inescapable, one tumbling upon another: the big pressman, buttoned tightly into a too-small chauffeur's uniform, steering the Maxwell through downtown Tulsa in silence in the late afternoon, his thick profile sullen, furious, and she'd known he was furious, could feel it like spitting rain from her position in the back seat, and he would not help her into the house but sat in the car staring straight ahead like a man who did not understand English when she'd begged him, begged him, to carry her up onto the porch; he wouldn't answer, would not speak, but stared at the windscreen, mute and angry, as the two light-skinned Negroes had been angry when she'd demanded they take her home, and how dared they? How dared they be angry? In her mind's eye she saw the two men on the street in front of the yellow shotgun house, in front of Graceful's house, their faces like the faces of gentlemen, their expressions hateful and closed.

"Another!" she barked at the champagne server. Shame flared into anger, for there was no other escape, and she shook her outstretched hand impatiently, frowned at the old man. Graceful stood four feet away, working steadily as if she did not recognize her mistress. The thick curve of the girl's mouth pressed tightly over her teeth as she picked up the used goblets, stacked them on the tray. Althea was struck once again by the impression that Graceful's face was suffused with tenderness, a kind of softness, beneath the hard, sculpted lines. "I'll have to come back for them others," the girl said. 'Want me to bring anything else up from downstairs?" A secret communication seemed to pass between them, some unspoken knowledge that Althea would never be privy to, and her fury rose higher, and she longed to say something, to give an order, but she couldn't speak. Graceful turned in her slow, placid manner and left the room, thickset, solid, her breasts swelling against the white starched cotton apron, her face still as stone.

"Getty's here after something," Franklin whispered against Althea's ear. "Bound to be. There's a new field opening—a mighty big one's my guess."

Althea caught sight of Nona Murphy slipping across the room toward them. At once her fury whipped away from Graceful, snapped onto the gliding Nona; she suddenly understood how it was that Nona seemed to materialize at her elbow when Althea least anticipated her: she was intentionally trying to sneak up on her. But then Nona paused beside a group of men, lifted her banded head as she said something to make them all chuckle, her figure slender, delicate, vaguely brazen in the soft buckskin. She never glanced in Althea's direction, and yet Althea felt her attention. An impulse slid over her to hide herself behind a statue, behind one of the giant fronds, or out on the terrace in the dark. She watched Nona tip her face at each of the gentlemen, trill her laugh. "Y'all are so *bad!*" Nona wagged a finger side to side, and the men laughed, and Nona laughed again as she sauntered away from them, aiming directly for Althea and Franklin near the punch table. Althea gripped the crystal stem of the goblet, pulled a brittle smile to her lips.

"Althea Dedmeyer, aren't you a caution? Go and dress up like the ladiest lady, come in heah and drink this naughty champagne! I declare!" Nona leaned toward Franklin, the honey in her drawl thick as mead. "Your wife is so *bad!*"

"Looks like we're all bad!" Franklin said. "If the law gets a good whiff of this party we might all be spending the night in jail."

"I wouldn't worry about *that*, sir. Sheriff's right out yonder on the terrace, imbibing some good bonded bourbon right alongside L.O. and a bunch of others, including none other than Josh Cosden himself! They're all waiting on you to come back. I heard L.O. say those very words: 'Where's Franklin Dedmeyer, where's our new Baron of Deep Fork!'" She blinked her kohl-rimmed eyes and dimpled a sweet smile up at him. Franklin tipped his head toward her.

"The dull conversation of those oilmen, Miss Murphy, tempts me from present company about as much as an invitation to dine on a mess of swamp rabbit could tempt me away from a feast of pheasant under glass."

"Don't be an ass," Althea muttered. She retrieved her silk fan from her pocket, whipped it furiously in front of her face. *What does she want?* She waited for Nona's little asides and glances, the insinuating smiles and drawled-out inanities to declare her purpose. But Nona went on simpering at Franklin, flattering him even as she mentioned the name of every tycoon at the party. Not that Althea had ever understood what Nona wanted: even after she'd figured out the surface motive, what it was Nona was most immediately after, she still never quite felt that she knew the reason behind it, what Nona *wanted*. It was as if Nona's mind, her hungers, were hidden behind a sealed wall, beyond Althea's powers to comprehend.

Nona suddenly purred up at Franklin, "Guess who just came through the front door!" She swept her wide green gaze to include Althea. "None other than that handsome partner of yours!"

Althea stepped toward the ballroom, but instantly stopped herself. Nona's eyes were riveted on her.

"I know I'm not a bit mistaken, because that scamp don't have a sign of a costume on!" She shook her feathered headdress, pouted up at Franklin. "Some folks, I don't care what you say to 'em, they're gonna dress just any old how. You'd about like to not even invite 'em, except. . . ." Her face was still tipped toward Franklin, but now her gaze was on the tuxedoed oilmen, Skelly, Getty, Sinclair, gathered in an elegant black-and-white triad near the mantel; she went on in a seductive whisper: "Some of the biggest fish got the toughest mouths." She cut her eyes at Althea. "Isn't that right, Thea?"

Althea saw instantly that her notion had been right: Nona had tricked the partygoers so that the wealthiest, the absolute oil elite, for the most part, were not in costume—and yet the pattern was unclear. Wasn't Josh Cosden in costume? And Waite Phillips and Tom Gilcrease, and the famous Marland, who'd just opened the Burbank field? No oil gambler was more successful than these. Nona's reasoning was indecipherable, just as it had been that afternoon in the rose garden when she'd come to borrow Graceful. Althea had only finally understood what she'd wanted some three weeks later, when Nona again came sauntering up the walk in a sequined silk afternoon dress to beguile that commitment from her, as she'd gone around "borrowing" all the decent houseservants from all the best families in Tulsa—and why? There was unfathomable purpose working in that feral mind of hers, Althea sensed it, just as in the rose garden she'd known by how her eyes darted everywhere that there was one other thing Nona wanted.

"I'll tell you what, though." Nona straightened, toyed with a bit of fringed buckskin dangling from her sleeve. "Your Mr. Logan's got somebody with him dressed up to beat anything I ever saw. You ought to see people turn and stare."

Althea glanced through the doorway. She couldn't see Jim Dee anywhere.

"I guess whoever it is might just walk away with that little prize L.O.'s gonna give out at midnight. That's what *I* think. If somebody don't have a fit and faint. That whole ballroom went dead quiet the minute they walked in. I mean, they shut that room like a *door*! Only I guess y'all couldn't tell it"—she smiled sweetly at Althea—"on account of all the noisy men in here!" She trilled her little laugh. Franklin was already halfway across the floor, making his way toward the ballroom.

"Franklin!" Althea called out to him. He stopped instantly, turned, and hurried back with his elbow extended. He dipped his head in a little cursory bow. "Ladies?" he said, and held his other arm to Nona. "Shall we?" Althea took her husband's arm in a kind of stupor, a muted dream, and she walked with him, Franklin's big thighs bumping her hoopskirt, making it sway and bounce, while Nona squeezed up close against his other side.

"Franklin Dedmeyer, you are the long-leggedest thing!" Nona laughed. "I'm gonna have to stand on my tiptoes and *run* to keep up with you!" Franklin slowed his rush, gathered a new and avuncular dignity as they passed into the ballroom.

The orchestra continued to play and a few people were dancing, but the center of the great hall was empty, the masqueraders pressed back near the walls, as a low, excited buzz hummed just at the level of hearing. Althea tried to understand the sound's meaning, but it was as unintelligible to her ears as the rhythmic whine of cicadas in summer, a lyric, undulating *whyyyyyyy*. She saw Jim Dee standing just inside the entrance talking with L.O. Murphy. He was wearing work khakis and a knotted red kerchief, his tawny head bare; he looked as rough and unkempt as Tom Slick, and Althea's heartbeat quickened at sight of him, but she had only an instant to notice him, because the creature beside him, the cause for all the stir and buzz in the ballroom, drew her eyes immediately, as it drew to itself all attention in the room. Looselimbed, scarecrowish, it slouched near the wall as if it did not intend to insert itself too deeply into the gathering, or as if it could not stand on its own. Its head was cocked sideways, hands tied behind its back, a thick flaxen rope around its neck. But what made the thing so hideous was not the sheer vulgarity of portraying a lynched man, or the purple tongue swelling from the thick lips, but the fact that the creature had painted its face, had drawn a line down the center from scalp to throat and smeared one half white as alabaster, the other half black as soot.

The buzzing sound in the room rose louder, and at once hushed again, like wind dying, as Chief Bacon Rind appeared from somewhere, walked past the bizarre tableau without looking, without speaking to L.O., and continued on to the entrance hall with the short woman in the blanket behind him. They had no wraps to retrieve and so walked straight through the carved doors left standing open and out into the cool October night. But then, as other guests—a few couples, a foursome—began to edge forward with downcast eyes to make their awkward excuses, their too-early farewells to their host, the situation gradually came clear: the servants had all disappeared. There was no one to retrieve the guests' wraps from the cloakroom. No one to serve up more illicit champagne or bootleg whiskey to distract the guests from the room's sudden chill. No Negroes passed through the ballroom balancing canapé-laden trays; no colored servants stood behind the linen-covered tables, no brown hands carved thick slabs from the haunches of barbecued buffalo and beef.

The realization seemed to pass in a wave from the front hall, through the ballroom, all the way to the dance floor near the terrace at the back. There was confusion, indignation, a few titters of scandalized amusement. The orchestra ceased to play. Althea had the sense that the room's legs had been knocked from underneath it, and it had gone down—whump—on its back, the wind knocked out of its chest. She glanced over at Nona, who stood on the other side of Franklin with her wide eyes flicking this way and that, as if she'd never seen such an appalling turn of events. Althea might not know the secrets that drove Nona Murphy, but she recognized the lie in the bronzed face: Nona wasn't appalled. She was not even surprised. She was, more than anything, tickled at the shock to Tulsa society. Nona suddenly detached herself from Franklin's side and started across the room, the down of the white feathers in her headdress waving airily, fanning the currents like cottonwood silk, as she glided over the empty floor in her supple buckskin, her feet buttersoft, silent on the marble in the near-silent hall. Her laugh trilled, echoed toward the vaulted ceiling, as she took the apparition by the bound arm, said in her drawl, "Law, child, you liked to scared all the niggers to death, comin in here lookin like that. They're gonna think we're gettin ready for another little Tulsa necktie party, you scamp!" The lynched man didn't lift his head from his shoulder, didn't blink or flinch, or seem even to breathe.

Now Franklin stepped away from Althea and strode across the room as the murmurs began to rise again, the low whispers and grumbles, for this was a subject unfit for the season's premier *bal masqué*. This was appalling, unheard of, intolerable; it could not be borne. Nobody looked at the lynched man. One could have almost thought the thing was invisible, an apparition that only one's own eyes could see—except for the fact that the room's gaze was trained very studiously away from the halfwhite/half-black corpse. Althea watched her husband join his partner, the two of them dipping their fair heads toward each other in a kind of swanlike gesture as they met. Instantly she swept her gaze to the ballroom, searching for the brown face that had become somehow the only sight that could ground her. But there were only two dark visages in the room: the costumed minstrel, whoever he was—a white man in blackface standing in front of a huge sepia-toned tapestry of a foxhunt—and the half of the lynched man's face that was folded down toward its shoulder. As she watched, the monstrosity raised its head, stared directly at her. The creature's eyes were open, unblinking, locked on hers across the vast swirling distance; both halves of the split complexion were squared in alignment, and Althea at last recognized her brother. The abyss opened in front of her.

She closed her eyes, willed everything away. Everything. This moment, that miscreated freak across the room. Jim Dee. Franklin. The loathsome Nona. Tulsa. The past. All. All. But when she opened her eyes, Franklin was listening as Jim Dee talked in hushed urgency. L.O. Murphy stood off to the side, an unlit cigar in his mouth, the war bonnet cocked at an absurd angle, a baffled, angry expression on his face. Nona's little hand was wrapped around the sleeve of the lynched man, while she simpered up at him. The world was here, in all its grotesquerie, without escape—though Althea longed for it, yes, not merely to run away, but to disappear. Vanish. *I want to die,* she thought calmly. And then, *No!* No. She did not want to die. She wanted . . . something. She gazed across the room, slowly lifted a hand to her forehead, touched a stiff curl, dropped the hand to her side again.

Nona stood very close to Japheth, as if they were the warmest intimates, but how was that possible? Where could they have met? Glancing up with the sly, secret smile on her lips, she motioned Althea to come over. All at once Althea knew what else Nona had wanted that day in the rose garden, or, rather, who: she'd been looking for Japheth. The knowledge seeped in as a kind of surprised aftertaste, as when one learns the name of a certain spice in a recipe and the mind says, Yes, I should have recognized that, but the tongue has known from the first savor. Her brother's eyes held on her, clear and shining, obsidian even across that great distance. She started toward him. She was aware with some part of herself that her husband and Jim Logan were arguing furiously in hushed voices off to the side near the doorway. She sensed L.O. talking behind his hand to a cowboy in a big hat and leather chaps, sensed the cowboy hurrying off in the direction of the terrace, even as she felt the several gentlemen behind her watching from the arch of the libation room: every eye in the chandeliered hall followed her as she walked across the floor. If she'd had capacity for irony or humor or self-reflection she might have almost laughed, for her fondest vision of herself had always been that of a beautiful girl in an exquisite gown entering a softly lit ballroom with all eyes upon her. But the submerged source was fully present; it left no room for anything but itself. Her revulsion was powerful, the compulsion stronger. From the corner of her eye she saw her husband and Jim Dee break from the doorway, but she didn't pause; she glided serenely over the floor, the bell of her skirt swaying, her feet burning inside the antique shoes.

"Holy Christ, man!" Franklin said, as the three reached Japheth simultaneously. "What the devil's the matter with you? Good God, Thea!"

Althea paid him no attention. Her brother seemed to be grinning, seemed to be whispering, though she couldn't hear him; she could not quite see his lips move. Her blood coursed furiously. Her ribs could nearly burst with loathing. She longed to do something, *do* something, she could take both her hands and . . . Memory swelled, images swept over her. A sound started within her, a low tremulous vibration. She pushed it down, clamped the unvoiced scream tightly behind her jaw, held it within the boned cage of her breast.

"Hello, Sister." The lynched man's lips still did not seem to move, or perhaps it was only the illusion of light and shadow on the painted face. Abruptly he flopped his head to his shoulder again, shut his eyes, pushed the purple-stained tongue out from his lips. Nona whispered, "Oh, watch this, watch this!" She called across the ballroom, "Evening, Sheriff!"

The sheriff, wearing his khaki uniform, strode nonchalantly toward them. The cowboy in chaps and a big blond man dressed as Teddy Roosevelt trailed after him. At the back of the hall, several men emerged from the terrace darkness, shotglasses and lit cigars in hand, to see what all the quiet was about. Japheth held his same neck-snapped slouch, but a little quiver passed over the painted face. The purple tongue disappeared inside the thick lips. Nona didn't let go her grasp on him, even when the sheriff and L.O. moved in close.

"Oh, come on, now," Nona drawled, "where's y'all's sense of humor? What a bunch of old party poopers. L.O.?"

"Excuse me, Sheriff." Franklin stepped forward as if to take the lawman to the side and talk privately, his earnestly tilted forehead saying surely they could settle this uncomfortable little breach of manners in a discreet fashion.

But Japheth suddenly lifted his face, grinned broadly. "Why, hello, Sheriff Woolley. How nice to see you again." He slipped away from Nona's grip, slouched back against the wall, hands behind him, his demeanor more nonchalant than the sheriff's own. "Hadn't seen you in a month of Sundays, or a month anyhow. Hadn't it been about that? Or no, no, it was still summer, I guess. With all that rain that night a man couldn't much tell."

The sheriff's expression was chary, a little bewildered, but he rocked back on his heels, thumbs hooked in his gunbelt, waiting.

Japheth chuckled softly, rolled his neck around as if he had a crick in it, said, "Oh, I guess you don't remember me, sir. I can understand that. There was such a crowd. Such a crowd." Nona laughed. Japheth turned his painted eyes to her. "Mrs. Murphy, you've been so kind, such a fabulous hostess, I wonder if you couldn't untie me here." Their shared glee was obvious; no one could mistake it, or their collusion. Casually, Japheth turned his back toward her, and Nona fumbled with the rope at his wrists while he talked on, addressing first L.O., then the others. "I know y'all wanted us to stay in costume till midnight, but you can't imagine how crippled a man feels with his hands tied. It was some trick, tying them. You might not credit it, Sheriff, but that's a feat I pulled by myself. I asked Mr. Logan to give a hand. But I'm afraid he's on the taciturn side, just wouldn't help out a bit. He's a fine driller—the best in the business, they say—but I don't know, sometimes he does get his tail over a crack."

There was a beat of murderous silence as Japheth stared at Jim Dee while he rubbed his freed wrists; his hands had been painted, too—one black, the other white—along with wrist and forearm. He grinned at the semicircle of men's faces. "Of course, I didn't have any trouble with this." And he tapped the hangman's noose about his neck. It was strange how clean and new it looked, pure flaxen-yellow, the dangling end cut neatly across. "We got practice with these type of knots, right, Mr. Murphy? Right, Cletus?" And he looked intently at the one dressed as Teddy Roosevelt, who in turn dropped his pince-nez, stepped back. "This criminal element don't watch out, we're going to get plenty more practice, isn't that right? You know, Sheriff, that very evening out on the Red Fork road, I said to myself, See here, Tulsa's going to show them. The criminal element better keep its head down in this town." No one present, not even Nona, could have understood the sweet pleasure within Japheth, to face down the sheriff who'd hunted him, to say baldly: I was there, sir. Right in front of your noses. You've been looking for me all over the country. I was there. I am here.

"Not to mention the niggers," Japheth said. "Niggers got to quit showing out, don't they? I been hearing good things about this new Klan, any of y'all been hearing about it?" He perused the nearby faces, the distant crowd of masqueraders who were by now creeping forward, straining to hear what was being said. "They tell me folks are joining to the tune of a thousand a week down in Texas. Of course, it's not the highest element in society, not like present company, but I'll make a prediction right now, I'll predict that before two years are out we'll have a Klan member right in the governor's office, right here in Oklahoma. I'd bet on it. Would anybody care to bet?"

Silence came from the nearby circle; the revealed faces were frowning, including the sheriff's, but there was fascination as well, a kind of wondrous anticipation to find out what would come next. Nona's face was rapt, her green eyes glittering, wide and innocent. Only Althea seemed not to be listening. She stared out from her silver mask, not at the lynched man but at a blank space on the wall to the side of his head. On the fringes of the ballroom the murmuring had renewed, the hanged man's words whispered in undulating waves back to the terrace. Slowly the gathering moved toward him, seemingly outside its own will.

It was curiosity that kept them from dispatching the one who'd slipped in to hold up a mirror, make them recall what their minds had comfortably shut away. No one talked about the Belton lynching anymore. The papers still mentioned the grand-jury investigation from time to time, but since no one expected, or certainly wanted, anything to come of it, the probe was not a topic for town talk. Lynching had, by joint silent agreement, become a taboo subject for social discourse, but here was this creature among them, declaring it for some unfathomable reason, and the masqueraders waited to find out what it meant. All looked for signs. They gazed round the room, eyed one another, glanced in the direction of the lynched man, trying to discover the secret symbols—for there were always signs, weren't there? If the face had been all black, the message would have been clear—as the message had been clear in a recent ad placed by a local store in the *Tulsa World*, neatly bordered and highlighted: *K!K!K!,* the ad said, *Just say "KKK" to the grocer. Kellogg's roasted KORN KRISP. You and your children deserve KKK.* If the face had been all white, it would have clearly been a direct reference to Roy Belton, and they'd have grasped the warning to all such hijacking hooligans, as well as the naughty slap that the spectacle was to Tulsa's sense of decorum. But it was the half-colored, half-white face that confused the gathering, made the meaning less discernible, more mysterious.

"Of course," Japheth said, smiling, "that new Invisible Empire's got nothing to do with present company. Far as I hear, it's all just a bunch of small-town do-gooders. So far." His eyes lifted to take in the garish grandeur of the mansion. "Mrs. Murphy." He nodded very formally, bowed to Nona, turned to L.O., and did the same. "Mr. Murphy. Allow me to compliment you on the taste and elegance of your lovely home." The weirdly divided face was made stranger by Japheth's sudden clean diction and formality of manner: one of his favorite chameleon tricks was to be crude as a hayrick one moment, suave and polished as a debonaire the next. "I was saying to Mr. Logan as we were motoring up from Bristow—"

"See here! Who are you?" L.O.'s eagle feathers were trembling. "Who let this fellow in?" He wheeled around to vent his rage on the Negro door-men, but, seeing no dark face anywhere, he turned in fury on the two partners. "Logan, did you bring this abomination? Dedmeyer, what are you trying to pull? I'll have the lot of you tossed out. Sheriff?" But L.O. couldn't wait for the laconic sheriff to make a move; he whipped his war-bonneted head at Franklin again. "You're up to something, you son of a bitch, I know that. I been knowing it. Laying out for weeks, and when you do come in, you strut around the lobbies tight as a tick, or else I hear you telling crap to any fool you can get to listen, spreading that conniving pile of lies and mystification."

"I think you'd better calm down, L.O." Franklin's voice was tolerant, a little patronizing: it was the voice he'd evolved years ago to try and quiet Althea's rages.

L.O. turned to the audience. "One minute he's acting like he's got the biggest strike since Spindletop, next he's crying poor, crying duster, cry-ing broke like a lying son of a bitch."

"Listen here, friend," Franklin's soothing voice began, "let's take a deep breath. . . ."

"Listen here, fella," Japheth said in unctuous, pitch-perfect imitation, "let's not say anything that'll make us sorry."

L.O. whipped on Japheth now, both fists raised like a boxer, like the feisty street-fighter he'd one time been. A crone's shriek rose into the great goldenlit space, and the room was stunned once more into silence. None could tell the scream's source, but as it echoed, Althea suddenly leapt at her brother with her hands clawed, reaching for his face. Franklin stepped in front of her, gripped her hands, as Nona gasped and rushed forward, and L.O. shouted to the sheriff, who quickly moved in, as did the cowboy and Jim Dee and several others. The men grabbed hold of Japheth's arms, detached Nona's hand from his sleeve. There followed an almost balletic, inverted *danse macabre*, as the handful of men mimed the movements of a lynch mob; they surrounded the noosed man in silent slow motion, hoisted him, struggling, cursing horribly, spitting from his purple-stained mouth, his black and white hands twisted behind his back and held tight. The only voiced sound in the room was Japheth's cascade of curses as the men half dragged, half carried him out of the hall. The room's gaze passed over them, though without pause, pretending not to register what it was seeing.

The silence extended itself a beat longer. The masqueraders' eyes returned to the empty wall, where the phantasm had appeared. There stood now only the two women, the belle and the buckskinned hostess, both staring out the open doors, and the silkshirted pirate with his arm around his wife. A clarinet tootled a few aborted notes, the piano joined it, and then the orchestra swung into a tinkling ragtime, as the masqueraders turned back to themselves. Gradually, in the tiniest increments, they began to move, to breathe, to pretend that all was natural, all was normal. Men turned to one another and spoke business or politics. Ladies excused themselves to the powder room, disappeared in rustling taffeta and satin whispers.

In the same manner that the city's mind had sealed over the swinging, stripped, beaten body of Roy Belton on the Red Fork road two months before—had opened, received the horror, knit itself quickly, like a scab—just so, the gathering in the Murphys' ballroom now sealed its mind over the vulgar invasion that had pierced the room. The floor filled again with masqueraders, moiled with sound and color, the loud and rowdy laughter of the inebriated guests underlaced with a kind of glittery hysteria, a scandalized excitement, now that the horror had been removed from their sight. No one noticed when the belle in the pink ballgown pulled away from her husband and hurried across the room, disappeared down an empty hall. A mulatto man with a penciled mustache and shining, straight black hair stepped to the front of the bandstand and began to sing into the microphone, his voice at once tinny and smooth, nasal as the muted moan of a trumpet. One by one the Negroes began to reappear.

Althea ran into the powder room, slammed the door shut behind her. Two women in red net dance-hall dresses bent over a low ebony vanity, leaning into the mirror, applying rouge. A velvet fainting couch reposed in one corner, a teardrop chandelier dangling over it. Gold-embossed fixtures adorned the basins; a naked cupid stood on tip-toe opposite the ebony vanity, peeing into its own little seashell. One whole wall was a mirror. A colored girl, innocent of all that had transpired in the ballroom, stood beside the basin with a stack of small white linen towels she was supposed to hand to the ladies to dry their little fingers. Althea kept her eyes trained away from the mirrored wall as she snapped at the attendant to come help her with her underthings—quickly! Quickly! The attendant set her towels on the lip of the basin and pro-ceeded to amble toward where Althea stood just inside the doorway.

"Ma'am?" the girl said. She was round and light brown, her brownish hair fuzzy beneath the white cap, and she moved slow as syrup, and Althea could have knocked her in the head.

"Help me!" The words echoed back in her memory, to the day in Greenwood when she'd cried out in the newspaper office, and she bit the inside of her jaw till the taste of salt made her stop. She hissed at the girl, "Can't you see I need help?" She snatched up the filmy skirt of the ball-gown to reveal the layers of petticoats in white complicated strata over the hoop-slip and bloomers and lower rib of the corset, an hourglass vise of bone at her waist.

The girl looked at her blankly. She put a tentative hand out and tugged ineffectually at a dangling corset lace. "What you want me to do, ma'am?" she said. *Fool! Help me. Help me. It's your job to help me, what else are you here for?* The dance-hall women were staring at them from the vanity mirror. "Oh, for God's sake!" Althea whispered. She pulled a mass of petticoats up to her chin, turned around, bunched the mass in one hand, waved the other behind herself: "Untie me!" She felt the girl's fingers fumbling at the small of her back, where the hoop-slip was tied beneath the petticoats. "Hurry!" she spat. "You idiot, just untie the lace!" At last the hoops fell to her feet in collapsing rings, and Althea stepped out of the slip, rushed past the two staring women into the next room.

The pink-tiled inner room was mercifully mirrorless. Althea reached up and untied her mask, laid it in her lap. Still she did not weep, though it was what she wanted. But her old habit was gone, self-pity swamped by the source which held capacity only for grief, absolute sorrow, hate, pity. The source, in turn, was blocked cold with fear. She shuddered deeply, rubbed the indentations around her eyes. She sat staring, unseeing, for a long time.

When she emerged from the toilet she saw that the two white women were gone. Her hoop-slip lay collapsed in the same place near the door, a small pointy-toed footprint exiting in plain outline on the circle of white. The attendant was bent over, peering at herself in the vanity, her lips pursed, frowning, as she plucked with plump fingers at her hair. Suddenly, inexplicably, Althea was swept in a tide of roiling fury, and she shrieked at the attendant, "What's the matter with you? Pick it up! Pick it up!"

The girl jumped, her eyes huge as she jerked her face to Althea, and then she turned and ran toward the fallen slip as Althea also rushed forward—to do what? Beat the girl, slap the girl, as she'd wanted to do from the minute she saw her. The girl snatched up the slip and held it in front of herself like a flaccid shield as the door opened and a dark-haired ballerina and a blond cowgirl sashayed in, followed by a sober-faced woman in a gray dress carrying a placard that said ONE WOMAN, ONE VOTE. Althea stopped. Unprotected, having forgotten to defend herself against it, she caught sight of her own image in the wall of mirror, and what she saw bled the rage from her as quickly as it had come. Yes, her hand was raised to strike the girl. She allowed the hand to drop to her side. The three women sidled into the crowded room, and Althea stepped back to allow them to pass, but her eyes were on the strange woman in the mirror, whose pink dress, without the buoyant hoops to support it, sagged forlornly; whose hair was wilted, whose lace bodice was limp. The lip rouge applied hours earlier now lingered on the rims of empty champagne goblets somewhere in the mansion's basement, and the lips in the mirror were bloodless and thin. The cut lines from the face mask appeared as scarlet slashes along the upper ridges of both cheekbones, like stripes of paint, or scars. But it was the eyes staring back at her that so completely stilled Althea: they were stark, big, dark, and glittery, and they had in them the same look that had glared at her across the ballroom from her brother's contemptuous, raging, hate-filled eyes.

Her soul screamed, a mute howl that could not make its way to the surface. She saw the attendant, big-eyed and scared, clutching the white hoop-slip to her breast; she heard the women's voices behind her, but the sound came from a great distance, like the sounds of the many voices calling outside the corncrib. The frightened girl stared at her from the other side of the abyss, the gulf of black terror: the girl stared at her from across the ravine of cut red earth and sandstone where the water trickled in the bottom the color of new blood, and the voices called, *Le-e-e-etha! Le-e-e-etha!,* coming nearer. Her throat made choked, garbled, near-silent drowning sounds. Mouth working, the soundless scream clawing her breastbone, Althea reached out a cold hand and jerked the attendant away from the doorway; she stepped into the massive hallway, where at one end chandeliered light glowed and there was the tinkle of piano, the wail of clarinet and trumpet, the sound of laughter, and she turned the other direction, ran down the vast, empty, echoing hall.

In the ballroom the masquerade went on at an exhilarated pace, fueled by the free flow of liquor and the titillation of the scandalous event taking place, not in secret rooms or on hidden roadsides, but right out directly in Tulsa society's glittering presence. The euphoria was fed by the sense of mystery in the room, the ravenous curiosity, the questions that were whispered behind hands and fans: What did it mean? Who'd dare do such a thing? What was the message? Most significant of all to the masquerade's mind: Who among the party guests was in on the secret? Several of the masqueraders behaved as if they knew very well the meaning of the lynched man; they raised their brows significantly, nodded sagely, closed-lipped, in response to the whispered questions; others gaped their own ignorance, for they wanted no one to suppose they'd had anything to do with it. The mystery was of the grandest, most delicious character, and the gaiety in the great hall rose in proportion to the wildness of the rumors flying from one end to the other as the orchestra played "Pickaninny Sleep Song."

L.O. Murphy had made a great show of dusting himself off when he came puffing back in ahead of the others, his white tuxedo smudged and dusty, his white war bonnet askew; he'd called out for the guests to partake of the feast of quail and prairie chicken, buffalo and beef and wild turkey, he'd had prepared and spread for his honored guests' delectation: Eat up now, folks, y'all come on and eat! With tremendous restraint, it seemed to him, L.O. ignored the sullen glares of the Negro servants (though privately he thought he'd fire the uppity lot of them if they'd belonged to him), and with great joviality he grabbed a passing porter, held him by the arm, and called out, "More wine, Sam! More wine! Fetch up some bottles of that French stuff! We're sparing no expense here this evening!" He went around one by one to the most important guests to reassure them that the intruder had been effectively dispatched, no need for the little ladies to worry, until finally it became clear, even to L.O. Murphy's dull perception, that the spectacle, far from dampening the gathering, had in fact enhanced his party's cachet. L.O.'s deprecations changed swiftly from apologetic to prideful, the words coated in false chagrin. So full of himself and his success was he that he didn't notice his wife gliding on her silent feet into the foyer, didn't see when she slipped out the front door.

As for Franklin Dedmeyer, he'd assumed his own wife was merely rushing off to powder her nose while the turmoil died down, and so he'd allowed his concerns about her to slide to the back of his mind while his full attention keyed in on business, for it was trouble at the drilling site Jim Logan had come in such agitation to tell him. They went on arguing in hushed voices, and only once did Franklin's words digress: "Why in God's name'd you let him come in here looking like that?" he grumbled, partly to shift the subject away from the thick bentonite clay they'd drilled into, partly because he couldn't understand why neither his brother-in-law nor his partner had any better sense.

"Me let him? I don't let that loco do nothing." Jim Dee wiped a little nick of blood from his lip. There was blood on his shirtfront; his red neckerchief was twisted to the side. He spread the fingers of his right hand, examining the swelling knuckles. "Son of a gun does just what he wants, which is mostly set around and let me and Ben do all the damn work."

"Well, he won't be sitting much longer. If you see his face within a mile of the location, you've got my permission to lay some birdshot in it. Looks to God like you could've reined him."

"Hell, man, I didn't know he was going to do that. Nobody knows what's in that weird head—a sane man couldn't dream it." Jim Dee brushed at his shirtfront. "He must've had that noose in his pocket or something. All I knew, when he came to the car he had his face painted up, said it was for the party. I didn't spend a whole lot of time worrying about it. We got bigger troubles than that lunatic brother-in-law of yours. That hole's swoll up like biscuit dough. I told you that formation's too damn cavey—"

"All right! I heard you," Franklin said. "Go on and pull it! You'll get your damn rig!" He caught himself, seeing how his outburst made nearby heads turn. But the delay was going to cost on too many levels to count, and Franklin's rancor was increased by the fact that he knew he should have let Jim build a rig from the outset, like he'd wanted, instead of trying to save a few dollars. Franklin went on, his tone slightly more subdued: "Send Koop to Bristow Tool first thing Monday morning. Or, no, maybe you'd better go in yourself and make the order. I'll be down in a day or two."

"I didn't come to ask your *permission*, Your Lordship." Jim leveled a dangerously mild gaze at Franklin. "I already been to Bristow, I was there yesterday morning. They cut us off. Zeke won't turn loose of a screw or a timber unless you come in there yourself and give him something on the note."

"All right, all right," Franklin said, frowning, "I'll come Monday." He had no cash, no collateral left; he'd sunk everything into tying up the nearby leases, but never mind; he would figure something out. He cocked his head toward the hallway. Althea had been gone an awfully long time. "Have you seen Thea?"

Jim's hazel eyes held on him in a cold, appraising look. "I haven't seen your wife," he said finally. "I'm trying to tell you something, don't you hear me? The old lady's gone."

There was a beat of silence, and then Franklin shrugged, his eyes skimming the crowd for his wife's pink ballgown. Why'd Logan keep harping on that? Colored folks and Indians disappeared all the time; hadn't their own Gracie run off without a word? "She'll turn up, I tell you. Quit your worrying. Those people go off to visit relatives or something, they don't have sense enough to leave a note on the door saying when they'll be back."

"You don't hear a goddamn word I'm saying, do you?" Jim Dee's voice dropped to a harsh whisper. "That fool brother-in-law of yours never got the old lady's mark!" Immediately he began to backpedal. "Or he did, maybe. He said he did, I don't know."

"What do you mean, *he* never got it?"

"I had other things to worry about. That's your blame job."

"Not when I leave it with you, it's not. You said you'd get right back out there."

"I had to get that well spudded in! You don't like it, you can just take care of your own damn end." Jim Dee's voice suddenly turned mild again, disinterested-sounding. "Hell, you can't tell anything about what he says. That lunatic's a full-out liar. Anyhow"—he shrugged—"you better get to Sapulpa and check on it. He said the paper's gone."

"What paper's gone?" Franklin said. "You don't mean the lease?"

"Told some cock-and-bull story about he got my lizzie stuck on the way to Sapulpa, said the courthouse was closed when he got there and he had to get a room to wait till morning, said when he went in to file and reached in his bag the paper with the old lady's mark was missing. I don't know what to make of it. He's your damn kin. Listen here, I knew good and well that hole wasn't going to stand up." Quickly Jim Dee returned to the subject of the wrongheadedness of commencing the well with a spudder, for on that issue he'd clearly been right, Franklin wrong.

But Franklin couldn't hear his partner's blaming words for the roaring in his own ears. He understood fully the meaning of what Jim had come to tell him: it was all going to be ripped away. Before the dream was in his hand, it was going to be filched from him. If the Tiger lease had never been filed in the name of Delo Petroleum, any wildcatter could come along and steal the field out from under them. Franklin cursed himself silently. How could he have failed to perform that one most critical act himself? It was a blank spot in him, he couldn't imagine what had been in his mind, that he'd left that most vital task to someone else. He nodded cordially at Tom Slick, who appeared to be eyeing him from over by the meat table, and at once a great suspicion seized Franklin: what if the appearance here tonight of Sinclair and Getty, Cosden and Slick and the others was somehow connected to this calamity? Jim Dee was saying something, but Franklin, consumed with dread, could only think how all his leasehound work—the weeks of sneaking around Creek County, on down into Okfuskee, leaving small deposits here, larger ones there, securing dozens of leases—all that work was for naught, because he knew what his partner didn't: Gypsy Oil already held claim to the land most directly abutting the old lady's allotment. It was only a miracle or an oversight, or, as his fear now told him, an act of dreadful cunning, that Gypsy hadn't yet drilled an offset well on the line. Franklin's discovery well, the Iola Tiger No. 1, was a phantom. The lease had never been filed.

Unconsciously Franklin's eyes searched for Althea. If his wife in her secret apocalypse sought grounding in the brown face that revealed nothing, for Franklin there was and had only ever been Althea. Not seeing her anywhere, he felt the old worries rising, and it came to him why he hadn't been there to take care of that crucial filing. Of course. When he'd tried to telephone Althea from the hotel in Bristow, the exchange rang and rang and rang. He'd had to go home to see about her, and it was a good thing he'd done so, for how had he found her but lying sick in bed with her feet wrapped in bloody rags? He'd tried to call in Dr. Taylor, but she wouldn't hear of it. He could get no explanation from her except that she'd gone for a walk by the river and had wandered too far, that's how she'd got such terrible blisters. But, Franklin, she'd cried, listen! She'd clutched his hand, staring up at him. Listen! I know where Graceful is! The flighty thing ran off to Bigheart, of all things. Mr. Sutphen said so. Franklin? Darling? No doctor, please. Just bring Graceful home. He'd gone to Sutphen's and hired a new maid, Althea wouldn't have her; she wouldn't let up: oh, she had to have Graceful to tend her, Graceful surely would make her feel better. And so Franklin had agreed finally to take the train to Bigheart. But really it had not helped much, having the girl back. There was something changed in Althea, something he couldn't put his finger on. Where was she? She'd been gone half an hour.

"Excuse me a minute," Franklin said, and he bowed slightly, as if Jim were a stranger, and began to make his way across the noisy floor toward the libation room. His partner stared after him, took a step to follow, but then he checked himself. Jim Dee's gaze swept the room as if he, too, were looking for someone; the hazel eyes were deeply skewed, his lips pursed. Turning, he walked swiftly to the foyer, paused for one last glance around the ballroom before he strode outside.

Althea fled along the hallway, past the open door to L.O. Murphy's trophy room with its many stuffed heads of bighorn sheep and bison and grizzly, all bought from a seller in Fort Worth, Texas; past the library with its thousand leatherbound volumes, purchased *en masse* and shipped by rail from a dealer in New York; to the very end of the south wing, where she came upon a great walnut staircase leading up to living quarters or guest rooms, and a more cramped set of tiled stairs leading down. She didn't hesitate before selecting the tiled steps, and she ran down into the labyrinthine lower level, designed with great craft by the Chicago architect to allow for the greatest invisibility of the many servants needed to run such a grand home. Althea wandered along a dim, cramped passageway until she saw light ahead, and she hurried toward it. Then, for the first time, she faltered.

The light poured from the service kitchen, candescent, yellowish, teeming with Negroes moving about in the brightness. Althea shrank back into the dark corridor. She watched the servants' faces as they worked, some loading food onto trays, some unburdening trays of dirty dishes, some cooking, some washing pots, others drying crystal glasses; it seemed to her they all bore Graceful's expression, that same enigmatic closed look. But as she peered directly at the faces, Althea grew more and more frightened: she was seeing in too much detail. In the brilliant yellow light it seemed she saw the very pores of their skin, every nuance of texture and color; she saw their big or small eyes, their nappy black hair, their pomaded brown smooth hair, their noses, their lips, the shapes of their heads. It was the same as how she'd seen Graceful, acutely, on the back porch that morning, long ago, it seemed years ago, before the abyss cleaved the world. The sounds of the orchestra drifted down a service stairwell on the far side of the room, and the music swelled each time the door at the top of the stairs opened to receive another servant toting a tray piled with the leavings of the partygoers upstairs.

At every new entrance Althea looked to see if it was Graceful, but the girl's face was not among them. The returning servant, male or female, would hand off to a pair of waiting hands in silence, and in their faces was that terrible, closed mystery, that furious constraint, like Graceful's, as they passed trays of half-eaten slabs of meat and crusts of toasts and mauled canapés from hand to hand. Their silence frightened her. What had she thought? That they'd all be happy darkies singing and clapping in the kitchen? Althea's fear disgorged itself into resentment, into the same dull rancor she'd felt inside the girl's house in Greenwood, and it had the same source: her slighted sense that these people had something or knew something she did not know, and would never understand.

The elderly champagne-server appeared from somewhere, coming directly toward where she stood in the dark passage. Althea made a convulsive movement, almost cried out. The man stopped dead; a surprised bleat erupted from him, and all movement in the kitchen behind him instantly ceased. Upstairs the orchestra swung into a jazzy upbeat tempo, but the servants stood watching in the lighted kitchen, trying to peer into the passageway; they did not resume their work.

"Ma'am," the server said at last, "I got to go in that door there behind you. Ma'am? Mr. Murphy want me to carry up some more wine."

"What? Oh, yes, of course." And she stepped aside. As he emerged from the wine cellar with laden arms, she caught him by the sleeve. "Where's Graceful?" The old man didn't answer. "Please. Tell me. I know you know her. She's my— I'm Mrs. Dedmeyer. Graceful works for me."

"I don't know. I'm sorry, ma'am." Very deftly, without seeming to do so, he pulled away and started back toward the kitchen. Althea rushed forward and caught him again. "Where is she?"

He didn't look directly at her, but neither did he lower his head. "I'm sorry, ma'am," he repeated. "I don't know who you talking about." The old man gazed straight ahead; his features were in profile and she couldn't make out his expression. She released the sleeve finally, and he stepped away in a kind of agile, respectful two-step, walked swiftly through the silent kitchen, disappeared up the far set of service stairs. Suddenly Althea was furious, and she ran after him, but he'd already gone. She was caught in the center of the too-bright kitchen with the many faces watching her. Drawing herself up, she looked at them all imperiously, her eyes sweeping the room, and it was a lie, it was not even old habit now but sheer bluff, and had she known how unkempt and shameful she appeared to them she'd have been a hundred times more mortified: they thought she was drunk.

"Where is she!" Althea demanded.

It was a long time before a woman in a white headrag standing beside the huge oven said, "We don't know, ma'am."

And another said, very politely, "Who is it you want, ma'am?"

"My maid. My maid, Graceful. It's time to go."

"Who she, ma'am?"

"Graceful!" The idiots. "Graceful Whiteside!" There. She'd said it. The name had slipped out smooth as cream.

The headwrapped woman said, "We don't know any Graceful Whiteside. None of us." And she folded her arms and glared a challenge to the rest of them.

But the polite voice came back: "Maybe she gone, ma'am. A bunch of us . . . some folks . . . left while ago."

"Left? Why?"

Here was the gulf fixed. The people stared at her across the expanse of gleaming kitchen, which was in fact a chasm, a great cleft in the world. Althea couldn't conceive that her brother's appearance in the upstairs ballroom had any larger significance than the personal horror it was to her own soul: the questioning whine had been a mystery to her, its source unfathomable. Furthest of all from her imagining was the living, breathing memory of the men and women before her, who, for their part, couldn't dream of the ignorance of the disheveled whitewoman standing in the middle of the kitchen floor. They disbelieved her, they suspected her, they lowered their heads in fear, or glared at her in rage from their unfractured, unsuppressed, long night's memory of lynchings, beatings, tortures, black bodies burning. They knew well that the lynched man was a sign for blackfolks' eyes, saying, Hearken, niggers, this shall be your sons, look here, bow your heads, niggers, we do not need a nigger in hand to warn you uppity Greenwood niggers: get down off your high horse, do not think you can be like whitefolks, do not dare to think you can be equal, self-sufficient, rich.

Althea looked at them a moment, and some returned her gaze and some did not, and the woman in the white headrag eyed her with such formidable defiance that Althea, baffled and intimidated, turned away, retreated into the dim corridor, fled once again up the back stairs.

Out, out into the darkness at the side of the Murphy mansion, down the long sweep of sodded lawn, soft beneath her feet. The full moon made the open spaces day-bright, but dying leaves clung to the trees at the edge of the lawn, cast trembling shadows, and the shadows shuffled and whispered. She turned only once to look back. Lights glowed in every room in the ugly rambling yellowbrick aggregation. Long black motorcars drove up the circle drive, disgorged or received passengers. A pair of liveried doormen stood at attention on either side of the carved doors; voices and laughter floated in an aural mist along the surface of the damp lawn. The orchestra music was muted now, perhaps by the constant drone of laughter and engines, or because of the thundering pulse in her own ears. Althea started to run again, not toward, not away from, but simply to be running, to disappear.

Graceful walked fast in the cold moonlight, almost running, except that her gait was too controlled. The night was frosty and she wore neither sweater nor jacket, but the heat inside her and the swiftness of her stride allowed that she was sweating by the time she reached South Carson, and still she didn't know what she would do. She'd be fired, of course, for walking off without permission from the job the Dedmeyers had hired her out to do. No matter. She was not going to stay in this place anyway, where that white devil would come around. If it had taken a moment for Althea to recognize her own blood-kin, Graceful had known him instantly. Her body had known, in fact, before her mind fully owned it: hatred swept her at sight of him, a hot, wretched, flaming surge, like a flashfire in her chest, searing her instantly from cheek to groin. She'd whirled away, not in fear, but to give vent to the horrific might of her own hate, her scalding rage, her helplessness before all that she felt, seeing that painted, choked, harlequinesque mask.

When she turned off the rustling, oak-canopied street, she fancied she saw him lurking in the dark on a neighbor's side porch. She hurried over the flagstones at the side of the garden, her breath pinched tight, and she was gasping by the time she slammed the bolt shut inside the house; she moved through the dark house and slipped into the tiny maid's room, where, without reaching up to pull the light cord, she sat down on the bed, panting, and tried to think.

Again and again her mind returned to the painted corpse with the noose around its neck, as one revisits in horror and fascination an old nightmare. It was now, for the first time, that she thought clearly of T.J., and she understood finally what the workers in the kitchen had known at once. Whites had lynched a whiteman in this town, they would a hundred times rather lynch a Negro, as they'd lynched Everett Candler, as they would lynch T.J. if they could ever get hold of him. She had to try to send word to T.J., she ought to warn T.J.!

Although she was already sweating, Graceful went warmer, flushed with an old, familiar shame. She had abandoned her brother in the filth and dark inside the army tent. Hedgemon Jackson, too, had left him, had followed Graceful to Tulsa, and so that was also her fault. Half the evenings of the world Hedgemon Jackson would be standing in the alley behind the Dedmeyers' house, waiting to talk to her, and sometimes she'd go meet him, just to have someone to talk with, someone to tell her how things were in Greenwood. Didn't Hedgemon say T.J. was going to come back to Greenwood? And if Graceful asked, When? Hedgemon would say, I don't know, soon as that lynch talk die down. But the lynch talk would not die down. Hadn't the white devil declared that to the world?

And anyhow, what would T.J. do in Greenwood? He couldn't go home to Mama's. He'd better not go to Mama's. *I'll go up to Greenwood in the morning, tell Mama to tell Delroy to tell T.J.: don't come home.* At once she was ripped with longing for the yellow house on North Elgin, for her sisters' complaining voices and Willie's broad grin, and for her Mama, just to see Mama, to be with Mama, just to go home. Her hand touched her belly. The old feeling of powerlessness came on her, caught by the forces inside and outside herself that had so little to do with her own will. *In the morning,* she said, but she knew she would not go.

A muted sound, the scrape of chair wood on tile in the kitchen, stopped her round of thoughts, stopped her heart. She sat breathless, listening for the intruder, but then she heard another sound: human, wounded, like whimpering, although it was not quite that. She got up and went to see.

The woman sat at the little wooden table in the dim light of the kitchen, the tulle-and-lace ballgown foaming around her as she pressed her face into her open hands. If the whimpering sound had been coming from her, she was quiet now, though her back and shoulders shuddered with spasms. Graceful didn't speak, for she was sure to receive the long spew of complaint and blame, and she knew she would not bear it, not one more time, not another ugly word; she turned to go back to her room, but the woman jumped up, crying out, "Oh, there you are! Thank God!"

Graceful turned to stare down the expected tirade, but what she found was an expression as mystifying as Mr. Dedmeyer's face through the hotel window: a look of gladness on the woman's face, of gratitude almost, and the look stopped Graceful completely, turned her still and cold with suspicion.

Althea rushed on as if nothing had happened, no lynched man, no rebellion on Graceful's part by having walked off the job; as if it were perfectly normal for the two of them to be standing facing one another at midnight in the lightless kitchen. "I was looking all over, my God, I looked everywhere, how'd you get here so fast? I practically ran. Well? Come, come, come upstairs and help me get out of these things, Lord, what a time I had getting into this garb, it takes a strong hand to cinch a corset properly, naturally a lady can't do it by herself, that's why in the old days they had— Oh, well . . ." And she began laughing. "You should have seen Mr. Dedmeyer, God, he's no help, the man is all thumbs, completely, just a nincompoop when it comes to ladies' unmentionables, as any man is, or should be, but I lost something, I dropped my— God, I was so mad at Nona Murphy. At myself, really, I never should have let her have you."

She paused, breathing hard, staring at Graceful in the wan light reflecting off the white floor, so that Graceful understood that the look on the woman's face wasn't because she was glad to see her, but because she was wrought up, crazy, madwoman crazy, and for Graceful the whole complexity of her feelings about the woman gave way to pity and fear.

"Maybe you better go on to bed, ma'am."

"I need you to help me."

Graceful returned her stare, silent. If Mrs. Dedmeyer could get herself dressed for the party while she, Graceful, waxed banisters and lugged goblets and food trays and polished tile floors on her hands and knees at the Murphy mansion, the woman could get her own self undressed. "I'm not no lady's maid, ma'am," she said. She looked steadily at Althea. "I'm a domestic who work in the kitchen and keep the house clean. I'm not no slave to loan out to the neighbors. I was going to tell you in the morning, but I might's well say it now. I'm giving my notice. I'll stay till Mr. Sutphen send you somebody if you want, but this here is my notice."

"No," Althea said. Her voice was as controlled as Graceful's, as firm. They looked at each other a moment, and then Graceful turned to go. Althea followed her to the maid's room, stood in the doorway while Graceful sat on the bed in the dark.

"You can't leave." It was a simple declaration. "I forbid it."

"I'm not no slave."

"No, no, I don't mean that . . . I'm sorry. It's— Graceful, I can't—"

Althea looked at the figure sitting on the bed in the small square of moonlight from the high, small window. The girl's cheekbones were distinct; her narrowed eyes were almost closed. Althea's memory arrived fully born: the afternoon she'd come home from Little Africa, when she'd collapsed in the foyer and wept till she could weep no longer, and then slept on the hall floor, only to waken hours later, alone, with the street light streaming through the stained-glass window, too frightened to cry, or to cry out; the memory of how she'd crawled up the stairs on her hands and knees, grunting, panting, clawed her way up onto the bed, under the covers, to stay there for days, not eating, not bathing, lying curled beneath the sour sheet while her feet wept bloody water, and she'd dared not sleep, for when she slept she was tormented with nightmares, and it was on the last night that the old memory came, the first memory, the ancient one, and after that it wouldn't leave her, nor could she wall it off, make a curtain, because she could not cut away the image of herself, her own real self, the Whiteside girl, holding the small ivory legs, the tiny white feet in her hands to better swing the misshapen sloe-colored head, the blueblack mass attached to the scrawny, pale buttocks. . . . Who was it who'd stopped her? Who knew of her murder and her sin? And who would absolve her? The one who witnessed. Only the one who bore witness had the power to release her. Althea had no words for what she'd understood then: that it was the girl who knew the truth in her, the girl who would somehow save her, or judge her— or, no, not judge her. Forgive her. Know her and forgive.

"No. Please listen. I need you," she whispered.

Graceful's narrowed eyes became slits in the darkness. "What for?"

"I . . . can't . . . explain. Did you know . . . you know something?" Althea voice lilted into a peculiar, hollow friendliness. She took a step into the room, and then stopped. It was such a tiny space. It was so dark there, so airless. "My name when I was a girl growing up—my family name is Whiteside. Isn't that funny?"

Graceful was silent.

"I mean, I thought it was odd when the little boy came with that note—"

Willie! Graceful thought, and her heart twisted.

"—had that name on it, I thought, why, there must be some mistake. But you, well, it didn't surprise you, so I thought, well, my stars, what an odd coincidence. I mean, I thought it was odd. It's not so common a name, really. I mean, I . . . it just sort of seemed . . . Not that I think we're . . ." Althea's voice drifted into silence, and the silence grew long in the cramped room. The grandfather clock ticked in the front hall. Outside, a balmy southwind had blown up, and the ground leaves skittered at the basement window and the oak leaves yet on the trees rustled along the drive. Inside the room, there was only the sound of their breathing. When Althea's voice came again, there was simple truth in it. "Graceful, I'm asking you. Please stay." Still the girl didn't answer. After a while a thought occurred to Althea. "Is it because I sent you to the Murphys'? I won't again. That was a mistake. That was stupid, really, I don't even know why I let Nona talk me into it, she is such a sly fox. I don't know what I was thinking. That won't happen again." She waited for Graceful to say something; she expected a sullen acquiescence, for Graceful to say, All right, ma'am, that'll be fine, ma'am, in her soft, infuriatingly slow voice, but the girl remained silent, and despite herself Althea's voice rose in desperation. "Whyyy?"

The silence went on a beat longer, and then: "I'm not going to stay and work anywhere that man come around."

"What man?" Althea was mystified. "Not Mr. Dedmeyer?" Graceful's head moved in a barely perceptible shake, a faint no. "What are you talking about?" And the girl looked up at her, and in the slanted eyes and hard face was pure revulsion.

"Him," Graceful said. "Your brother."

"Oh." There began to rise in Althea a kind of strange, satisfied hope. Why, yes, the girl loathed Japheth as she loathed him, and Althea didn't question why such a thing should be so, she thought only that here at last was both explanation and answer, something concrete she could control. "Oh, you don't have to worry about him. He won't be here. I promise you. He'll never darken my door again."

"He's your brother." The meaning in the flat voice was, He will have to.

"He is not. He isn't. Not really. He's just . . . some person. . . ." Althea's voice faded. There were no words to explain such things, not this mystery, this trouble, this old, hard past. She changed the subject. "Mr. Dedmeyer's going to be gone a lot for the next couple of months. Won't you just stay until he comes home? Just that long. I'll see if we can afford a bonus or something." Desperately she reached for the old concerns, a kind of vacant normalcy. "I mean, I'm not promising anything, but I'll ask him. You're already making a very good salary, I mean, it's not the money, surely? No. No. Of course not. How about this: how about you'll stay until after the first of the year? Just through Christmas, and then if you still want to go, well, that will be fine. It'll be too hard to find somebody here right before the holidays. Won't it?" She reached up to smooth her hair.

"How you know he won't come?"

"He won't, that's all." The odor of pomade, familiar, medicinal, infused the room with its oily scent of petrolatum masked with spice. "I promise you," Althea said. "He won't." There was silence. "Just two months." It was not a question but a statement.

Graceful stared straight ahead. "I can't stay two months and then go."

"Why? What is it? For God's sake, what more can I do?"

"Nothing, ma'am. You're fine. Y'all been fine." Which was not true. Oh, the man had been fine, Mr. Dedmeyer, he'd treated Graceful with nothing but the nicest condescension, whenever he was around. And the woman had spewed out only two tirades since Graceful had come back, though she followed her everywhere, sneaking into rooms behind her back; she was worse now than in the beginning, last summer, when Graceful had first come to work here and realized Mrs. Dedmeyer was following her around room to room, spying on her. Graceful looked up at the white

236 · RILLA ASKEW

face in the doorway, and the image struck, as it had struck on Mr. Berry's jitney when she'd fled this very house, this very room, where that white devil laid down on her, and Graceful made a jerky move to rise, to escape the nightmarish vision of the mouth opening, and the hawk's hunt-cry shrieking out from the blackness, but the woman stood in the doorway, blocking her, too close, choking her back, and she couldn't touch the lady, make her move. "Please, ma'am!" she whispered.

"Hssssht!" Althea grabbed Graceful's arm, held it tight, digging her fingers in, listening as the front door snicked shut. There was the muted click of a man's shoe on the tile, one cautious step. They listened, their breaths stopped, hearts pounding. Neither of them thought then how they were joined together, but in those few seconds the gulf receded the tiniest increment, shrunk by the force of what they mutually dreaded. The footsteps left the hall and started up the stairs, and Althea recognized the tread and weight of her husband's step, and the knowledge passed silently to Graceful, without word or signal, so that the two breathed again, in union. Althea eased her clutch on Graceful's arm, and in the small room they stepped away from each other, even before Franklin's muffled voice wafted down the stairwell, calling out softly, fearfully, hopefully his wife's name.

"The fools," Nona hissed into Japheth's ear, though there was no need to whisper. They were far from the buff mansion, far from champagne, lights, harp, voices, far from hungry eyes and attentive ears. She'd found him at the end of the lawn, where the men had thrown him, the white half of his face glistening with black swells where the dark blood streamed. Carefully she'd pulled the buckskin skirt above her knees to keep it pure of grass stains and knelt beside him. With a small, delicate hand, avoiding the blood, she'd shaken his shoulder, again, yet again. It had taken some ten minutes to rouse him.

He blinked at her. The moon's light turned night to blue day on the sweep of lawn above them, but for a very long time he seemed not to see her. "I never dreamed for a minute they'd act like that!" Nona pouted. The white half of his face grimaced as he twisted to sit up; she couldn't make out the black half at all. "You'd think most of them wasn't right out there on the Red Fork road with us. Now they're gonna act like butter won't melt in their mouths." He struggled to his feet, began to walk away. "Where are you going? Wait!" Nona jumped up and ran after him

She tried to keep up with him as he left the damp lawn, walking fast, making his way down the hill toward the Arkansas River. In the moonlight, in the distance, she saw him plunge into the undergrowth near the bank, and she hurried after him, but the ground was harsh beneath her naked feet, and she had to cull her way through the scrub like a berry-picker. By the time she reached him he'd already washed the blood away, washed most of the black cork and white clay from his face and hands. He crouched on the bank, staring intently, slit-eyed, at the glowing refineries across the river.

"You all right?" He didn't answer. Nona stood preening a moment, smoothing her hair, brushing imagined dirt off the buckskin. "D'ja ever see such a bunch of hypocrites?" Her laugh trilled, and then her voice dropped an octave. "'Dedmeyer! Did you bring this abomination?'" she imitated her husband's bombast, then her voice silvered into oily tenderness: "'Now, listen here, friend, let's just calm down a minute.'" She laughed again. "Tell you what, this town's going to talk of nothing else for a month! Nothing!" She was so taken with her triumph that she didn't notice the silence of the one crouched beside her. "We sure stirred up a little storm for the old sanctimonious frauds, didn't we? Like Cletus Floyd-Jones wasn't out there in the big middle of it, shouting orders like an old army sergeant, 'Y'all fetch that rope over here!' And now he's gonna act so shocked. Did you see his face? 'My word, Sheriff!'" she tsked. "'What're we going to do about this fellow barging in here reminding us of our nasty little selves? Why, we better beat the hell out of him like we done Roy Belton!'"

She caught herself, reached down and caressed Japheth's shoulder, a little breathless, aroused by the scent of violence, though the evidence had been washed clean, all but that which could not be bathed away: the cut above his left eye, the bruised swelling along the bridge of his nose, which she could see even in the cold moonlight. "Well, you know good and well why the sheriff got so mad," she cooed. "He's fixing to lose the 'lection over that lynching and he knows it! Don't tell anybody, but he'd've lost if he *hadn't* let them take that scamp out his jail. He's bound to lose either way." She laughed again, looking up at the swollen moon.

Nona was too excited to perceive the force rising from the sand earth. Her mind was filled with images of the last Saturday night in August, a sultry night so different from this one, hot, dank, the sky thick with storm scud and the bass rumble of distant thunder, black clouds racing across the moon's half-face so that it had appeared to be the moon itself running madly across the dark heavens. They'd brushed against each other by accident at first, or perhaps it was accident, but she hadn't moved away. L.O. was over with Cletus Floyd-Jones and some reporter interrogating the prisoner, and Nona stayed just exactly where her husband put her, gazing straight ahead at Roy Belton smoking a cigarette and mumbling answers to their questions, while the side of a strange man's thigh pressed against hers. She knew he was a roughneck, or she believed he was, though she didn't look at him, and she'd have been content with just that, would have liked it, in fact, preferred it: to stand side by side with a stranger, touching the side of a man's thigh with her hip for half an hour, and then walk off and never see his face, never look at him. But just before they put the noose around Belton's neck, the stranger leaned toward her, breathing scentless breath on her cheek, said, "He's doped."

"No," she said.

"Sure. Look at him. Look how glassy his eyes is. Somebody doped him." She looked at the condemned man, uncertain if the whisperer was right, but then Belton swayed a little as the rope thunked thickly around his neck, and she decided the stranger was telling the truth. "How'd you know that?" she whispered.

"I ought to know if the fool's doped. He's my partner."

Nona looked up at last, titillated, shocked, pleased. The newspapers kept saying Belton had a partner who'd escaped. She saw his face then, shadowed beneath a soft hat-brim, flickering in the torchlight, slender-featured, sensuous, distinct. He winked at her. "Just kidding. You ought to see your face. Name's Charley Ware. You?" And she told him, not just her name, but many things, while the prisoner choked and kicked and fell silent, while the body dropped to earth when they cut him down and the people rushed forward to snatch bits of rope and cloth and skin. Told him her husband's name and how to get in touch with her once he'd settled in at his sister's, and she told him where his sister lived. He spoke Letha's married name, and she described for him precisely the house on South Carson, all the while scanning the crowd of a thousand, passing again and again over the highest and the lowest, the young and the old, male and female, wealthy and working class and rock-sucking poor, all strata of Oklahoma converged on the Red Fork road for one purpose—except they weren't mixed black and white and red, as the whole population was, but white only. That was the very night she'd come up with her idea for the lynched man's exhibition at her masquerade.

Even now the brilliance of the idea electrified her. Nona's mind skated again to the hushed ballroom, the shocked faces, vanished servants. She laughed. "Oh, I got to get back, L.O.'ll have my hide!" In fact, it was the chaos, the consternation and turmoil she'd created, that she wanted to return to. Again she touched his shoulder. "You gonna be all right?" He kept silent. "Ring me up Monday," she whispered, though there was still no need to whisper: they were far, far from anyone. "Regular time. I'll tell you when I can come. Charley? All right?" She was confused, unprepared, more astonished than her own astonished ballroom had been a half-hour past, when the slim, dark form leapt up at her from the bank of the river.

He couldn't stay longer, exposed on this sandbar beside the meandering water gliding slowly south, too wide, in its vulnerable crawl. Japheth found a sandstone boulder, stripped off his bloody shirt, used it to bind the stone to the body's belly, and with uncanny strength he dragged the lifeless weight over the sand. He kicked off his boots, hurled them one at a time into the water, waded out. The body tried to sink before he'd got it well into the current, but he put his arm around its neck, the way one rescues a drowning victim, and swam out to the heart of the river, and then he let it go. The white buckskin gleamed only an instant in the moonlight before it disappeared. Japheth kept swimming, across the dirty Arkansas, thick with sand, slick with oil washed down from the Cleveland field, rank with the spewings of Josh Cosden's refineries on the other side. He moved in a slow, leisurely breaststroke, his dark head gliding on the surface.

If the river was cold he didn't feel it, any more than he felt heat or strain or fear. He was aware only of the viscous flow buoying him downstream, the scent of deepearth dregs merged with the water, floating on the surface, foul, gummy, ignitable. About the woman whose life he'd squeezed from the copper-stained throat he felt nothing. One moment she was the cause of his ignominy, his outrage and defeat, and the next she was a passing danger, for she knew too much, but neither of these truths caused him to kill her; he'd killed her simply, coldly, without feeling, in surrender to the force rising inside him.

After a time he stopped stroking, allowed the current to move him, his gaze on the small licks of fire darting up from smokestacks on the far bank, where the foul odor belched. When the river had carried him well south of the refineries, Japheth began to swim again, but lazily, without purpose. His first impulse to escape was eased now, and he drifted in a kind of pleasurable dream. The polluted waters swelled the darkness in him, enlarging that absolute to which he'd surrendered long ago, as the lynching of Roy Belton had swelled it, as the killing of Nona Murphy made it grow, as each breath and thought and stroke increased it. The odor of alchemy wafted downwind from the receding smokestacks, where the earth's blackblood was being distilled into gasoline, into casinghead gas, fuel oil, kerosene—into power of force—and he inhaled it as he glided down the wide khaki river.

He walked out of the water naked from the waist up, though in the moon's glow he appeared to be wearing a white shirt, for his skin was dark where the sun had touched, fishwhite in the covered places. The pale chest and back and arms were bruised all over, and greasy with oil. For a long time he stood on the bank, shivering, chillbumps mottling his flesh as he peered through swollen eyes across the river at the lights of the Magic City; the malice in him widened before he turned and moved quickly over the sand beneath the cold eye of the moon, ducked into the tangled undergrowth.

There was the freezing all-night walk to Sapulpa, where he garroted a drunken pipecat for his boots and dry clothes and a pistol, shot a line rider at dawn for his Ford motorcar. Afterwards he drove directly to Iron Post, but the old lady's cabin was still empty. He spent the next several days in Bristow (hadn't he learned long ago that fools never hunt in the obvious places?), loitering around the speaks on the eastside, buying drinks with the dead men's money, trying to find out something. He scanned the papers, listened to oil talk and gossip, but never did he hear word of the Tiger woman. No word of his first murder either, though the second and third duly received their two inches of space in the Bristow and Sapulpa papers, along with several other notices of hijackings and killings in the oilboom towns. He'd thought it would make a tremendous scandal; he was disappointed to find no mention of Nona Murphy at all.

But soon Japheth dismissed her as his mind turned fully to his next purpose. He loaded commodities into the stolen Ford secreted in the brush along Sand Creek: a month's worth of dried beans, cornmeal, tinned meat, blankets filched from a clothesline, a checkered coat and new tan derby he'd taken off a drunk drummer passed out in the alley behind the dry-goods store. Once, he met Jim Logan coming out of Bristow Tool, and Japheth stepped into a nearby doorway. The driller continued along the street, got into his own battered Model T. Japheth smiled, fingered the faint babyhair mustache he'd started to grow. On his list of those he would obliterate, Jim Dee Logan ranked near the top.

That sweet enmity, in fact, almost made him incautious: he drove out to the location in bald daylight, seeing the driller's scowling face before him. As the stolen Ford topped a rise, he spied the X of a crown block above the snarl of oak. Japheth stomped the footfeed harder, thumping in the rutted road. But sense and stealth returned to him before he rounded the last curve, and he cut the motor, coasted to a silent stop. Quietly he set the brake and pushed open the door, moved along the rutted road until he stood just in the curve's bow, looking up. Gorge rose in him.

In the litter-fouled clearing, where a week ago there'd been only a clogged spudder, some broken casing, and a pond of mud, now, on this gray November morning, some fifty yards from the old hole, a fully outfitted cable-tool rig stood. The perfectly crosshatched grid towered eighty feet above the trees. Two roughnecks hustled around the derrick floor, a third balanced himself on a girt forty feet above the earth, holding on to one of the sway braces. The belt and engine houses weren't closed in, the floor remained exposed on sills, but the rigging-up had begun; he could see the derrick man setting the rig irons. Ben Koop was bent over in the engine house tying the boiler in to the engine. Jim Logan was striding the length of the platform, shouting orders at the roughnecks in a spume of oath-laden urgency.

Crouched on the leaf-strewn earth, Japheth watched the crew prepare to spud in the new well, and idly he wondered at how they'd got a rig built so fast, where Dedmeyer had scrounged up the money, but mostly, watching Logan through slitted eyes, he relived the beating he'd received from the half-dozen pompous oilmen, and from this one, Jim Dee Logan, high-and-mighty driller. At length the boiler roared to life and the bandwheel began to turn, and as the heavy spudding bit started to rise, Logan straddled the hole in the derrick floor; he steadied the cable with one hand and with the other he guided the thousand-pound bit as it plummeted. It met the soft earth with a thud. Japheth heard the sound of fists on his own giving flesh. The bit raised and dropped, raised and dropped, and the hidden earth beneath the floor opened, the subterranean water gurgled in, and the rocks below the world's surface were pulverized with a rhythmic *pound-poundpoundpound*. In that great disguise of sound Japheth returned to the stolen car, cranked the motor. He backed up along the track, dreaming sabotage, dreaming night destruction and ruin, dreaming murder.

B areheaded, barehanded, Jim Dee revolved the spudding bit each time it came up out of the hole, turned it with ungloved hands, daring the half ton of metal to crush his flesh, take off his head. By the time they'd made enough hole to switch to regular tools, his callused palms were fissured with tiny cracks, his lips and cheeks chapped with cold. He didn't pause but stamped over to check the loose brake on the bull wheel, hollering at Ben Koop to slap a tong on that screw, hurry up, dammit, they had a goddamn well to drill.

Within minutes he was lowering the two-ton string into the hole. He worked the tool string with one hand on the drilling line, reading the mud and rock below, while Koop hurried from engine house to forge to temper screw on his short legs, his red turkey-neck stretched heavenward, the sinews in his arms tight with knots. They worked rapidly, wordlessly, driller and tool dresser meshed in the mute rhythm they'd synchronized at Drumright seven years before. Neither man had any use for the rites and rituals of religion, but the two shared, sacredly, the sacrament of work. Once a well was spudded in, they hardly ate, seldom slept until the hole had proved or been abandoned. Koop and Logan had made better than five hundred holes together, and they shared a union that was like a marriage, more compatible than most marriages; they didn't need to talk, because work was the sacrament, and work was not about words; it was about the feel.

Within days they'd drilled through the treacherous bentonite into shale, into sandstone, were passing a thousand feet, and the drilling went on, unceasing, but there was something about this hole that did not feel right to Ben Koop, or, more accurately, there was something about his boss. Never had he seen the driller distracted, but twice now he'd had to remind him to watch that slipping brake on the bull wheel, and once he saw him drilling a loose line, so that Koop feared what he'd never seen from the hands of Jim Logan: a crooked hole. That time he'd called out and caught him, but mostly the toolie said nothing, just kept his eyes open and went to pull the tools before Logan hardly seemed to know it was time to dress them, and in general found ways to make up for the driller's puzzling and dangerous distraction.

If Jim Dee was distracted, he was no less relentless: he worked like a man hounded by demons, born to pound holes in the planet, a natural-born driller, which he was, though he'd lived aimlessly for a quarter of a century before finding it out. It seemed now like fate that he'd been passing through Indian Territory in those first days of the oil boom, though at the time he'd thought it just a run of bad luck: I.T. was the very place he'd avoided since he walked out of his father's house at the age of eleven, changed his last name, and headed west. For years he'd wandered through California, Texas, Utah, Arizona Territory, driven by an itch to roam coupled with a lust for work received from his father, from the long line of men before his father, who worked because work was the salt and meat of living, because work was the one salvation they could believe in. He had tried his hand at cowboying, coal mining, panning for gold, but no job of work could assuage the restless burn in him.

He'd been on his way from Denton, Texas, to a rail job in Kansas City when, sitting on a siding in Sapulpa one noon in 1906, he heard that the toolie on an oil rig near Kiefer had been blown to bits when the nitro wagon hit a bad bump. Shredded like wheat, the fellow said, right along with the shooter, you couldn't tell whose parts was which. Takes a fool to hitch a ride on the nitro wagon anyhow, but they were sure looking to hire another, and damn quick, though a man needn't apply unless he could sling a sixteen-pound sledge one-handed and wanted to travel from rig to rig to rig. Jim Dee thought the job might suit him, and he'd gone to Kiefer that evening and hired on.

Before the next day was ended—June 7, 1906—Jim Dee Logan, born Lodi, had found his life's work. He saw right off that it wasn't worth beans to dress tools, because the driller was the force on the rig: the driller was blacksmith, steamfitter, plumber, carpenter, mechanic; the one who gouged a hole in the world with a ton of steel and never paused any longer than it took to sink a well or plug a dry hole, strip the rig, load up, and move on. He hired on as toolie in the Glenn Pool, but six months later Jim Dee had made driller, and he'd been drilling ever since, never stopping as long as there was hole to make and light to see by. He'd partnered with Franklin Dedmeyer during the mad Cushing glut with the understanding that he'd be the sole driller on every one of their wildcat wells.

Now, though, when the crude-saturated Deep Fork Sand was only a few hundred feet down, Jim Dee couldn't keep his mind on his work. He barely glanced at the cuttings in the bailer, would log them carelessly, haphazardly, or dump them in the slushpit without bothering to record them at all, while his mind circled in resentment and doubt. Almost seven years he and Dedmeyer had been together, and that, too, was like a marriage, a bad one, but Jim Dee knew his partner very well. And one thing he knew was that Franklin Dedmeyer never willingly surrendered a sliver of control. Other oilmen might trade and barter endlessly, might sell off shares on a proven lease to develop promising new ones, but Delo Petroleum's meager history could be directly traced to that closed-fistedness on Franklin's part: if they ran out of capital he'd call a halt to drilling until he had the money coming in from elsewhere; he simply wouldn't trade lease shares for more operating funds—or he never had. It was a peculiar trait in a wildcatter, not a very good one, but Jim Dee had never tried to persuade him otherwise, because if it weren't for Franklin he'd still be a hired-out driller jobbing around, and because, secretly, he had that same greedy streak in himself. Always he'd believed that when they finally made the big strike the wealth would be split fifty-fifty between them.

And now Franklin had let L.O. Murphy in on the lease. He hadn't consulted Jim Dee about it, had just showed up in a hired buggy the next Monday after Murphy's party and told him Delo's credit at Bristow Tool was good, go order what he needed, hire in a crew quick, and get that rig built. Zeke Loveless at the tool supply was the one who told him who was signing the checks, and Jim Dee had been furious, but his blood could smell the earth's blood flowing in the Deep Fork bottoms, and he'd had to go on. He'd made out the order, hired the crew, built the rig. Now, though, the closer they got to the source, and the more the oil called out to him, the more he loathed the idea that somebody else was going to have a piece of it. This strike was going to pass Cushing, he knew it, beat Cleveland and Burbank, rival even the legendary old Spindletop. Greed turned to suspicion as he mulled over the fact he'd seen nothing to prove Franklin's claim that he'd tracked down the old colored woman, got her X on the wildcat lease, had it all legally signed and notarized and filed in the Creek County Courthouse in the name of Delo Petroleum Corporation. Franklin hemmed and hawed when Jim Dee asked to see his lease copies, had promised to bring them, but he never had. Inside Jim Dee the suspicion swelled like the waterlogged bentonite clay, became thick certainty, clogging not just his mind but his capabilities.

By the bright Tuesday morning before Thanksgiving, when Franklin rode out in L.O. Murphy's new Pierce-Arrow, with L.O. himself behind the wheel, puffing a fat cigar, that certainty in Jim Dee had turned to viscous, numbing rage. It was powerful enough that he did what for fourteen years he'd done only to pull tools or lower casing or fish the swallowed-up tool string out of the hole: he shouted for Koop to disconnect the piston arm, and the ceaseless rocking of the walking beam ended, and the pounding at the earth's core went suddenly still.

From his position on the derrick floor Jim Dee could see a woman in the back seat, sitting sideways in a veiled tulle hat and a man's duster. His brain tried to dismiss her as Murphy's little trollop of a wife. But one does not fail to recognize an icon carried in the mind so many years. Jim Dee squinted skyward. The sun was wasting. He turned and glowered at Franklin, at L.O. Murphy, but his scowl was for Althea, and though her face was hidden behind the gauzy veil, he knew she saw. He watched her open the car door, open a parasol, lift it over her shrouded head; he kept his eyes on the men, but his awareness was on Althea as she picked her way through the mud, her arm on Franklin's arm.

Of the several reckless acts Jim Dee Logan had performed in his life, sleeping with his partner's wife had been the most lasting—though it hadn't been anything nearly so intimate as sleep, but a hard, awkward coupling on the sweaty dufold in the rented house on Olympia, with the cicadas whining in the yard trees, the sticky August light filtering through the venetian blinds, both of them listening every minute for Franklin's step on the porch. There'd been no pleasure in it. She was bristly as a currycomb, all teeth, nails, bones, tension, and it had happened just once, three years ago last August. But for Jim Dee, who was used to taking his relief from deft if bored professionals, it had not been about that anyway. It had been about . . . what? Not her beauty, which was harsher each time he saw her, and in any case was completely obscured now by the veiled hat. She paused, lifted her head as if to peer up at the towering derrick, and he surrendered to the old wordless connection that had little to do with carnality. Her will was part of it, that gritty hunger in her, which his desire responded to, and there was the fact that he knew, or he believed that he knew, every minute, what she was thinking.

Franklin called up to him, "How's it going, buddy?" The power was still roaring in the engine house but the shout carried well; it was that condescending "buddy," as if the driller were another hired hand, no more skilled than a boll weevil, that caused Jim Dee not to answer. L.O. Murphy strutted along in front, reached the belthouse before Franklin and Althea were halfway across the clearing. He stepped up onto the walkway as if he owned the rig, and probably he did, probably his assets had paid for every cable, brace, tool, and timber. A grunt escaped him as he climbed onto the derrick floor; he swept past Jim Dee, went immediately for the logbook, calling out, "How many feet now, you reckon?"

Jim Dee didn't answer. He stood with arms folded, leaning on the Samson post, staring down at Franklin guiding his wife onto the planks. "What the hell'd you bring her for?" he called, but he couldn't keep the calm in his voice over the sound of the steam engine, and so he hollered for Koop to cut it off. The toolie shot him a look, but he went and cut the boiler. Jim Dee's voice was mild, detached, when he said to the cold air, "Ain't you heard it's bad luck to bring a woman on a rig?"

Franklin laughed. "Aye, Cap'n. See, darling, I told you he'd give us a hard time. Watch your hem there. I'm afraid there's no place to sit. Jim won't build a lazy bench, I told you. He doesn't care much for an audience."

"Waste of wood." The tone was bland as pudding, but the hazel eyes skewed down as he watched Althea step up before her husband onto the derrick floor; he tried to pierce the netting that spilled from the wide hat-brim, covering her face, her neck, foaming into a great filmy bow beneath her chin.

"You don't have to stop for us, buddy!" Franklin was in a magnanimous mood, his head thrown back, voice booming. "We're glad for the noise. Stand right there, darling." He positioned Althea beside the bull wheel as if she were a mannequin. "We were talking on the way out." His excited gaze swept from his wife, to L.O. Murphy poring over the logbook, back to Althea again. "We're glad to put up with a little grease for the privilege of seeing it, isn't that right, darling? Crank her up, Benny!" he yelled. "Thea's never watched a well blow in!"

But Ben Koop took his orders from the driller, and since Logan remained leaning on the Samson post, Koop continued pumping the forge bellows as though he hadn't heard.

"Let's have a look at that log." Franklin started toward L.O. "I'll tell you what, if you can make sense of this driller's shorthand you're an abler man than I am." He glanced at the greasy, graphite-blackened book, frowning, and set it back in the cubbyhole; he took a couple of steps toward the belthouse. "Say, we'll go down and try to get a look at that seep in a minute. The water's half over the bank and all muddied to Jesus, I don't know that we'll see anything this time of year, but we can try."

"I'm in on your bragging, Dedmeyer." L.O. reached for the drilling log again. "If it's a dry hole it's coming out of your hide." The tone was jovial, his florid face wreathed in cigar smoke, but the threat underneath was perceptible enough.

"I got a thick hide, friend. I believe another slice or two out of it won't take me to the bone yet! L.O.'s been anxious to have a look at his big investment," he muttered to Jim Dee, then he turned grandly back to L.O. "No better time to come have a look than the day she's drilled in, right, partner?"

Jim Dee heard how he himself had been transformed in Franklin's loud munificence from "partner" to "buddy," L.O. Murphy converted from "that chiseling s.o.b. Murphy" to "partner," and the viscid rage swelled in him. He stepped away from the post. "I want to know what the hell you're up to."

"Up to?" Franklin tried to laugh. A baffled look crossed his face.

"You know what I'm talking about."

"What?"

"My blame lease copies, for one thing."

Franklin's face darkened. "Is that what you called us out here about?"

"Called you? I ain't called you for nothing, but I'm getting ready to call you *on* something. You told me six times you were going to bring them, I ain't seen 'em yet."

"I'd like to know what's got your nose so out of joint. When did you ever want paperwork brought out to a location? Place for that's the safe-deposit box at the bank. What are you going to do with them out here but get the blame things lost?"

"That'd be my lookout, wouldn't it?" Jim Dee turned suddenly to Althea. "What have you got on that ugly widow's hat for?"

"Why, to protect myself," she said vaguely from behind the veil. "My complexion. The wind . . ."

"You look like you're ready for a funeral."

"We scrounged up that duster to protect her pretty dress, too, didn't we sweetheart?" Franklin said, as if it weren't a strange comment, weirdly intimate from one man to another man's wife. "Darling, don't you want to go sit in the car? It'll be warmer." Smoothly, Franklin stepped across the platform, took Althea's arm. "When that gusher blows she'll rain crude from here to Christmas."

"What makes you so all-fired sure she's coming in?" Jim Dee scowled at Franklin. "Did I say a goddamn word about any goddamn show?"

"Watch your language in front of my wife. You're treading dangerous water, buddy."

"You call me *buddy* one more time, you're going to be wearing this tong for a hat."

"What's got into you? I never saw you act like this."

"Listen!" Althea hissed, the word released like steam in the cold air. She had untied the netted veil and rolled it up to the hat's wide brim; she was staring at the muddy curve where the track turned out of the clearing. The bright, still air, hushed with the absence of machine sound, rang crystalline with silence, so that the vibration in the distance spiraled through the bare arms of the blackjacks: the low signature grumbling of a tin lizzie motor coming along the built road.

The Model T chugged into the clearing, stopped nose-to-rear behind the Pierce-Arrow, snubbed up incongruously against it, like a plowmule cinched to a racehorse. When her brother stepped from the mudcaked car, there was a faint huff from Althea, a sudden expulsion of breath. He was thin as a knife blade, pale, famished-looking, wearing a dirty tan derby and a shiny check-vested suit, his chin and upper lip graced with fine, sparse dark hair.

"Good morning, people," Japheth said. "Sister." He tipped the derby. "What good luck to find y'all here. I didn't expect to find you all here together." And the insouciant smile he lifted toward them told Franklin it had been Japheth, not Jim Dee, who'd left word at the Hotel Tulsa that Delo Corp was wanted out at the location; told Althea it had been her brother's hand which had penned the scrap of paper she'd found in the mail box: *Come with them. J.D.*

"What the hell do you want?" Jim Dee gave voice to the unvoiced question ricocheting in the clearing.

"Why is it folks always think I want something? Just thought I'd drive out and have a look."

"You been banned from this location," Franklin said.

"How's that?"

"You damn well know what I'm saying."

Ben Koop began to edge toward the engine house to lay his hands on the twelve-gauge shotgun propped in a corner. L.O. Murphy relit his cigar. He was irritated at how close Japheth had parked behind his Pierce-Arrow, could see clearly that the fellow was up to something, but he hadn't yet recognized the piebald lynched man who'd ruined his masquerade: the very man L.O. believed his wife had run off with. Within a day of her disappearance L.O. had hired an ex-Pinkerton detective to track Nona down, and in the meantime he'd had it noised about that his wife was in Georgia visiting relatives. It wasn't the first time she'd disappeared: he'd found her once in Dallas with a cattleman, once in a Colorado silver-mining town. If any of the masquerade guests had noticed that he was alone as he wished them good night when the ball was over, none had commented on it to him, and L.O. had pushed that night's turmoil to the back of his mind. But there was something about this fellow that didn't sit right, and as L.O. puffed on the Cubano to get it lit, he watched the man closely.

"Speaking of location." Japheth stroked the down on his upper lip, smiling faintly. "This well's just about six miles from where Letha and me grew up. Isn't that strange? Life has a peculiar way of looping back on a person." He looked steadily at Althea. "No matter how desperately that person tries to go in a line straight ahead." His gaze passed to the curve of trees by the water. "About like the path of that Deep Fork yonder. That's how that crazy river does, you know it? Acts like it's going one direction, but if you try to walk it, you'll find yourself looping back where you came from, like a nightcrawler. You ever done that? Hold a nightcrawler in the middle, watch it twist and curl back on itself?" It was hard to tell whom he was asking. "I have. A snake'll do that, too."

Koop had retrieved the shotgun, was coming along the walkway with it, not aimed, but cradled loosely in his arms. Japheth smiled, shook his head. "You intend to use that, you'd better be ready to shoot Sister, too. She's a witness." He held his hands up, fingers spread. "I'm unarmed."

"Trespassing is grounds to shoot a man in this state," Franklin said. "You're on my land."

"Whose land?"

Franklin felt both Jim Dee and L.O. turn and look at him. "What's that sign say?" he snapped, after an instant's hesitation.

Japheth stepped backward, feigning surprise. He read aloud the painted board nailed to a tree: "'The Delo #2, Drilled by Delo Petroleum Corporation.' Ought to say the Iola Tiger #2, hadn't it?"

"Sign says it's Delo's well," Franklin said. "You are no part of Delo Petroleum, so I suggest you remount that automobile, turn it around and head back to town."

"Whose well?" Japheth's voice was smooth, unguent. "Whose well, Mr. Logan?" He tipped his head. "Mr. Murphy? Your partner here wouldn't be hiding anything from you, would he?" Something in Japheth's sneer, the cocked turn of his head, suddenly made L.O. recognize him.

"It's that son of a bitch!"

"What?" Japheth's smile vanished.

"Where's my wife, you bastard?"

Japheth began to back toward the automobiles. "I don't know anything about your wife, Murphy! I'm here on oil business! Dedmeyer's lying to you! Both of you!"

L.O. had already started toward him. "I'll wring your goddamn neck."

"Wait!" Jim Dee stepped in front of Murphy. "Let's hear him."

"Don't you all know when you've been taken by a liar?" Japheth paused near Murphy's Pierce-Arrow. The smile he turned up to the driller was pure venom. "I guess you know your partner's jacking you over with Murphy here. The minute the field proves, you're going to find out just how tight they got the noose around your neck, and I'll tell you why: Mr. L.O. Murphy wouldn't come in for any less than half." His voice rose over L.O.'s threatening rumble. "Or that's what he *said*. But just to let you in on a secret, I happen to know he was desperate to get in on this deal. So desperate he couldn't be bothered to go look for his missing wife— Oh, sir, this is a swell automobile." Japheth's head swiveled as if he'd just noticed the Pierce-Arrow. "Beautiful. You know," he offered confidentially, "from what I hear, you might try Saint Louie when you get around to it, heard she ran off with a cornet player. Of course," he addressed the others, holding them with the purity of his audacity, "Mr.

Murphy's desperation was matched by Delo Corp's, no doubt about it. But he's a skillful old poker player and he put on a good bluff, didn't you, sir? Got in for half, like you wanted."

Japheth crept slowly forward in the sudden silence. "Now, we all know Franklin Dedmeyer's not about to split half in half again and take only that. Not Franklin Dedmeyer, wildcatter deluxe. After all, he's the one had to go track down the old freedwoman, get her mark on the papers, on account of me and the driller messed that deal up. You had to get the lease filed properly, didn't you, Brother? Isn't that what you said? Of course you've got to squeeze out your old driller friend, you can't take a measly little quarter-share. Oh, don't feel too bad about jacking over a seven-year partner, son of a bitch's been doing it right back to you. That's something you didn't know, isn't it? Logan cut me in months ago. But then he tried to renege on the deal." Japheth cocked his head toward the driller. "A full third partner, yessir, just for me driving out to Iron Post to get the old lady's *X*. Reckon why he'd want to do that? Wouldn't pay her a nickel, though. Hell, I didn't have nothing to negotiate with but a stick of dynamite, no wonder I couldn't get the job done." He smiled at Franklin. "What do you suppose went with that two hundred you gave him? He didn't hand it over to the old nigger, I can testify to that. Now, that's one lie from Logan, but it's not lie number one. Lie number one would be how he's been screwing your wife. I always figured he cut me in—"

"He's a liar!" Althea shrieked. "He's lying!"

The cry echoed away, and in its absence the roar of the forge fire behind the engine house huffed like distant wind.

"Somehow I knew you were going to say that, Sister. But how's a body to believe it when a liar calls a man a liar? Say, that's some sour faces y'all are pulling. What have you people got to be sour about? I'm the one's been lied to. That's all right, though. I can deal with liars, I got no special prejudice against them. Everybody's liars. Take Letha there, for instance, her whole life's a lie. Or maybe she just neglects to mention a few facts. Like how she's got five living sisters. You wouldn't think a little thing like that could slip a person's mind, would you? Used to be seven girls altogether, but Winema's dead. Did I tell you we lost Nema, dear? Same damn flu that took Mama, back in '18, that blame epidemic flu. I guess I forgot to tell you. Must be a family trait, this absentmindedness. It's really something, isn't it, Brother?" Japheth lifted the derby, swiped the back of his forearm against his brow as if to wipe sweat, though it was cold in the clearing, cold and stunned and silent. "Looks like there's just no end to what you don't know about your wife."

"Shut up," Althea said.

Japheth turned his slitted gaze on her. "She came back to see us one time," he said. "Wagging a sack of horehound candy. Lord, we scrambled and fought over that junk. I was just a little bitty thing, but I remember." He seemed to be addressing an invisible audience, but his eyes never left Althea's face. "I guess she was already on her way to being a *fine* lady. You ought to see how she lives now. Got a big fancy white house in Tulsa, got her own personal nigger. That's true. She's got a pretty nigger maid'll do just whatever you order her to do. Man, if I had one of them, I'd eat breakfast in bed every morning. I surely would. I used to dream about that, somebody to do all my work for me. We worked hard, all us kids. We had to. Daddy took off and left before I was born, or that's what they tell me, I don't remember. Sure remember how we worked, though. Except Letha, of course. She was already gone."

He paused, scanned the men's faces. "She tried to kill me before she left," he said matter-of-factly. "I didn't know that for a long time. It's funny, I used to think there was something special about her because she was gone and nobody'd talk about her, and then she showed up that time with a sack of candy, looking so pretty to my four-year-old eyes, I guess, in that goosefeather hat. I thought she was my dream mama. I didn't know she'd tried to beat my head in. I don't guess anybody ever would have told me, I just heard it by accident. Learned right then it pays to keep your ears open. I come in from the barn one morning, Jody and Mama were in the kitchen screaming at each other. I was six then, maybe. Yeah, six. Mama's yelling, You're going to end up like your sister, and Jody's shouting back, I ain't like Letha! I never tried to kill a hours-old baby, for one thing! Well, of course, I didn't know they were talking about me. Jody's screaming, You did it, Mama, you put her up to it! and Mama's hissing, If you don't shut that smart mouth of yours I'm going to come over there with this skillet, and Jody yells, You know the reason Japheth ain't right in the head is because she dropped him on it the day he was born!"

His voice dropped to a suave whisper. "You know, that was a real revelation to me, all that news at once. I never knew they thought I wasn't right in the head. Mama wasn't yelling at all then, she was hardly whispering, I had to lean my ear close to the door—Mama's hissing, Shut up! She never dropped him!" Now Japheth's voice oscillated between a young girl's high-pitched whine and the rasp of an old crone: "*She did, Mama, she did!* Shut your mouth, girl! *She was going to beat his brains out! I saw her!* Get out of my sight before I snatch you baldheaded! *She had that ugly baby slung up over her head right over the rocks.* I'll shut it for you! *If that old Creek woman hadn't stopped her she was going to smash him like a gourd!* Shut up! Shut up! *I won't shut up! I saw it! She's wicked bad and good riddance to her, but I ain't like that, don't you dare say I am!*

"Hunh!" Japheth spat. "Saved by an Indian on the day I was born. That's funny, isn't it? Ugh. Meat. Bread." He gazed at his sister; his finely arched eyebrows, the feature that most declared his kinship to her, lifted in elegant contempt. "You remember them kids?"

"What do you want?" Althea rasped

"There's that blame question again. Well, I'll tell you. I want my share, that's all. Just my fair share. Now, a few weeks ago I was in for a third. Of course, that was before your husband here ran out of money and got in such a greedy big hurry, had to bring Murphy in to get hold of some capital." Japheth crooked his neck to peer up the eighty-foot derrick. "But Murphy's built us a pretty little rig here, hadn't he, Dedmeyer? I'm a reasonable man." His gaze passed slowly from one to another. "I'm willing to talk."

He started toward the Ford, but stopped abruptly, snapped his fingers. "Oh, you know, Brother, I been thinking. Hadn't you better let them know you never found that old niggerwoman? It's a shame to put all this money into a lease that's never been filed." His emollient voice rose in the clearing as he grinned up at Logan and Murphy. "Y'all don't believe me, go to the courthouse like I did and check." He clanged the car door shut, stuck his head out the open window. "Now, y'all please don't kill yourselves trying to sort out this mess of lies. I got some business to go see about." He tipped the filthy derby, started the motor; his eyes were on his sister when he called out over the noise of the motor, "After that, I'll be back."

Japheth drove away exulting, his insides raw with glee. He'd triumphed for an instant, and he suffered a kind of gnawing joy, but the winning wasn't complete. Its pleasures only whetted his hunger. The day was bright and cold, and he couldn't abide the thought of sitting alone in the thicket of brambles and riverwillows at his campsite. He drove on to Bristow, to a gin mill on the eastside, ordered a shot of white mule, stood at the bar eyeing the other drinkers as he savored the memory of the stunned, frightened faces on the derrick. He longed to have someone see how he'd beat them, his victory craved an audience, but the strangers at the bar couldn't bear witness; they didn't know what he'd been through. Japheth's mind turned to the final vanquishment. A dozen ways he dreamed it, and in every vision it was his own sly machinations that destroyed his enemies. He left his drink on the splintered wood, walked out blinking into the sunlight, got back into the murdered line-rider's Model T.

For the fourth time since September, he followed the rutted wagon road to Iron Post. The old woman was the last piece. As soon as he found her, he would have them all bested, completely. All of them.

The triumph was so real to him that he expected to see smoke rising from the rock chimney when he rounded the last bend. He was furious to find the old woman's cabin still empty. He sat in the car, thinking of the ways he would make her pay when he found her. She'd messed up his plans from the beginning, and his first plan had been so artful, so easy, because the driller had played right into it. Logan had blown the lease money almost as soon as Dedmeyer gave it to him, spent the whole two hundred on casing like an old sot on whiskey, and Japheth had been able to jump in, offer to fix it with the old woman. The plan, of course, was to claim the lease himself, but he'd been willing to bide his time, wait for the drilling to progress, because Japheth was no idiot: he was glad to let Delo foot the bill. For over a week he'd had Logan in his palm, would have had that horse's ass Dedmeyer, and so, finally, Sister herself, just exactly where he wanted, but the old niggerwoman showed up in a wagon with a dirty Indian, so that Logan started asking questions. Japheth had had to come out with the damn Delo lease, try to get her to sign it, in order to make the driller shut up—and the old woman had sat in her chair and stared at him, her nigger face closed; there'd been cunning in her, he thought, and stubbornness—but no submission, no fear. He was livid, he could have killed her right then, but he was too smart.

Instead, he came back the next night with a few sticks of dynamite for persuasion. When the bitch cur started toward him, growling and snapping, he blew a gratifying hole in her belly with Koop's twelve-gauge, and the other dogs yelped and took off. He crawled under the cabin and set the dynamite charges, and then went to hide in a nearby oak thicket till the old nigger should come home. It had poured rain all night, but he'd kept waiting, until dawn, until noon, until he knew she wasn't coming, and the hunger and fury and wet misery had driven him out of the timber, back to the Deep Fork, and as he bumped and slogged along the muddy road in Logan's tin lizzie, he'd promised himself that, when she did come, he would kill her.

The third time had been the day after he strangled Nona. The bitch dog's carcass, rotted and half eaten in the yard, spoke to him before he got out of the car. He could see the old redbone on the porch, lying flat, its ribs showing. The hound whined a little, thumped its tail once when Japheth climbed the steps, but the dog was too weak with starvation to stand up. Japheth shot the redbone, not to put it out of its misery but out of spitting frustration, and he tore up the inside of the cabin for a warning, though his heart wasn't in it. Even then he'd had a feeling she wouldn't be back.

Now he sat in the stolen Ford and glared at the cabin, its very presence an affront to him. The bones of the bitch cur gleamed in the yard, white in the afternoon sun, scattered, the skull dragged off somewhere. Beneath the shade of the porch roof he could see matted red hide flattened against the porch slats, as if the redbone's liquefied flesh had melted into the wood. No, the old niggerwoman had not been here. She defied him, still. He climbed the cabin steps; the stench of animal decay, the odors of disintegration were like musk to him as he pushed open the door. The one dark room was in chaos, chairs broken, crockery smashed, how he'd left it, only covered now in cobwebs. The thought flitted that she might in fact be dead, as Dedmeyer was gambling on. No. Japheth wouldn't allow that Iola Tiger could be dead. It didn't fit his plans. He seized a coal-oil lantern from the mantel, broke the globe, sprinkled the kerosene, but there were only a few drops left in the reservoir, and so he went back outside and fetched the gasoline can from the turtlehull, and when he sloshed the fuel on the puncheon floor the scent of petroleum mixed with the other smells and rose up in a kind of intoxicating fume of power inside the cabin. He paused in the doorway, inhaled deeply, tossed a lit match, and ran.

He was standing in the yard, watching fire lick the log walls through the broken window, when the explosion came. The concussion thrust him back, a satisfying blow against his chest, surprising—he'd forgotten the dynamite charge under the house—and though the log cabin was too strong to be blown apart by such a small blast, the force of it opened holes in the floor and ceiling, and the wind rushed in and fed the fire. Japheth watched, arms folded, leaning against the Model T at a safe, thrilling distance, as the logs went up like tinder; he wished he'd set more than three sticks of dynamite under the cabin. He wished the old woman was still inside.

After a few minutes he took a pistol from under the front seat and hid in the blackjacks east of the burning cabin with a mind to pick off a few nigger neighbors when they showed up to put out the fire. But no one came, even though the smoke billowed black in the November sky, signaling over the treetops. Nothing happened. The flames roared a while, and then the fuel was used up, and the fire began to wane. Japheth grew bored, grew empty. There weren't even any dogs to kill. He got in the Model T, drove back to his campsite.

But something had changed. No longer could he bear to conceal himself in the brush, weaving plans. Sons of bitches didn't do what his mind dreamed they'd do anyhow. He tried to keep his thoughts focused, but inside Japheth two forces pulled against each other: one called him to his old pleasures of sly, scornful scheming; the other, birthed by the beating on the Murphys' moonlit lawn, rushing into him from the oilsoaked sands of the river, swelling as he'd squeezed the life from Nona's slim neck, called him to pure destruction.

The next morning he drove to Sapulpa, to the Creek County Courthouse, and found that Dedmeyer had already filed a forged lease. His mind boiled with outrage. A damn forged lease, of course it was forged, and Japheth would prove it to them, prove it to the courts—as soon as he'd tracked down the old freedwoman, got her to sign over to him every last lying drop. He would need her alive for that. He'd have to put his mind on where to find her. As he perused the record of filed leases, Japheth realized for the first time that Gypsy Oil, not Delo Petroleum, owned the leases on the abutting allotments. How had Dedmeyer let a thing like that slip past? Japheth smiled. A new plan began to unwind itself.

On the way back to Bristow he stopped at a juke joint near Kellyville, and throughout the afternoon he leaned on the bar, sipping choc beer, plotting, but he couldn't keep his mind on his plans. The more he drank of the thick, milky liquor, the more he kept seeing his sister's features, her black, scornful eyes and haughty sneer, or, in his mind's eye, he'd watch the driller's scowling face turn away from him, dismissing him in contempt. Japheth drank in silence, glaring now and then at some white man or Indian whose glance caught his attention; he dreamed a dark, unfocused vengeance, on the old niggerwoman who'd defied him, the toolie who'd held a shotgun on him, the two pompous husbands who'd tried to bully him. But the sweetest depths of his hatred centered on the one who'd beaten him bloody on the moonlit lawn, and on the other, the sister who had tried to smash his head in before a time he could remember.

By nightfall Japheth was back at the Deep Fork, hiding in the brush, watching. They were all still here, except Sister. The men stood in a small circle, warming themselves by a campfire. At first Japheth felt a kind of dull, half-drunken pleasure, seeing that Dedmeyer hadn't gone home with Aletha, but then he realized that his brother-in-law stayed, not because of Japheth's triumphant accusations, but because he expected the well to drill-in any moment. They all expected it. No one was willing to leave the rig, even to sleep.

Just after daylight, Japheth watched in impotent fury as Logan and Koop screwed on the control head, fit the Christmas tree. When the rumbling started in the earth's bowels and a spray of gas and oil began to sizzle around the drilling line, there was only hushed excitement on the derrick floor. The control head vibrated mightily, and the driller opened a valve, slowly, and a stream of oil shot into the tank. Carefully, excruciatingly slowly, Logan opened all the valves on the Christmas tree, but within minutes he was shouting at Koop, "Shut her in! Shut her in!" The five-hundred-barrel tank had filled in less than twenty minutes.

On the rig the men were weirdly quiet, eyeing one another, eyeing the woods, as if they expected the very blackjacks to betray them, proclaim their unprotected strike to the world.

They shut the well in till they got hold of more tankage, turned the oil into the line so fast an outsider could believe nothing had happened—but it was already too late. Within an hour of the strike Japheth was sitting in Gypsy Oil's front office in Bristow, suggesting they might want to send a scout to the Delo location at Section 35-T, 16-N, R8E, on the Deep Fork. The next morning Gypsy recommenced drilling on the Yargee lease, a half-mile west of the Delo location; this time they were making hole right on the line.

Logan and his crew had to pull tools and rush over to where the two Creek allotments joined one another; they had to start drilling offset wells immediately, fifty yards across the line, because the law of capture said oil belonged to whichever company pulled it up from the ground. Gypsy Oil could siphon every drop from under Iola Tiger's allotment if Delo didn't match each hole Gypsy drilled, rig for rig.

By week's end, Gypsy was spudding in their fifth well, and Dedmeyer and Murphy had hired four new crews, and the drilling went on furiously along the line, day and night.

Japheth hated to lose that amount of oil to Gypsy, but it was worth it, his mind told him, to get Delo away from the original location. Fools might hunt uselessly in the hidden places forever, but Japheth knew—had known as he watched the first greenish-black spewings around the drilling line—where the old niggerwoman would finally show up.

An old hen will steal her nest out, won't she? Lay her eggs in the hay meadow, way up in the barn rafters, anywhere she think that farmer can't find them. Her mind say, Them's *my* eggs, I'm going to hide my eggs till my little chicks come. Un huh. That is just what I done. I couldn't steal the Lord's earth out from under them whitemens, so what am I going to do but steal out myself? For a long time after the dark one leave that morning, I just sit on my porch, thinking. Afterwhile I gets up and walks off from that house where I lived with Bluford in all our time to-gether, my own Bluford, leave the dogs whining in the yard, just step off the porch and walk away. I wasn't afraid. I know how whitemens will set dynamite, knock a person in the head, do whatever they want to get hold of lease rights, but fear is not how come me to leave. The greed-devil got hold of me, that's what.

I come down to Boley and stay awhile with my daddy, but you think I tell my own daddy what I'm about? No sir. I don't tell a breathing soul. I do not tell God. That's how the spirit will do when it's been corrupted, and here is the full power of corruption: you don't have to have them little eggs in your hand, you only got to dream them, your mind say, *They mine.* Seven times seven days I lived in that narrow twisted greed place, look like this in my soul: burnt up, hungry, twisty pig trails going around and around in the same tracks, saying *Mine,* saying *Now,* saying, *Give me,* saying, *They, They, They*, saying *Hate* and *More* and *Too Late*. I quit doing the work the Lord have set for me. How am I going to help a child come in the world when my whole brain is eat up with lies? My mind telling me like this, say, That's *my* land, allotted to me by the U.S. federal government, what's in it and on it and under it supposed to be *mine*. Mind say, They haven't got my mark on the white piece of paper, let's just wait now. We going to bide our time, hide out in Boley and wait on them. When that oil come spouting out the ground they going to wish they did bring me my money, because we fixing to go right back there with our own piece of paper, see what kind of smile these whitemens got for theyself. Who's this *we* I'm talking about? Me and the greed-devil, I believe.

Weather turn cold finally, and my mind say, They bound to have got it by now, and I prepares myself to go. How? By right doing and right thinking and right praying? No ma'am. By calling on the Lord's power, how He have given it in medicine, in tobacco and cedar smoke and prayer? Never cross my mind to think about purification. All I'm thinking is how to get me a lawyer. A *lawyer*, child, that is what I got my crazy mind on. Quick as I get a good look at that oil, I'm going to go up to Tulsa, find me a colored lawyer knows just how to work whiteman's law. My mind whispering, Hurry. Go yonder and see what they doing. Hurry. Catch them stealing your oil out from your native earth.

So. I proceed on back to the Deep Fork, and this time everything change. I come alone, come walking. I taken the train up from Boley, because nobody's going to notice a lone colored woman riding in the colored car, and I think at Bristow I'll hire a buggy to carry me out to that place on the river. But when I climb down off the train I see that Bristow town is just wild with the greed-hunger, whitemens everywhere, noisy, rushing, they all in a fearsome hurry, seem like any direction I look is a danger. Seem like every person I see, colored, white, or Indian, is scheming to steal my oil money. You see how the greed-devil got me? I ought to been afraid of so many things, all I'm scared of is somebody going to take from me. I never once question how I get to thinking so strange. That day's a cold, gray day, look like it's fixing to sleet or spit rain or something, and I don't know what I'm going to do when I get yonder, but I don't want to join up with nobody. Nobody. My mind say, All right, we going to walk.

Trucks and wagons pass me, carrying pipes and lumber and big machine tools, they all going the same way I'm going, headed south. My mind say, See now, they carrying these things yonder to steal what rightfully belong to you, and I walk faster, choking in the cold dust from them trucks. Way down past the Little Deep, I come off the road, set out across the prairie. I don't aim to go by Iron Post, just go quiet around it, like you'd sneak past a sleeping yard dog. My mind won't let me think on Bluford, won't let me think on my house. Rain come finally, a cold fretsome rain, spitting needles at my face, I go in a empty barn shack, stay there all night listening to that freezing rain peck the tin roof. I am cold, I'm wet, hungry, miserable, miserable—but you look at the power of that force: next morning I go right back to that frozen mud-rutted road, set my face toward the Deep Fork again.

Late next day is when I come to the place where the road divide. Me and Istidji never seen no fork such as that one; these whitemens have cut a new road, and the many stumps are still raw where the trees have been hacked down. Off somewhere at the end of it is that terrible *bang bang bang bang,* and not one but many, yes, Lord, many, many, layered over each other like a great thunder. The old fork is the one that twist down to the river, where Istidji carried me that long time back. That's the road I take. Night is coming, and I am far from my peoples, far from home, far, far from my Lord. Let me tell you something, God have made no more haunted place on His earth than the Deep Fork bottoms at nightfall, but I keep walking on.

By the time I reach the water, the sky is darkening purple, the woods are turning black, but I can see a timber ladder rising like it want to climb up to heaven. It is no Jacob's ladder, though, I know that for true. The wheel-in-a-wheel is gone. That pounding sound is still booming soft through the treetops, way off west, but the clearing is quiet—not ordinary cold winter quiet, but more like something have gone out of the world. I stand back, just looking. Nobody around. Whitemens can't find it. That's what my mind say. They have quit pounding here because there's no oil under my earth. And, oh, the grief come on me, a terrible, unnatural grief.

Low and rushing then, finally, I hears it, a steady humming. The clearing is quiet, but it is not silent. Listen. Hear it? *Hmmmmmmm.* The earth's pulse. *Hmmmmmmm.* That's the sound of the world's blood pumping, pumping, up from the core through steel tubes into pipes into them huge round tanks hulked off in the distance. No kind of machine is pumping it: that oil is coming up through the power of its own force. Oh, they have found it all right, tapped the earth's bones, un-huh, and that black blood spewed forth, and now they siphoning it into pipes, into tanks, they going to try and hold it, but that force is not tamed.

Well, well, a voice say, look who's here. He step out from behind the sky ladder. You sure saving me a lot of trouble, old woman.

He look different, eaten away, the bones in his face sharp, his skin lighter, like a man locked away from the sun, like a jailed man. But the eaten-away look is not the whole change. He stand back, peer all around the clearing, up the road behind me, eyes squinched down to slits nearly, he say, How'd you get here? The light is drained away, but I can see his face floating like a ghost face. He keep studying the road behind me. You came out here by yourself, didn't you? he say, and then he start toward me.

I feel that hunger force, the greed rising, and something else, but I can't name it, swelling in that clearing.

They take me for a fool, he say. He talk soft, coming toward me. You ever heard of fool's gold, old woman? They got a million dollars' worth of fool's black gold. He stop sudden, listening. You hear that? he whisper.

I think he's talking about the low earthpulse under that sky ladder, but, no, he look off behind the trees, where the pounding is coming from, over west.

Know what that is? he say. Night drilling. Guess where.

He stare past me at the empty road. A smile slice his face then, a cold, white thing in the darkness. He turn and look at me. Tell me something, old woman. What would it take to get that driller to walk off from a hole, come down here where I want him?

An owl start up hooting then, way off in the shadows by the water, and my soul is frightened, it sense something so terrible, so awful, it want to shrink down.

He keep looking at me, say, They're sure going to be surprised to see you. His smile look like a pale glowing fishbelly in the dark. In my mind I see a half-blueblack half-fishwhite baby. I see a great mound of white flesh, moving, crawling, I see blood and water, red dust swirling in high wind. Everything fall together inside me, and I see that misshapen infant I taken out his sister's hands. That same one.

Now—now, when it is too late—I'm going to know him.

My mind full of every picture, the little foxface girl running, shrieking, so I got to turn back, go quick to the ravine behind that house, see the darkhair middling girl raising up that blighted baby, she's holding him over her head, to smash him, smash that infant down to the earth. In my mind I cry out, how I cried in Creek language that gray noontime twenty years ago, *No!*

His long white fishhand come from behind him, where he been hiding it, he's holding a coiled rope. See, old woman? he whisper. I knew you'd come.

I try to turn, try to get away from that place, but he flip the rope around me so fast I can't run. He cinch my arms down, pull the rope tight, and take to shoving me up the road, to the place where the road curve, push me against a post oak at the edge, wrap that rope around, tying me to the tree. All while he's wrapping, he talk soft and steady, not to me, though. He's talking like he got people listening inside his head. He's saying about it would of been so easy, he wasn't in no hurry, he had them fools right in his hand, and on and on. In my mind I see that dressed-up whitewoman in my dooryard, see her scrawny backside, how she turn and walk away. I see blood up and down the front of that little muslin dress. The same one. They both two the same. My whole self is shaking. I can feel that power-force swelling. I don't know what it is.

He knot the rope, step back. It's full dark now, I can't hardly see him. When his voice come it is like the night talking, and the sound is flat, no rise or fall to it, he say, You're going to sign this. I can see a white flutter, he's holding out a piece of paper. Right in front of those fools, he say, in your own ignorant nigger-hand. He lean toward me, breathe on me his breath that have no smell. I know then he don't know me, or he don't know me for the birthwoman who saved him. He only know me for a freedwoman been allotted this cursed piece of Deep Fork-bottom land. He whisper, You and me's fixing to drive up to Bristow this evening. You're going to tell the law just exactly what I tell you to say.

Then he turn and walk off.

I am caught in a deep place, trying to know what my soul is feeling. I am trembling now, oh Lord, in my soul. It's not death I'm afraid of—death is so close it breathe on me, too, but death's going to carry me to my Saviour, I'm not afraid to die. What make me so scared is what I feel rising in the clearing, swelling, I don't know what it is—not evil, my mind say. Evil is born of the spirit, it's a spirit force. This force here come from the material world. There under the sky ladder, that hole yonder: that is where the force pour into the world.

Over in the dark by the river I hears a little boom, and then a great *whoosh*, and one of them big tanks lights afire. That whole clearing turn bright as noon—I sees him walking back toward me, slow in the road, swinging his arms like he got all the time in the world. He have a knife in his hand, I can see the light glint on it. He stop in front of me.

We got us a little wait, he say.

Off west I can hear motorcars coming, and when they get near, he cut the rope, fast as anything, go to push me out to the road. Here come a long black car roaring around the curve, and behind it two trucks, coming fast. They all got to stop sudden, squealing, because us two standing in the middle of the road. That yellowhair man, Mister Dedmeyer, he jump out, come running up fast, and behind him is the lighthair Logan, and the little redhair banty man, they all running, other whitemens jump off the two trucks, everybody cussing, shouting.

The dark one stand still, smiling, he got that knife point stuck against me. Now the yellowhair man get close enough to see me. He stop cold. The others stop behind him. Everybody get quiet. I hear the fire now, like a roaring, feel the heat on my back.

Much obliged y'all come to help me, the dark one say.

Move out of the way, Mister Dedmeyer say.

The dark one start in to talk about me like I'm a stump, say, Ain't you even going to mention what I got here? Found her right here at the location, ain't that strange?

Mister Dedmeyer won't look at me. He shout about they got to get in there, that separator's fixing to go. The lighthair man, Logan, take a step forward, but the dark one lift up the knife, say, Naw, now, I wouldn't. And Mister Logan stand still.

The dark one keep talking, like he can't stop hisself, like he been sitting out here in the haunted bottoms so long his mouth want to boil over with words. He talking 'bout it's a dirty shame this poor old nigger ain't seen a drop of lease money. Yonder's her well, he say, you people can't find it in your hearts to pay her a red cent.

He put the knife to me, right up against my belly. I can feel the point of it touching. That's all right, though, he say. She's done signed this lease here. And he wave that piece of paper in his other hand, like a weapon, like it have its own power, like I already put my mark on it. But that piece of paper is not the power. The dark one sneer at the whitemens, say, Ain't I told you people Dedmeyer's a liar? That lease at the courthouse is a fake. It ain't got Iola Tiger's mark on it. Am I right, old woman? Right? And he push the knife against me, slip it like a silver flash against me. But that knife is not what cause me to tremble.

Mister Dedmeyer say, Somebody shoot that son of a so and so, we got to get in there.

But the others don't move.

See, now, the dark one say, that's how it is. Folks aren't usually just jumping to risk their lives on a fire ain't theirs.

That lease is worthless, Mister Dedmeyer call out. And then he start talking all about how I can't make no such decision on account of I'm crazy and I'm ignorant and I ain't got good sense. He say he already got me declared, he's my guardian, I can't sign a thing without his say-so.

But I hold my peace, trembling. It don't matter what that yellowhair say. Don't matter if I put my mark on that paper or don't put it, don't matter if any one of us standing in that road lives or dies. Because I know now what my soul feel pouring through that clearing: it is two forces joined together—the spirit force of evil and that power from under the earth, joined together. I feels them, united, pulsing up from below, unleashing a terrible destruction into the world.

There's another little boom sound then, and another tank lights up, *whoosh*, and the other whitemens all take off running back to the trucks, motors start, they're yelling, shouting, and the front three, Logan and Dedmeyer and the redhair, they stand still one second, and then they too turn and run. The dark one let me loose. He have forgot all about me. I feels that knife point just fall away. He's jumping up and down in the road, cursing, shouting, waving that white piece of paper. Them trucks fixing to drive over him, look like, trying to get to where that oil is burning. I just turn and walk away. Go into the brush like maybe I can hide there. But I can't hide. Can't nobody hide anymore.

T he winter stretched before her, interminable, hopeless, moving
toward a spring she neither expected nor desired. She thought it
would last forever: endless ugly gray days strung together with jeweled af-
ternoons of brilliant sun and sudden warmth. On the bright days in particular, Althea took to her bed. She ordered new heavy damask drapes to
replace the lace curtains at the window. Perhaps once a week she roused
sufficiently to put on the veiled hat and take a cab to the Exchange National Bank to draw funds; she portioned out the money to Graceful for
the shopping. From time to time she'd appear at the bottom of the stairs
and bark a few orders, tell Graceful to polish the teakwood and silver, or
she'd slip into the library and stand with one hand draped along the
ebony curve of the telephone, her eyes gazing in the middle distance as
she tried to think of whom she wanted to call.

But a life lived on a lie, once the lie is extracted, becomes remarkably
flaccid, limp of purpose, soft and tenebrous around the hole where the lie
stood. Mostly Althea read in her bedroom, sensational novels that held no
threat of edification or truth. She'd draped the mahogany mirror. That
trick had come about by accident one evening when she flung her silk
robe against the wall and it inadvertently landed on the vanity, but the relief was so enormous that she'd left the robe across the mirror's face for

three days before replacing it with a triple-folded swatch of the lace curtain that had once filtered light at the window.

Downstairs, Graceful went about her duties in a kind of leaden re-
moteness. She was grateful that the woman stayed in her room, but with
the husband gone there was too little to do. Mrs. Dedmeyer hardly ate
enough to justify heating the stove; the woman wore the same dressing
gown for days on end, so there was almost no laundry to put through the
Eden, and she no longer tracked in mud from the garden, so that the
kitchen floor stayed clean for a week after Graceful mopped and waxed it.
Often Graceful would find herself standing at the back door, staring out,
unseeing, as her mind explored the interior of her body. One noon in the
third week of December, she felt the child move. A faint flutter, like moth-
wings, like delicately batting lashes, but it was inside her: inside her, and
separate from her, and one with her. Living. Her soul tore.

Christmas came and went, a day of hurtful sun and church bells peal-
ing in the distance, along Boston Avenue downtown. Mrs. Dedmeyer
didn't seem to notice its passing, but Graceful was aware every minute of
the day's meaning. She prepared the woman's breakfast (which would be
left entirely untouched on the tray outside the bedroom door: the only
sign Althea was aware of the date), seeing in her mind pictures of her
mama and sisters and brothers in the house on North Elgin, the rush and
secrets and cooking and Willie hanging at the table, saying, How much
longer, Mama, how long? Graceful hadn't cried since the afternoon by the
creek near Bigheart, but on Christmas Day her insides cramped and
raged and trembled, and she thought if grief could kill the unwanted thing
inside her this day's hurt would kill it, and she surrendered to the ferocity
of the pain, guiltily, in that awful hope. But the next morning, when she
got up to light the stove, the eyelash heartbeat flutter yet quivered in her
belly, the living life. It was then that Graceful sat down at the little table
against the wall inside the kitchen and wept.

She was sitting just there, again, many days later—how much later?
Two weeks? A month? After the year turned, the days flowed one into another without definition. But she was sitting just the same way, her hand
on her womb, touching the swelling mound as she stared out at the gray,
cold porch, when she sensed Mrs. Dedmeyer standing in the passage.
Graceful didn't flinch; for some minutes she didn't even bother to glance
up. The woman's silent, sneaking approaches had always been the condition of working in this house. Graceful expected a feeble carping: Mrs.
Dedmeyer's tirades now were faded, toothless; they barely irritated.

Woman need to eat more, Graceful thought indifferently. *She 'bout to dry up.* But Mrs. Dedmeyer didn't speak, and at last Graceful looked up. The woman was staring quizzically at her, a sort of half-distracted, half-interested gaze.

Slowly Graceful rose from the chair, stood waiting beside the little table. The black skirt of the maid's uniform rode up toward her breasts, and she reached to smooth it down. "Ma'am?" she said at last.

But the woman remained silent, staring at her as if she only half perceived her, as if in the back of her mind she calculated something. "My word," she said at last, faintly, the sound drawn out in a kind of distant wonder.

Don't tell me she don't know, Graceful thought. Each morning when she delivered the linen-covered tray upstairs, she waited for the woman to say something, but Mrs. Dedmeyer only asked about the mail, any telephone calls; often she didn't speak at all but merely motioned impatiently for Graceful to set the tray down and leave. *Take a blind woman not to know.*

Blind was the choice word. On some level Althea had known, yes— she'd perceived it even as far back as the Murphys' party, when she'd seen the softening in Graceful's face—but she had no willingness to receive it. Now, sunk since November in the blue misery that desired neither light nor air nor food nor future, she was blind to all the world, including, perhaps most especially, Graceful herself. But the accident of coming upon her in that classic gesture, hand touching swollen belly, a sign she'd seen her own mother make so many times, forced the unwanted knowledge into Althea's cobwebby brain. She narrowed her eyes. "Graceful?" she said at last. "When's that baby due?"

Graceful gazed ahead, mouth closed.

"Have you made arrangements?" At the girl's continuing silence Althea swept into the kitchen, crossed the gleaming white floor. She stopped a few feet away, eyeing Graceful's skirt. "Looks fairly soon to me."

"Not soon." Graceful had never reckoned the exact time, because reckoning would force her back to the night of the seed's planting; she refused it. All she carried were the vague words: *when warm weather come.* It was not warm now but a day of sleety rain changing to all-rain changing back to sleet, a slate day that had seemed all day to grow darker. *She going to make me go, on a spitty day of cold rain. That's how she do.* "You be wanting supper, ma'am?" she said dully. The woman's appetite was so fitful that Graceful had quit trying to predict it, just prepared what she wanted for herself, dished up a small amount on a fine china plate and carried it upstairs. Sometimes the woman ate; sometimes she didn't.

"Why . . . yes." Althea's voice was surprised. "Yes. I believe I will have a little something. Just a bite. Graceful?" Her tone softened, became hollow, less true, but infinitely nicer. "Is the fa— Do you have somebody to take the baby? I guess you've taken care of things?" She'd almost said *father*, but she didn't want to shut the girl's face even tighter; she didn't want to acknowledge anything of the girl's separate life. She wanted only to hear that arrangements had been made, that this bump in the monotony of her own existence would quickly be rolled over, smoothed down. Well, that was how other people's live-in help did, wasn't it? Left their offspring with relatives or . . . somebody . . . and stayed through the week in the servants' quarters over the garage or in the maid's room, returned to Little Africa on Thursdays and Sundays to tend to their own. Some did. Most did. "Are you—" She couldn't bring herself to finish the sentence: *going to leave me?*

"I got a fryer cut up in the icebox," Graceful said. "Do chicken sound good to you?"

"Chicken'll be fine. Not fried, though, chicken and dumplings, how you used to make them for Mr. Dedmeyer." Althea frowned; a shadow passed behind her eyes. She put a hand to her temple, stood quite still, breathing deeply through her nostrils. When she spoke again her voice was low, well modulated; she didn't look at Graceful, but her tone was direct. "I don't know if Mr. Dedmeyer . . . I don't know what's going to happen. What I mean is, where, or, that is . . . how are you going to . . . have the baby? I mean, are you going to go . . . Do you people . . . have midwives or . . . ? What I'm trying to say, if you . . . Will you have to go back to colored town?" She was pained, embarrassed.

But there the question was in the damp air of the kitchen: the very question that Graceful herself had skeered away from, dreaded, lain awake nights asking without ever reaching an answer.

"I don't know, ma'am."

"What do you mean, you don't know? What do colored girls usually do?"

Graceful continued to stand with her face lifted, nostrils flared; her eyes canted toward Althea for an instant. What did the woman think, having babies was different for colored women? At last she muttered, "Some have a midwife. Some go to the doctor. Some just . . . have they child."

Another moment of silence passed. The freezing rain ticked at the porch roof. Althea shivered, drew her wrapper around herself. She looked out the window. In this cold rain Franklin would be . . . What would he be doing now? There'd been no word since his telegram saying there'd been some trouble in the field, a rig fire; he'd arranged for her to draw an allowance at the Exchange National Bank. The wire mentioned nothing about him coming home. Althea's gaze remained on the fogged glass as she asked vaguely, "What about you?"

"I haven't made up my mind. Just deal with it . . . when it come along. That's all."

Althea's full attention returned to Graceful. "You can't do that. You have to plan for it. I mean, doesn't a doctor have to see you or something? You can't just call them up out of the clear blue . . . ?" But her thoughts trailed away. Perhaps they could. Perhaps that was the way colored people did things. "Well," she said, and crossed the floor briskly to the sink, try-ing to dismiss from her mind the declarative fact that her own mother never made plans for childbirth; for Rachel Whiteside, in the four preg-nancies that Aletha Jean as middle child could remember, the birth-woman had come only once.

Althea jerked the spigot on fullforce, and the rusty water gushed. She held her hands under the stream, spoke loudly over her shoulder. "You have to give me some notice. You know you can't just go off and leave me." She splashed her face with the cold water, elbowed the spigot closed, stood with her hands and face dripping. Her teeth were chattering. She wore only the thin silk gown and wrapper. Suddenly she looked down at the dark splotches where the water streaked the blue silk. When had she last dressed herself? Washed her hair? What if Franklin should come home and see her like this? Oh, she'd have to draw a bath; she would put on the rosepink tea dress. She would have Graceful come up right away, freshen the bedroom—dear God, when was the last time that girl changed the sheets?

Rousing herself to start snapping orders, Althea turned, and was sur-prised to see Graceful still standing in the too-tight maid's uniform, still staring at the floor in silence, her face closed in the old manner. The girl's hand was on her distended belly; it was not a tender gesture but more a tentative prying, the way one's fingers return again and again to a half-healed sore. Graceful's face lifted; she met her gaze.

Without words, facial tic, gesture, the knowledge passed between them: not the full truth, not the abhorred name of the father, but even to Althea's self-absorbed mind Graceful's dread and wretchedness were plain, and she understood that there was no husband, no boyfriend. "Graceful? You don't have to go back to Greenwood." She tried to make her voice sound efficient, empathetic, though it feathered out almost wistful. "Wouldn't a colored doctor come here? I mean, it could be here, as far as I'm concerned. You could have it here."

The girl didn't answer. After a moment she dropped her hand away from her womb, crossed the floor to the icebox. "You want your supper upstairs?"

"No. No. The dining room will be fine," Althea said. She stayed in the kitchen, watched Graceful moving slowly, methodically, mixing flour, rolling dumplings between her palms, and in the back of Althea's throat there was a tense, relieved satisfaction.

From the cocoon of her darkened room Althea emerged, if not transformed, at least focused on the world in a new way. In the few seconds of wordless exchange, when she'd recognized not just the girl's pain but their mutual isolation, their dependence on each other, Althea received a new purpose. She told herself that she would, magnanimously, allow the girl to stay here and have her bastard child. She would, in fact, help her. The next morning, she went to the Ladies Auxiliary League and procured several lying-in dresses, a bit faded and threadbare perhaps, but perfectly serviceable. She bought a new feathertick to put on Graceful's cot, that the girl might sleep more comfortably, and she told Graceful to order an extra quart of milk from the milkman every other day—And drink it, if you please, you'll lose a tooth. Althea's old vision of herself as a patroness of benevolence and grace returned, but this, too, was changed, tempered by the puzzling sadness that would well up from time to time, surprising her, flooding her chest as she watched the girl work.

More than once Graceful wished the woman would take to her bed again and shut the door. Althea no longer appeared out of nowhere in little catsneak creepings; she openly followed Graceful around, not issuing orders as before, but solicitously directing her in how to do things, getting in the way. She didn't lessen Graceful's load—in fact, her emergence from the bedroom caused more work than Graceful'd had to do through all the late autumn and winter—but she often trailed behind her saying, "Here, let me get that." When Graceful hoisted a heavy laundry basket to her hip,

Althea would grasp one handle awkwardly, bump Graceful's hips or belly, nearly force her out the door backward, or she'd walk ahead of her and limply hold open the screen. Yet in some ways Graceful was glad for the whitewoman's company. At least she, Graceful, no longer had to sit alone in the kitchen for hours, thinking, or trying not to think. And when she lay down at night she was too exhausted from the day's work and the demands of the growing baby to lie staring into the darkness. Her most immediate dread had been assuaged: for a little while longer she would not have to find another place. She could stay at the Dedmeyers' until it came.

And then there was that: the indefinite pronoun shared. In the same way that siblings in a family with a violent father might never put a name to the force that rules every breath but refer only in low tones, without need of explanation, to "he," just so "it" dominated the lives of the two women. Each took the oblique pronoun to mean, equally, the unborn child in the womb, the newborn when it should finally get here, and the event of the birth itself: an unseeable and unknowable future fated "it." They seldom spoke the word aloud, but it was the shared unspoken knowledge of an unnamed force, and it silently joined them.

Spring came early and hard, not stealing slowly, fitfully awake, but bursting fullblown out of the southwest, ferocious with nightstorms, blustery with daywinds, and by the second week in March the redbud trees had bloomed all over the city, and by the third week the beautiful blossoms were gone, ripped from the trees by the violent wind, skittering in tiny magenta flutters along the paved and unpaved streets, bleeding in matted wavelike piles soaked by the plunging rains. Graceful seemed with each passing day to grow slower in her movements, more calm, or perhaps she was merely in a stupor: she seemed to move as through a swamp, her very center of gravity settling deeper and deeper, sucked down toward the earth. But Althea grew more restless. Daily she paced the house, unable to settle on something to do, and as the weather warmed she grew increasingly frightened. The sun had returned, but her husband had not. Still she had no word from him; she had tried calling the Laurel Hotel in Bristow, but they said there was no Mr. Dedmeyer registered there. She pored over the oil reports in the newspapers; she knew the Deep Fork field had been fully defined, that it was producing fifteen thousand barrels a day for Delo and Gypsy, a good strike, though it was no Burbank or Glenn Pool: it wasn't the big one. Why wouldn't he come home? The only way she knew he was still alive was by how the bills were always paid, and when she went to the bank on Mondays to draw her household funds for the week, that precise amount, and no more, was in the account, along with a terse note signed in Franklin's hand for her to be allowed to withdraw it.

At first Althea kept her fears fused in her mute bones, and only at night, in her room alone, did she give in to them. Then she would stand at the undraped window and shake her fists at the passing storms, or pace up and down, cursing under her breath. But she did not take to her bed again. In the daytime she'd sit in the swing on the side porch, gazing at the clustered dandelions and tender poke shoots erupting all over her rose garden, telling herself she was to begin weeding today, this very afternoon, but always she would end by going into the house and calling out some mindless chore for Graceful. Their lives were so unvaried, so mired in the routine of meals neither cared to eat and a too-big house shined and mopped and waxed which no guest ever entered, and their turgid conversations were so mutually understood, so internally referential and plain, that the two women were like an old married couple. "That do?" Graceful would say, meaning, *Is this sideboard polished to suit you?* or *Is that all the laundry you want done?* or *You want toast with your eggs this morning? I don't aim to mix biscuits,* and Althea would nod or murmur "Fine," or perhaps "No," or "Once more, if you don't mind." Althea might say, "It's going to be too late for Easter, I think," or "Weather's going to be hot as sin by the time it gets here," meaning the child and the impending birth, and Graceful would not even bother to nod but would simply acquiesce or deny with her dense, torpid silence. Eventually Althea began to speak about Franklin.

Her words were cryptic at first, as elliptical as their other exchanges, though more nervously rendered; she would say things like, "You'd think he'd have finished by now. Wouldn't you think he'd be tired of hanging around that trashy town?" or "I'll bet he'd give anything for one of your fried pies. Doesn't it look like he could come home on Sundays? At least?" and, later, "There were some things I shouldn't have done," and, finally, "He won't forgive me. I'm afraid he's not ever going to come back. He . . . might not come back. Oh, Graceful, what am I going to do?"

Graceful never answered, never commented, but received, unruffled, in that placid pool of her seeming equanimity, what Althea told her. She had her own troubling thoughts, and they paralleled Althea's and contrasted them, thoughts that said she ought to phone the *Star* office this morning, just speak to Hedgemon a minute or two, see if he'd heard anything from T.J. Maybe she could ask him to go by Mama, go see the children a little while, so he could tell her how they looked, how they were. Then she'd catch a glimpse of her ever larger and larger self in the library mirror, and the impulse to telephone Hedgemon would vanish. If she called, he would ask to see her. If she called, he might refuse to keep picking up her letters from the post box and carrying them to Mama. Often she'd gaze down at herself, saying silently, *After it come*, meaning in an inverted way, *after it's gone*, as if the act of birth would wipe out all her troubles.

The sixteenth day of May was sweltering, with a gauzy haze of sunlight that shimmered all around the house, veiled the street, hid the full length of the garden. Althea had gone so far as to don her gardening dress and dig her sunhat out of the hall closet, but at ten o'clock in the morning she still sat in the porch swing, fanning herself with it. Inside the house she could hear Graceful moving slowly through the dining room with the dustmop, *thump* and, feebly, *thump*, and after a long while a faint little *tump*. Then she heard the dustmop handle crack against the wood floor at the same instant Graceful cried out.

Althea cursed herself as she hurried through the French doors, for of course she knew what it was, as she'd known all along that this moment would come, and never, damn her for a thoughtless fool, had she prepared for it, really. Her mind flew through all the possibilities she'd dreamed up and never settled on, and she stopped on the opposite side of the walnut table. The girl's back rose and fell in shuddery breaths as she leaned on the breakfront, resting her full weight on the polished wood. After a long while Graceful straightened, stood up tall, but she didn't turn. The two looked at each other in the mirror.

"Well," Althea said, the word at once a flat comment, a question, and a kind of chagrined shrug. Graceful answered only with her steady gaze, but between them passed the wordless acknowledgment that, yes, her time had come, and then she was cramped with a fresh pain. She tried to hold the sound inside, but the sound and the pain were one, and, gasping, she let the sound loose, a sharp high cry, as if that would spew out the pain, but the pain went on stretching and closing and clamping, and she cried out even louder, a near scream; she heard the sound as if it did not belong to her mouth. The pains had been coming since before dawn, low, grasping her insides, like her monthly gone mad, or like she needed to empty herself, and she'd entered the little bathroom a dozen times, but that couldn't help. She'd tried to keep on working through them, because motion helped, or it seemed to help, and she'd been able, through the morning, to hold in the sound, but the pains had moved around to her backside now, and they were worse, twisting, cramping, stabbing her spine; she wanted to bend over with them, but she was too big to bend. She leaned on the breakfront again. From a great distance she heard the whitewoman's voice.

"What do you want me to do? Do you want me to call a doctor? What doctor? Give me a name!"

The pain ebbed, fell away, was gone finally. Graceful stood once more on her own weight, panting slightly.

"I told you we had to make some arrangements," Althea snapped. She came around the table. Graceful was nudging the head of the fallen dust-mop out from under the breakfront with her foot; grunting a little, she leaned over as if to reach down and pick it up. "What are you doing? Give me that! Jesus." Althea snatched up the dustmop, leaned it against the wall. "Well?" she said. "Here we are. What did I tell you?"

She was furious that she had not made a plan—or that was not quite true, she'd made several plans, she'd simply not settled on any. She'd toyed with the idea of calling Dr. Taylor, but she was almost certain he would not treat a colored girl, and what if there should be a problem? No colored person could be admitted to Hillcrest or to any other white hospital in town. A white doctor was no good. She'd thought of bringing in the handsome light-skinned doctor who had bandaged her feet; she didn't know where he was, but she could find her way to the newspaper office and the editor would tell her. Good God, no, what was she thinking? She was not going to go traipsing into Little Africa again, that was out of the question. Sometimes, though, she found herself imagining the yellow shotgun house, seeing herself on the front porch at the door, the dark woman from the photograph, wearing the same elegant white turn-of-the-century dress, standing inside the screen, and Althea speaking to her, warmly, urgently, saying, Your daughter's in my home; she needs you. But no. If Graceful wanted her mother, she would have gone to her. Althea understood very well that the girl did not want her mother. She'd questioned her several times about a colored midwife who might be willing to come, but the brown face would instantly close down, and Graceful would murmur something like, I got to aks around.

Well, it was only a baby, good Lord, women had been having babies since the beginning of time. This colored girl did not need a doctor; she probably didn't even need a birthwoman. But what if something went wrong? What if the baby got stuck? What if—? Thoughts of the actual labor would erupt, always, into memories of the one terrible birth Althea had witnessed, and immediately she had to reduce everything to that vague future "it": she would turn her mind to the weedy garden, the cherry banister that needed oil, something, anything, in order not to see. And so they'd never decided on anything, never made the proper arrangements, and now here the goose was trying to have her baby in Althea's immaculate dining room, and the old returning visions of fluid and blood roared through her, and she said, "Get in the bed! This minute. You can't have it standing up like an old milk cow."

The girl groaned and leaned on the breakfront again, and the groan grew louder, grew high-pitched and shrill; it frightened Althea. The cry became a howl, a gaping, wordless wail that rose in union with the pain, and Althea said, "Come on!" Terrified lest water and blood pour down on her beautiful polished hardwood floor, as it had poured down on her mother's roseprint rug, as it had poured from between her mother's legs, darkening the red earth beneath her mother's feet, Althea shouted again, "Come!" She tried to take the girl's hand pressed to the breakfront, and Graceful instantly grabbed her fingers, gripping like the clamp of teeth, squeezing until Althea herself yelped with pain, and still Graceful held on—gradually, slowly easing her clench as the wave passed.

She let go of the whitewoman's hand, embarrassed. Lord, she had never thought it would be this bad, why they never told her it was this bad? She was sweating; the shapeless shift she wore was soaked under the arms, all down her front. The woman was griping again, what she say? Would the whitewoman in her awful ways never shut up?

"Come on, here, I'll help you."

They had to stop again as they crossed the kitchen, once more in the back hall for the pain to pass, before they reached the maid's room. Graceful did not want to lie down, but she couldn't stand up, and so she sat on the edge of the narrow cot, leaning into the pain, groaning, until the groan became the released sound, and it was so bad in her spine, so bad; she tried to reach behind herself to press against her own lower back, but the pain came too hard, and all she could do to ease it was yell. She was still sitting so, spraddlelegged, arms braced on the feathertick, riding into the beginning of another pain while the woman's distant voice carped around her, when her water broke. It poured from her like a flood that would never stop, like she was wetting herself without control, and she batted the woman's hand away, but the woman's hand was firm, insistent, and Graceful let her pull the soaked shift up over her head, but she stayed inside the pain, and when it began to recede she felt a piece of cloth come around her, a clean, soapsmelling sheet.

"Lay down," the woman said. "Aren't you supposed to lay down?"

Graceful shook her head, not so much to say no, but in confusion, exhaustion; she didn't know what she was supposed to do. She allowed the woman to help her to lie down on her side as another wave began to cramp and twist. "My back," she grunted. "Push my back." It took Althea a minute to understand what the girl wanted, but when she reached over the huge body and put her palms on the girl's naked lower back, Graceful gritted out through clenched teeth, "Harder. Ma'am. Harder," and then surrendered to the groan that turned to cry and then to howl. When the long wave of pain had passed, she said, panting, "That help. Some."

"Well," Althea said, and then, uselessly, "here," and she pulled the sheet up to cover the girl, though it was so hot in the little room she herself was pouring sweat, and the smell, dear God, it was enough to make a person retch. "I've got to go put some water on," she said, although she didn't know what for, but she'd always heard that: first you boiled the water. She wanted to get out of that room. Graceful lay very still on her side, eyes shut, and Althea, thinking she hadn't heard, started to repeat herself, but the girl moaned and reached out for her hand, said, "Here it come." She squeezed Althea's hand so hard she pinched the bones, and she began that strange, strained huffing as she reached with her other hand, snatched off the sheet, pleading, "My back. Ma'am. Please." She gripped Althea's fingers tight, and Althea tried to pull away, she tried not to look down at such a swelling of brown skin, such a living mass of brown womanflesh; she didn't want to see Graceful's navel pushed out, tumescent, like a man-thing on the great brown swollen globe, she didn't want to see Graceful's breasts, the excruciating intimacy of Graceful's belly and thighs, and her mind said stupidly, That brand new feathertick is going to be ruined. "Ohhhh," Graceful groaned, "push on my back. Push my back. Ma'am!"

There was nothing else to do. Althea twisted free of the girl's grip and reached across her, put her fingers on the girl's spine, and pressed hard with the slim strength of her slight arms, but the angle was awkward, there was no room, she was actually pulling the girl toward her rather than pushing, and she could feel the heat of the girl's body beneath her, felt the great soft flesh and the drumhard belly rise and fall with the girl's yell. When the wave had passed, Althea straightened up immediately and took a step back; she said officiously, "You're going to have to turn over, Graceful. I can't get a good grip from here."

Again Graceful lay motionless with her eyes closed, as if in a deep sleep, but when Althea prodded her shoulder, she mumbled, "Yes, all right." With a low groan she allowed Althea to help her turn to her other side, allowed her to spread the sheet across her once more, but the instant the next pain came she threw it off. Althea didn't need to ask this time. She pushed at the girl's lower back with all her weight. She could feel the hard muscles radiating from Graceful's spine, could feel the incredible strength of the girl's body, like the strength of the whole world converged, homed on the one task of laboring forth this baby. She pressed harder and harder as each pain welled, and Graceful rode with the pain, yelled with the pain, not in fear or hurt but for the release of its sound, so that the two women, joined in near silence through the cold months into spring, were married now in a loud, wordless, voiced rhythm as the birthpains came closer and closer together, multiplying in intensity, purpose, strength, and for Graceful the whitewoman was a only pair of hands kneading their feeble relief into the torment in her back, and for Althea the laboring girl was only an extension of her own barren, fading self, but it was the pulse of the labor that dictated their actions, as it dictated their union, as it dictated the moment Graceful had to roll over, and Althea had to help her to sit halfway up, head against the wall, and Graceful did not yell any longer but grunted deep in her diaphragm, an ancient sound, as she bore down.

What had been too flesh-real and private to be looked at an hour ago was now no more separate from Althea than her own skin. "Lean back," she barked. "Brace yourself. Here," and she tried to soften the wall with a pillow as Graceful pushed. "Oh, it's coming," Althea said. "It's coming!" The top of the child's head, wet and matted, showed in a round mottled patch, and for the slenderest part of an instant the old memory welled in Althea, but the dark head receded, sank back inside its mother's flesh, and every pore in Althea's being hummed, unmindful of self; she forgot everything but getting the baby free of the womb, the dark tunnel, out into the world. Graceful wasn't sounding the pain now, but Althea was, or she was talking loud, chanting, "Here it comes, it's coming, good, honey, you're doing good, oh, oh, here it is now, Graceful, push!" But the patch of head, having swelled forward, receded once more. "Almost," Althea puffed, and then her chant rose again, "It's close now, here it is, one push, now, here it comes, we're so close now, come on, come, baby, push, mama, push—"

And when the baby's head emerged, facing up, Althea reached forward and turned one tiny shoulder as naturally as if she'd been told what to do, and the other shoulder came, the whole slender slick body slipped out, and Althea held him, gasping. Or no. She was crying. "A boy!" she said, as if Graceful couldn't see with her own eyes. Breathing hard, sobbing, half laughing, half crying, Althea held the living child in her two hands, unable to think what to do with him. She was exhilarated beyond anything she'd ever known. The baby blinked at Althea, silent, slick as salve, his fists and legs moving, his belly still corded to Graceful, his mouth open wide, nose clotted, round face shiny with mucus. You were supposed to spank them, Althea thought. Weren't you supposed to spank them? She gave the child a faint, trembling little shake, and he gulped for air, began to cry. Althea laid him on the bloodsoaked sheet between his mother's knees, took the hem of her gardening dress and began to wipe his face.

It was only then that she looked up and saw that Graceful, too, had been crying. Graceful was still crying, but her tears were not like Althea's tears, nothing like. In the brown, twisted face Althea saw an agony that was beyond her ken, unknowable to her: a sorrow that went to the heights and depths of the world and had nothing to do with her, and everything to do with her. The sadness that had hinted itself from time to time in the past months now rushed through Althea, multiplied a hundredfold, unfathomable, its source and meaning nameless, boundless. She watched, understanding nothing, as Graceful reached down between her legs and picked up her child.

PART FIVE

———

Fire

Greenwood
Tuesday
May 31, 1921

The call came in to Mr. Smitherman's office a little after four-thirty in the afternoon. The new sheriff didn't stay on the line long; he said only, "We got this boy up here and I think we can keep him, but there's a lot of talk going round, a lot of talk. I don't know if you've seen the evening paper, but looks like there's going to be trouble. You might want to come down."

Smitherman clicked the earpiece in its cradle, stood for a long time staring at the oak casing on the wall before him. In his mind he saw the hard-burned image of limp, hanging bodies, the evil fruit of Southern live oak and elm, and a powerful dread was on him, and anger, and a furious fixed coldness. *No more!* his mind said.

On the top floor of the county courthouse at Fifth and Boulder, a young black man named Dick Rowland stood at the rear of a jail cell, his pulse pounding too loud in his ears for him to be able to pick out specific words from the angry murmur he heard rising from the street below. He was being held for assault on a white woman, though he and the elevator girl both knew that the car had jarred and he'd stepped on her foot—that's all, he'd stepped on a whitegirl's foot—but he knew, too, that the truth had no more power than that old deceitful word *justice* in the face of a mob's will to murder, and so Dick Rowland's thoughts were little different from the silent, bloodracing thoughts of Roy Belton as he sat in this same Tulsa jail cell on a stormy Saturday evening last August, or of Everett Candler in the Oklahoma County jail the following afternoon. No different from those of seventeen-year-old Marie Scott (Negro) in the predawn hours of a March morning six years ago, just before she was dragged screaming from the Wagoner County jail and lynched a block away; or of Oscar Martin (Negro) before he was hanged from the second-story balcony of the courthouse at Idabel; or the four horse thieves (White) left twirling silently in a barn near Ada; or the unnamed drifter, an anonymous black man, strung up from a light pole and shot on the main street of Holdenville last December: of any prisoner anywhere who ever waited in a jail cell sweating, praying, crying to believe, right up until the final writhing moment, that something would happen to stop men's killing hands.

At half past four, in the house on South Carson, Graceful was cutting lard into a pie crust on the kitchen counter; her baby slept, its lips nursing air, inside a pillowed basket on the tile floor at her feet. Outside, in the muddy garden, Althea knelt beside her riotously blooming Cimarron Tea Rose, mulching the roots. Her husband sat alone in a great leather chair in the lobby of the Hotel Tulsa. He had returned home just over a week ago to find his wife quiet and careful, a new little mulatto baby in the maid's room. He spent very little time at the house. Franklin took out his gold watch to check the time; frowning, he snapped the watch shut, tapped the ashes of his glowing cigar into the brass tray standing at his elbow.

On the north side of the city's invisible border, inside the printing plant in back of the *Star* office, Hedgemon Jackson worked with Lawrence at the great presses, darting forward to lay down sheets of fresh newsprint, jumping back out of the way. Out front, on Greenwood Avenue, a certain Creek freedwoman emerged from attorney I. H. Spears' law office, paused a moment, looked around. A faint shudder passed over her. She turned, made her way toward the Woods Building on the corner. Farther north, in the shotgun house on North Elgin, Cleotha Whiteside stirred her cavernous kettle of fresh-picked poke salat, while her daughter LaVona desultorily squeezed suds from the clothes in the tin washtub beside the back door. Willie played in a yard across the street with some other children. Jewell was down on Archer helping to decorate the hall for the high-school senior prom. Cleotha's new daughter-in-law lay hugely pregnant and useless on the bed in the middle bedroom. Over on Latimer Street her brother Delroy lay on his back on the garage floor beneath the

Nash truck. And in a dim and odoriferous choc joint near the Frisco tracks her eldest son was playing pool.

T.J. moved around the felt square noiselessly, on thin cardboard soles; his cuestick danced in the air, came down, slipped silently between kneeling fingers, stabbed suddenly. The balls snapped apart with a sound like cracked bones. Whether he missed a shot or ran the table, T.J. didn't speak. The big brownskinned war veteran he played against was also silent: Carl Little kept an eye on the game from his position against the bar, where he leaned on the roughcut slab in a cream-colored suit, sipping choctaw beer. Reports of the boy's arrest had spread quickly through Greenwood, and at the other end of the room angry voices rose in the smoky light.

"Dick Rowland ain't touched a whitegirl, he got better sense than that—"

"That don't matter, fool, they'll lynch a man for breathing the same air as a whitewoman—"

"I'm just saying—"

"You know they fixing to do that boy like they done the whiteboy last summer. . . ."

Downtown, on the white side of the divide, the crowd in front of the courthouse was getting larger. Day laborers coming off shift were joining the scores of out-of-work oilfield men and half-grown schoolboys milling on the corner near the newsboy hawking the bulldog edition with the cry, "Nigger nabbed for assault on white woman!" There were several here who'd been in this same location nine months before, on the last Saturday night in August, when the young man on the top floor who dreaded them and hated them and prayed for deliverance from them had been white. Across the street, leaning against a brick building, was one who'd hidden himself in that Belton lynch mob; he held back now, a shapeless hat pulled down over his eyes. The sun was still too high, too hot and bright, ruthless in its telling glare.

Japheth listened to the mob voices, but the men were spewing only the same boring maledictions, cursing the same unimaginative oaths, sucking from the same tin flasks secreted in the same mudcaked workboots. A wave of profound emptiness passed over him. This lynching would be tiresome, dull, ordinary; it would prove nothing new. Squinting against the westering sun, he peered from beneath his mashed hat-brim at the barred windows on the third floor. His lips lit suddenly in mockery of the old insouciant smile. Well, yes. He might as well wander on uptown, to the good choc joints in Little Africa, drink a beer, see how the niggers were taking this bit of news. Covertly, gracefully—at the precise moment one of the men in the crowd spat and asked in indignation, "Are we gone let these niggers rut all over our wimmin?" and the other men answered back, "Hell no!," Japheth slipped away from the corner of Fifth and Boulder, began walking north.

He stopped only once, to buy a copy of the evening *Tulsa Tribune* from a newsboy near the Frisco station, before he sauntered across the tracks in bright daylight, as other white men did after dark when they made their frequent, secret forays to the gambling houses and brothels, the juke joints and speakeasies on the north side of the tracks.

No stir occurred as he passed from the bright yellowgreen afternoon light into the sawdust-floored cavern nearest the station: Japheth's entrance was sleek, glabrous, like a grass snake gliding over a doorsill.

The only light in the joint came from a high, barred window at the rear of the room, two kerosene lanterns in sconces behind the bar, and the lone, bare incandescent bulb hanging over the pool table. Japheth ordered a choc beer, moved into the dim light at the end of the bar, spread his paper out on the roughcut slab, and silently sipped the thick milk-colored liquor as he read. The owner kept an eye on him, not so much because of his skin color, which was so blackened with weeks of sun and dirt as to be indeterminable—he could have been Indian, maybe, or Mexican, or Gypsy—but because Japheth was a stranger. The uneasiness and anger were running high in the room, and any surly newcomer might set off a brawl.

A couple of hod carriers rushed in, brick-dusted, mortar-smeared, sweaty; they'd walked off their jobs downtown and hurried home to Greenwood to bring the latest lynch-talk news, and one of them, seeing Japheth's newspaper spread on the bar, said, "There it is. That's the paper right there!"

Subtly, so subtly one could hardly distinguish the motion, Japheth lifted the paper so that the bold black letters of the headline were illuminated in the lamplight. The headline read: TO LYNCH NEGRO TONIGHT.

"See!" the first hod carrier declared. "They aim to do it tonight!" And the other one shouted, "They won't wait till night, they're not afraid to be seen. No law's going to come after them. We got to arm ourselves and get back downtown, quick!"

Voices were raised in agreement, but a muffled voice said, "They say tonight right here in the paper, don't they? Y'all don't want to go off half-cocked." Only the two pool players and the owner, who were nearest him, realized that the words came from the slouch-hat-shaded figure at the end of the bar. Worried that a fight might break out, the owner moved nearer, swiping at the rough slab with his rag. The big man in the cream suit stood to one side with his pool cue balanced loosely in his hand. The service insignia and war medals gleamed on Carl Little's vest. His white silk derby, brushed to a high, buff sheen, was pushed to the back of his head. Without taking his eyes off the stranger, he said to T.J., "Your shot."

But T.J. did not step forward; his eyes were fixed on the newsprint. TO LYNCH NEGRO TONIGHT. Before T.J.'s eyes swam not symbols on a page but the clear image of his friend's face as the nine whitemen dragged him from the back seat and wrestled him to the elm tree. Midst the angry voices raised in the beer joint, he heard Everett Candler's polite, terrified voice on a dusty road at sunset, calling the whitemen *sir* and *mister*, showing his teeth.

"I been renting from Dad Rowland since I first come to Greenwood. We can't let them lynch his boy."

"We're not. We not about to!"

"This ain't about Dick Rowland, this about every black man in this country."

"You got that right!"

"You going to shoot pool," the big vet snapped at him, "or stand there gawking?"

T.J. bent over the cue, lined up his shot. In his mind the memories tumbled, the white lawmen outside the house and Everett's daddy firing from the window, the rusty six-gauge in his own hands, how easy the whiteman fell. It had happened so fast. He'd thrown the gun down the cistern, he would run, they'd never know, they would never find him, but they took Everett. They took Everett instead, and T.J. had to follow.

"They gathering already. There's a hundred or better at the courthouse right now."

Had to stand outside the jail and watch the whitemen bring him out, put him in the front car. Had to go after them, catch up with them, only to hide cowering, unarmed, unmanned, in the rustling corn.

"They fixing to take him, you watch!"

T.J. jabbed at the cueball, seeing again the stunning competency of those colorless hands, as efficient as if they'd whipped such a knotted loop around a hundred black necks, and Everett, with his own hands tied behind him, swearing hopefully, politely, that he'd had nothing to do with shooting no whiteman. They had been silent, the nine whitemen, except for the one who told Everett one time to shut the hell up.

"When we going to stand up and make 'em quit?"

"Right now! Who-all's got a gun?"

"My army pistol's right here in my pocket, loaded and shined—"

Everett's narrow, scuffed, useless shoes jerked in the air, dancing upon nothing; then the gunshots, and those same twitching shoes were instantly still, and the blood on the duck suit so brilliant in the dying sunlight, carmine red on white cotton, and the nine men turned and walked back to their cars, their weasel faces—unmasked, grim weasel faces that would burn in T.J.'s memory forever—showing only a mild satisfaction, as if they were glad to have done with a nasty but necessary little job. Inside his mind, T.J. watched again as the three cars drove away in crimson dust; again he turned to the elm tree, to know again, in the same sinking blood-rush, why they'd hung Everett as well as shot him. Because the image of the hanging black man was part of the terror. Because Everett's body had to hang there for black men to find, for a sign, for a warning.

"I got a shotgun home and a couple of pistols, Luther Adair's got some fine carbines—"

"A bunch of us got service revolvers, ain't we?"

"Oh, yeah, we good enough to get killed in their goddamn war, but we're not good enough to try on clothes in their goddamn stores—"

Feet poised, toes down, in graceful silent pointe, silhouetted on the horizon, through the brilliant sunset, through the purpling dusk, going darker and darker with the loss of light, until the limp form was only a blacker black against the night sky while T.J. crouched in the corn, wanting to go to him and cut him down. Wanting to run. But fear whispered that the whitemen were waiting just beyond the curve of road in the distance, murmured that they would come roaring back in their automobiles, that T.J. would be caught in their headlamps, unarmed and helpless and terrified, as he was terrified now, in the dim light of a choc joint in Greenwood. But not helpless. Never would he be caught helpless again. T.J. reached beneath his shirt to touch the butt of the Colt tucked between belt and skin.

"Who's got shells? We're going to need plenty ammunition—"

"Sook, run up yonder to the Dreamland, see who-all's up there, tell 'em to meet us at Archer and Greenwood in half an hour—"

"I'd wait for first dark, fellas." Japheth folded the paper, laid it face-down on the bar. "They're not going to move before night."

The vet in the cream suit called out, "You don't sit around till they strong! You got to strike like a thief in the night!" And then, more softly: "Ain't y'all learned nothing? We got to go down now, while they still congregating, before they expect anything. And we can't go aiming to shake our fists and threaten somebody, we got to go ready to shoot to kill."

"You right, Carl!"

"Let me run home and get my Winchester."

"I'm ready this minute. Let's go!"

"You people better be ready to kill a bunch of them peckerwoods," Japheth said, "or they're going to come burn you out. Don't you know that?"

"Where you think you at? This is Greenwood, mister."

"We're going to *defend* ourselves. We'll defend our homes."

The men began to move in a ragged wave from the far corners of the room to the lighter area around the pool table, and for the first time they looked hard at the stranger. Japheth's features were shadowed and blunted, but he had no mastery over the ravenous hatred in his hooded eyes, and it was this the men recognized. Someone in the back of the room said, "Shit, that's a whiteman."

T.J.'s hand clamped tight on the cuestick.

"You all ready to kill white men?" Japheth asked.

"If I have to." The vet gazed steadily at him from beneath the clean buff brim of his hat.

"Tell you what, sons, *I'm* ready." Japheth tapped the folded newspaper. "This is as much my fight as it is yours."

"How's that?"

The darkness in Japheth's mind raged with a thousand answers, how his enemies had insulted him, tricked him, beat him, banished him; in the months since the tank fires at the Deep Fork, he could not go among them without a fight. They had joined forces against him; they would beat him mercilessly. In Japheth's mind the loathing swelled large, but his cunning homed to the one answer that could be heard by the men facing him.

"That was my partner they took out the jail last August and lynched on the Red Fork road."

"Like hell it was."

"He's a liar!"

"What you want here, whiteman?"

Japheth put his back to the bar, held his beer glass in front of him. "I'd like to go burn the sonsabitches out," he said. "I'd like to wipe the street with their sniveling faces."

T.J. reached again to touch the gun beneath his shirt, as the voices in the room lifted in a deep, threatening chorus, and the stranger's nasal tones whined among them, an eerie, angry call-and-response.

"If it was up to me, I'd take a torch to white town this minute!" Japheth said.

"You here to stir up trouble, mister, you're about to find more trouble than you ever dreamed."

"Kill every goddamn one of them."

"You best get on out of here, sucko."

"I'm telling you it's my fight, too!"

"Fixing to be your fight sure enough!"

T.J. watched the whiteman's face, and it was to him the same as the nine weasel faces on the dirt road at sunset, and the whiteman's hands tight on the beer glass were the same as the bloodless hands holding the rope; his gut twisted with hatred and the old pointless, empty longing to go back and undance Everett's feet, to erase the hours of terror in the rustling cornstalks, the nights cringing in the storm cellar. To remember it a different way: that he had not slipped away at dawn and left his friend silhouetted on the graying horizon, motionless, silent, hanging from a tree. Quietly T.J. leaned his cue against the pool table, slipped his hand under his shirt.

"You think they only lynch niggers?" the voice whined.

"Shut your mouth, whiteman!"

"I stood by and watched them lynch my friend!"

T.J.'s hand stopped. The chorus of threats stopped.

"What else could I do?" the voice whispered. "I stood there and watched it!" As if the voice came through him and not of him, Japheth went on in a kind of chanting singsong: "They acted like it was a party. The cops kept the crowd back, but it was just to give them a clear space to lynch him. He was my partner. He was just a kid. He was too damn stupid, I told him so, I told him when he shot that cabbie, and I told him later, when he blabbed about it. He wouldn't keep his stupid mouth shut. They gave him a cigarette, but he never finished it. He didn't die right off, he jerked a long time. A long damn time." Japheth's gaze swept across the men in front of him. "What could I do, one man alone? That was a thousand men, women, and children on the Red Fork road. Once that mob had aholt of him, I couldn't do nothing. The time to do something is *before*! We got to go downtown and stop them!"

"We're *going* to stop them!"

"You got that right."

"We going down there this minute!"

The chorus lifted again, not in threat to the stranger but in unity with him, and the men turned, moving toward the chartreuse light slanting through the open door. The big veteran in the cream suit led them, and T.J. was with them, not at the front of the crowd, not hanging back in the rear, but slipped in with the others, unobtrusive.

"We ought to go set some of their damn homes afire!" Japheth's voice twisted higher as the men spilled together out the door. "We got to go on the offensive, burn 'em out before they come up here like that mob in Chicago done!"

But it wasn't Japheth Whiteside who lit the fire. For all his malevolence and hatred, he hadn't the power to bring into materiality the paroxysm to come. Japheth was in service, as others were in service; his voice one among many, as the gathering in the choc joint was only one of hundreds taking place in those hours throughout the city, on street corners and courthouse steps, in cafés and billiard parlors and law offices, on both sides of the divide.

Downtown, scores of white men balanced themselves on car hoods or stood up on crate boxes, spewing bloodlust and hatred, while others gathered in closed rooms to discuss how to calm this lynch-mob fever. In the lobby of the Hotel Tulsa, Franklin joined a group of oilmen gathered with anxious faces near the front desk. Inside the courthouse, in his office, Sheriff McCullough hung up the telephone; he stood a moment in silence, one hand scratching his brushy mustache, before he turned to a deputy and said, "Kelly, go get Brill and Duncan and y'all take the elevator upstairs. Prop a chair in the door so they can't call it down."

In North Tulsa, as the knot of angry black men, with Japheth in the midst of them, spilled out onto Archer and began walking east, several community leaders were gathered around Smitherman's desk in the *Star* office, composing an urgently worded telegram. They had tried, without success, to place calls to the mayor, the governor, the police chief and commissioner. This telegram was to be sent directly to Governor Robertson's home, with similar wires fired off immediately to Congressman

L. C. Dyer and to that most eloquent decrier of lynchings, Mr. W.E.B. Du Bois himself, who'd visited Greenwood just two months past and declared it the finest example of Negro self-sufficiency in the United States. The men in Smitherman's office believed that the combined forces of articulate Negro voices and powerful white men of good will could prevent this lynching. Standing at the file cabinet, Hedgemon Jackson took down their dictation in his elegant backtilted script.

On both sides of the Frisco tracks, knots of edgy men, black and white, mirrored each other, excepting in this: On the white side of the divide, the gatherings as yet had multiple purposes—some came together to foment mob violence, others to avert it; some gathered out of curiosity, or hatred, or to taste sanctioned murder; some had missed out on the Belton lynching and did not want to miss this event. On the north side of the divide, the people of Greenwood, although not in agreement on method, were of one mind in their resolve—they were going to prevent the lynching of Dick Rowland. In Smitherman's office, as in the furious minds of the men marching in phalanx toward Greenwood Avenue, as within the myriad gatherings all over North Tulsa in those hours, there was but one unified purpose: whiteman's lynch law was not going to rule this promised land.

It was one of those weird yellagreen twilights like we're apt to get of an evening in early summer. All off toward the river and looking back to the east, both directions, the sky appeared like it was lit up with sulfur from horizon to horizon, that kind of bright weird yellagreen. You ever seen it? Looks like it just never will get dark. Not that we were waiting for dark—no, sir, I don't mean that. To tell you the truth, I can't say exactly what we were waiting for. Just milling around, how folks will do. It wasn't to lynch that boy. The coloreds and the commies are the ones who keep saying that, but we weren't aiming to lynch nobody, we were just milling around. Me and Stinson had come off shift at six-thirty, and I mean that whole town was buzzing. You could feel it clean up on Second Street—the ironworks was right there by niggertown—and a couple of fellas had already run in and told us a nigger'd raped a white girl and so forth, but that wasn't so much what we were het up about. We'd just come downtown to see what was going on.

Well, sure, we wandered on over to the courthouse, that's where the crowd was. Not that it was that big a crowd, I mean, not so big as folks are saying. There weren't two thousand white men on the streets, not then there wasn't, maybe later, along about daybreak, when we had to go in and clean that nest out. But right then I bet you there wasn't over a couple hundred—well, maybe a few more than that, but we weren't doing anything, just messing around.

Naturally folks aren't just jumping to talk about it. None of us expected it to get so out of hand to that degree. But, listen, the coloreds brought it on themselves. They did. Look at the papers, they'll tell you. Right there in the *Tribune* the next evening it told it: that whole mess started on account of a bad element in the colored population, just a handful of bad niggers stirred up by the reds. These Bolsheviks have been trying to come in here for the longest, agitating, telling the coloreds they ought to expect "social equality" and all that nonsense, and I guess those poor folks in Little Africa didn't have any better sense than to listen. But I'll tell you what, you let the coloreds get their minds wrapped around that kind of notion, first thing they're going to do is look for a white woman. Ain't it? You know it and I know it. So you've got to watch them. You've got to come down hard on 'em, you can't be letting them get away with what that boy in the jail tried to get away with. But, no, I don't believe anybody was trying to lynch that boy.

Oh, there were some, sure, had some pretty foul mouths, saying all about what they'd do to any nigger they caught with a white woman, which I'm not going to repeat. It don't bear repeating. There's always going to be a bad egg or two. But most of us, we were just looking for a little something to do. It was a nice evening out, warm, but the weather hadn't turned hot yet, and that yellagreen twilight just lingering for hours. Maybe one or two of us had a little something stashed in a boot, or somebody'd slip down a alley and take him a nip. It was just a kind of little social gathering. I heard that a couple of men tried to get in at the courthouse and the sheriff run them back out, but I didn't see that. But listen here, if that bunch of colored boys hadn't marched downtown, nothing would've happened. I believe that for a fact.

It'd finally got dark—that twilight drained off sometime when I wasn't looking—and it was pretty well dim on the side streets, but the courthouse was lit up, and the streetlamps, and somebody'd scrounged up some pineknot torches from somewhere, so there was light enough right there where we were. We'd swelled up a little bigger, our bunch there on the street. Fellas kept coming. Sometimes, a situation like that, it'll peter out afterwhile if it looks like nothing's going to show. Folks said Sheriff McCullough'd jammed the elevator on the third floor so nobody could call it down, and then set his men around at the top of the stairs with shotguns so they could take a potshot at anybody trying to get up to where that boy was—I don't know if they would've really shot a white man, but they might—anyways, it looked like the sheriff meant to put up a show. So who's to say but what folks would've just gone on about their business afterwhile if the niggers hadn't rushed us?

Along about ten-thirty or eleven, maybe, everybody standing by me hushed, just all at once. I seen everybody looking north, so I turned to look, and here they come out of the darkness, this whole wall of black faces materializing out of that black. They weren't coming fast, they weren't running, just walking, and it was spooky, now. It was weird. Walking right down Boulder Avenue toward us, dead silent, maybe fifty or a hundred of them abreast, and I mean to tell you they were armed. And they didn't try to hide it neither. You see what I'm saying? Arm them up and send them out to war in a white man's army, let them get these "social equality" notions running in their blame knuckleheads, that's how they'll act. Well, you've got to put a stop to it, don't you? You got to nip that kind of crazy malarkey in the bud.

Just to give you an example: this bunch of colored boys came right directly at us, and when they got to where our bunch was knotted up there on the steps they didn't even flinch but just kept coming, straight up to the door. I'm surprised it didn't start that minute, I'm surprised somebody didn't haul off and start shooting right then, and I don't know why somebody didn't. I reckon we were too dadgum surprised. And then these *Negroes* had the gall to offer their services to the sheriff! You believe that? It's the devil's own truth. They'd come up to see if the *sheriff* needed *their* help to protect that colored boy up yonder on the top floor!

But I'll tell you what, that sheriff could've done a whole lot better job calming things down if he'd acted right. He never took a gun off a single nigger. He never acted like they were out of line in any way. He'd ought to arrested every last one of them, but I heard him stand there and talk to them reasonable as anything. He had his pistols out, but all he said was, Y'all go on home, boys, we got everything under control.

Well, naturally, with a sheriff as mealymouthed as that, the niggers just kept standing around like they owned the place. They had I bet you thirty shotguns, a whole bunch of army-issue .45s, I don't know what-all. You see what I'm saying? You can't be soft on 'em. Nobody wanted to hurt anybody, but those colored boys are the ones that brought it on themselves. Give them an inch, they're going to take over the whole damn country, that's what they're aiming at, most of them. Now, a few of them turned and started back down the steps, acted like they'd got some sense finally and would go on home and settle down. I seen a couple boys I recognized, that shoeshine boy that works at Louie's and Mr. Stedham's chauffeur, I think, and a couple others, and, really, up till that evening I believe the majority of our coloreds here in Tulsa knew how to act. Most of them were pretty good niggers, or they used to be, but niggers are just like anybody, there's good ones and bad ones, and there's not a creature on this earth lower than a bad nigger, and that night at the courthouse there were sure some bad ones in that bunch. I couldn't begin to tell you where they'd come from. Folks were saying a nigger mob was headed over from Muskogee with some dynamite, but I don't know if that was some of the Muskogee niggers or not. Might've been some of these agitators and Wobblies you're always hearing about. What I do know, that was about the arrogantest crowd of niggers you'd ever want to look at. Black as the ace of spades, some of 'em, and some near about as white as you or me, and every damn one of them had their noses stuck up in the air. And they had all them goddamn guns. That kind of behavior makes a fellow plain mad.

Well, somebody got mad. Wasn't me. I'm not saying who, if I knew, which I don't. No, I'm not saying. But look here, what do you expect? Here's this one big buck nigger on the steps, he don't act like he's going nowhere. Had him on a pretty white suit and a pretty white derby hat, and, oh my, didn't he think he was fine? Had a big old revolver about the size of my mama's skillet laid across his arm, like this, just kind of cradled sideways like a baby, and he wasn't waving it or anything, but you could tell he thought him and his white suit and his big gun was just about the cat's meow. So somebody says, What're you doing with that gun, nigger? And this nigger comes back in a slow voice like fleas are going to drop off him, he says, I'm going to use it if I need to. And this other fellow, I ain't saying who, just some white fellow, he tells the nigger, Naw, you ain't, you better let me have it. That nigger looks at him a minute, comes back with, Like hell I will.

Well, what are you going to do? You can't let them act like that. The white fella had to go to take that gun off him, didn't he? He had to. I don't know who shot first, don't know if it came from that nigger's gun, but I don't think so, because it sounded to me like a .22. All I know, there was one shot, and then there was a hundred, and I seen about a dozen men drop, black and white both, right in those first few seconds, and, man, I dived for cover, and them niggers took off. They ran a gun battle all the way up Boulder and some of our bunch took off after them, but I stayed there at the courthouse for a while. A doctor showed up from somewhere and tried to help one of the niggers that was dying yonder on the sidewalk, but some of our fellas wouldn't let him, they said to let the nigger lay there and writhe, which maybe that wasn't right, but the way the fellas seen it, it wasn't right for a white doctor to give aid to the enemy, because, the way the fellas seen it, right then, we had us a war on.

W hen the telephone in the library began to ring sometime after midnight, both women were still awake. Graceful lay on her side in the maid's room with the baby asleep in the curve of her arm, her body fatigued and trembling on the narrow cot as she stared into the darkness. At the shrill cry of the black gnome on the library table, her heart contracted. She knew the call was for her. Never had she received a telephone call in this house, such a thing was unheard of, but her heart knew at once that the insistent ringing in the library, that bell-cry of trouble, was for her.

Althea was sitting up in the fringed and shaded lamplight of her bedroom, propped against the feather pillows with a gardening book in her hands, though she wasn't reading, but listening, to the ticking house, the ticking hall clock, the ticking of her own heartbeat, waiting for something, though she would not admit to herself that what she was listening for was Franklin's tread on the stairs. Since the night of his return more than a week ago, when he'd stood several minutes in the bedroom doorway, staring at her in silence, she'd waited for him. Each afternoon, bathed and dressed for dinner, her hair arranged, she sat waiting in the parlor, sewing, and though their dinners passed in that same bloated silence, and though he retired each night to the guest bedroom across the hall, Althea's fears were eased. Her husband was home. But he was so late this evening, far too late, and she'd heard no word; she was afraid he'd gone away again, that he wouldn't come back. And so when the phone rang she was swept with relief, an easement followed instantly by greater fear.

They met in the front hall. The phone shrilled and shrilled in the library. They hesitated before each other, unsure for an instant. Of course it was Graceful's charge to answer the telephone, as Althea had taught her, greeting the caller with a pleasant "Good afternoon, Dedmeyer's residence," or "Good morning," or "Good evening"—but what of a call in the middle of the night? There was no etiquette for catastrophe. Althea rushed into the library and jerked the phone from its cradle.

"Hello!"

"Graceful?" a soft Negro voice said.

Althea was so surprised that she simply handed the receiver to Graceful, stepped back. She watched the girl's face in the reflected light from the streetlamp, heard her dull greeting, and then, after a long time, heard her ask, "Where they at?" Graceful listened to the lengthy answer in silence, without a murmured yeah or un-huh or any of the verbal courtesies that told a speaker his listener was attending to his words. After some time she said, "Where's Delroy?" And then, "Did anybody go by Mama?" Althea could hear the low hum of the man's voice rising and falling through the receiver, but Graceful's face revealed nothing, as ever, though there must surely be a death in her family, or a near death, somebody dying, to account for the boldness of a Negro man calling up in the middle of the night. "I'll be there in a little bit," Graceful said. And after a beat, "I *am*, Hedgemon." The insect voice rose louder in the black scoop, but Graceful's mask remained unchanged. Later she said, "All right," and put the phone down without saying goodbye. But she didn't turn to leave the library, not even when her baby began to cry in the maid's room. Althea could see her chest rising and falling in long, slow, deeply drawn breaths.

"What is it?" Althea tried to give her voice a kind of friendly, concerned kindness, though it echoed back to her own ears sounding false.

Graceful didn't look at her. "Nothing, ma'am." The baby was crying hard now. "I got to go."

"Go where?"

"Home."

"Is something wrong?"

"They having trouble, ma'am. I got to go." And she disappeared into the dark hall.

Althea followed, flicking on lights as she went; she stood at the door and watched Graceful in the square of light falling from the hallway as she picked up the wailing newborn and put him to her shoulder, patted his back.

"What kind of trouble?"

In evidence of the profound change between them, Graceful sat down on the bed without apology or permission, opened her gown to nurse the baby. "He say it's a war."

Althea wasn't sure she'd heard correctly over the baby's cries.

"A what?"

But Graceful didn't answer.

"Who told you that? That's ridiculous!" The idea was absurd. How could they have got into another war so soon? The papers had mentioned nothing about it. Why, the Great War was the last war, the one to end all others—surely they weren't already having trouble with another country? "War with who?"

Graceful looked at her in silence. After a moment she turned her gaze down to her baby. "Whitefolks," she said, without looking up.

Her meaning began to seep into Althea's understanding. "Oh," she said after a long time. The baby was quiet now, nursing. "Oh," she said again, her mind flying through a dozen scenarios. Almost as quickly as she'd received the word, put the word *race* in front of it, she dismissed the idea. Negroes were always exaggerating those things. *War* was such an extreme word, it implied armed conflict, engagement—*combat,* for heaven's sake. Maybe there was some unrest over that colored boy raping a white girl, which the papers were so stirred up about, but surely *war* was not the right word. Althea had an impulse to ask for details so she could patiently reject the notion, calm the girl's fears. But something in Graceful's face made her too timid to ask.

"Well," she said at last, dismissing the whole issue, returning to her first thought, that a death in Graceful's family had been the reason for the late-night call. "I'll have Franklin take you in the car tomorrow morning." Again she tried to find the proper placement for her voice, the correct tone of solicitous concern joined with serene certainty that Franklin would in fact be here in the morning. "Who was that on the phone?"

Graceful stood, put the baby on the bed, placed the pillow beside him, stepped over to the wall and pulled one of her plain dresses off the hanger, tossed it on the foot of the cot.

"Graceful! Answer me!"

But the girl went on getting dressed in the dark as if Althea were not present, and the telephone began shrieking at the front of the house, and Althea whirled, certain it was the same caller, and went to answer it herself. She would get to the bottom of this. So prepared was she to grill the soft-spoken colored caller that she was stunned to hear her husband's voice.

"Darling, I'm sorry to wake you. You were sleeping?" Franklin's voice was agitated, breathless. "I wanted to tell you not to wait up for me. There's some serious trouble downtown. Darling? Are you there?"

Darling. He had called her *darling.* After a beat she answered: "What kind of trouble?"

"Oh, it's a— Some Negroes— Never mind, I'll tell you when I get home, but listen, Thea, I wanted to tell you: don't let Graceful come up here. Maybe you'd better make her— I don't know. There's some talk. You might want to put her and the baby in the basement. Just to be safe."

"The basement!"

"Or . . . I don't know. It sounds crazy, but it is crazy, the whole town is mad, I've never seen anything like it. There's a thousand or two thousand in the streets, I don't know how many, they tried to break into the armory—"

"The Negroes broke into the armory?"

"No, no, some of these rabblerousers. I can't tell you now, just, she might hear about it, and want to—"

"She heard. Somebody called. She's on her way."

"No, run catch her! Or, no, no, don't you come outside. Let her go if she's gone."

"She's getting dressed."

"Well, go talk some sense into her. Tell her they're shooting every Nigra on sight."

"What?"

"Dear God, can't you understand me? It's a race war! The coloreds are shooting white men, whites are breaking into pawnshops, they're arming themselves like it's Armageddon. She can't come up here, it's a battlefield all over downtown!"

"Come home!"

"I can't, somebody's got to—" He broke off in silence, and in the interval she heard for the first time the faint popping of gunfire through the receiver.

"Got to do what? Franklin, come home." Now it was the whine of sirens, which she heard simultaneously through the telephone and through the library windows, off in the distance, to the north, downtown. "Oh, my God," she said, "Franklin! Come home this minute!"

But her husband's voice was tinny, far away, distracted. "If you want that girl to stay alive, you'd better stop her. I've got to go. I'll be home as soon as I can." And the line was dead before Althea could say his name again.

The light was on in the maid's room. Graceful was dressed, shoes on, her hair pulled back tight into a stiff, brushy tail at the nape of her neck. She was bent over the cot, changing the baby's diaper, her hands folding the tiny white square in deft, quick strokes, sliding the open pins through her hair to grease them before stabbing them into the cotton; she jerked the baby's gown down, pulled the drawstrings around his feet like he was a sack of potatoes, and almost in the same motion turned, without acknowledging Althea, and snatched up a burlap sack from beside the bureau, began to stuff it with diapers.

"What do you think you're doing? You can't go up there!"

But Graceful kept on snatching items off the bureau, and Althea cried, "Graceful! Listen to me! That was Franklin. They're shooting people on the streets! You can't take that baby up there!" For the first time the girl seemed aware of her, not that she turned to look at her, but the swiftly moving hands suddenly slowed. "They're shooting Negroes on sight, do you hear me? You can't!"

The sounds of many sirens snaked through the walls into the tiny room at the core of the house. Graceful's hands stopped moving, and in a moment the burlap sack thunked to the floor. She sat down on the cot, staring straight ahead. For an instant the mask held, and then the smooth features crumpled, and Graceful began to sob. She sat with her shoulders back and her head raised and the whole of her chest moving in deep, ragged sobs, tearless, shuddery. Her face was twisted. The baby lay blinking in the light, staring up at his mother.

Althea stood uncertainly in the doorway. If Graceful had collapsed, buried her face in her hands, if there'd been tears, Althea would have probably reached down to pat her back, for that awkward impulse burgeoned in her at once. But Graceful's stiff, erect figure, her contorted features as unreadable in their extremity as ever they'd been in their masklike stillness, cut off the impulse, made Althea clumsy, unsure of herself. The baby began to hiccup, the tiniest little normal sounds, incongruous against his mother's dry sobs and the distant wailing of sirens. At last Althea announced matter-of-factly, "Mr. Dedmeyer will be home soon. He'll know what to do."

Graceful didn't look at her, but the sobs began to ebb, the silences between the ragged huffs growing longer, punctuated by the baby's tiny rhythmic hiccups. After a long time she spoke softly, dreamily, without explanation, as if she were recalling a long-ago experience. "He say they trying to hold Greenwood, but they keep falling back. Whites be taunting them from the train station, shouting about they going to come in and shoot everybody in their beds. Going to catch them kneeling at prayers and shoot them in the head." She paused. "He thinks they might have got T.J. He's not sure." After a moment she said, "They been trying to kill T.J. the longest time."

"Who? Who was that on the phone?"

"Nobody. Hedgemon. I got to go home," she finished dully. Graceful stood and moved to the bureau as if she were fatigued beyond telling. She ignored the hiccuping infant, ignored Althea, began once again to stuff the burlap bag with bits of clothing she pulled out of the drawer.

"You can't take that baby."

"I can't leave him," Graceful answered simply. Her hands did not stop.

"What are you going to do up there? You can't do anything."

"Somebody got to tell Mama."

"You can't." It was almost a whisper. "Didn't you hear what I said?"

"I got to go home."

For the first time since the birth, Althea touched her, but it was hardly the rhythmic intimacy of that event: she stepped into the room and grabbed Graceful's moving arm, clutched it so fiercely she could feel the soft give in the little layer of flesh over the hard muscle beneath the cotton sleeve. "You can't get through downtown! Didn't he tell you that?"

Graceful stood as a statue facing the blank wall, her features hard and empty, nostrils flared, and yet expectant, as if she were waiting for the fullness of the event—not this old back-and-forth tug of power between them but what was taking place in the city in that hour between all blacks and all whites—to seep through to this whitewoman.

In fact, Althea understood the peril of what was happening downtown far more realistically than Graceful. She'd heard the staccato gunfire through the telephone wire; more than that, she'd heard Franklin's voice, and the sound of it, strung at the far-tether of fear and excitement, echoed back to her. Unconsciously she aped him: "They're shooting every Nigra on sight, you fool! What do you aim to do, wag that baby through it?" She let go the girl's arm. Graceful continued to stand motionless, staring at the wall. The baby was quiet now.

"All right," Althea said. "Tell me what you want done. I'll go."

At last Graceful turned to face her, and the half-lidded stare she leveled at her was cool with challenge. "They shooting whitefolks, too," she said.

Althea took a step back. She hesitated, trying to adjust her thinking, but quickly she rejected the outrageous notion. Her sense of white immunity was too ingrained, her assumptions of feminine privilege too deeply set. If there was danger downtown, she, as a white woman, was exempt from it. "That's ridiculous," she said. "Is it your mother you want?" Suddenly she saw the solution. "I'll go find Mr. Dedmeyer, he's right downtown somewhere." Her chest relaxed with the notion. "He can come home and get the Winton and we'll go fetch your mother, bring her here in the car. Would that satisfy you?"

But Graceful was bent over the sleeping baby now. She hardly heard what the woman was saying. A new recognition had begun to open inside her: Mrs. Dedmeyer was right. She couldn't take him. Not just for the reasons the woman said, but for her own reasons. She studied the baby's face, her feelings alternating in the familiar seesaw of tenderness and ice. He was light as a tan eggshell, but not white. Not wholly white. When he was asleep, as now, his little pink tongue bulged from his mouth like he hadn't grown into it yet. The boy had her lips and flat nose, her almond-shaped eyes. Chinaman eyes, the other children used to call them. The same narrow eyes as T.J. and Jewell. But the baby's eyes were closed now.

"You could keep him," she said. She raised up, the fatigue like an iron press on her belly and shoulders. "He could stay here with you."

"My God, no! How would I feed him?"

"He won't be hungry for a while." But even as she glanced down at the baby she knew he'd awaken in a few hours, and if she were beside him he'd drowse and nuzzle her breast and nurse awhile, go back to sleep. And if she were not there he'd cry until he'd worked himself into the trembling, leg-jerking, hiccuping hysteria from which he could not be calmed.

"I have to go," she said.

"Well. You can't. I forbid it."

In the silence that followed, a lone siren sounded, seemed to grow louder as if it were coming toward them, and then it turned northward, drew away. Still the siren wailed, thin and eerie in its isolation. Faintly, very far to the north, there was a continuous peppery knocking, like a mad woodpecker deep in a far woods who couldn't stop. Inside the maid's room there was only the sound of their breathing, the aloof, distinct ticks of the grandfather clock in the hall. Looking at the stubborn face before her, smooth and brown and stony as a buckeye, Althea understood that she could forbid the girl nothing: she could not make Graceful do anything that was outside her own will.

"We'll go together," Althea sighed, as if this had been at the back of her mind all along. "You'll be safe with me. We'll go find Mr. Dedmeyer. He'll take you and the baby home." Immediately her hand went to her hair, loose and uncombed on her shoulders; she glanced down at her nightgown. "Let me get dressed." As she turned to go, a new thought occurred to her. She looked back at Graceful's thin, shortsleeved dress of bright print cotton, unmistakably a colored girl's dress. "You too. Come upstairs. We've got to find something to cover you up."

Althea flung clothes from the wardrobe onto the carpet, pawing through hobble skirts and shirtwaists, looking for an outfit loose enough to fit over Graceful's solid shoulders and hips. At last she pulled out a floorlength green evening dress, loose-fitted and flowing, somewhat faded, and hardly of the latest style, but far too good to put on a colored girl. However, it couldn't be helped. "Put that on," she said, and hurled the dress at her. Graceful backed into the hall with the dress in her arms. "Hurry up!" Althea called. With a satisfied sense of purpose, she turned to put on a light housedress; she jerked the hairbrush through her thick mane a few times and twisted it into a knot, shoving the hairpins in as she crossed the room, knelt on the rug to dig her gardening shoes out from under the bedskirt. She wouldn't make the mistake a second time of walking to town in dress shoes.

Graceful returned and stood waiting quietly at the door. Althea, glancing up to bark another order, felt a slicing pain in her chest. Framed in the doorway, with the bed lamp's light on her sculpted face, the dim hall behind muting the silhouette of the green sateen dress flowing around her, the girl looked regal. In spite of her darkness, or because of it, she looked majestic, like a forest queen. How was it possible, Althea wondered, that for all the unwilling attention she'd paid, she'd never realized that Graceful was beautiful.

"Well, don't stand there like an idiot," she snapped. "Go get the baby and meet me in the front hall. No. Here. Wait. Come here a minute." And she went to the wardrobe once more, reached overhead for her hatboxes, pulled down a stack of them, and spread them on the carpet, opening lids and tossing them to the side until she'd found the one she wanted. "Come *on*," she said, and snicked her tongue against her teeth in impatience. Graceful came slowly into the room, her heavy brown maid's shoes peeking out from beneath the hem at each step. Althea merely glanced down at them in silence. There was no point in even thinking about that; there was no way any of her tiny shoes would fit those big feet. Graceful stopped, caught by her own image in the mirror, but Althea pulled the girl around by the arm and set a veiled hat squarely on her head, though the clever feathered concoction had been designed to tilt cunningly to the side. She tugged the veil down to cover the girl's face, stepped back to look at her, frowning. "Well," she said. "It's dark out."

They made their way along the front walk in silence. The beautiful new Winton Six gleamed dully in the driveway. Franklin had driven it home and parked it, and left it sitting each morning while he took a private car downtown. None of the wealthiest oilmen drove themselves. Althea thought as they passed it that she was going to make Franklin teach her how to operate that automobile, and people's notions of ladylikeness could just be damned. If the scandalously absent Nona Murphy could learn how to operate the thing before she took off with that ragtime player or wherever she went, Althea could most certainly learn how to drive. It was absurd, having to walk all the way downtown, for of course no street-cars were running this time of night, no cabs.

In silence the two turned north, an incongruous pair hurrying along beneath the streetlights; or, rather, it was Graceful whose appearance was most strange: a tall, elegant, overdressed lady in hat and veil walking fast in the mild darkness with an infant slung over her shoulder. The baby was swathed head to foot in a blanket. They no longer heard the ratchety gun-fire, and Althea's mind relaxed in a sort of relieved exhalation. Thank God, the disturbance was finished. Now it was only a matter of finding Franklin. But as they crested the little rise above Fifteenth Street, they both saw at once the first faint ruddy glow in the distance, lighting the sky behind downtown, and immediately their swift pace quickened, led by Graceful, who, unhindered by the yards of material in the voluminous skirt, took such long, free strides that Althea had to double-step to keep up with her. Soon they were nearly running.

They were not the only ones hurrying toward the center of Tulsa in that hour. Throughout the city, north and south, telephones jangled in dark houses. Telegraph wires were singing. Footsteps thudded on brick and stone and hardpan; fists pounded on doorposts; automobiles roared to life in garages and carriage houses, rumbled toward that line of steel rail slicing east to west across the midpoint of Tulsa: the visible line marking the invisible partition that separated north from south, black from white.

Like parallel magnetic bars, the silent, inert Frisco tracks seemed now to draw to themselves the life of the whole city.

In the lobby of the Hotel Tulsa, Franklin Dedmeyer lit his fifth cigar of the evening. The gunfire had become sporadic, scattered, and it came from well north. Hearing the lull, he contemplated going outside to see if the worst had passed. But through the plate-glass window he could still see armed men running in the street, and he thought maybe he should wait a while longer. No matter. He'd been waiting all evening, had started out in the late afternoon impatiently awaiting the driller's arrival on the three-twenty from Bristow, his anger growing with each passing half-hour, because it seemed that Jim kept him waiting far too often these days. But then the trouble had started, and Franklin had dismissed Jim Logan from his mind, as he was later to drop all thoughts of his wife the instant he'd hung up the desk telephone after speaking with her. His mind was too saturated with all that he'd witnessed: The young dead man's oozing neck, for instance. The odd, strained faces of the businessmen coming in from the streets. The gun battle he'd watched moving slowly north after the first eruption—Negroes in slow, organized retreat, taking cover behind automobiles and building corners as they fell back, firing constantly at the disorganized batches of white men in pursuit.

It was during that running gun battle that the hotel manager had lugged the young man's body into the lobby. All the porters and bellhops had disappeared, and there'd been no one to help him, and so Franklin and a couple of other oilmen had gone to offer their aid, but there was nothing to be done. The young man, a white boy, was dead, though he continued to bleed profusely all over the carpet. Someone said he'd stuck 'his nose out the side door into the alley a moment ago to see the action, had instantly fallen backward, shot in the neck.

Franklin had taken a seat then at a small round table, well back from the window, at the east end of the lobby, near enough to see out but far enough back to be out of the way of flying bullets. From time to time he'd get up and go stand near the front, close enough to hear the news as it dribbled in excitedly from the street, but at a great enough distance to not attract others' attentions; he waited at the fringes, listening to what others were saying while denying any connection, and though he had clearly wanted Althea to think he was doing something to stop this horrid business, in fact, he had done nothing. In fact, it was just as he was speaking with his wife that he'd first seen the roadster race by with the shouting white boys hanging all over it, perched on the running boards, clinging to the hood, waving their guns from the turtlehull above the back fender. Connected to the bumper by a taut, vibrating rope, a dead Negro man bounced on the pavement behind them like a loose sack of grain. Franklin had hung up on his wife, returned to the little table, lit a cigar. Now he watched the car pass again, going north this time. It had passed by several times. The dead Negro was so mauled that if he'd not seen them go by the first time Franklin would have had to guess what kind of bloody thing the car was dragging. Other automobiles filled with armed men continued to race past the window, and still more men on foot, and boys, a lot of young boys, some of them hardly out of kneepants, most of them carrying pistols, walking fast, running, all headed north, toward the Frisco.

From her position at the window in her front room, Cleotha Whiteside, too, saw armed men running. The porchlights were on at many of the other houses on Elgin, and in their muted glow she saw shadowy figures of men hurrying south along the avenue, but, unlike the flow in white Tulsa, which moved only in one direction, the traffic in North Tulsa flowed two ways. Already women were carrying their children away from the gunfire, north beyond the section line, to stay with friends or family until the inconceivable fighting should end. Cleotha's gaze seldom stayed long with the people hurrying past in the dark street, but returned again and again to the ruddy glow on the horizon. She was trying to guess where the burning was. It looked to be somewhere along Boston, but she couldn't tell which side of the tracks it was on.

She had a powerful urge to go see, but she did not want to leave the sleeping children again. She'd left them once already, early in the evening, before the shooting started, and she'd worried the whole time, and not just because she'd feared that Elberta's baby, so long overdue, would finally make up its mind to come while she was gone. She'd told Jewell to go fetch the birthwoman immediately if the pains started again, as they'd been starting and stopping for days now. "You go straight to Miz Tiger's," she'd told Jewell, "and bring her back the minute Berta start, if she start again. Hear? Don't come looking for me. I'll be home soon enough."

"I want to come with you, Mama. Bessie and Louise are still down there." Jewell was the one who'd first come panting into the house with

word of the trouble, holding her hand to her side, gulping air, telling how
Mr. Ferguson had rushed into the hall where they were decorating and
told everybody to go home because there was going to be race trouble. Before Jewell finished gasping her excited words, Cleotha had turned and
gone into the bedroom for her hat, because of course she had to go right
down to Deep Greenwood and get T.J., because race trouble was the very
trouble he didn't need to be anywhere near.

"Annmarie still down there," Jewell pleaded. "Everybody's down
there. Mama, let me come with you. Please?"

Cleotha had turned a hard look on her best-behaved daughter. "You
got no business in that mess on Greenwood. You hear me?"

Jewell nodded slowly, with her head down, cutting her eyes up at her
mother. But even as Cleotha hurried away in the eerie twilight, she'd been
nagged by the thought that Jewell would sneak out and follow her. She'd
stayed half an hour on Greenwood, her eyes searching the crowd for T.J.,
growing more and more terrified by the race talk, men ranting on the corner like preachers, others grumbling and shouting their approval, but the
whole time she couldn't get her mind easy about Jewell. The notion had so
pricked at her that finally, despite having seen no sign of her son, she'd
turned and hurried home, only to find Jewell standing at the window, with
the curtain lifted, trying to see south, almost exactly as Cleotha herself now
stood. Of course Jewell had stayed home and done like her mother told
her; she was a good girl. She'd always been a good girl. Cleotha knew she
should have turned right around and gone back to look for T.J. But she
hadn't. And then the distant shooting had started, and she wouldn't—not
out of fear for herself but because she wouldn't leave the children alone.

Standing at the window in the dark house, Cleotha allowed her mind
to touch each of her children: the three youngest asleep in the middle
room, along with her son's young wife, whom she could hear moaning
faintly from time to time; her mind reached for the silent, angry eldest son,
whose troubles had so seized her thoughts and attentions for almost a
year. And Graceful. Cleotha's chest constricted. She hadn't seen Graceful
since the night she'd sent her out with T.J. and Delroy from that stinking
shack in Arcadia. Seldom did Cleotha Whiteside doubt any of her deci-
sions concerning her children, but she grieved that one. What she'd
feared had never happened—whitefolks had never come around looking
for T.J.—but, as a result of her acting on that fear, the one thing she'd
never imagined had come to pass: her daughter had gone away from
home. From that night, almost as if Graceful had traded places with her

brother, she'd quit the family entirely. At first T.J. swore he didn't know where she was, but finally Cleotha got it out of him that she was working for a white family in Oklahoma City, and not long after that, Graceful had started to write. In every letter she promised to come home soon, but she never came. *Well,* Cleotha thought, watching the beautiful orange semicircle lighting the southern sky, *at least she's safe with her white family down in Oklahoma City.* But where was T.J.? Cleotha noticed then, with a little lifting of the tightness across her breast, that the gunfire had stopped. People were still going by on the street in the front of the house, but, she thought with relief and a little prayer of thanksgiving, the trouble must be over.

Berta moaned again from the inner room, louder this time, and Cleotha thought she heard the girl whimper. Then there was a terrified scream, and LaVona's voice squealed, "Mama!" The screaming continued, one long, high, hysterical yodel, and Cleotha rushed into the middle room to find her two daughters standing scared-looking beside the cot, where Berta sat up, wild-eyed, staring at the wet bedclothes beneath her, yelling at the top of her lungs.

"Oh, hush!" Cleotha pulled the girl around by the shoulders and shook her. "You hush up this minute! What's the matter with you? Ain't nothing but your water broke! Jewell! Get your shoes on and— No. No. Nevermind. Just . . ." Cleotha couldn't think. She prayed that this was another false alarm, even as she tugged at the soaked sheets, told Jewell, "Bring me some towels. And go put the kettle on." Her youngest daughter started to whimper. William was pressed up against the wall with his hand in front of his mouth, grinning broadly in his confusion and fear. "LaVona, you hush too, I'm going to give you something to cry about. Take Willie and y'all go in the front room. Keep an eye out the window for your brother, he's going to be home any minute. Hush, girl!" She turned on Elberta. "T.J. going to be here in a minute, can't you hear? That ain't nothing but water! Now hush!" But the girl wouldn't hush. Her hands were on her huge belly, and she screamed now with the pain coming, and Cleotha knew this wasn't any of those practice pains her young body had flirted with for days. Berta's water had broken. The baby was going to come this time, sure.

In a moment Jewell was standing beside her with her arms full of towels and her dress on and her shoes on and a very grown-up expression on her face. "I'll go quick, Mama," she said.

"You're not going nowhere." Cleotha took the towels from her, bent over the cot.

"But, Mama, how we going to get Miz Tiger?"

"We're not."

Jewell sucked in her breath. Cleotha did not even glance up but went on shoving the clean towels under the thighs of the shrieking girl. "You put the water on like I told you?"

"Yes'm."

"Go in the front room, then, you don't need to be looking at this." But Jewell didn't budge, and Cleotha didn't say it again, as she realized, not for the first time, that the swollbellied girl on the cot bawling and carrying on was no older than Jewell anyway. "Stand around and gawk, then," Cleotha murmured. "See what happen to a girl who don't keep herself to herself. Quit that screaming, missy!" She poked Berta. "I'm going to put you out on the porch!" But her words had no effect on the terrified Berta, and Cleotha went on shoving towels pointlessly under the girl's legs as she tried to think what to do next. Cleotha had never attended a birth. She'd given birth to seven babies herself, yes, and lost two, but she'd never witnessed another's, and all she remembered of her own labors was the sweet time afterwards; all she knew about birthing was how to lean into the pain, how to push. *Can't be that much to it,* she tried to tell herself. *Just hold your hands out, tie the cord and cut it when the child come.*

But Berta would not quit screaming, and Cleotha couldn't tell if the pains were coming that close together, neverending, so fast, or if it was just the girl's fear and hysteria, or if, as Cleotha herself feared, there was something wrong. She couldn't tell anything. She didn't know anything. She turned finally to Jewell, dressed so neat in her pink school dress, with her hair freshly plaited—when had she had time to do that?—and her almond eyes gazing directly at her mother in confident expectation. Cleotha turned her ear toward the south and listened with her whole soul to all that was happening outside the walls of her house. Silence. Nothing. No, there was a siren, wasn't there? Down toward the tracks? Well, yes. That would be the firewagon. The firewagon come to put out that orange glow on the horizon. There was no sound of gunfire. The crazy trouble was over now. Surely it was. Cleotha looked back at her waiting daughter. "All right," she sighed. "Go quick. Go straight there, straight! And come right back. Tell Miz Tiger she been—"

But Jewell was already gone.

I nside the *Star* office, Hedgemon Jackson was alone. He, too, heard the lull in the gunfire. From his position at the window he could see armed men in the upstairs windows of the building on the corner, taking aim toward the south, but nobody was shooting. There was no movement on the street; the shouts, the thudding footsteps had ceased. The fire in the distance was getting bigger, the night sky dancing yellow, but Hedgemon couldn't see what was burning. Greenwood Avenue was dark, no street-lamps lit anywhere, the businesses all shut tight, but the fireglow showed up the brick buildings across the street as plain as a drawing; he could see other faces watching from other windows and doorways; he could see gun barrels poking out between venetian blinds. Sometimes he heard whitemen's voices coming from the train station, shouting taunts and curses; sometimes he heard scattered shooting, but the gunshots, when they came, were lusterless, drowsy-sounding, like the growl of a sleeping dog roused just enough to give warning. He looked at his watch again. It was after three o'clock. His glance returned to the telephone on the wall, as it had done a hundred times in the past hour.

He was supposed to be waiting for calls from the governor and Mr. Du Bois. Or else it was the mayor and Mr. Du Bois. Somebody and Mr. Du Bois, the Du Bois part he was sure of. It didn't matter. If a call came in from anybody he'd dart out the door and up the street to Mr. Smitherman's house so fast they'd think he was a jackrabbit. The only men with guns he'd seen were colored, but Hedgemon trusted nothing. Since Mr. Smitherman rushed in looking wild and frenzied, saying that Tulsa had exploded like a firebomb and the city was in the middle of a race war, Hedgemon understood that anything could happen. Mr. Smitherman had gone right to the telephone and placed several calls. As soon as he rang off, he'd started back out the door, calling over his shoulder to Hedgemon that he had to go home and see about his family, but if Mr. Du Bois or the governor (or the mayor or some white somebody) returned his call, Hedgemon should come get him. *Wait here, son, these are important calls, very, very important, wait here where you'll be safe.*

And Hedgemon had waited. He'd heard the battle coming nearer, until finally he could see men running in the street, armed men, darting in and out of doorways. He looked for T.J., who'd been in the crowd headed downtown, but he never saw him. He did see Carl Little trot past, a pale moving target in a cream-colored suit. A flush of jealousy surged through Hedgemon at sight of Graceful's old boyfriend, but the feeling was soon swept away in the strange excitement and fear. After a while there weren't so many running; there was only the sound of riflefire from hidden places on either side of the tracks. The shooting slowed to peppery sniping, and yet Hedgemon waited. He was a good boy, a good employee, and Mr. Smitherman had said to wait for the call from Mr. W.E.B. Du Bois, and Hedgemon waited, though he no more believed that call would come than anything. It had been two hours since he'd got up the nerve to phone the whitepeople's house and speak to Graceful, for which he was both sorry and not sorry, because she'd said she was going to come. He'd told her to stay with the whitefolks until he called to say it was over, but she had not really said that she would.

Hedgemon stared at the dark, quiet street, trying to decide if it was safe to phone Graceful, safe for her to come on now. He wanted to see her. He wanted to talk to her. At last he left his post at the window, telling himself he ought to just call and make sure she was all right. But when he cranked the telephone, no operator came on. He whirred the handle harder and harder, jammed the bar down a dozen times, but the deadness in the black cup was like an ocean pressed to his ear. The wires were cut. He returned to the window. No movement on the street. Silence. He pressed his face to the glass, trying to see south. But Graceful wouldn't come to Deep Greenwood anyway. If she came north again, she would go home. He turned to look up the street, past the business district, toward Mr. Smitherman's house. If the phone was dead, Hedgemon thought, he didn't have to wait anymore, right? Whether the callers tried or did not try, it didn't matter, because no calls could get through. Right?

He reached for the door handle, but a burst of gunfire from the west made him jump back, a ratchety nonstop barrage, like a hundred guns firing one after another. The chattering fire was followed by silence, but Hedgemon knew what had caused the sound. Colored folks didn't own machine guns. Only whitemen. They'd cut the telephone wires coming out of Greenwood, they had set fire to some of the buildings, now the whites had mounted a machine-gun on the hill by the granary. Anything was possible. His eye was caught by a movement in the street, and he turned to glimpse a man running north, and then a slim figure in a pink dress, darting across the avenue toward the Woods Building, a delicate lightfooted girl, running. He had only an instant to recognize Graceful's skinny little sister before the girl suddenly whirled, a lithesome half-turn in midair, like a dancer, and fell down in the middle of the street. She lay still, unmoving.

For what seemed like an eternity Hedgemon watched the dark flower blooming across the pink material, irregularly etched, blossoming from her collarbone, spreading toward her breast. He thought maybe it wasn't Jewell, maybe he'd been mistaken. The girl's face was turned away from him. But in himself he knew the tiny form on the street was Graceful's sister. If Graceful ever dreamed that he'd watched her sister fall and done nothing, she would hate him with a hatred from which there'd be no pardon, ever. Hedgemon opened the door and ran into the street. There was another scattering of gunfire from the tracks, and an answering volley from the top of the Woods Building, but Hedgemon kept running, and when he got close he saw a big woman kneeling in the street beside the pink figure. He bent to scoop the girl in his arms, but the limp body was heavy, and he was thankful when the woman took the girl's legs and hoisted them around her waist. Together they carried Jewell into the *Star* office and laid her on the floor.

They stood each on either side, looking down. The flower on the pink cotton did not appear black now; this close, in the reflected firelight, the blood was dark red. Jewell's eyes were half open, her mouth was slack. Hedgemon had never seen a dead girl before, but he knew Jewell was dead. Slowly, very slowly, he began to realize the truth of the thing that was happening. The truth that he could have died just now, running out in the street. You did not have to be caught in the wrong place at the wrong time. You did not have to sass or rob a whiteman or look at a white-woman; you didn't have to lift your eyes the wrong way. You could be a young girl in a pink dress running, or an old woman in the street bent over to help her, you could be anybody. If they saw you they would kill you.

"What in the world this child doing out on the street?" the woman said. And then, "Must be the baby come, un-huh." She bent over Jewell, straightened the girl's crooked head, touched a finger to each eyelid, and rolled it down. She muttered something else, which Hedgemon couldn't make out at first, and then he knew she was saying prayers. After a while the woman raised up again. Her hair was plaited in a thick braid down her back, her face was smooth, thick-featured, mahogany red. She looked at Hedgemon, looked hard at him. "What are you going to do, son?"

"Do?" Hedgemon felt his heart jump. "What do you mean, do?"

"You going to help me carry this girl home? Or am I fixing to have to go to that house alone, tell her mama where she's at?" The woman's gaze returned to Jewell. "She a sweet child, too. I hate to leave her, but I can't carry her myself." She paused, and Hedgemon could hear gunfire again, faint, off to the west. "Lord, Lord," the woman said, "what was that mama thinking, to send this child out on such a night?" She exhaled a long breath. "Baby don't wait for a peaceful night, anyway. Don't wait on good weather. Child have its own time. Its own time is God's time." She met Hedgemon's eyes again. "So?"

Hedgemon didn't know what the woman was talking about, or why she spoke of Graceful's sister as if she knew her, but he understood that she wanted him to carry Jewell home. Home through the firelit streets where whitemen had mounted machine guns to kill Negroes, through a world where anything could happen. He stared at Jewell's face, peaceful now, with the eyes shut: she'd been living, running, a tall, agile, strong girl moments ago, and now she was dead. His mind whirled as he realized that he couldn't be sitting here with a dead girl when Mr. Smitherman came in to-morrow morning. But he couldn't go back out there. And yet maybe Graceful would love him, finally, if he did such a thing, carried her dead sister home. The longing in him was terrible; the longing was as bad as the fear. He thought, Delroy! Sure, he could telephone Delroy and tell him to come in the truck to get his niece, and then he thought: No. White-men cut the phone lines, didn't they? Cut the wires to keep Negroes from talking to each other, to keep them knifed off from the outside world, and he thought, *They're shooting any black face they see. They will shoot me.* The woman was watching him, but he couldn't meet her eyes or speak.

His mind whispered, *Maybe she's there already. Maybe Graceful gone home to her mama's house.* Hedgemon felt rather than heard the woman start toward the front door.

"No! Wait! Not that way!" Before he understood what he was doing, he'd pulled her away from the glass. "Go out the back," he said. The woman was nearly as tall as he was. Her skin in the fireglow was a deep, ruddy color. She waited, watching him. "Go up the alley toward the section line," he said finally. "We can cut over from there."

He squatted beside Graceful's sister, folded each of the girl's limp arms across her belly, and then he wrapped his arms around her and pressed her to his chest, lifted her—she was heavy, so heavy for such a slight girl—and carried her over his shoulder toward the back of the office. The woman went before him, opened the door leading to the big room, where the presses were silent. The alley was silent when they emerged from the back of the building. All of Greenwood, it seemed, was silent, but for the roar and crackle of the fires farther west. For a moment, as he hurried north with the old woman beside him and the weight of the girl across his back, Hedgemon had the feeble hope that it was finished, that the white-men were done with them.

Franklin stepped into the street with his head lifted, feeling the air. Men were everywhere, and little boys, running. He followed the flow of foot traffic until he came upon a crowd in front of McGee's Hardware, where the big window was smashed and a man in a police captain's uniform stood inside, handing out guns and ammunition as fast as his hands could deal them. A man on the corner called out, "Did you get deputized yet?" When Franklin looked at him blankly, the fellow said, "Hell, man, jump up there and tell him to deputize you! They're deputizing every two-legged white man that's got a weapon. If you ain't got one they'll give you one. They need all the help they can get. There's a nigger army coming from Muskogee, hadn't you heard?"

Franklin shook his head, turned away; he withdrew immediately to the safe surroundings of leather and brass and cigar smoke inside the hotel, where oilmen and business magnates stood about in little concerned clutches of threes and fours. He did not join them, only lingered close enough to hear snatches of conversation: . . . ought to go in and clean out that nest of vipers . . . turn that hellhole into an industrial-and-wholesale district . . . nothing but a red-light district full of choc joints and whorehouses . . . place for a new train station . . . crying shame, all those colored shanties sitting on that prime real estate.

A young man in white seersucker and a straw boater came rushing in, shouting, "They're taking the depot! Come on!" and some of the businessmen followed the young man into the street, but Franklin stepped into a recessed alcove at the end of the lobby, behind a brass spittoon. From here he could see most of Third Street through the window and, on Cincinnati, a river of men, streaming north. The voices inside and the muted yelling voices outside swelled and echoed each other, a garble of voices rising and falling, half-understood phrases: . . . secure the Frisco! . . . damn buildings across the tracks . . . wait for daylight anyhow, the niggers got . . .

Where the hell was Logan? Franklin was convinced that he was still waiting for his partner, though it was almost four in the morning and there was a small war raging between First and Archer, the heart of the battle centered at the Frisco station, where Jim Dee should have arrived hours ago if he was coming. Still, for the hundredth time Franklin consulted his watch. In a great show of impatience he snapped it shut, turned again to the window, where the glow on the northern horizon had grown brighter. The crowd had set fire to some Negro shacks, he'd heard, but the colored snipers had driven them back, and so, when the firetrucks arrived, the crowd of whites surrounded them, wouldn't let them through, and the firemen had returned to the station, let the fires burn.

"They ought to set fire to the whole mess," a familiar voice said behind him. Franklin turned to find L. O. Murphy clipping the end of a cigar with gold nippers. "They're trying to, we're damn sure going to, but that goddamn police inspector Dayley's perched in front of the depot, threatening to shoot the first white man who goes across." L.O. examined the leaf carefully, put the nipped end in his mouth. "He won't be inspector much longer, pulling a stunt like that. We've got to get in there and clean out that cesspool."

"I was wondering where you were. Logan stood me up again."

"When are you going to get rid of that insolent son of a bitch?"

"When I find a man half as good."

"Never mind about that. Listen, go home and get that Winton I sold you and bring it around. We're going to need it come daylight."

"For what?"

"I told you. We've got to clean up that cesspool of a niggertown. Should've done it a long time ago. If you own a weapon you'd better bring it. The whistle's set to blow at daylight, that's the signal."

"What are you talking about?"

"There's only one way to stop typhoid, set a torch to every goddamn thing that's contaminated, and these Tulsa niggers are sure as hell contaminated. Haven't I been saying that, just exactly? We've got a dozen planes sitting at Arbon Field this minute, gassed up and ready to take off, but they'll have to wait till it gets light enough to fly. Then, by God, we're going to run the niggers out of Tulsa."

"What's the matter with you, Murphy? This is none of our business."

L.O. blinked at him. "It's every white man's business. Go get the car and meet me at the Frisco station in an hour. We're finally going to put that part of town to good use." He turned, made his way across the lobby to join the other businessmen. Franklin lowered his head and peered through the plate-glass window, patted his vest pockets for a cigar.

Althea had never seen so many men in one place in her life—so many humans, if they could be called humans. To her mind they were little better than animals panting through the streets with their guns and tongues hanging out. She kept just back from the edge of the building, watching the stream of men pass. Oh, would they never all get to where they were going and get out of the street? In irritation she turned to see if Graceful was still sitting where she'd put her. The dark form in the dark dress blended with the dark alley, but the baby was wrapped in a light blanket, and she could see that it was still lying loosely, unattended, in Graceful's lap. The nitwit had run out in the street chasing after a roaring man-and-gun-loaded roadster, and Althea had had to grab her and pull her into the alley, make her sit down on the store's back step. The girl had been slumped like a ragdoll ever since, barely keeping hold of the swaddled baby in her lap.

Now what were they going to do? It was another five or six blocks to the Hotel Tulsa, which was the logical place to look for Franklin. Althea's agitation eased a little as she thought of her husband. Franklin would know how to negotiate this mess. But how was she going to get Graceful through that mob of trotting white men? She'd like to just let her wait in the alley, but some of them might find her, and then no telling what would happen. Althea glanced at the road again, but the flood of men, rather than lessening, seemed actually to be swelling, as if it flowed from an inexhaustible source. On the far side a tawny head glided smoothly in the crowd. Her heart stopped. What was he doing in Tulsa? On such a night?

In the midst of a trashy, filthy, vulgar mob of poorborn white men? Althea stood on her toes to see better, but already the dark-blond head had vanished in the river. Instantly she convinced herself it wasn't Jim Dee, only someone who looked like him, and she turned and started back into the alley as the baby began to cry.

Graceful stared straight ahead. She seemed to hardly know the child was there. Althea picked up the wailing baby, put him to her shoulder and patted his thickly padded bottom, but his cries didn't lessen. "Here," she said, and laid him back in Graceful's lap. "Feed him." Graceful gazed down at the sateen bodice stretched tight across her chest. Dark spots welled in two places, where her breasts were leaking milk. Althea said impatiently, "Oh, good God, here," and pulled the girl forward by the shoulder; she reached behind and unbuttoned the back. Graceful put the baby to her breast mechanically. Her naked torso was revealed in the dim light of the alley, for a ballgown was hardly a nursing dress, but Althea barely noticed; her mind was elsewhere. She turned an ear toward the men's voices, the old restless impatience coursing in her, as she tried to think what to do next. Probably she should just turn around and take the girl home. It was going to be too hard to reach the hotel in the first place, and Franklin would never be able to get the Winton through that mass of men running in the streets anyway.

"When you finish, put your hat on and we'll go." She narrowed her eyes then, glanced around, but she didn't see the feathered hat anywhere. She hadn't even noticed when Graceful took it off. The dress was ruined, greasy milk spots down the front and filthy all over the back, no doubt, from the alley floor, but Althea had known she was discarding the dress by the very act of giving it to a colored girl to put on her body. For some reason, however, she'd thought to salvage the hat. "Where is it?" she snapped. She couldn't take the girl through those wild streets bareheaded. "What did you do with my hat?" She didn't wait for Graceful to answer. "Hurry up now and finish. We can't take all night. What's the matter with you?" She reached to tug the bodice up but was stopped by the sound of the girl's flat, listless voice.

"They finally done what he say they going to do. All that time he know it, and now it's done."

"What's done?"

"He know all along they were going to. Now they done it." Graceful inhaled so slowly, so deep in her lungs that the baby's head rose and fell several inches with the strength of the breath. "I shouldn't have treated him so. Sass and talk back. I should have stayed. If I stayed, maybe he wouldn't have come back to Tulsa. He wouldn't be dead now. Look what they done to him." She raised her eyes to Althea. "You see what they done."

"What?"

"Lynch T.J."

"Who's T.J.?"

Graceful stared straight ahead, said dully, "My brother."

"Nobody's been lynched. That's not your brother raped that white girl? Is it?" In her mind's eye Althea saw the solemn little colored boy in the studio photograph on the dresser inside the yellow house. "Listen," she said, her voice very businesslike, authoritative, "I want you to understand that nobody's been lynched." She took the baby in one arm, reached awkwardly to tug the bodice up over Graceful's breasts. "Nobody," she repeated, though she was in no way certain that a lynching wasn't just exactly what that mob of men was running toward. A lynching and a bonfire as well, it appeared, for the whole of the northern sky was glowing. "Come on, now. Let's go."

"They lynched T.J.," Graceful repeated dully. "Tie him up to a car, drag the flesh off him, drag the skin off my brother till he don't even look like himself."

"That wasn't your brother. Don't be ridiculous. Graceful, that was not your brother!"

Graceful suddenly got to her feet and started toward the front of the alley.

"Stop!" Althea screamed. But Graceful had stopped anyway, standing in the breach with her shoulders heaving horribly. Althea snatched up the hat from the alley floor and reached her in an instant; she said again, "That was not your brother! Hear me?" Because she was unwilling that it be so. Because if they were going to drag niggers behind cars it should be nameless niggers, bad niggers, dangerous ones who raped white women and carried knives in their boots, not little boys who stared solemnly from photographs, and Althea said it again, hissed the words, "That wasn't him!"

Graceful said, "Don't you think I know my own brother?"

"No. You do not. You're—you're distraught, that's all. It's sad. It's terrible, but it doesn't have anything to do with you."

Graceful stared at her a moment. She turned to look again at the men running in the street. The baby was crying. She held him so carelessly, so loosely, that his big head lolled back on the fragile neck.

"You're going to break that child's neck!" Althea took the baby from her. "Cover yourself," she ordered, and Graceful pulled the sleeve up. "Turn around." Althea put the bawling infant to her shoulder and tucked the hat beneath her arm as she tried to fasten the dozens of tiny mother-of-pearl buttons, but it was entirely too awkward. "Take this baby," she said, and handed him back to Graceful. "Hold his head! Here." She plopped the hat on Graceful's head, twirled her like a seamstress's mannequin, and now Althea's fingers flew as she buttoned the ballgown. "All right, now, we are going to go back to the house. I'll carry the baby. Walk straight. Don't look at them. Keep your hands down, hide them in the skirt. Like this. Don't talk. We'll walk home, and in the morning Franklin will carry you to your mother's house in the car. Do you hear?"

"I got to go home."

"We can't get through that mess."

"I got to go home."

"All right," Althea sighed, but her heart was racing. "We'll go around. Do you know how to go around?"

Graceful was silent a moment, staring at the roiling street. "Can't go around," she said. "There's no way to go around."

"Yes there is. You'll have to show me. Wait!" Althea cried as Graceful started into the street. She pulled the girl to her and reached up to straighten the hat; she tugged on the black veil, smoothing it, trying to tuck it into the high collar. "Here, let me have him." Althea held the baby in one arm as she draped Graceful's hands inside the folds of the skirt again, wondering why it hadn't occurred to her to put gloves on those dark hands. She covered the baby's head with the blanket and grasped a firm hold on Graceful's arm, but when they emerged from the alley they were taken up like drift in the rushing current. Without willing it, completely powerless against it, they merged with the river of white men sweeping north. Along First Street the river swelled outward, became a sea of armed, hatted men pressing forward and yet held back by some massive obstacle blocking the flow. Althea couldn't see what held them back.

"You ladies better get off the street," a voice said behind her. "Them niggers are armed, ma'am, hadn't you heard?"

Another voice cursed and spat. "I'd whip my wife if she come out here."

"This sure as hell ain't no place for a lady."

"You sure it's a lady?"

A burst of low, ugly laughter made Althea clamp Graceful's arm harder, pulling her toward the west. The baby was bawling, bawling, and Althea wanted to shake him to make him stop. The crush of men, chests and elbows and foul breaths and curses, began to thin around her, seemed to part and allow her to go through; in a moment she understood that it was the wailing baby that made the men separate and make way for them. "Let the nurse through," she heard someone say, "Let 'em through!"

"Lady, you better get on home, away from this business, you don't want to see what we're going to have to do—" The man was talking to Graceful.

"Ma'am, hadn't you better take that baby someplace safe?"

Slowly it began to filter into Althea's perception that the men thought Graceful, in her sateen ballgown and black-feathered veiled hat, was the lady and Althea the nursemaid to the squalling child. Mortified, drenched in shame and fury, she tried to stop in the street, but she was shoved from behind, forced forward in a world turned upside down by men's eyes, for she'd put her own clothes on the back of a colored girl, had come away from her house in her filthy gardening shoes and plain housedress, without a sign of a parasol or a decent hat, and what the men saw was what she most dreaded in the world: her own lowborn, ugly self. Where was Graceful? She'd lost hold of her, and she could not stop the force that propelled her. Althea was swept around a brick corner, and the press of men at her back lessened a little, spreading out on either side as the street opened onto the railyard, where a crowd was gathered around something on the ground. Fire licked up in the blank eyes of a building on the far side of the tracks. The odor of gasoline was strong, as was the odor of whiskey, the smell of roasting meat.

Between khaki pantslegs she saw the thing on its back among the cinders, its legs bent at the knees, stumps of arms reaching up. At first she couldn't tell what it was, because the hands had been burned off, or chopped off, and the skin was charred black, but it was the mouth, finally, the gaping, white, lipless smile, that made her understand it was a dead Negro; its lips had been burned away, or cut away, so that it seemed to grin up at the ring of laughing firelit faces. Not all of the white faces were laughing. Some seemed to hardly notice the corpse in the cinders; others looked greedy, as if they'd like to burn and kill again what was already dead and burned. Some were drinking from tin flasks, or squinting overhead at the great slash of leaden sky swathed in red, or looking hungrily northward, like jackals, like wolves, she thought, and suddenly a burning claw of rage and loathing came up in her throat: she saw her brother in the distance among them, or she believed it was her brother. But she was shoved from the back again, and she lost sight of the swarthy face; for an instant she watched the nearby faces, shadowed, flickering in the firelight. On the other side of the circle was a familiar face, though she couldn't quite place it: ruddy, sunworn, eyes narrowed against the smoke from the smoldering tar as he peered down at the blackened corpse, and she thought then that this was her brother. No. NO! Dear God, what was she thinking? *He is kin to me*, her mind said. *They're all kin to me.* The baby was crying, and she smothered his face against her shoulder.

Graceful! If these men saw Graceful, if they realized she was colored, they'd do the same to her. Althea tried to turn around, but the bodies were pressing at her back, jostling, pushing, the baby was crying, and men's voices were shouting, the sounds were so loud, and the crackling fires roared. Suddenly the wind turned, blew the thick smoke from the building across the tracks toward them, mingled it with the stinking creosote beneath the dead Negro; the wind whirled up glowing cinders, floated red-limned black ashes through the stinging air, made some of the men cough and choke, and the crowd opened a little, enough for Althea to catch sight of the tall figure in the black veil standing, swaying, at the edge of the track. How had she got all the way over there? Althea started toward her. But in the next heartbeat she realized that if the men saw her with a colored girl they'd believe she was a nigger lover. She hesitated. Oh, *would* this baby never shut up its bawling!

A darker thought touched her, and she stopped completely now, paralyzed, for she understood that if the men saw her carrying a colored baby they would think it was hers. The newborn's eggshell skin wouldn't save her: he was too clearly a colored baby. He was a child born of both races, and she had to get rid of him, had to give him back to his mother, but the press of bodies was too close around her, she couldn't see Graceful, and now two recognitions came to her at once, mute, but fully alive and understood. Graceful's skin would betray her. No matter how well disguised she was, how dark the veil hiding her face, Graceful was not safe anywhere on this night inside her brown skin. The other thought, more terrifying than the first, and entirely inconceivable before this moment, was the understanding that Althea's white skin wouldn't save her. If they thought she'd lain with a black man—

Oh, the men's bodies were so close together, the stench was wretched, rising all around her. A voice at her shoulder said, "Sweet Jesus, what'd you bring a baby out in this for?" And another said, "Daylight's coming!" Desperately Althea looked around for a place to stash the baby, somewhere hidden, that the men might not see.

In the east a thin line of red made a slit in the gray at the horizon. A metal silo loomed out of the smoke, and Althea started toward it, holding the baby so tight to her breast its cries were muffled, like a kitten mewing under the house. Some men were running, and as she came up on a little rise by a tin storage-shack she saw hundreds of people, thousands, moiling in the railyard. A dozen uniformed white men stood on the tracks with guns drawn, facing the crowd, but it was the Frisco rails themselves that seemed to hold the mob back, dammed the flood, forcing the crowds to swell east and west along the tracks. Men and little boys and a good number of women stirred restlessly along the rails as far as she could see, all facing north, as if for a road race, as if they were chafing at the line before a land run. Althea pressed herself against the corrugated wall of the tin shack, trying to hide herself and the baby.

A nightmarish whistle sounded, a piercing shriek that split the universe, followed by a breath of stunning silence. Then the people moved in a wave across the railyard, overrunning the men in uniform; heads bobbing, knees jacked high, voices hollering, they crossed the rails, running. Automobiles and oilfield trucks crammed with armed men roared among the racers, and past them, into Little Africa, shooting, shouting, as the mad woodpecker waked in the silo overhead with its ratchety endless roar of knocking, which was not knocking but machine-gun fire from the high, square window of the granary.

In the same way it had taken time to see the human form in the charred corpse in the cinders, now it was a minute before Althea understood what was happening. She saw men breaking windows in the stores across the tracks, splashing kerosene, shouting orders; she saw a woman, a perfectly well-dressed white woman, lug a bolt of cloth out through a shattered door; the woman dropped the bolt in the street, disappeared back inside the store. Althea's mind didn't want to receive what her senses were telling her. A dozen or more buildings were burning already in Greenwood. The sound of breaking glass reached her again, and again, and again. Dear God. They were going to wipe them out.

The memory flashed of the morning she'd stood on the little rise above the tracks in her kid-leather shoes, looking across at colored town gleaming in the sun like a distant city across a river. Now black smoke billowed, bowed low, darkening the coming daylight, but she could see the hundreds of white men and women looting those same stores, breaking windows. The heat from the flames radiated toward her; the very tin of the shack behind her seemed afire with heat. Over to the west a pair of armed men herded a family of Negroes out the door of a little woodframe house. The Negroes, a man and a woman and three children, were in nightclothes. They walked down the porch steps with their hands in the air, even the children. Althea could think of nothing except to hide herself. The smoke was horrific, but it wouldn't cover her. Where was Franklin? And Graceful? What had they done with Graceful? Althea peered through the smoke, but she saw only white faces now, and the baby wouldn't stop crying; he was hungry again, or wet, probably, or burning up in that smothering blanket, or simply terrified by the noise and smoke, as Althea was terrified, and furious, and despairing. She held the baby to her chest, patted his back, but there was nothing she could do for him. There was nothing she could do for any of them, for Graceful either. She'd tried. Hadn't she tried?

"Shhhhhh, baby," she whispered. "Shhhhhh. Hush, little baby," she crooned, "don't say a word." Her voice cracked. She hunted for a cleft, a crevice in the tin in which to hide; seeing a door in the side of the shed, she quickly went to it and pushed on it, but the door was locked. Althea turned to face the riot again. Well, it was not a riot anyway, was it? Not a war, as Graceful had called it. It was—what? She had no word for what she witnessed, the thunder and rattle of gunfire, smashed glass shattering, the hiss and snap of flames, and everywhere the rolling, choking smoke. Shifting the baby to the crook of her arm, she peeled back the blanket to give him some air. He was such a limp little thing, so tiny and boneless. His cry was weakening, growing bumpy; he arched his back, opened his mouth, turned his face toward her. She placed the knuckle of her forefinger between his lips, and the baby quieted, sucking hard. He stared at her a moment from almond-shaped eyes the color of granite. Slowly his lids drooped, and then closed, but he continued sucking. Althea surrendered to the sensuous pleasure of the soft gums on her finger, knowing he would not stay contented very long. Maybe she could just carry him back to her house on South Carson, maybe the rioters in the streets wouldn't know he was colored. His hair was black and curly, yes, but not frizzy, not nappy; it lay in little sweat-matted swirls on his crown. And his skin was so light, the color of age-faded beige silk, nearly transparent in places, like the finest membrane. Gazing at him, she thought that perhaps his nose wasn't so broad after all. There was something almost feminine in his face, his lips like an open rose, and his eyebrows distinct for such a tiny one, finely arched, naturally arched, like her own. Althea lifted her head. *Like my own.*

The knowledge settled in her with a terrible force. She tried to dismiss it, wall it off, deny. But Althea's powers of deception had been stripped from her long months ago, on the banks of the Deep Fork, when she'd stood listening to her brother's bitter voice speak truths she'd kept hidden a lifetime. There was no need to filter and calculate, to review the signs that had passed to show her. *Kin to me,* her mind said. She raised her gaze to the fires burning in Greenwood, the fury and chaos, the feast of destruction. Graceful was even now making her way through that devastation to the shotgun house on North Elgin. Or she was dead somewhere, or dying. A drone hummed high in the sky. Althea squinted against the smoke, saw an airplane coming from the northeast, flying low. The meaning didn't register. There was but one obsessive thought in her mind: she had to carry this baby at once to his mother, give him back quickly, before it was too late.

T J. peered over the edge of the roof at the whites pouring across the tracks. His hand was on the butt of a carbine rifle he'd picked up from a fallen soldier, but the rifle was useless. He had no more cartridges. The pistol tucked in his waistband was also useless; he'd fired all the shells. He eyed the assault for a few minutes; then he turned over and lay on his back on the tarpaper, gazing at the sky lifting pale bird's-egg blue above him. Automobile motors rumbled in the streets below, blended with the pop-pop-popping of many pistols, the crack of riflefire, the sounds of tinkling glass. Above him the light blue sky swirled with pink and yellow, a gorgeous pastel dawn, a fine early-summer morning, June 1, his father's birthday. T.J. marveled at how tranquil he felt.

A high distant hum came from the north, grew to a buzzing, and then a loud roaring overhead, as a shiny new biplane, wings gleaming, flew in low, banked away from the smoke; it was followed by another, and another. T.J. could see a whiteman leaning from the open seat of the first plane, firing a rifle over the side, down on the streets of Greenwood. A canister plummeted from the second plane, trailing fire, and where it landed there was an explosion, and a roof somewhere on Frankfort or Easton burst into flames. Quickly T.J. rolled over, crawled on his belly to the rear of the building and heaved himself over the side; his dangling legs searched for the open window from which he'd hoisted himself to the roof in the darkness, hours ago.

When he swung himself into the dawnlit room, he was relieved to see that the woman and her little girl were gone. Good. She'd done what he said. He didn't know her name, had never seen her before he knocked at her room at midnight and asked to use the window, but when she'd begged him for news of what was happening on the streets, he'd told her, Take your little girl and go north, past the section line. Whites coming at daylight, he'd told her; won't be no place down here safe. She'd looked at him helplessly, unbelieving, and turned back to her little girl asleep on the dufold. T.J. hadn't had time to mess with her; he'd set the chair in front of the window, looped the carbine over his shoulder, crawled out. All night he had sniped from the rooftop, as long as he'd had ammunition. Twice he was certain he'd got one, a dark head falling back, and it was nothing like shooting the whiteman who chased Everett's daddy. That had been accident, the shotgun in his hand by instinct, not to *kill* the whiteman, but to stop him. Now he knew there was only one way to stop whitemen. T.J. carried in his mind the image of white weasel faces, Everett's silhouette on the horizon, fallen black men around him as the line retreated toward Greenwood. He was going to kill every white face he could see, but he had to find more shells.

He took the stairs four at a time, was almost to the ground floor when a voice caught him. "Son! Son!" A tiny elderly woman was hunched in a doorway on the second floor. She was dressed up like Sunday in a fine navy dress, a string of red beads at her throat. Her hair was white; her fingers, gnarled as willow roots, were wrapped around the knob of a cane she grasped in both hands. "Help me! I can't run!"

"You safer here than on the streets," T.J. said.

"They're burning everything. They'll burn the hotel down over my head."

There was a crash of shattered glass at the front of the building, followed by a splintering sound, and T.J. stepped over to the woman and picked her up piggyback. The cane clattered to the floor, her old lungs grunted as he hoisted her, but she weighed no more than one of his little sisters, and he ran with her toward the back hallway, away from the sound of the breaking glass.

Out the back of the building and into the alley and through it till they reached the Midland Valley railyard. In the distance he could see people running north along the rails, women dragging their children by the hands, old people in nightclothes tottering in the center of the tracks, and men, too, young prime men, running, his people running. T.J.'s soul rebelled. No! He'd not come down to the streets to run but to fight. The gunfire behind him was constant, wild, unconnected, issuing from a hundred directions. Smoke billowed, dipped low; the old lady started to cough. He ran with her out into the open space of the railyard. What had he done with the rifle? He'd left the carbine on the rooftop; he must have, because he didn't have it. But his Colt was tucked in his belt, he could feel its smooth, bloodwarmed barrel against his skin; he'd find more shells, find someplace to stand and fight, he thought, as he jogged along the side of the tracks, running north with the others, running with the old lady on his back. He heard her faint wheezy lungs. Then she grunted hard and slammed against him, shoving him forward, and the stick-thin arms around his neck went slack; she began to slide backward. T.J. crouched low, hunkered forward so that the old lady's body might not fall off, and on he went, running.

Graceful, too, was moving north. She wasn't running but gliding serenely among the white rioters on Elgin Avenue. If any had paused in their frenzy to notice, they'd have been struck by her purposefulness and composure, but the rioters were looking for loot and for niggers, and the tall, veiled lady in old-fashioned evening dress met neither description. She passed Johnson's Shoes and the confectionery, where whitepeople streamed through the shattered doors in antlike relays, carting vats of cherries and chocolate syrup to add to the pile of round black tables and brass chairs; carrying leather workboots and children's oxfords to toss onto the great, tumbled, multicolored mountain of shoes. Already small fires were flickering inside the stores. Hours earlier, when she'd seen the mauled black body being dragged in the street and believed it was T.J., Graceful had entered a deep, listless mourning. Her brother's fear in the tent at Bigheart instantly became prophecy, she herself the unheedful sinner, and for those few hours in the alley, she'd been lost.

But the sight of the blackened corpse in the cinders had wrenched her from grief to purposeful fury: it might be T.J. on his back in the railyard, might not be; might be Delroy, or Hedgemon, might be a woman, even, because there were no clothes or genitals to show who it was. With the odor of burned flesh in her nostrils, Graceful had crossed the tracks. The masses of whitepeople breaking and pouring north made her struggle easier, that was all. She held no conscious thought of Mrs. Dedmeyer, or the baby, though the tingling gut-deep pull went on coursing from her breasts to her parched throat, her belly, her privates, because her body would not so easily relinquish the child. By the time she started up the hill, her milk had let down again. A baby was crying somewhere. She stopped, turned to look behind.

The whole of Archer was in flames now; smoke blackened the daylight sky. Graceful pulled the veiled hat off in order to see better. The cross streets were afire as far north as Brady. Open carloads of whitemen with shotguns and rifles, men with badges and hats and guns, patrolled the roads, but they were not trying to stop the white looters. They were gathering up Negroes. In the distance she saw a young woman with a crying baby in her arms being pushed along the avenue by a whitewoman. Two men in stocking feet, with their arms raised over their heads, were being marched south by three young whiteboys with guns. The front line of looters had passed the stores now; they were starting in on the homes a few blocks below where Graceful stood. The sound of breaking glass was everywhere. She watched a half-dozen whitemen trying to wrestle an upright piano through the doorway of a two-story brick house. A whitewoman stepped out the shattered front window with her arms full of silverware; she dashed down the porch steps and hurried south, dropping spoons and forks as she ran. Graceful walked on, her breasts weeping, her breath labored, her step calm and deliberate, but quickened. She had to get home.

Throughout the city all living creatures were moving, the rats and cats and stray dogs fleeing the fire, as the black population fled, and the white rioters swelled north and east and west from the train tracks, burning, looting, or taking Negroes into custody and marching them to the newly spawned prison camps at the fairgrounds and the convention hall. Near the Frisco station hundreds of National Guardsmen, sent by the governor, were disembarking from a train just arrived from Oklahoma City, and those already on the ground were moving, too—not north, to stop the riot or to put out the raging fires, but south, toward City Hall, to prepare and eat breakfast. The sheriff was driving east in a closed car, with two deputies guarding the prisoner, as they spirited Dick Rowland out of town. Franklin Dedmeyer hurried south on Carson Avenue in the bright morning sun, his palm at his forehead in a salute, for he'd misplaced his hat somewhere. Miles away, Althea walked north, with the child in her arms. Mr. Smitherman, having watched the *Star* office surrender to the fire, was in that moment crossing Dirty Butter Creek with his wife and children and another family in a Ford motorcar, as Hedgemon Jackson, for the fourth time since daylight, climbed the front steps of the yellow shotgun house, where, inside, in the cramped middle room, Elberta's baby moved through the moist tunnel, in the darkness, the violence, the crushing waves, without light. Even the blackened corpse in the railyard was moving, as it was hoisted by disinterested hands and tossed onto the flatbed of an oilfield truck, to join the other black bodies stacked like cordwood near the cab.

Behind a car shed near the train tracks, T.J. eased the old lady to the ground. He stood pondering her a moment while he caught his breath: a tiny slackmouthed brown woman, a stranger in a navy dress, dead. Still panting, he stepped to the corner of the shed and peered south, where the smoke covered everything; he turned and squinted west. The whites had mounted another machine gun inside Greenwood; it was raining fire now from the top of Standpipe Hill. Another glance at the dead woman. Nothing to do for her. Nothing he could do, same as there'd been nothing to do for Everett Candler, except kill whitemen. He had to get hold of some ammunition somewhere. T.J. slipped from the protection of the car shed, walked fast along Latimer Street, and then he was trotting, and finally running toward his uncle's garage. Behind him the dead woman lay like a thin shadow in the alley, curled around itself.

The old stable that Delroy used for a garage was empty, a few tools and engine parts scattered on the dirt floor, the Nash truck yawning, its hood raised, front wheels on blocks. T.J. ran next door, but the house, too, was empty, Lucille and the kids gone, the beds unmade. He hurried to the closet in the front room, tossed clothes and hats on the floor, but he knew Delroy didn't own a gun; there'd be no bullets here. Pulling his pistol from his waistband, T.J. went to the window, pushed aside the curtain; he could see two whitemen coming along Rosedale, and the fury in him was terrible, to have a gun and no ammunition. He could kill them so easily from here. T.J. shoved the empty gun back in his belt and rushed to the kitchen, slung drawers open, grabbed a butcher knife and a paring knife, and ran out the back door, hunkered over, crossed the yard to the garage. A voice down the street hollered, "There's one!" and guns popped below him, but T.J. ducked in the stable door.

When they came in, he was up in the old hayloft, pressed against the back wall. He was hiding from whitemen, yes, but it was not the same as cowering in the cornstalks: if they tried to climb the ladder, he was ready. Both kitchen blades raised.

"Watch out, them sonsabitches'll snipe ya," one whispered.

"Burn this dump down," the other answered. "He'll show his coon ass quick enough." There was the muted sound of boots scrabbling on the dirt floor, the clank of metal on metal. "Me and Skinner torched a whorehouse on Archer, Christ, you ought to seen the monkeys run!" Both men laughed. T.J. could smell gasoline.

"Shit, it's livelier'n shooting ducks at the fair," the first one hissed, and then there was the whoosh of flames. "Let's get out of here!"

T.J. didn't let himself think; he stepped to the edge of the loft and leapt down, and where the blade entered there was no resistance, the butcher knife slipped slickly in the soft side, like cutting lard. He twisted the blade as the whiteman gasped, tried to holler, but T.J. already had the man's gun, and he shot the other one as he turned his surprised weasel face toward him, and then this one in the head, and then was sorry to have wasted the bullet. Whitemen died easy. He felt their pockets for cartridges, took the rifle and the two revolvers, let the fire have the two men.

Inside the yellow shotgun house Iola Bloodgood Tiger took the child in her two hands and laid it on the mother's belly. The shriveled cord pulsed feebly; the baby's skin was withered, ancient-looking, as if she'd already begun to die in the womb, but the child breathed, and her cry lifted to join the sounds coming from the front room. Iola turned to tell Hedgemon Jackson, All right, we can go now, get them in the front room ready. The young man had been at the door a dozen times in the last hour, saying, They're burning Greenwood, we got to take these children and go! Behind him, always, she could hear the old mother weeping in the front room—

—sometimes wailing, sometimes sobbing, sometime little low whimpers like a child. Sometime no sound at all but the old mother walking back and forth across the floor. That sound of weeping been accompaniment for the little mother's birth groans all night, and I heard them like a song, right up till that child come into the world dying. For true. Birthcord flat and twisted. Baby look like an old woman, skin wrinkled, frizzly hair sticking out all over, little fingernails long enough to scratch. I have seen such things, more than a few times, because sometime a little soul don't want to come out. Sometimes it stay in the womb so long the child have to be born dead, because life will go right out if the child won't breathe this world's air, and sometimes it kill that mama, too. I would not blame any child coming into such a world as we showing that morning if it take one look and go right back to God, but this child do not go back, she lay slick on her mama's belly, crying like a cat.

I don't know how that little mother is going to travel, but she is going to, because we are all going to, because we do not have a choice. This is what I tell myself when I turn to speak to that tall boy. But he's not standing at the door now, how he been so many times through the labor, and when I go in the front room I don't see him there either, only the old mother on the divan with her dead daughter, touching the girl's face in her lap like the child is sleeping, and her other two young ones ringed on both sides. All night, whatever way the old mother is crying, that's the same way her two children cry—if she sob they sob, if she cry silent that's how they do, the little boy and his sister. Right now Mrs. Whiteside is facing straight ahead, making a slow shuddery sound deep in her chest, and the children match her, breath for breath. But the tall black boy is not here. He's not dancing fidgety at the window like he done all night, watching. I say to the old mother, Child born, and she nod, but she don't look at me. Girl child, I tell her, and I ease myself to the window, look south. The whole world have disappeared into smoke. I got to step outside to see how far the fire is.

Everything looks different in bright morning to how it looked in the dark when we carried the dead girl up on the front porch, when I stopped and looked south, seen the lone pillar of fire burning way off in the distance and little lights winking everywhere. Now the world have come to full daylight, but the light is turning dark from a hundred clouds of smoke rolling toward heaven, and when those many clouds gets up high they join together, make one huge gray boiling cloudbank to rise up over the world. Behind me, before me, all around me I hear the guns rattling, because death is coming from all directions, we are fully surrounded. What have I tell you about such force? That power's been unleashed, and there's no might on this earth going to turn it back under, no return till the story finish, and we a long way from finished. This hour of destruction is no more than a eyeblink to God.

I stand on the porch and look toward where the fire's crawling, and I see whitefolks running, blackfolks running, or walking slow with their hands in the air, I see men in cars rumbling everywhichway. Then I spy the tall black boy in a yard just down a ways, and I holler, Boy! We ready now! The child come! But he's turned away, looking south into the smoke.

All at once he start running away from me. I thinks to myself, Well, son, you been wanting to run all night, haven't you? Now you going to take off just the minute I could use you. I was so pure disgusted I turned and went back in the house.

The dead girl lay by herself on the divan, so peaceful looking, so pretty, except for the dark dried blood spread out on her chest. I hear the old mama in the middle room, barking at her two childrens, fetch this, do that, and when I go in I see she is wiping the infant clean with a wet rag. She have covered the little mother with a fresh sheet. The girl's face is swollen, her eyes look terrible, the afterbirth laying on the floor beside the cot, and the old mother ignore it, just step over it to carry the baby to the other bed. She look straight down at the little mother, say, Missy, you going to have to walk. I say, Miz Whiteside, you carry the baby, I'll help her. But that woman ignore me, turn to the chifforobe, jerk a dress off a hanger, say, LaVona, take Willie's hand, don't you let him go, I don't care what happen. Here, girl, sit up. And she go to help that little mother lean forward so she can slip the dress on over her head. The girl groan, say, Where's my baby? Mama? Is the baby all right?

I say, Your baby just fine, honey. Hear her? And, sure enough, that baby is crying strong now. I go to pick her up, she jerk her arms and legs good, the skinny wizened thing, little naked ancient child, hard as blackjack sticks, face like a bone; she's wailing loud, demanding, she ready to nurse this minute, but we got no time to wait for that. The two younguns standing in the doorway, the girl holding to the boy like she'll die if she let go of him, the old mother's putting a shift on the little mother, what am I going to do but wrap that baby up? I wrap her snug in a piece of blanket while Mrs. Whiteside help the little mother to stand, she wobble a minute on shaky legs, sit back down on the bed. Mrs. Whiteside lift her up again, hold her under the armpits to make her stay standing. She look over at me. Seem to me like it's the first time she have truly seen me since we come in the door, me and the tall boy, carrying her dead girl. But now she look directly at me, she say, Mrs. Tiger, where's Hedgemon?

I shake my head. He's gone, I tell her. He run off.

The woman stare past the two children to the front room. I can see her thinking, Who's going to carry my daughter? And I wonder the same. Mrs. Whiteside and me together could carry the dead girl, maybe, and the two childrens could take turns with the baby, but who's going to help the little mother? She can't walk. I don't believe she's going to walk a block without her womb fall out in the street. The woman keep looking at the front door, but her soul's eye is on the dead girl in her pink dress laying on the divan.

I say, Miz Whiteside? We got to go now. They coming. Fire's coming. We got to take these children and go north.

The old mother turn to me. She stare at me for a long time, silent. In a bit she turn to the two younguns, say, LaVona, you going to have to go with Mrs. Tiger. Y'all got to mind her now, hear me? Willie? You hear? The children nod. She come take the baby from me and put her in the little mother's arms, push that little mother away from the cot toward the front door. But when that little mother get to the front room and see the dead girl, she start to wilt down. Like a tallow wick on a hot stove she melt toward the linoleum, and when she get to the floor she let out a long whimpery wail.

Hush! That old mama's voice so fierce, the girl quiet at once; even that just-born babe in arms hush up her mouth. Outside folks are shouting, motorcars roaring, guns chattering, but inside is so quiet. The old mother whisper, My child come back to me dead, but your child is living. You going to take her. Take Willie and LaVona, because they are your flesh now. You got to help them. There's nobody else to help them. Daughter! You hear me? The little mother nod her head. Mrs. Whiteside turn to me, her eyes dry as breath, not even shiny now with wet. She say, Wait for us somewhere by Turley, if you can find a good place to wait.

They're burning everything, I say. They'll burn this house down with you and your child in it.

I got to stay with Jewell. That's all she answer. She disappear in the middle room, come back with a knotted handkerchief, hold it out to me, say, We thank you for your help. I don't put my hand out to take it. Very soft, in that dry feather-whisper, she say, I have lost enough children this night, Mrs. Tiger. Take my children someplace safe. Then in a loud voice she say, TeeJay going to be here in a minute. Him and Delroy coming soon. She keep talking in that loud everyday voice, like the world's not on fire, like the whites not swarming like an army into Greenwood to kill colored folks, like blackfolks not shooting whitefolks either, and her daughter's just having a little nap on the divan. She say, Y'all wait for us at Turley, or Bird Creek, or Dirty Butter, whichever look best. We'll find you. Soon as Delroy get here with the truck, we going to come. LaVona! What did I tell you? The girl grab her brother's hand, quick. The woman look steady at me when she put that knotted hanky in my hand. I can feel the little stack of coins tied so smooth in it. Her eyes never blink. We just going to be a

little while, she tell me. We'll soon come. She turn and hold the screen
open. I pick up the baby, put my hand under the arm of the little mother,
help her up from the floor.

On the porch Mrs. Whiteside bend down and hug those two young
ones, and they both take in to crying, but she say, Hush! And instantly they
hush. The smoke is rolling thick now, the little boy start coughing. The old
mother don't look at us anymore; she pull open the screen and go back in
the house, sit down on the divan, take the dead girl's head in her lap.

Japheth moved openly among the rioters—not unobtrusively as he'd
slipped among the lynchers when they hanged his partner, but brazenly,
at the center, the coreheart of violence. In the first moments of eruption,
when the armed black men, firing, began their retreat toward Greenwood,
Japheth, seeing who was winning, turned immediately and joined the
white mobs. It was Japheth, yes, whom Althea had seen at the burning of
the corpse in the railyard, as it was Japheth who'd found the gasoline can
in the first place, doused fuel on the dying body, shouted, Let's burn the
nigger! Japheth's hand that struck the match. Japheth's voice crying from
the steps of Mount Zion Baptist, The niggers got an arsenal in here, burn
down the church!

It was Japheth who sauntered forward now among some white men in
the yard of a fine brick home on Detroit Avenue, where a Negro doctor in
a houserobe and slippers walked down his front steps with his hands
clasped on top of his head. Japheth whispered to a teenaged white boy
with a pistol, That nigger raped a white woman, or The nigger's got a gun,
or That uppity nigger's got better things than you'll ever have, or some
words, Japheth said some words, and the boy pulled the trigger, shot Dr.
Blanchard pointblank in the chest. The others nearby whooped or
shouted, What the hell are you doing? Japheth turned, made his way to
the next block.

In a strip of dirt yard he paused, looking north. The street was filled
with Home Guard, hundreds of white men waving their guns, bellowing,
as they rounded up Negro prisoners, set fire to Negro homes. A familiar
dark-blond head moved among the others, hatless, the frowning face unmistakable. Japheth started toward it; then he stopped, his eyes narrowed,
his cunning returned. He watched as the driller and several others separated a group of black men from some women and children, searched

them, took whatever money they had in their pockets, and herded them into two silent clutches. In Japheth's mind the images rolled: thudding fists on the Murphys' lawn in the cold moonlight; the scowling, scornful face in the clearing. He retreated into the narrow space between two houses, crouched low to the earth to gather himself.

Some of the Home Guard began to march the black men down the middle of the street, four abreast, arms high in the air. They were coming directly toward him. The driller was in the midst of them, anonymous in oil-stained khakis, looking like any white man, but Japheth knew him. He raised the barrel of his gun. In a moment they'd be beside him. He would call out softly, Logan! and no one but the driller would hear. A delicate squeeze, and the sound of the discharge would be lost in the sounds of other bullets, in the roar of fire and voices, but Japheth would call out his name, and the driller, dying, would look up and know by whose hand. As Japheth waited, anticipating that delicious moment, a faint pop came from somewhere, and Jim Logan fell. There was a staccato burst as the Home Guard shot three of the unarmed Negroes, another shot from the sniper, and a second white man dropped, and Japheth sucked himself back into the crevice, the great ravenous place in him exploding in fury. The sweet moment had been stolen. Ripped from him by niggers! Japheth slipped back farther, hid himself deep in the cleft between the two Negro houses. In the crevice, in the dark, he tended his rage.

When he emerged from the narrow space a half-hour later, he was starving. Dark skin was the marker. Dark skin was the sign and permission. He found a black man hiding in a basement across the way, and he shot him, but the man wasn't destroyed. Japheth doused the man with gasoline, lit him, watched the body burn a few minutes before he climbed out the basement window. His gluttony, whipped by fire, enhanced by the earth's blackblood refined to the incendiary liquid he carried, was aimless, insatiable. He walked to the next street, found an old couple praying on their knees in their bedroom, shot them each in the back of the head, piled their curtains and bedclothes on the mattress, sprinkled gasoline on the pile, lit the sheets. But even before the flames licked up, Japheth walked out of the house, hungry. At each death the craving within him swelled larger; at each fire the great ravenous place increased. By the time he emerged from a gasoline-soaked house onto a porch on Elgin Avenue and saw the tall, graceful figure walking out of the smoke toward him, the gluttony in his soul was as large as the world.

N orth was the direction she'd begun, north she continued, striding fast in her gardening shoes, until she came to a place where a church was burning, a massive church of brick and stained glass, but the flames licked up tall through the broken windows and men swarmed around it, shouting, and Althea turned aside, went west a ways before she turned north again, climbing now as the land climbed. She held her brother's child tight to her breast, secret from the world, owned within herself, as she moved through the morning light, the hot light of early morning. The yellow light of September. It had been early September, yes, and she'd walked such a long way, through a sea of black faces, faster, the swells rushing over her, faster, until she was running in this same place, this same street—or, no, not this street, another, where a brown-skinned grocer swept the plank sidewalk, where a café owner was setting out a sandwich board, and somewhere, at the end of the block, a black woman in a flowered dress stood in a glass doorway, saying, You welcome to come in and rest your feets awhile.

Althea stopped, looked around, but there were no colored people readying for work, no shopkeepers, schoolchildren, mothers tugging their youngsters along; only burning houses, and Negroes walking in the center of the road with their hands in the air, shoeless, hatless in the smoky light, and the hatted and booted men behind them, around them, holding rifles and shotguns, men in open cars roaring in the dirt street, churning dust to rise up and mingle with smoke. She walked on, holding her baby brother carefully; she was sweating in the heat, coughing, and the baby was crying, its face muffled against her. In the distance she saw the back of her green sateen dress moving away, growing smaller, disappearing, as if she were watching herself draw away from herself in a dream. No. She'd given that dress to Graceful. It was the flax-colored dress she wanted, not that old green one. She put the baby to her shoulder, hurried to catch up, but the green dress was gone.

Just ahead a handsome man in a maroon bathrobe and slippers was coming down his porch steps, his amber-colored hands clasped on top of his head. Althea's heart jerked with recognition at sight of the doctor's shining black hair and thin mustache. She started forward to ask how to get to Graceful's mother's house, for of course he would know. He'd driven her there in his touring car. But the doctor was surrounded by white men, and she hesitated. There was one among them, a familiar sylphlike figure, whispering in the ear of a young white boy, but his face was shaded, concealed by the dirty brim of a slouch hat, and she couldn't quite see. Then the sound popped and the doctor fell, and she heard the shouts, saw that one slinking away. Althea recognized her brother. She turned at once and followed him, followed in the grip of blood-recognition, without thought of what she'd do if she caught up with him, without any effort to catch up, but only to keep him in sight. He slipped into a crevice between two houses, and she stopped, waited in the street for him to come out again, but a new burst of gunfire made her run for protection. She sank down beside a frame house, crouched low, patted the baby's shuddery back.

The guns peppered the air for a moment, and then there was silence, only for an instant, but she heard them calling, the voices faint in the distance, Leeeetha, Leeeeeeetha. It was dark in the shadow of the house. The baby was crying. She lifted his tiny scrunched face close to her face. The velvety forehead was warm, emollient, bathed in the spiced scent of his mother's pomade. "Shhhh, baby," she whispered. It was dark where she was hiding. She couldn't run because she had torn her dress off. She was naked. It was dark in the slatted light of the corncrib. She remembered the plump milkwhite legs in her hands, the surprising heft when she lifted him, the rubbery weight. The birthwoman shouted a Creek word, something she couldn't understand, but Aletha saw fear in the brown face, saw shock and judgment. The abyss opened before her. In the bottom of the ravine she saw the red water trickling. She'd thrown the baby down, run away. Run to the corral. No. What was she thinking? Yes, she'd called the red calf, and when he came trotting she'd raised the chopping ax, hit him in the head, the blood spurted, and she hit him again, and again, but it was nothing; it was only how they slaughtered hogs in winter, it wasn't why she hid the bloody flaxen dress beneath a stone, hid herself naked in the slatted dark while they called and called, because she'd killed her brother.

But the baby wasn't dead. He was here. He was alive, in her arms, shuddering. She touched her lips to his forehead, his warm temple. He smelled of milk and urine, petrolatum, newborn skin. Somewhere a siren wailed. More gunshots. The baby coughed in tiny little spasms as the smoke rolled into the sheltered place, dipping low. Althea sat motionless. Something welled up from deep within her breast. She put her fingers to the baby's face. His skin was so fragile, soft. She brushed her face against him, his soft eyelash-flutter cheek against her cheek. "It's all right," she whispered. The feeling kept rising, spreading honeylike through her. She was weeping, and she didn't know why. Out in the street the gasoline engines roared, the voices went on shouting. But they weren't calling her. She kissed the baby's soft crown.

Dear God, the world was burning. One could not mourn private sin when all the world was burning. Althea leaned against the house, forced deep shuddery breaths into her lungs, bit down on the inside of her jaw. Slowly the shudders began to ebb, the honeyed feeling seeped away. She tugged the blanket up around her nephew's face. He was quiet now. In another few moments she got up from the soft early-summer grass, settled the baby against her arm, walked out to the street.

There were bodies in the road, colored men and white men lying dead beside each other. Althea turned her eyes away. She peered south, but the world was a wall of fire to the Frisco line. She couldn't take the baby there. She saw no way to turn back, no way to go around; she had to move forward, that was all. Keeping to the near side of the road, she hurried past the dead men; she wouldn't allow her gaze to settle on the lightsoled bare brown feet, the shattered limbs in cotton shirts and filthy seersucker suits, the oil-stained khakis dark with blood.

Before Graceful cleared the crest of Brickyard Hill, she saw Hedgemon Jackson bounding down the slope toward her. She hadn't seen him in many months, but all she could think was that he shouldn't be here, on Elgin Avenue, on Mama's street, just a few blocks down from Mama's house. "What is it?" she called, but already her heart was caught. Hedgemon's face was stark, the muscles jiggling beneath the skin as he ran toward her. Graceful walked faster. They met in the middle of the block, and Hedgemon stood in front of her, panting; he raised his hand as if to touch her, let it fall.

"What they do to him?" Graceful said. "Where is he?"

Hedgemon bent from the waist a little, put his long hands on his knees. "Not T.J.," he puffed.

"Who, then?"

He shook his head, raised up, looking over her shoulder, past her, to the fires in Greenwood. His face had filled out; he looked mannish now. "Hurry. We got to go." He was breathing hard, but already his feet were edging backward as he reached for her hand.

Graceful slapped his palm away. "Tell me!"

"Last night. Berta." He was still trying to catch his breath. "Berta's baby start to come. Your mama. She send—" His beautiful longlashed eyes flicked sideways, guilty. "Send Jewell. Down to Greenwood— Graceful! Wait!"

She was past him, moving in strong strides toward Mama's house. She could see the edge of the porch now. Was that Willie in the yard? She started to run.

"Graceful!" Hedgemon was trotting after her. "Wait!

There was the screech of automobile tires, voices yelling, whitemen's voices. "Stop right there, nigger! Put your goddamn hands in the air!"

"Wha'chu running for, nigger?"

"Somebody grab that gal!"

Rough hands grabbed her from behind, and it was the same as the first whiteman's hands, the brother's hands, and the cold rage swelled up as other hands clutched at her; she tried to keep running, but they had her by the arms, the skirt. "Where'd you steal this dress, nigger?" She struggled to get free, she had to go, her mama needed her, Jewell might need a doctor, they couldn't keep her, she had to get home.

"You been looting white ladies' bedrooms, gal?"

"Keep those hands up, nigger! I'll shoot 'em off!"

Hedgemon was in a yard a little ways away, his hands high over his head, palms toward her, his face frozen in fear. Graceful felt a wash of unforgiving fury, and then the white hands were shoving her, turning her in a circle. Somebody said, "Get that white woman's dress off that nigger!"

and the voices laughed. White hands plucked at the yards of material, jerking it, pulling at it. Somebody grasped the lace collar, yanked it away from her throat. The flimsy material ripped like rotted cotton.

"Whooooeee! Looka there, they're going to strip the bitch."

With a mighty flailing heave, she twisted away, and the sateen at her waist shrieked in one long tear as she broke free. "Get her!" She ran, but something hit her in the back, a fist or a rock, knocked her to the ground, knocked the wind out of her, and her face smashed against the earth. They were at her back, and it was the same as in the maid's room, the same, they would do the same thing to her, and Graceful rolled over, she fought them with a strength beyond her strength, she lashed out in terror and fury, but she couldn't stop them; they were everywhere, tugging, whooping, laughing, clawing. She felt the sateen bodice tear, heard it rip down the back as the tiny buttons gave, and then she felt the hot, blank air upon her chest. Graceful folded up, crouched in the grass, shrinking away from their white weasel faces, their spotted faces, colorless laughing faces, ringed around her naked on the ground.

Naw, now, that gal tore her own dress off. I don't know where you're getting your information, but, what I seen, that colored gal went to hollering when we tried to arrest her, and then she just laid down and wallowed in the grass, screaming and carrying on like she'd got a scorpion in her britches. Next thing I know, she's naked. That's all. Who knows what those people get in their crazy heads. We were just doing our job. The governor'd declared martial law, see, and our orders were to disarm the coloreds and march 'em down to Brady, to the convention center on Brady, and that's just what we were doing, rounding up loose niggers like we been deputized to do. Well, some of them cooperated and some didn't. That black buck she was with put his hands up right off, so we didn't have to shoot him, but I'll tell you one thing, I's about ready to shoot that white woman. Dear God, what a witch— and you can drop that w and put a b in front of it, you'll hear a word closer to the damn truth. She come swarming up there, wagging that baby, hollering, "What do you think you're doing? Take your hands off!" and on and on. Lord, you could hear her a mile. We tried to tell her she could have her niggers back if she wanted them but she was going to have to come down to Conven-

tion Hall and sign them out, same as anybody else. They were going to issue tags for the coloreds, see, once we'd got them all
gathered up, and then they'd let white folks come vouch for the
good ones. That way we'd know which ones was good niggers and
which wasn't. Any upstanding white person could sign for their
chauffeur or housemaid or what-have-you, there was no problem,
but you were going to have to do it proper, do it right, go down
yonder to the holding pen and make it legal, according to how the
mayor and them had figured it out.

Well, we tried to tell that to the woman, but you couldn't tell
that banshee nothing. We were about ready to arrest her too,
make her stand yonder with that sullen colored boy. Tell you
what, if you could've shot them for looks, that boy would have
been dead on that count, for sure, but he stood quiet enough, kept
his hands over his head, and anyhow we were busy trying to get
that wench to stand up. A couple fellows prodded her with their
boot toes or the barrel of their gun, but she was hunkered down
like a bobcat, you didn't want to wade in too close. Naked as a
jaybird from the waist up. It was funny, but then again it wasn't
funny. I thought Stinson was going to shoot her in the head and
be done with it, he was that mad, but you felt kind of sorry for
her, too. Somebody'd ought to give her something to cover herself up with, that's what I thought. But we had us a job to do, and
that colored gal wouldn't cooperate, and here come this white
woman, making matters worse, screeching around—

"Stop! This instant! You fools! You absolute idiots. Give me that!" Althea
tried to grab the barrel of a rifle poking Graceful's buttocks. The man
jerked it away, stepped back with the gun turned on her, and then he spat,
lowered the muzzle, said, "Lady, hadn't you better go home?"

"What in God's name do you think you're doing?"

"We been deputized to round up niggers. What is it? This gal steal
your dress? Get up from there, gal. Stand up!"

"Watch him, now, watch him."

"He's all right. You all right, nigger? He's fine. He's a good nigger. You
a good nigger, boy?"

"Look out, Tim, don't get too close. That wench's liable to bite your
pecker off."

"Leave her alone!" Althea screamed. "Leave her!"

"Lady, you better stand back and let us do our job."

"I'll have every one of you arrested! Do you hear me? Sheriff McCullough's a personal friend of my husband."

"Somebody shut that woman up."

"This girl works for me. Stop! Stop that!" She turned on a snickering boy using the barrel of his pistol to try to pry up one of Graceful's clamped arms. The boy was laughing. "Let's see her titties, I never seen nigger titties! She's nekked! It's a nekked nigger! Let's see!" A carload of men squealed to a stop on Elgin Avenue, and the same impulse that had caused Althea to run shouting when she crested the hill and saw Graceful on the ground, now caused her to wheel and turn on the newcomers as a she-bear rears up to swipe at a pack of dogs, but she had no weapons, no claws or strength, only her impotent shrieks and her sex and her white skin to fight them with. A half-dozen men poured from the automobile, joined by others swarming up the hill on foot. The men swaggered into the yard. "You fellas need a hand? My, my, my, what have we got here."

Althea recognized a clerk from the shoe department at Renberg's, and she called out to him, "Make these idiots stop!" The clerk, so obsequious and flattering when he knelt to help her try on shoes, shoved past her as if she were nobody, as if he'd never seen her before, waving his gun in the air. "Y'all step aside! We'll get that nigger on her feet!"

"Take your hands off her!"

But the clerk and a second man were already hoisting Graceful by the arms, holding her up to stand exposed in the midst of them. The baby was wailing. Graceful stared straight ahead. Althea kept repeating, shrilly, pointlessly, "Leave that girl alone! She works for me!" as she rocked the shrieking baby, patted his back. Behind the shoe clerk she spied another familiar face, an oil acquaintance of Franklin's, she couldn't think of his name but she recognized him from the dining room at the Hotel Tulsa. The oilman stood off to the side, armed with a little pistol and a cardboard star pinned on his chest, big-bellied, puffed up in a fine summer suit, his graying hair neatly coifed, like Franklin's. For an instant she was flustered by thoughts of her husband. Was Franklin running around bullying people with a gun and a paper star, like these men? And Jim Dee, hadn't she seen Jim Dee running in the street with the others? No. Jim Dee was in Bristow. That had been her overwrought imagination, hours ago, a lifetime ago, in the alley downtown, before—

Japheth. She had forgotten about Japheth, almost from the moment she'd seen him slip between the houses. But, no, that wasn't him either. That had just been her wild imagining, like thinking she'd seen Jim Dee. She searched the dozens of white faces. Men in battered felt hats and porkpies and summer boaters jostled one another, bullying, bellowing, bloated with their own lawless authority, but Japheth wasn't here. Of course he wasn't here. Her brother was dead. "Hush, baby," Althea whispered. Graceful's lips were drawn tight over her teeth. Still she didn't meet Althea's eyes. The baby was crying so hard, his face covered by the blanket. It was murderously hot, hellish hot, the fires like a furnace at her back, and the ceaseless voices kept barking.

"Stinson, you and Lambert haul these two down, we'll meet you at the section line."

Althea peeled the blanket back from the baby's face.

"Eskew, take your bunch and fan out west."

The baby's face was wrinkled, sweaty, dark with rage.

"Me and Cletus'll go back downtown and see if we can't scrounge up some more ammunition."

Althea lifted her gaze to the deep indentations in Graceful's arms, the brown smooth upper arms clamped tight in chalky fingers, the marbled marks on her breasts, her belly swelling above the sagging half-chemise. The cotton slip was ripped and dirt-smeared, its limp drawstring dangling. With no thought but to cover up what she did not want to see, Althea unwrapped the child, held the blanket out to Graceful. It stank of urine. The baby's gown was sopping wet. Althea stood holding the little strip of blanket, foolishly shaking it up and down as if to say, Take it!

When Graceful turned at last and looked at her, the fixed expression on the smooth, slanted face startled Althea, and then swept her with fear and pain. Graceful stared at her from hooded eyes as if it were Althea who pinned her arms, Althea who cursed and shamed her, who lit the fires, burned the blackened corpse beside the tracks. The girl hated her. How could that be? Hadn't she tried to save her? Hadn't she put her own dress on the girl's back, set her own hat on the pomaded head? Hadn't she done everything for her, for months now, since the very day the girl had come to work in her house—

"It's not me!" Althea hissed. "I didn't do any of this!"

Graceful turned away. She stood with her face lifted, shoulders down, unclothed and dignified in the white fingers' grasp.

From the back of the crowd a voice piped, "For God's sake, somebody cover that wench up, y'all are going to start a riot."

"Hah!"

"Gimme that!" The shoe clerk jerked the blanket from Althea's hand, flung it over one of Graceful's shoulders. As if the gesture had opened their collective eyes, they all turned to stare at the white woman's colored baby.

"Wouldja look at that!"

"Yella as my daddy's toenail, ain't it?"

"No wonder she's th'owing such a fit!"

"She's a nigger?"

"Naw, she ain't a nigger, she's been screwing niggers."

"That's a mulatter baby, sure enough."

A disgusted voice said, "Take her into custody. We'll bring her in with the rest."

"Dear God, no!" Althea held him away from her. "He's not mine! Look. Look at her, she's the mother. Graceful, take your son!" She thrust the baby out, her hands circling his little hiccupy chest; the baby's head lolled, his legs kicked inside the gown. The girl stood across from her, without moving.

"Take him!"

The girl stood across the abyss of cut red earth, the slashed crater in the world where the water rolled in the bottom the color of new blood.

"Step over yonder," a voice said. "Move."

She had to drop him. Yes. She would simply open her hands and let the shrieking newborn fall to the earth. Drop him! she told herself.

"We can't take in a white woman, Jack."

"We can if she's got a nigger baby."

Althea felt suddenly that she held in her hands the power to undo sin. Her own sin, the past. She pulled her arms in, put the baby over her shoulder, muffling his cries; gently she patted his back. In a clear, calm voice she said, "This baby's starving. He's got to nurse." Graceful met her gaze, and the whole history passed between them, separate, skewed, held in common: the single narrative of their bound-together lives. "I can't feed him," Althea said. "You know he'll die." There was a beat of silence, punctuated by the baby's wails. Graceful didn't speak, but Althea saw the slow exhalation through her flared nostrils, the little surrender, before the girl flicked her eyes to the tall black boy, who stood with his hands in the air, lightish palms open, staring from confused, scared eyes. Althea took a step forward. Several men made abortive half-moves, but no one stopped her.

"Which one's the mama?" someone whispered.

"Hell if I can tell."

"Lady, is that your maid?"

"Let her go," Althea directed the shoe clerk in the same calm voice, and the clerk and the other man released Graceful's arms. Cradling the baby horizontally in her arms, she held him out.

From the porch across the street, Japheth watched. The sweet scent of gasoline radiated from his hands, clothes, shoes, the wooden pillar before him, the shingles of the house. He inhaled deeply, breathed the fumes like source as he watched his sister raise the tiny figure, lift the baby crosswise, an offering, and in his mind's eye he saw two girlish hands rising over the fishwhite line down the center of her dark head, the relentless repetition of a life's litany recalling what he could not possibly remember: the blood-smeared girl in dark pigtails raising the bloody newborn over her head to kill it, kill it, kill him. Japheth was cold now, deepearth cold, though the fires burned all around him. It didn't matter: he could feel how it didn't matter. Hatred for the sister was no more personal than for the black ones; it was all the same, it had nothing to do with them, or with him; it was only the need now to satisfy the deadening hunger. Hate, transformed from rage into lust for slaughter, had become only this dull, cold will to annihilate the world. He walked out of his hiding place as Graceful reached for her son.

He was a shadow flying from her side-vision but Althea knew him, even before she let go the child, spun to face him, thinking to fight him, to hold him, embrace him, thinking she had to protect herself. She struck at the air as one flails at a fluttering night moth's wings; there was no flesh to strike, only the warmth of delicately splashing liquid, the sharpness of the smell.

"Holy Christ!"

"Get back!"

Japheth dropped the can, stood back away from her, fumbled with the box of matches, and in the eternity which was no more than the slivered part of her next heartbeat, she knew what he'd done. She felt the force in the gasoline darkening her gardening dress, knew there was no power on earth to combat the death he'd drenched her in. Somewhere there was a great shout. Her brother came toward her with the tiny flame lit, and she reached for him. There was a white searing flash, Graceful screamed a name, but it was not her name. A body was on top of her then, rolling her on the ground.

Sound like one loud shout to crack heaven. I was already moving, hurrying them young ones away from that hellplace. I done seen the world collapsing, flames licking, when I step off the porch of that yellow house. I'm not going to stand in some yard looking behind like Lot's wife, I gathers them children, put my arm around that little mother, she holding her baby, we halfway up the street time that shout come.

The little boy, he give a shout, too, twist loose, take off running back yonder, and before I can understand anything, I got to turn, I got to see them two flags in the street—oh, yes, that dark one and his sister. They tiny small, way down the hill, but I sees 'em, Lord, I knows them at once, and I say to myself, Yes, this hour won't pass without them. I see the dark one is nothing now but that destruction force walking: empty hands, eyes, feets, evil walking. In my soul there's a great eruption, and I wishes him dead off the earth. I see it plain in my mind, same as I see that whitewoman move, and in that same heartbeat the brother go up in flames.

Whooosh! He light up like a pineknot, just *whooosh!*

Stand straight up burning an instant before he run; run just an instant before he fall. Then they all running, all them whitemens running, shouting, and the little boy is running, little girl screaming, Willie!, she take off down the hill after him, and I see that tall black boy then, way down there among them, the tall boy helped me carry the dead girl, the one I thought run away, he's sprawled on top of that whitewoman on the ground.

You couldn't hardly tell what was happening. You had your pistols trained on them, you were trying to keep order, see, but you didn't know which ones to shoot. That son of a gun just appeared out of nowhere, out of absolute thin air, seemed like, but you didn't know what he was doing till he'd already throwed the gas on her, and then it was too late. Who'd dream it, anyhow? She was a white woman. We didn't get deputized to burn up white women, I don't care what she'd been doing. It happened so damn fast. Somebody shouted at her, but her dress had already caught. I don't know how come that colored boy didn't get his head blowed off when he jumped on her, except that white fella had caught fire, too, and our eyes were all on that. Lord have mercy. His clothes must have been just soaked in fuel oil, because he went up like a gas rag, he only run a few steps before he dropped. You'd think he'd have been screaming, that white woman was sure enough screaming, we all were shouting, but that fella run silent, burning, absolutely silent. By the time you could get your mind wrapped around what was happening, he'd fell to the ground. He was still flaming, but you knew inside them burning clothes he wasn't nothing but a crisp. I tried to think to do something. Stinson's standing yonder going, Christ, oh, Christ. They'd got the fire put out on the white woman, and it looked like she wasn't dead yet, she wasn't screaming, but I could kindly hear her moaning, that colored gal was bent down over her, kneeling over her, and she had that little yella baby on her, suckling greedy, like it's about to starve to death. I tried to think what we were going to do with the white woman. We couldn't take her to the internment center in that condition. Somebody'd already told me the white hospitals was full. I couldn't think clear. I turned and told Stinson to shut the hell up, but he kept standing there, repeating himself, saying, Jesus, would you look at that, Jesus. Christ Almighty. Lord God.

W ith the child in her arms Graceful knelt beside the woman. Mrs. Dedmeyer's eyes were closed. Her face was bright red, scalded-looking. The charred housedress curled away from her in black, flaking strips, and beneath it her throat, her upper chest were seared pink. She was moaning. Her eyelashes and eyebrows were gone. A great feeling of pity welled up in Graceful and she reached a hand out, drew it back quickly, afraid to touch her. *I tried to warn her,* she said to herself.

But Graceful knew that the sound exploding from her throat had not been for the whitewoman. *NO!* she'd screamed in a rush of terror and hatred when she saw him running with the gasoline can in his hand, *NO!* her soul screamed, her mouth screamed, and it was with joy and relief and loathing she'd realized it was the woman he was running toward, not her, not Graceful, and in that same breath she was glad. *Look out!* she shouted when she saw the matches, because then Hedgemon was running, and when the fire went up between them, the whitewoman and her brother, it was Hedgemon's name Graceful screamed. She saw him burning alive, the hated father to her son, burning alive, running, but she felt nothing when she saw it, not even relief.

The other whitemen were everywhere, shouting; some were near the fiery body, circling it, holding their arms out like scarecrows to keep each other back. Hedgemon was on the ground on the other side of the woman. A deep moan rose from the woman's throat, and when Graceful looked in the peeled, scalded face she could see two hugely dilated pupils staring up at her from narrow slits, like shining black berries inside the puffed lids. Mrs. Dedmeyer lifted one of her hands, seemed to be trying to say something, but one of the whitemen shoved Graceful aside and she had to catch herself to keep from tumbling over, she had to clasp the baby, and whatever the woman meant to say was lost in the shoving hands, shouting voices, the whitemen swarming all around.

"Graceful!" a high, child's voice called. She looked up to see Willie pounding down the hill, and behind him LaVona running. Graceful scrambled to her feet, covered herself and the nursing baby with the blanket, looking north to see where Mama was coming; she saw instead, from the corner of her eye, a whiteman raising the butt of his rifle. She wheeled around as the man clubbed Hedgemon in the side of the head. Hedgemon fell over, put his arms up to protect himself, and the whiteman turned away, and then, as if in afterthought, turned back, raised the rifle stock, clubbed Hedgemon again. "Hedgemon!" She took a step toward him, but Willie raced into the yard then, his thick legs pumping, his eyes terrified, round face shiny with sweat, and yet beaming with his wide beautiful grin. He threw himself on her, hugged her waist, and she could feel his wet face on her skin. LaVona came after him, sobbing hard as she grabbed Graceful around the neck, and within Graceful was such a storm of love and shame and fury. The humiliation she'd refused when the whitemen stripped her, when she'd stood defiant before them, saying to herself, *They dogs anyhow, it's no shame to be naked in front of dogs,* now overcame her as she tried to hold the blanket up with one hand, keep her bared torso covered, hide the nursing child. "Where's Mama?" She had no free arm with which to hug them. "Where's Jewell and T.J.? LaVona!" And LaVona stared at the baby's blanket, but she was crying too hard to answer, and Willie was crying, holding on to her, and beneath the scrap of blanket, the baby nursed as if he'd never get his fill. An oilfield truck crammed with colored prisoners roared down Elgin Avenue, ground to a stop beside them; a voice shouted, "We got room for a couple more, how many y'all got?"

"Two nits, two lice!"

There was laughter, more shouting, and she felt Willie being jerked away, felt the blanket pull loose as he tried to cling to her, and there was no time for shame or questions, because a gun barrel gouged her lower back, dug deeply into the skin above her hip, pushing her toward the truck, and everything moved so fast; she was afraid they would shoot Hedgemon where he lay groaning on the ground, and she cried out, "Hedgemon! Hedgemon! Come!" He rolled to the side as if to rise, and Graceful scanned the street then, looking north toward home, thinking she might still see Mama and Jewell and T.J., she might be able to warn them as she had not been able to shout in time for the children, Run, Mama! Hide! Don't come down here! The edge of Mama's porch was obscured now, but in the distance she thought she saw the slender outline of Elberta, though that made no sense. Elberta wouldn't be out alone, and the truck would have stopped and got her anyway, it had come right down Elgin Avenue. They were picking up all Negroes, they wouldn't have passed Elberta by.

But Graceful had no time to think, for she was being manhandled onto the back of the truck. The flatbed was jammed tight with bodies, some of them lying down, wounded, but most crouching or sitting, crushed together like livestock. Whitemen with guns were standing on the running boards, or on the bed up front, leaning against the cab, where two men with rifles perched on top. There was no room, but Graceful and the children were shoved from the ground, forced to climb up, and she struggled to hold the baby; a brown hand reached down for her, and some women squeezed aside, made a place for them. The baby was wailing again, furious to have been pulled away from the breast. Willie and LaVona were with her, but she couldn't see Hedgemon. "Hedgemon!" she called as the truck ground its gears.

"Hey, gal! Catch!" A whiteman on the ground threw something at her; it landed across her face, began to slide back, and when she grabbed it up, she found it was the voluminous sateen skirt from the green dress. "It's ruirnt now," the man called. "You might as well have it." She wouldn't look at the whiteman, but she did draw the skirt around her shoulders, covered herself. A voice hollered from the street, "They're plumb full at Convention Hall, can't cram another nigger in there without it's a midget! Take this load on to the fairgrounds!"

"All the way out there?"

"Hell, yes, even the ballpark's full, we're liable to be hauling 'em to Claremore before it's all over!"

She was wedged in tight, facing the back of the bed, and yet there was nothing to hold on to, and when the truck lurched, Graceful grabbed for Willie. Her eyes searched the street as the truck began to roll. Mrs. Dedmeyer lay very still on the grass, her arms flung out to the side, her thin chest, from this distance, looking childish, flat, pale. The men were moiling in every direction. Farther back in the yard, the dark brother's body was still burning. A half-grown whiteboy darted forward, stomped at the fading fire a second, jumped back. Desperately Graceful searched, but she couldn't see Hedgemon, and then the mob parted a little, and he was there, standing in the road, under guard, his hands on top of his head. A thick trail of blood eased down the side of his face. Hedgemon's eyes were on her. Willie was wedged next to her, completely silent, and she only knew he was crying by how his shoulders shuddered. LaVona was behind her, penned inside the too-many bodies pressing at Graceful's back. She put an arm around her little brother, and he shoved his face against her, his head under her chin, hard against her collarbone. As the truck lumbered away, she stared at Hedgemon Jackson over the top of Willie's head, trying to understand what his eyes were saying, until she lost sight of him in the sea of white faces.

Cleotha hadn't heard the back door open, but when the thunks and crashes started in the bedroom, she knew instantly who it was. Gently she eased Jewell's head off her lap, went to stand in the archway. At sight of her eldest son's thin form hunched over the dresser, her throat emitted a little chirp, like a bird's. T.J. whirled, slamming the drawer shut; he stood panting in front of the mirror. "Mama! You still here! Where's my shells?" Cleotha didn't answer, and T.J. turned and rushed into the kitchen. The spoon drawer clattered. The pantry door opened and slammed shut. T.J. reappeared in the kitchen doorway. "Those boxes of cartridges I had hid, what y'all do with them?" His eyes were wild as a mare's.

"I don't guess you're wondering what went with your wife."

"I had two full boxes, Mama. Twenty-two shells. Where they at?"

"Your sister is dead."

He stared as if he couldn't comprehend her meaning. Then he went to the chifforobe and jerked it open, began pawing through his mother's and sisters' dresses.

"You got a new baby daughter." She waited a moment. "Your wife and your child just gone with Mrs. Tiger. They're on their way to Turley."

T.J. backed away from the chifforobe with a small paper box in his hand. "Where's the rest of them? This isn't all of them. You ain't let Willie get hold of them!" He rushed toward her, forcing her against the door frame as he pushed past her into the front room, hurried to the south window, brushed the curtain aside to see out.

"Your sister is dead," Cleotha repeated. T.J. ripped open the box, pulled the pistol from his waistband and started loading the chambers.

"Son! Look at me!"

His eyes flicked toward her, turned to the open front door as he finished loading. "You got to get out of here, Mama. Go up by Skiatook. Quick."

"Look at your sister."

His gaze roved the room, paused hardly an instant on the divan, returned to the screen door. "I see her. You aim to join her?" He started back across the linoleum, and would have pushed past her again had Cleotha not reached out and seized his arm.

"T.J., what's the matter with you?"

"They're killing every nigger in this country, you want to sit here in this house till they come—"

"I can't carry Jewell by myself."

"Leave her." They stood silent a minute, staring at each other. His eyes were half slitted now, not wild and rolling. Cleotha took into herself the fullness of the change in him, how the hate and fear had eaten out the tender place in her firstborn. In the hard bones of his arm, his panting breath, she felt the force with which the newmade cavity was filled. After a moment T.J. looked away.

"You go on ahead, son," Cleotha said, watching him. "Go find your wife and daughter." She waited for him to say something. Beneath her closed hand, his arm shook.

"Go quick, Mama. Whitemen's just down the street. You might have time."

"Willie and LaVona are with them, somewhere around Turley. Mrs. Tiger is going to carry them someplace safe."

"There's no place safe! Good Lord, Mama. They're going to burn this house down." He glanced at the girl on the divan. "Burn her up with it."

"We'll come just as soon as Delroy get here."

"You ain't coming with Delroy!" He turned on her now, glared at her as if he hated her as much as he hated the thing roaring and chattering and burning outside the door. "Your brother is dead!" he yelled in her face. "Jewell's dead! We all going to be dead, they're going to kill all of us, but I'm going to kill every goddamn one of them I can—"

"NO!"

The shout was so great it seemed all the world was silenced. When Cleotha went on, her voice was quiet. "No more," she said. "Hear me?

Been death enough already." T.J. was still trembling. She let go his arm, waiting. He didn't look at her as he made himself slim to get past her, went into the dark middle room, on into the lighter kitchen. Cleotha's eyes were dry when she watched him go out the back door.

That shout sound like the last trumpet, the last denial and fury, the last time the world going to say No! To this day I tries to understand to myself what I seen. I can't explain it. Sometimes I think she do it, that white-woman, his sister: she turn and throw fire on him to finish what she start twenty years back. Some other times I believe he do it himself, set his own body afire, because that force for destruction don't care what it burn. Or else me. All this life, these many years since, I been thinking sometimes that maybe it was my own mind that do it, jump up and cause a spark to set fire to him, that same one, the boychild I kept her from killing on the day he was born. Maybe in that hour of destruction I tried to repent myself.

Me and the little mother stand on the hilltop, watch the little Willie boy and his sister run right into the arms of them whitemens. The little mother cry out, but her and me both know there is nothing we can do. Them two young ones are gone. We got to save her little baby, save ourselves. We turn and go, fast, fast, through the fiery furnace. I will tell you something, that little mother way more stronger than I thought. She have a young strong body, yes, but what give her the most strength is that new baby; she's running to save the life of her child. All around, on every side, peoples are running. We all trying to flee that destruction, but the little mother can't go so fast. In a minute we got to stop again, let her rest. I turn around, see the world collapsing, bowels of the earth opening to suck that place in. Flames licking. Black smoke rising. Then is when I seen what the truth is: we only going to save ourselves for a little while. That force is not finished. We can't hide from it. We can't get away.

To this day I been studying in my mind why the Creator set me in it, to bear witness to the end and the beginning—or his, anyway, that dark one—because he's dead in his flesh, maybe, but that force is not dead. Evil can't be destroyed. You try and destroy it, evil just change its shape, become something look different on the outside. Inside, it always act the same. I don't know why the Lord let me get caught by the greed-devil, or why He cause me to have to stand on a hilltop and watch them fires rag-ing before I get free. I don't know why it is, I can't see yet, but I know one thing: we peoples have joined them two forces together, turned that power loose in the world, and I done my own part. Oh, yes. Listen. Evil is spirit force, yes, but it have to manifest in the material world. That deep-earth power belong to the material world, but it is capable to manifest in the spirit. And we have let it. We have loosed our own destruction.

Whose hand set them houses afire? Not God's hand. God don't make that gun on the hill to spit and chatter, He haven't created machines to fly in the air above smoke and drop fire in jars and bottles, to make fire on God's people, by God's people, to kill God's people, Lord, Lord. How do He say the world's going to be destroyed? Not by water but by fire next time, the Book tell us that, but it is not going to be God who do it, we do it, you and me do it, because that power come into the world by human hand, and it is going to live in the world through human hand, and we can't none of us turn it back until the whole story done.

Cleotha was standing in front of the divan, bending over it, when she heard their boots on the porch. The glass in the front window shattered, and a voice called, "Anybody in there?" She pulled the pink dress back up to Jewell's throat, dropped the washrag into the red water in the basin on the floor.

"Come in," she said, straightening, turning. "Door's open."

But the men smashed the screen anyway, butted through the wire with a rifle stock, splintered the wood frame, broke the rest of the glass out of the window beside it, before they stamped into Cleotha's front room. There were only three of them, but they made as much noise as an army.

"Come on out now, Auntie, we got orders to take everybody in."

Cleotha turned back to the divan, reached across Jewell to smooth the skirt of the girl's white Sunday-best dress lying like a buoyant lace antimacassar across the back.

"Oh, Jesus, what're we going to do with that?"

"I don't know. Go see if there's any more of them in yonder."

She had waited too long to begin to wash her daughter. The long, limber body was already rigid. The pink school dress, tucked up modestly around her throat again, was stiff with blood. It would be hard to take off. Cleotha listened to the sounds of drawers being jerked open in the next room, things smashing against the wall. In the kitchen she could hear glass breaking. She knew these sounds' meaning as clearly as she'd known her son was hunting bullets when she heard him in the middle room a short while before. She seated herself on the divan, lifted Jewell's head into her lap, stroked the glassy cheekbones, the smooth, firm eyelids. Her daughter's beautiful brown skin was cold, despite the searing heat.

"Get up from there, Auntie. We don't want to have to shoot you."

She looked up at the man. His gun was pointed toward the floor. He wore sooty overalls and a checkered shirt, and beneath his shapeless, sweat-stained hat, his eyes were flitty, blue, uneasy-looking. "Don't make it hard on yourself," he said. His attention was taken by one of the other men returning from the back of the house. "Anything in yonder?"

"Naw, just some nigger trinkets." The new man went to the front window, jerked the flower-spattered curtain down, tossed it onto the braided rug in the middle of the floor. "Tubbs is getting whatever's to be got. What're you going to do with her?" He nodded toward the divan but didn't wait for an answer as he went to the south window and pulled that curtain down, too. The windowshade fell with it, clattered on the linoleum as he tossed the curtain on the rug. "Tubbs!" he shouted. "Bring that coal oil in here!" He went to the armchair and snatched the crocheted doilies off it, swept the framed photographs off the end table and plucked up those doilies, dropped them all on the curtains. He reached behind Cleotha to take Jewell's burial dress off the back of the divan, tossed the white dress on the rug.

The third man appeared in the archway. In one hand he held Cleotha's half-full kerosene jar, in the other the ornate gilt frame with the family photograph from off her dresser. "There's nothing here. Where's your jewels, old woman? You got your silverware hid?"

"Fetch that jar over here. You sprinkle the back room down good?"

"Waste of kerosene, but I did it. Let's go. Silas and them are plumb the hell up to the section line by now."

"Stand up, old woman. We got orders to burn this place."

"Who?" Cleotha said softly. "Who give you orders to do this?"

But the men did not answer.

"Light that and come on," one of them said, and two of the whitemen went out the door. The man in overalls went to the corner and jerked Cleotha's whatnot shelf off the wall. The delicate china cup Ernest had brought her from Boston tumbled and shattered, the porcelain cat he'd found in New Orleans, the blond angel with folded wings from Pittsburgh, the frame with Ernest's picture, all fell when the shelf came down. The man picked up the gold-embossed frame, ripped Ernest's broad smiling face from it, and tucked the frame in his bib pocket; he tossed the photograph on the pile. He broke the wooden shelf in two and tossed the pieces on the curtains and starched doilies, picked up the kerosene jar and began to shake it around.

"You know you going to have to burn me with it," Cleotha said.

The man straightened up, looked at her. His pale, uneasy gaze dropped to Jewell's face an instant, slipped around the walls of the room, past the pictures and the old lamp sconce and the place where the Last Supper was framed on the wall. Then the man turned and walked out the broken door. Cleotha expected him to come back, or for there to be others. She heard yelling in the street, but a few minutes passed and there was no sound of boots on the porch; she reached into the basin at her feet, squeezed the rag out, began once again to bathe her daughter.

The fires were raging on both sides of the road as the oilfield truck drove down Elgin Avenue, or Graceful believed they were still on Elgin, but she couldn't recognize anything. The streets of Greenwood had been transformed to an alien, dreamlike world; she couldn't tell where she was. The baby had begun to nurse again. Graceful was tortured with thirst. She thought she wanted nothing in this world but a drink of water, she was dying for water. The notion came to her that maybe she was already dead, on a truck, driving through hell. But, no, she could smell odors, soap and sweat and pressing oil, her brother's unwashed hair in front of her, and behind her the iron scent of blood, and smoke, everywhere the black choking smoke, becoming thicker as they drove. Her eyes teared; she began coughing. She needed water. A sip of water to drink. Willie sat up, coughing, too, now, and behind her in the truck other children were coughing, whining, crying, and women's whispers rose, harsh, frightened: Be quiet, honey, shhhh. In the street Graceful could see small groups of colored men being marched south, four abreast, surrounded on all sides by armed whites; there were whitemen everywhere, Lord, she had not known there were so many whitemen in the world. It occurred to her to wonder who was running their city if they were all here.

The truck passed a standing brick building, unburned. *That's the high school,* she thought. *That's Booker T.!* For an instant she knew where she was, but the truck made a turn, and once more she was lost. They were passing through an unearthly landscape, no longer lit with huge raging fires but flattened, black, ghostly. In every direction sprawled piles of burning rubble; small licks of flames flickered here and there. A few iron bedsteads, some blackened cookstoves jutted skyward, attended only by smoke tendrils rising in wisps.

The people in the truck were silent; even the children did not whimper. Off to the right was an area of hollow brick shells, low to the earth, the blackened centers burned away. Graceful saw several huge squarish shapes hulking in the rubble, and her throat tightened as she realized she was looking at Mr. Smitherman's presses. Near them, Hedgemon's old linotype machine lay on its side. They were passing Greenwood Avenue. Deep Greenwood. She couldn't tell which piles of bricks had been the Dreamland Theater, which the confectionery or Bryant's Drug Store, only the building that had housed the newspaper office, because the steel presses would not burn. She heard sobbing behind her in the hushed truckbed, muted beneath the grinding motor. *Fire take everything,* she thought. *Everything.* Then she thought, *They going to kill us all.*

But the white driver kept going, beyond the ruined landscape, beyond the steel border of what had been Greenwood, and soon they were driving through the white section. On the streets, in the front yards of houses, behind windows, and on shaded porches, she could see white faces— women, children, a few men—and some were laughing, some looking on in seeming sympathy, some staring as if gaping at a circus sideshow. Her eye was caught by one woman, standing in a yard beside a whitehaired old man. The old man stared steadily up at them, shaking his head. The woman's face was squinched tight, eyes red and swollen; she had a toddler child on her hip, and the little boy was teething a biscuit. Graceful turned away. She was so thirsty. Another truck was coming behind them, the back crowded with colored prisoners. Where the bed stuck out on either side of the cab, she could see women clinging on, grasping the oil-stained boards beneath them to keep from falling off. She bent toward her little brother.

"We're going where it's safe," she said softly in his ear, and then raised up to speak over her shoulder to LaVona. "You all right back there, honey?" She tried to make her voice airy, but it came out sounding like a frog's croak, her throat was so dry.

"What are we doing?" LaVona whined.

"Won't be long now," Graceful said. "These whitefolks taking us where it's safe." She shifted her baby to her other arm. With her free hand she stroked Willie's neck, rubbed a light sweaty circle with her thumb. "They going to give us a drink of water. Real soon." She squinted skyward.

Smoke lay over everything, but she could see the sun, high in the sky now, a bright, ferocious coin burning in the haze.

During the night one primary force had held sway, one rhythm building to a crescendo—pounding human feet, rumbling gasoline motors rushing toward the Frisco—but now, as the day opened, disparate rhythms made themselves known. The National Guard had begun, at last, to stop the white looters and burners, but they were moving north very slowly, disarming white men, dispersing the Home Guard, telling them to go on home. Some white citizens, in the safety of daylight, emerged from their houses and motored north to gape at the devastation, watch the police bring in Negro prisoners, and take photographs if they were so fortunate as to own a personal family camera. Others worked to organize the relief operation, to get food and water to the internment centers. Several reporters, having rushed to their rented rooms at dawn to dash off news articles, now stood in line at the telegraph office to send their revised dispatches out on the wire. A few men put themselves to the task of gathering the dead. Black bodies were stacked in front of Convention Hall, on the open beds of oilfield trucks, in piles at Newblock Park near the river, and still dozens of burned bodies lay about in the dirt streets. Most of the white dead had been taken to the city morgue or the white hospitals, although some of them, too, were burned, and the gatherers could not always tell black dead from white. An urgent call went out for gravediggers. But Tulsa's gravediggers were under guard at McNulty Baseball Park, Convention Hall, the fairgrounds, penned up inside the detention camps. There was as yet great general confusion, but it was becoming clear to the city fathers that one of the first orders of business was to issue release tags to the colored gravediggers, to get this mess cleaned up.

Franklin Dedmeyer sat bareheaded in the open Winton, sick to his stomach, sweating, trying to maneuver the car through the clotted streets. He told himself that the nausea came from too many cigars smoked, lack of food, lack of sleep. A flatbed truck filled with Negro prisoners lumbered past him, and he looked away, his chest so constricted he could hardly breathe. It had taken such a long time to get through downtown. There'd been broken glass from the pawnshops to drive around, police wagons parked everywhere, hundreds of men in the streets. Now he was at the edge of the tracks, and he could see the razed buildings of colored town, but he couldn't get through. Automobiles angled in every direction, horns tootling; firetrucks and police wagons blocked the roads, sirens wailing. The urgency ripped at him. He slammed the heel of his hand against the steering wheel, tried not to think.

He'd gone home at daylight, climbed the stairs to her room—their room—the bedroom he hadn't set foot in for over six months—not knowing what he meant to say or do, thinking only that he wanted to see her, to see that she was all right. He'd stopped short in the doorway, confused by the empty bed, the scattered hatboxes and dresses strewn about on the carpet. Then he thought of Jim Logan, and his confusion vanished, swallowed in sickening jealousy. He understood suddenly why his partner had failed to meet him: he'd stood him up so that Franklin would sit like a fool all night in the lobby of the Hotel Tulsa while the driller sneaked around to Franklin's own house and ran off with his wife. The illogic of the idea, the insanity, didn't occur to him.

He rushed immediately downstairs to interrogate Graceful, but the girl was not at the stove preparing breakfast; she wasn't on the back porch or in the pantry or the maid's room. The tiny maid's cubicle was tossed about in hurried confusion, like the upstairs bedroom, and her little baby was gone. Franklin went outside to the cellar door and opened it, called down into the dark, Graceful's name, his wife's name, descended finally into the damp darkness, feeling overhead for the lightcord, but the bulb showed only the empty basement, and he stood on the dirt floor, staring at the stone walls, knowing beyond sense, reason, calculation that Graceful and her baby had gone to Little Africa, and that Althea had gone with them. In an instant he was standing in the back hall, calling his wife's name, shouting it to the empty house. Then he was running out the front door, climbing into the Winton.

Franklin sounded the Winton's horn at a Model T stalled out in front of him. He scanned the road as far as he could see, but there was nothing to look at except Guardsmen, prisoners, burned-out buildings, fires on the horizon. He could feel nausea joining grief joining fear, threatening to boil up and explode from him, and he took his foot off the clutch, the motor shuddered and died, and Franklin got out of the car. Glass crunched beneath his shoes. He struggled to think rationally, but the world had gone mad around him; there could be no logic in the midst of madness. He had no idea how to find her. He began walking north.

For a time, as he moved deeper into the riot area, he peered into the faces of the people passing, but the dark and light faces threatened to disrupt his purpose, and soon he quit looking. He was drawing near where the fires were still raging, and the panic in his chest, the heat and smoke and nausea made him faint. He paused at the side of the road, but there was nothing to lean against. People were coming toward him down the center of the street. He hadn't eaten since yesterday. Hadn't slept since . . . when? He couldn't remember. Most nights he lay awake in the guest room, angry, silent, listening to his wife's silence in the bedroom across the hall. Oh, why hadn't they stayed quiet, the Nigras, everything would have been fine if they'd just stayed in their own part of town. He'd told her, he'd called and warned her. Hadn't he told her to put Graceful in the basement? Surely no sane woman would come out in such danger. No sane white woman. It was her damned peculiar softness for that hired girl. He'd never understood it. Gracie was a good hand, but Althea was entirely too tenderhearted about her, and now look—

Franklin raised his eyes. Walking toward him were twenty or so Negro men under guard. None looked directly at him. His eyes searched their faces, seeking something to justify the frenzy of destruction all around him, but in their set, dark features he saw only caution, fear, immutable anger. They marched past in silent formation, followed by uniformed white men with guns.

"Dedmeyer! There you are!" The voice bellowed from the passenger seat of a closed touring car in the street, pointed north. Franklin had to bend to see the face beneath the visor, flushed, excited, a fat cigar clenched between yellow teeth. There were pale, puffy bags under L.O.'s eyes, like little thumbs. He took the cigar out of his mouth. "Where the hell you been! Get in!"

Franklin stood staring an instant, confused, and then the thought came to him that L.O. Murphy had been out in this all night, that he knew where Althea was and had come to take him to her. Quickly he reached for the door handle, had hardly climbed in the back seat before the driver started off.

"You damn near missed it." L.O. craned his head over his shoulder. "They're scattering like chickens, heading for the damn hills." The interior of the car was sweetish, sour, choking with cigar smoke. "Spreading all up towards Skiatook, Owasso, who the hell knows, right, Tom?" The driver nodded. "Chapman's been up in his plane," L.O. said. "Told us you can see 'em for miles, just streams of 'em, runnin like ants. They'll be hid out in the creekbottoms if we don't act quick."

"Where—?" Franklin started to ask about Althea, but was struck silent. In the floorboard were three rifles, a shotgun, several boxes of shells. He must be the mad one. She wouldn't be out in this, she wouldn't.

"Hell, man," L.O. answered, "I just told you. The niggers're runnin off."

"Seems to me," the driver said dryly, "that about this time yesterday you were the one bellyaching about we got to run the niggers out of Tulsa."

L.O. leaned forward. "You can't let 'em off scot-free after this awful business; besides, who'll do the nigger work if we let 'em all get away?"

They were passing a group of prisoners, men in overalls, women in headrags, being marched south. L.O. twisted in the seat to follow them with his eyes.

"What are they doing with them?" Franklin's throat was parched, his belly burning.

"Arresting their black asses, 'cept I don't know where they're going to put 'em," L.O. said thickly. "Convention Hall's crammed to the damn ceiling, God Almighty, does that place stink." He ashed his cigar out the window. "Tell you what, if they let 'em get down in them canebrakes we'll have to use dogs to flush'm out."

"What are they doing with them?" Franklin said again.

L.O. glanced round at him. "Who?" His face was swollen, his eyes bloodshot. For the first time Franklin realized he was drunk. "Teachin'm their goddamn place," L.O. said. "For one thing. I don't know. Ask Tom. What're y'all doin with 'em?"

"I don't know. I think they're carrying some of them to the ballpark."

"Stop," Franklin said. There was no response from the front seat. They hadn't seemed to hear him. "I said stop!" The driver stopped the car as Franklin shoved the door open, climbed out.

"Dedmeyer! What the hell's the matter with you?"

Franklin reached in through the open window, smashed L.O. in the side of the face with his fist. Then he turned and started walking back. He would find Graceful. He'd go wherever they were holding the coloreds and track down Graceful, and she would tell him where Althea had gone.

But he'd taken only a few steps before he stopped, confused again, uncertain. Overhead a great black cloud boiled over the entire city. Down the street several corpses were being loaded into a wagon. In every direction the fires were burning. He stood paralyzed. How had such a thing happened? This was Tulsa, Oklahoma; this was America. It made no sense. Why hadn't somebody stopped it? All that he'd witnessed the night before, the cold, cut-off feeling he'd steeped himself in, his silence, guilt, terror, everything wrapped around him, and he stood at the side of the road, gazing down at his new well-shined cordovan shoes, covered in ashes, fine as sifted dust.

In the back of a farm wagon Althea lay on a stretcher. Her eyes were closed, the seared eyelids fluttering; behind the tender reddened skin, memory joined dream. The mule-drawn wagon, pressed into service as an ambulance, began to move slowly south. It would be many hours before she would come to consciousness in a crowded hallway at Hillcrest Hospital, and then her mind and body would be entirely consumed with living pain. It would be days before she'd remember the flash that killed her brother, longer still before she would recall her own hand reaching toward him the instant before the fire went up.

Japheth's blackened body lay atop other charred bodies in a truckbed designated *For Colored Only;* the truck was heading toward Newblock Park, where the bodies would be stacked in piles to be consumed by a different fire, neat, controlled, kindled by strict ordinance to prevent, it was said, the spread of disease. The white dead were laid out at the Tulsa morgue, waiting to be claimed by grieving loved ones, among them an unidentified dark-blond oilfield worker in stained khaki workclothes.

Beneath the baking sun on the open fairgrounds, Graceful held the sateen skirt out to shade her baby while she stood in line for a cup of water. She'd set Willie and LaVona to wait in the thin shade of the judges' booth. The livestock sheds were already full. On every side of her, spread out over the open space of the fairgrounds, blackfolks stood or sat without protection. They were mostly women and children, and very few of them had on hats, though several women had fashioned makeshift coverings for their little ones by piecing together sycamore leaves. Graceful glanced around, thinking she might try that for Willie and LaVona after she got them some water, though where the women had found the leaves she had no idea. There wasn't a tree of any sort in sight.

The Red Cross people had set up a tent; they were handing out sandwiches. She almost believed now that the whites weren't going to slaughter them—why would they bring sandwiches?—but she couldn't fathom what they meant to do with them. The line moved so slowly. Everyone was acting polite. Especially the whitefolks. Some of them were walking along the line taking down the names of white employers, saying that would help the people get out sooner. There were armed guards posted around the perimeter, to keep, she supposed, these dangerous half-starved colored women and children inside Exposition Park. Graceful looked up and down the line, across the fairgrounds, scanning the brown and black and copper faces, hoping for a glimpse of Mama and Jewell— and yet half hoping not to see them. Maybe they'd got away. The Negro men had been taken to Convention Hall, someone said, and the ballpark—the ones who'd been captured, that is. The ones who hadn't escaped, or been shot. That would include T.J., maybe. And Hedgemon. Her mind kept returning to the image: Hedgemon standing in the street as the truck carried her away, his hands on top of his head, his face bleeding, eyes saying something. What? *Wait for me. Meet me . . .* where? How would she find him? Find any of them? She realized that the women in line on both sides of her were looking around in the same way, frowning against the sun, turning their heads to search the hundreds of dark faces inside the fairgrounds. *We all been separated,* Graceful thought. *Every family in Greenwood been cut off from each other.*

"Who do you work for, dear?" A roundish whitewoman with powdery skin and small worried eyes stood in front of her holding a pad of paper, a poised fountain pen.

Graceful didn't answer. *We're hunting loved ones,* she thought; *we all looking for our family. Woman only want to know the name of our whitefolks.*

The woman tried to smile, but peering into Graceful's face, she hesitated a moment, uncertain; suddenly she dropped her gaze, frowned down at her pad, made a few superfluous checkmarks beside some names. Without looking up she said, "If you tell me the name of your employer we'll try to get word to them that you're here. They can come sign for you."

Still Graceful didn't answer. The whitewoman turned to the next person. "Who do you work for, dear?"

Then, with a little rift of pain, Graceful saw the thin, burnt form on the grass, the pale arms flung out to the side. Mrs. Dedmeyer. "Mrs. Dedmeyer," she said aloud. The round whitewoman looked back. "Mr. and Mrs. Franklin Dedmeyer," Graceful said softly, and the woman scribbled on her pad. "Sixteen twelve South Carson. Osage six, three seven six." The whitewoman moved on.

Behind Graceful someone's baby was crying. Babies were crying all over the fairgrounds, and yet her milk had not let down; she thought maybe it was because she was so dry; there was no liquid in her body to make milk with. The sateen was hot, draped around her as it was, like a shawl. Her baby was quiet. She held the skirt out, looked down at him. He was sleeping, his tiny pink tongue showing between tawny lips. One thing was certain. Whatever the whitefolks meant to do with them, her fate and the baby's fate were the same. By blood he was hers. By whitefolks' beliefs he would always be more colored than white. The baby yawned, smiled in his sleep. She put her finger to his cheek, traced the line of it, thinking, as she'd thought so many times, that very soon she was going to have to give him a name.

September
1921

On the last morning in September, Althea awakened before daylight from a dream of such grief and loss that before she'd come fully awake she knew she'd been weeping. The gaslight on the street had lost its power to the coming dawn, but in the bedroom the light was yet gray, shadowy. She lay still a moment, staring at the ceiling, trying to escape the dream's sorrow, and finally, unable to shed its residue, she rolled over, slipped from between the starched white eyelet sheets carefully, so as not to waken Franklin. His snores continued undisturbed as Althea left the room. She drew her silk wrapper around herself as she eased down the stairs.

Graceful stood at the enameled kitchen counter stirring up biscuits; she wore a cotton print shirtwaist with tiny yellow flowers embedded in a blue background, protected by an embroidered butterfly-bodice apron. Her hair was combed smooth. She didn't glance up when Althea came in but immediately turned from the mixing bowl to the coffeepot, saying, "I didn't expect you to be up so early."

The kitchen was hot already with stove heat, and Althea could smell a pie in the oven. A chicken was cut up and floured in a tin dish, ready for frying, and a big pot of something, stew perhaps, simmered on a gas burner. Graceful must have been up cooking since three or four o'clock. Althea watched her scoop ground coffee into the basket, light another burner, and put the pot on to percolate. Graceful turned back to the counter, sprinkled flour on the enamel, plunked down the biscuit dough, and began to roll it out.

"What time are you leaving?" Althea said finally. She went to sit at the little table against the wall, drew the wrapper more tightly around herself, as if she were cold. In fact she was perspiring; she ran her fingers along the nape of her neck, tugged at a few strands of her bobbed hair.

"Hedgemon say he'll be here about nine."

"No, I mean Tulsa. When are you—? Are you going today?"

Graceful went on cutting perfect neat circles with the biscuit cutter. "Tomorrow. I got things to do up home."

Althea nodded, watched the deft brown hands cut the raw biscuits so fast, so close together. "I don't guess you'll change your mind," she said. It wasn't really a question. In the silence she gazed out at the screened-in back porch; the day was drawing lighter now, though the sun was not quite yet risen.

"What's wrong, ma'am?"

"Wrong?"

Graceful stood with the biscuit cutter cocked in the air, looking at her. Almost as an echo, Althea realized she'd released a great plosive breath into the hot kitchen, a tremendous sigh. "Oh. Nothing," she said. "I was just thinking. . . ." She stood as if to go upstairs to dress, at once sat back down, and watched Graceful plop the biscuits in a pan, turn to open the oven door. A rich apple-pie cinnamon scent breathed into the room. Graceful put the biscuits in the oven, turned the flame down beneath the perking coffee.

"You want me to start your bacon now?"

"I'll wait till Mr. Dedmeyer gets up."

Graceful lit the burner under a large cast-iron skillet, and the odor of heating bacon grease joined the sweet pie scent, the homey smell of baking biscuits, all soon dominated by the scent of frying chicken. The familiar, clashing smells filled Althea with a wave of inexplicable sorrow.

"How long will it take you to get there?" she said.

"I don't know. Half a day maybe. It's just down by Okemah."

Althea nodded, watching Graceful turn the browning pieces. She couldn't seem to shake the dregs of her dream, though she couldn't remember it either, only the one image of the nursing child, and not just the image, the sensation, for it was her own withered left breast the child suckled. "Is that coffee ready yet?" she said irritably. Graceful poured out a scalding cup, brought it to her at the little table, poured one for herself, set it on the counter near the stovetop, went on frying chicken. Althea frowned. "How many chickens did you cut up?" she said. She thought to get up and go look, but she felt too tired.

"Four."

"My goodness. We can't eat that much in three days. The new girl will be here Monday." There was a pause. The grease popped and hissed as Graceful put in several new heavily floured pieces. "Take some with you," Althea said. "You can eat it on the train."

"Thank you, ma'am." Graceful glanced at her. "I already meant to." She dropped two more pieces in. Without changing her tone, she said, "I didn't think you'd mind I cooked the two frying hens I bought myself while I was cooking up you all's food for the weekend." It was neither challenge nor explanation.

"Oh," Althea said. She sighed again. They'd been over it many times in the past month; she had asked, promised, tried to bargain, but Graceful wouldn't bargain. Her mind was made up; she was going to go live with her new husband in one of the all-black towns, and there was nothing Althea could say to dissuade her. She was taking the baby, of course, her whole family was going, and really, Althea tried to tell herself, who could blame them. The city had made it so hard for the Negroes to rebuild; the city fathers had created those impossible fire codes, had turned back the donations that poured in from around the country to help the Negroes get started. All over North Tulsa, apparently, colored people were still living in tents, on mud streets, without heat or facilities or sanitation. It would be winter before long. Althea had not been up there to see, but Franklin said it was terrible. Graceful's family was not living in a tent, but there were fifteen or sixteen of them crowded together inside her mother's house. Althea tried to visualize how that many people could fit, eat, sit, much less sleep in the tiny shotgun house she had visited. Once, she'd asked Graceful how her mother's house was left unburned, but a cold, sealed, unreadable look passed over Graceful's face, and she'd turned away, her lips clamped in silence. Althea hadn't asked a second time.

"You know," Althea said, "if you could just wait a little longer, we could put in servants' quarters over the garage. You and . . . your husband— We could perhaps find . . . something. . . ." Her voice trailed away. Well, of course, that had been one of her first suggestions. Graceful had answered, Yes'm, me and Hedgemon and the baby and Mama and LaVona and Willie and Uncle Delroy and Lucille and their four children and Miss Campbell from Latimer Street and Mr. and Mrs. Douglas from next door and . . . Althea had let the notion drop. No point in bringing it up again. It was as if Graceful had had no family before the disaster, and now all of a sudden she had more than a dozen people to take care of, and she was so stubbornly attached to them, she no longer slept in the maid's room but went home every night.

The first evening after Althea was discharged from the hospital she'd asked Franklin to send Graceful up with some hot tea, and that was the first she'd learned that Graceful was walking home after work. There was no longer a colored jitney, of course, no streetcar service, and so Graceful walked seven miles each evening, Franklin said, through downtown Tulsa and the devastated colored section, through several checkpoints, with her green pass openly displayed so the patrols wouldn't arrest her—home to her mother's house. The following morning, Althea had greeted Graceful at the back door with, "You know, there's no problem with you bringing the baby to live here," and Graceful had answered, "We doing fine, ma'am, just how we are." Althea had had to pry it out of her, how many there were, where they were living. The new husband was listed as a kind of after-thought. It infuriated her, Graceful's stubbornness to go home every night, the new husband, all of it, but there was nothing she could do—no more than there was anything she could do now to make Graceful stay.

"Well," Althea said, and set her coffee cup down on the little table. "I'll go get dressed." But she didn't move. It seemed that beneath the popping grease she could hear the relentless tick of the grandfather clock in the front hall. "What time did you say they're going to be here?" she asked af-ter a moment.

"About nine."

"Well." Althea sighed again. She felt Graceful's eyes on her, and she stood up briskly, saying, "You might as well start the bacon. He'll be awake any minute," and left the kitchen quickly, went upstairs to draw a bath.

Inside the little bathroom, as the water pounded into the tub, Althea stood at the window. The emerald leaves of the magnolia tree in the side yard gleamed in the sunlight, blurry. She turned again to the mirror, to the strange woman in the mirror, an unknown face, browless, the skin pink and strangely smooth beneath short wavy hair: a youngish face, if one did not look too closely and discover that the smoothness came with a seared, masklike tightness. The tight skin across Althea's nose and cheekbones burned with the contortions of her weeping.

She heard their voices in the kitchen as she came down the stairs, Franklin's baritone, followed by a low, vibrating, rounded bass. Althea stood in the foyer, listening, her back to the hall mirror. The voices were muffled—a soft mumble from Graceful, and then the bass Negro voice, and then Franklin's. She tried to make herself go on into the library, but she couldn't. The stained-glass window beside the door threw the sun's brilliance in a dazzling iridescent oval onto the polished hardwood floor.

"Sweetheart." Franklin stood in his new fall suit in the library doorway. "I was just coming up to see about you. Graceful's got your breakfast ready."

"Aren't you going to eat?"

"You were so long with your bath I went ahead and ate a bite. I've got to get on to the hotel, there's rumor about a new field opening around Tonkawa. Got to keep my ear to the ground."

Althea nodded. "I forgot my hat." She touched her bare neck. "I thought I might sit out in the swing awhile. I was just going back up for it. Would you mind?" She tried to smile at him, but the drawn skin surrendered no more to smiles than it did to weeping.

"I think some fresh air would be just the thing for you this morning. It's a beautiful day!" And Franklin took the stairs two at a time, like a young man.

She continued to stand, waiting for Franklin to return. Beneath the two low alternating voices in the kitchen she heard the contented gurgling of a baby.

"Here you are, sweetheart. This one? It was on the bed. Not much brim to it." Franklin handed her a soft purple cloche hat designed to wrap close to her head; it offered almost no protection from the sun but the flaps could be pulled low over the ears and brow.

"That will be fine." She took the hat, turned to the mirror. Franklin came up behind her, put his hands on her shoulders. "You look beautiful!" he said with that loud heartiness that had become a permanent part of his tone. "I'll be home early for dinner. Looks like Gracie has cooked us up some tasty leftovers in there! Or would you rather eat out?" His brows lifted in a question as he tilted his head toward her. "No, no, of course not. Well . . ." He leaned down and kissed her on the back of the neck. "You'll be all right?" he said against her. She reached up and placed her right hand on top of his.

"I'm fine. Thank you, dear," she said.

Franklin retrieved his new fedora from the rack beside the door, glanced at her with a question, and this time Althea did smile, though it came out almost a grimace, a twisted little tugging at her lips, but Franklin smiled back at her, broadly, blew her a kiss. When he'd gone, Althea gathered herself and went on down the hall to the back of the house. She entered the kitchen through the rear hall door by the maid's room rather than through the dining room. This had become her habit. At the little table against the wall, a Negro man sat holding the baby. Graceful was not in the kitchen. The Negro stood up. He was very tall, very black. The baby looked so light, so very small in his arms, though Althea realized he'd grown a great deal since the night of the disaster. His face was rounded, alert. The Negro man held him about the waist, facing toward her, and the boy waved his arms, kicked his legs, gurgling. His eyes were brown, very bright in his light face, and he was drooling from teething gums. He smiled at her. He was, if anything, more beautiful.

"How do you do, ma'am?" the Negro said. "We just— Graceful setting the table—"

Althea looked up at the man's face, and her heart gave a little kick. She'd only seen him once clearly, and that was in the moment a white man lifted a rifle to club him, but she understood, in the great interlocking of pieces, that this was the Negro who had jumped on her, rolled on her, put out the fire that would surely have consumed her as it had consumed her brother, and she was at once filled with gratitude and fury. He stepped toward the dining-room passageway, called softly, "Graceful? Honey?"

Althea took a slow step into the room. It was something she'd never dreamed of, that Graceful had married the man who'd saved her. Why hadn't Graceful told her? And then Althea thought: Why would she? Never once had Althea mentioned the person who'd put out the fire; she had not, in fact, thought of that moment for more than a fluttery, frightened instant in daylight since she regained consciousness, a hundred and twenty days ago, in the hospital hallway, because to do so made her see her brother's hand reaching toward her with the lit match, her own swiftly moving hand flying toward his, grabbing his wrist. To see was to make herself ask the question she'd lain awake asking a thousand times in the long, tortured nights since; to ask was to ponder the unknown, unknowable answer: had she been reaching toward Japheth to hold him, draw him to her, or to turn the flame back on him?

"Miz Dedmeyer, this is Hedgemon." Graceful held the silver serving tray at her side; her face was as expressionless as ever.

"How do you do, ma'am?" the young man said again.

They stood facing one another, Graceful and her husband holding the baby just to the side of the dining-room passage, Althea across the gleaming white tiles from them near the pantry door. The young man bowed slightly, very formal, and it suddenly seemed to Althea that this was a moment of great import, great dignity, and if they had not been colored she would have invited them into the parlor, to sit stiffly on the edges of the silk and velvet chairs, receive tea perhaps; she would have created some kind of ritual, a formal thank you, a parting, a farewell. But of course she could not do that. They were Negroes.

"How do you do, Mr. . . . ?" Althea glanced at Graceful.

"Jackson," the young man said.

"How do you do, Mr. Jackson."

"Well," Graceful said. There was in her face a kind of softening. "Here he is." She took the baby from the man's arms, came across the floor. She stopped a couple of feet away, held the baby up to show him. "He's getting big, isn't he?" She nuzzled her brown face against his tea-colored one. "Already trying to cut a tooth, too." The baby was gnawing at her closed fingers, a long string of spittle dangling off her wrist. "That's how come he drool so bad."

Althea reached out her arms.

"He'll get your dress wet, ma'am."

"That's all right," Althea said, and after another instant's hesitation Graceful gave him to her. The baby immediately fit himself against her; he didn't feel like the fragile newborn she'd last held. He was so strong, bobbing one hand in the air, as if conducting an orchestra, and with his other hand he held on to Althea's sleeve. He was making babbling noises, looking up at her as if he had something to say.

"He's going to be a real talker," Graceful said. She took the edge of her apron and wiped his chin. "Aren't you, Theodore?" she said, and smiled at the baby. Althea realized that it was the first time she'd ever seen Graceful smile.

"Theodore? Is that what you named him?"

"Hedgemon Theodore Jackson, Junior," Graceful said. She looked in Althea's eyes. "After his daddy." Her face showed nothing, but in her tone, in the very lack of expression, was that specific truth neither could speak, and not just the one truth, but many truths, passing back and forth between them, so powerful, so full of hurt and love and sorrow, that Althea, feeling the skin tighten across her face, the great welling in her chest, turned and began to pace the kitchen, patting the baby's back as if he were fussy, though he was still making little repetitive cooing sounds.

"What's the name of that town again?" she asked sharply over her shoulder.

"Boley," Graceful said.

"Boley." Althea stopped near the back door. She looked out past the screen. The leaves on the great elm were already turning yellow. "Down by Okemah," she said softly.

"Yes, ma'am. Twelve miles west."

It might as well be twelve thousand, Althea thought. She could no more go to Boley, Oklahoma, to see her nephew than she could fly to the moon. That was one of the truths which had passed between them. When Graceful left this morning, they would not see each other again.

"Are there a lot of folks from . . . here . . . moving to Boley?"

"Some," Graceful said. It was quiet in the kitchen, and Althea turned around. Graceful and her husband were not looking at each other, but something was being communicated between them. "Your breakfast is on the table, ma'am." Graceful busied herself at the sink. "You don't want your eggs to get cold." Now she glanced at her husband, and he edged away from the dining-room doorway, as if to give Althea clear passage.

"Well, I mean, do you have people there? Do you know people?"

"Hedgemon know a few folks. Honey, take Theodore so Miz Dedmeyer can eat her breakfast." He took a tentative step in Althea's direction, but stopped when she made no corresponding move. Graceful sprinkled soap flakes in the dishpan. "I put the chicken in the icebox. There's some potato salad in there, and I cut up some of the pears Mr. Franklin brought." She stirred the sudsy water. "I left the soup on the stove for y'all's supper."

"Who are you going to work for?" The question was meant for Graceful; it was something Althea had wondered, though she'd never thought to ask her: if there were no white people in Boley, whom would Graceful cook and clean and wash for? How could she get a job? But Graceful mistook her meaning.

"Hedgemon knows how to run the linotype, the presses, he can do about anything around a printing press wants doing. They got a nice paper in Boley. We're going to see about that first. Elberta wrote Mama there's plenty of jobs."

"Who's Elberta?"

After a beat Graceful said, "My brother's wife."

"Your brother's down there?"

Again the silence, and this time it seemed to extend beyond the boundaries of the kitchen, to join, in great soundless waves, the silence that covered the whole city: the unspoken names of the dead, the disappeared. There were so many who could not be found in the chaotic days after the disaster, and the papers said that the missing Negroes had fled to avoid prosecution, though at first there were whispers about dead blacks buried in mass graves, or dumped by the truckload in the Arkansas River, or burned in gigantic pyres. Then, within days, the silence had descended, and names were no longer mentioned, not even the names of missing white men, the drifters and itinerant oilfield workers: aimless unclaimed men with no family to ask after them. Althea's brother's name was among the unspoken. Graceful's brother was perhaps also among them, but Althea wouldn't press further. There was one other secret she carried: the image of a tawny head moving in a river of white men. Jim Dee Logan had vanished from the Deep Fork, had not been seen or heard from in the oilfields anywhere in Oklahoma, since that violent night.

"Well. Goodness." The baby was starting to fret. Althea put her cheek to the top of his smooth head, began to pace the kitchen again, patting him.

"I left the cover on," Graceful said, "but them eggs already been cooked awhile."

"Yes. Thank you. I'll just— How near ready are you?"

"Just got to finish washing up. My things are all packed. Honey," she said quietly, "take him." This time Althea surrendered the baby, and when Graceful's husband held him he instantly settled down. "He behave better for Hedgemon than he do for me. Of course, Hedgemon's the one take the most care of him. Mama don't feel much like . . ." Graceful's voice faded as she turned to the sink. "I got to get cracking." And she plucked a handful of silverware up from the bottom of the pan.

Her husband went outside to sit on the back-porch step. Althea could see him balancing the laughing baby on his knees jacked up high on the bottom step. She went into the dining room and sat at the walnut table, removed the lids from the chafing dishes and served herself, listened to the pots and pans clanging in the kitchen as she pretended to eat. When Graceful came in to remove the dirty plates and serving dishes and the lone delicate gold-rimmed china cup, she'd already taken her apron off; she held the serving tray away from her chest as she disappeared through the passageway.

Althea followed, watched in silence as Graceful hurriedly washed up the last of the breakfast things, dried them swiftly, put them away. A small bundle wrapped in a brightly colored scarf sat on the floor beside the door. Graceful folded the damp tea towel over the rack at the end of the counter, turned for one last quick look around the sparkling kitchen, and, seeming satisfied, went to pick up her bundle. In Althea now there was a great urgency just to have it over. She came on into the kitchen, saying, "Here, let me get the screen," as if Graceful might need help wrestling the small bundle of worldly goods out the door.

Then they were on the footpath in the side yard, and Graceful's husband was holding the baby. Then they were out the gate, moving along the walk beside the fence, and Graceful turned back once. She stood for a moment, and it was too far for Althea to make out her expression, but it didn't matter; she knew that Graceful's smooth brown features were completely still, completely unreadable. Althea lifted a hand to say goodbye, and Graceful raised her hand briefly, palm outward. Then she took her son from Hedgemon, and the two of them walked on. Althea went to the porch swing and watched them, both of them tall, the baby hidden from her sight in Graceful's arms, until they'd crossed Fifteenth Street.

Long after they'd disappeared from her vision, Althea sat in the swing, motionless, her mind restless, unable to stay on any one thought for more than a few seconds. She had so much work to do, her garden was an absolute disgrace. The roses were blooming, of course, but the weeds were abominable. When was the last time she'd worked in it? Where in the world would she start? If she ever did want to try to get in touch with Graceful she wouldn't know how, because she didn't know her married name. Well, yes, of course she did. It was Jackson. Graceful Jackson. Well. That was the one thing she'd never asked, wasn't it, where Graceful's people had come from that had caused her name to be Whiteside. The baby's name was Theodore Jackson. Teddy. Perhaps they would call him Teddy. No, probably not. Come to think of it, there must be others. She surely had other nephews, and nieces. It wouldn't be too hard to find them. They were all living in Bristow. She wouldn't know her sisters' last names, of course, but Bristow was not a large town. Well. If she meant to get a lick of work done this morning she was going to have to go upstairs and change in a minute. Lord, it was hot for the end of September. Althea took her hat off, laid it in her lap, and with one hand smoothed down the skirt of her silk mourning dress.